Heaven Official's Blessing
TIAN GUAN CI FU

1

墨香銅臭

Heaven Official's Blessing

TIAN GUAN CI FU

1

WRITTEN BY
Mo Xiang Tong Xiu

TRANSLATED BY
Suika & Pengie (EDITOR)

INTERIOR ILLUSTRATIONS BY
ZeldaCW

Seven Seas

Seven Seas Entertainment

HEAVEN OFFICIAL'S BLESSING: TIAN GUAN CI FU (DELUXE HARDCOVER) VOL. 1

Published originally under the title of 《天官賜福》
(Heaven Official's Blessing)
Author ©墨香铜臭(Mo Xiang Tong Xiu)
English edition rights under license granted by 北京晋江原创网络科技有限公司
(Beijing Jinjiang Original Network Technology Co., Ltd.)
English edition copyright © 2024 Seven Seas Entertainment, LLC
Arranged through JS Agency Co., Ltd
All rights reserved

《天官賜福》 (Heaven Official's Blessing) Volume 1
All rights reserved
Interior Color Illustration by 日出的小太陽 (tai3_3)
Illustrations granted under license granted by 2021 Reve Books Co., Ltd (Pinsin Publishing)
US English translation copyright © 2024 Seven Seas Entertainment, LLC
US English edition arranged through JS Agency Co., Ltd

Dust Jacket Illustration by Arisk_k
Hardcover & Printed Edge Illustrations by zaxnianx
Interior Illustrations by ZeldaCW

Seven Seas press and purchase enquiries can be sent to Marketing Manager Lauren Hill
at press@gomanga.com. Information regarding the distribution and purchase of digital
editions is available from Digital Manager CK Russell at digital@gomanga.com.

Follow Seven Seas Entertainment online at
sevenseasentertainment.com.

TRANSLATION: Suika
EDITOR: Pengie
COVER DESIGN: M. A. Lewife
INTERIOR LAYOUT & DESIGN: Clay Gardner
COPY EDITOR: Dawn Crane
PROOFREADER: Jade Gardner
IN-HOUSE EDITOR: Lexy Lee
PREPRESS TECHNICIAN: Melanie Ujimori, Jules Valera
MANAGING EDITOR: Alyssa Scavetta
EDITOR-IN-CHIEF: Julie Davis
PUBLISHER: Lianne Sentar
VICE PRESIDENT: Adam Arnold
PRESIDENT: Jason DeAngelis

ISBN: 979-8-88843-320-1
Printed in China
First Printing: October 2024
10 9 8 7 6 5 4 3 2 1

HEAVEN OFFICIAL'S BLESSING
CONTENTS

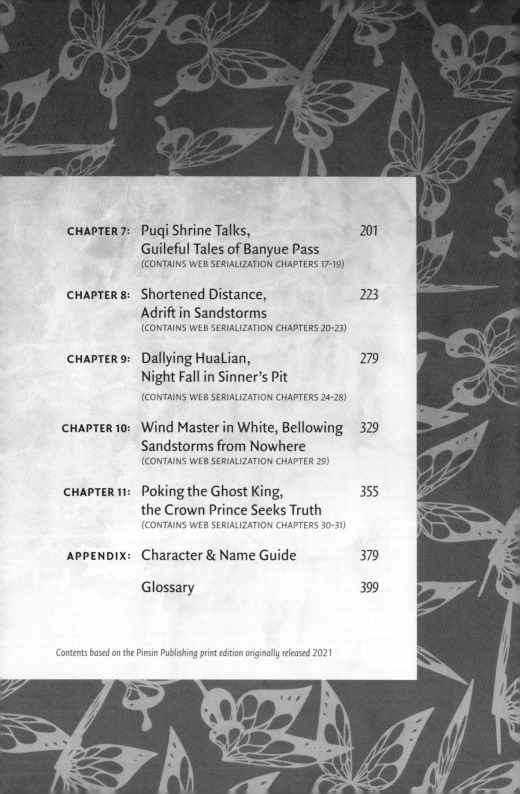

Contents based on the Pinsin Publishing print edition originally released 2021

Prologue
Heaven Official's Blessing

AMONG ALL THE DEITIES of heaven, there was one famous Laughingstock of the Three Realms.

Legend has it that eight hundred years ago, there was an ancient kingdom in the central plains called the Kingdom of Xianle.

The Kingdom of Xianle was a vast and bountiful land. There were four treasures within it: abundant and handsome beauties, vibrant music and marvelous literature, gold and gems, and their one infamous crown prince.

What would be the best way to describe this crown prince? Well, he was a unique man.

He was beloved by the king and the queen, and they doted upon him exorbitantly. They would often say with pride, "My son will become a great ruler in the future, and his good name will echo down through history!"

However, the crown prince was not interested in imperial power or wealth in the mortal world at all.

What he was interested in, in his own words, was:

"I want to save the common people!"

When he was young, the crown prince focused solely on his cultivation, and there were two short tales that were widely spread of his time on that path.

◇ ◈ ◇

The first tale took place when he was seventeen years old.

That year, there was a grand Shangyuan Heavenly Ceremonial Procession in the Kingdom of Xianle.

Although the custom of conducting these divine ceremonies has been out of fashion for centuries, it is still possible to deduce what a grand, jubilant occasion it must have been from remnants of ancient books and oral tradition.

The wondrous Shangyuan Festival, upon the Grand Avenue of Divine Might.

Seas of people gathered on either side of the grand street, with royals and nobles talking and laughing in merriment atop the high platforms. The glorious royal warriors bedecked in armor opened the paths, while maidens danced elegantly, their fair hands scattering flowers—and who could say whether the flowers or the maidens were more beautiful? From within the golden carriage came marvelous music that drifted across the entire imperial city. And at the rear of the procession was a grand stage pulled by sixteen white horses in golden bridles.

Upon this towering grand stage stood the God-Pleasing Warrior, the focus of everyone's attention.

At the Heavenly Ceremonial Procession, the God-Pleasing Warrior wore a golden mask. Dressed in glamorous attire and with a sacred sword in hand, he played the role of the subduer of evil, the number one martial god for the past thousand years: the Heavenly Emperor, Jun Wu.

It was the greatest of honors to be chosen for the role of the God-Pleasing Warrior, which was why the selection criteria were exceedingly strict. Thus, the one chosen that year was that crown prince. People across the kingdom believed that he would give the most thrilling performance as the God-Pleasing Warrior.

However, an accident happened that day.

During the third tour of the procession, it passed by a city wall that was hundreds of meters tall. At the time, the martial god upon the grand stage was just about to strike the demon down. It was the climax of the performance, with people on both sides of the street at the height of excitement. The top of the city wall swarmed with crowds clamoring to watch the show, pushing and shoving each other to get the best view.

At that moment, a small child fell from the edge of the wall.

The screams of the crowd reached to the heavens. Just when everyone thought this child would stain the Grand Avenue of Divine Might with blood, the crown prince looked up, leapt into flight, and caught the boy.

The people only saw a glimpse of a white silhouette that flew like a soaring bird before the crown prince landed with that small child in his arms. The golden mask fell, revealing the young, handsome face behind it.

In the next second, cheers erupted.

The people were thrilled and joyous, but the state preceptors of the royal cultivation hall were troubled.

They had never imagined such a huge mishap would occur.

This was ominous luck! The gravest of misfortunes!

Every trip the grand stage made around the imperial capital symbolized one year of peace and harmony within the kingdom. Now that it was cut short, did that not mean the invitation of disaster?!

The state preceptors were so distraught, they were losing hair as fast as the rain fell. After much contemplation, they called the crown prince over to speak to him. In the softest manner possible, they requested: "Your Highness, might you be willing to face the wall in reflection for a month? It does not really need to be a month, as long as the intention is there."

The crown prince smiled. "No."

This was what he said: "There is nothing wrong with saving people. Why would the heavens condemn me for doing the right thing?"

Uh...but what if the heavens do condemn you?

"Then it is the heavens who are wrong. Why would I apologize to those who are wrong?"

The state preceptors could not argue.

This crown prince was such a person.

He had never encountered anything he could not do, nor had he ever met anyone who did not love him. He was the justice of the Mortal Realm, the center of the world.

Although the state preceptors were frustrated—"What the heck do you know?!"—it was not their place to say much, and they did not dare say more on the subject either. His Highness would not have listened anyway.

The second tale took place in the same year, when the crown prince was seventeen.

Legend has it that, south of the Yellow River, there was a bridge called Yinian.[1] Upon this bridge was a ghost that had been lingering for years.

This ghost was exceedingly fearsome: it was clad in broken armor, the flames of hell blazed beneath its feet, and its body was covered in blood and pierced by all manner of sharp weapons. Every step it

---

1   一念 means "One Thought" or "Fleeting Thought." This is also the first half of the idiom, "Wrong decision made in a moment of weakness."

took, it left behind a footprint of blood and fire. Every few years, it would suddenly appear at night and wander back and forth at the head of the bridge, blocking travelers to ask them three questions:

"What is this place?"

"Who am I?"

"What is to be done?"

The ghost would then devour whoever answered incorrectly. However, no one knew what the correct answers were. As the years went by, this ghost devoured countless travelers.

During his ascetic travel, the crown prince caught word of this. So he set out and found Yinian Bridge and stood guard there night after night. Until finally, one night, he met the haunting ghost.

When that ghost appeared, it was indeed as horrifying as the legends said. It asked the crown prince the first question, and he answered with a smile.

"This place is the human world."

However, the ghost replied, "This place is the abyss."

An auspicious start. The first answer was already incorrect.

Well, all three answers are going to be wrong anyway, the crown prince thought, *so why should I wait till you're done?* And so he pulled out his weapon and lunged.

The fight was complete chaos. The crown prince was skilled in martial arts, but the ghost was terrifying and dauntless. Man and ghost fought so hard that the sun and moon began to topple. In the end, the ghost was finally defeated.

After the ghost vanished, the crown prince planted a flowering tree at the head of the bridge. As he did so, a cultivator passed by and happened to see him sprinkle a handful of dirt to consecrate the grave and send the ghost off.

"What is this?" he asked.

And thus, the crown prince replied with his now-famous line: "Body in the abyss, heart in paradise."

When the cultivator heard this, he gave a light smile. He then transformed into a divine warrior clad in white armor, with auspicious clouds beneath his feet. Then, he drew in the wind and rode off in holy light. Only then did the crown prince realize that he had just encountered the Heavenly Emperor, who had personally descended to the Mortal Realm to subdue evil.

The deities had already taken notice of this exceedingly outstanding God-Pleasing Warrior since his time in the Shangyuan Heavenly Ceremonial Procession. After the meeting at Yinian Bridge, they asked the Heavenly Emperor, "How does My Lord find this Royal Highness?"

The Emperor answered, "This child's future is infinite."

That night, a celestial phenomenon manifested in the skies above the palace, and storms raged.

Amidst the flashes of lightning and the roars of thunder, the crown prince ascended.

Whenever a mortal ascended, the Heavenly Realm always shook. When the crown prince ascended, the entire Heavenly Realm quaked outright with three times the normal tremors.

Achieving fruitful cultivation was always far too difficult. It required talent, training, and luck. It was often a long road of a hundred years for a god to be born.

It was not that there were no fortunate souls who became deities at a young age. However, the majority who tried exhausted their entire lives, trained for a hundred years, and still had no Heavenly Tribulations dawn upon them. Even if they did come to face a Heavenly Tribulation, should they fail the trial, they would die—or be ruined, if they managed to survive. Those who made the attempt were as numerous as the sands of the Ganges, but most were simply ignorant mortals who would spend their entire lives as nothing more than ordinary, never finding their own paths.

Yet this Royal Highness was no doubt the darling of the heavens. Whatever he wanted, he received; whatever he wanted to do, he succeeded. He wanted to ascend and become a god, so at the age of seventeen, he did just that.

He had always led the hearts of the people, and the king and queen loved and missed him dearly. So to honor their son, the king ordered great temples and shrines to be built across the land and for statues of the crown prince to be erected and worshipped by all. The more believers that were amassed, the more temples were constructed. That meant the crown prince's life would be more prolonged, and his spiritual powers would grow more powerful. Thus, in a few short years, the Xianle Palace of the Crown Prince became incomparably glorious, and for a time, its prosperity and splendor reached its peak.

Until three years later, when Xianle fell into chaos.

The cause of the chaos was tyranny, with rebels rising in revolt. However, while the flames of war were set ablaze all over the mortal world, the deities of the Heavenly Realm could not easily intervene. Their concerns were ghosts, monsters, and demons that encroached on the borders, and whatever fell outside of those parameters had to be left to its own devices.

Think about it: conflicts were everywhere in the Mortal Realm, and everyone believed they were justified. So if any god were to stick a foot in... Today, you would back your former kingdom, tomorrow, another would avenge his descendants. Thus, would there not be gods who wanted to fight each other all the time, who would fall into a life of disgrace?

That was why the crown prince needed to keep his distance. But he did not care for that reasoning in the least.

He said to the Heavenly Emperor, "I will save the common people."

The Heavenly Emperor possessed a thousand years of divine power, but even he did not dare let those words hang off his lips. When he heard this, it was easy to imagine how he felt, yet he could not do anything to stop the crown prince.

So he said, "You cannot save everyone."

"I can," the crown prince declared.

Thus, he descended to the Mortal Realm without looking back.

Naturally, the whole nation of Xianle rejoiced. However, ever since ancient times there had been one truth the people always spoke of in the human world: there would never be a good outcome when gods descended to the Mortal Realm without permission.

And so, not only were the flames of war not extinguished, they blazed even wilder.

It was not to say that the crown prince did not try, but it would have been better had he not intervened at all. The harder he worked, the more of a mess the war became: the people of Xianle were devastatingly battered and crushed, the wounded and casualties innumerable, and in the end, a plague swept through the entire imperial capital, and the rebel army broke through to the palace and ended the war.

If it was said that Xianle was originally hanging on by a thread, then the crown prince came and cut it directly.

After the kingdom fell, the people finally came to realize one thing: the crown prince they worshipped as a god was never as perfect or strong as they imagined.

To speak harshly, was he not just useless trash who could not do anything right?!

Without anywhere to vent the anguish and pain of losing their homes and families, the battered people furiously poured into the palaces of the crown prince, toppled his divine statues, and burned down the divine temples.

Eight thousand temples burned for seven days and seven nights, burned until there was nothing left. From that moment on, the martial god who protected peace and safety vanished, and a God of Misfortune who brought disasters was born.

When the people call you a god, you are a god. If they call you crap, you are crap. You are whatever they say you are. It had always been thus.

The crown prince could absolutely not accept this reality, and he had an even harder time accepting the punishment he received for his transgressions: banishment.

His spiritual powers were sealed, and he was knocked back down to the Mortal Realm.

He'd grown up endlessly coddled and pampered. He had never tasted the suffering of the human world before, yet this punishment hurled him from the clouds down into the mud. And in this mud, for the first time, he understood the taste of hunger, poverty, and filth. This was also the first time that he did things he never thought he would do willingly: he stole, he robbed, he cursed loudly, and he gave up on himself. He lost all dignity, no self-esteem remained, and he was as unkempt as one could be. Even his most loyal servants could not accept this change in him and chose to leave.

"Body in the abyss, heart in paradise." This phrase had been engraved on stone monuments and plaques everywhere in Xianle. If not for the war that had burned almost all of the kingdom to the ground, if the crown prince were to see the remnants of those words, he would probably be the first to rush to destroy what was left.

The person who had said those words had personally proven that when the body was in the abyss, the heart could not be in paradise.

He ascended to the heavens quickly, but his fall from grace was even faster. That awe-inspiring impression at the Grand Avenue of Divine Might, the evil he met at Yinian Bridge; it all seemed as if it were only yesterday, and the Heavenly Realm merely sighed for a while before letting go of what was past.

Until one day, many years later, a huge rumble thundered from the sky. This Royal Highness ascended for the second time.

Throughout history, heavenly officials who were banished either never regained their glory or fell into the Ghost Realm. It was rare to turn over a new leaf after banishment. This second ascension was truly grand and spectacular.

What was even more spectacular was that, after he ascended, he charged all the way into the Heavenly Realm and rampaged in full fury. Thus, he had only been ascended for the span of one incense time before he was knocked back down again.

One incense time. It could be considered the swiftest and shortest ascension in history.

If the first ascension could be considered a beautiful tale, then the second ascension was a farce.

Having been banished twice, the Heavenly Realm looked upon this crown prince with full contempt. And in that contempt, there was caution. After all, he was already threatening and on edge after the first banishment; now that he had been banished twice, would he not go berserk and take his revenge on the world?

Yet who knew? After being banished this time, he did not go berserk and even adjusted earnestly to banished life. There were no issues at all, and the only problem was that...maybe he was taking things a little too seriously?

Sometimes he would busk at the end of the street, expertly playing any instrument and singing any songs, and even shattering boulders on his chest as part of his act. While there had long been word that this Royal Highness could sing and dance and was a master of many talents, it was unbelievable to witness all his talents in such a fashion, truly inspiring complicated feelings in anyone who saw. Sometimes, he would diligently and humbly collect scraps.

The deities were shocked to their cores.

It was unthinkable that things would reach this point, where now, if one was to say "the son you gave birth to is the crown prince of Xianle," it would be a curse more malicious than "may you die without sons."

He was once the noble and gracious crown prince, a heavenly official who was part of the divine ranks. But in truth, no one else had ever screwed up so badly. And so, this was the story of the man who was known as the Laughingstock of the Three Realms.

After laughing, those who were more sentimental might also sigh. The darling of the heavens, who once stood at such a height, had truly and thoroughly vanished.

Divine statues collapsed, a native kingdom was destroyed, and not a single believer remained. Gradually, he was forgotten by the world. Thus, no one knew where he had drifted afterward.

It was already a great shame to be banished once. No one would be able to get back up after being banished twice.

Many more years passed. Suddenly one day there was another huge rumble in the sky. The heavens fell and the earth cracked, the ground trembled and the mountains shook.

The lanterns of everlasting light shuddered, the firelights danced in fury, and all the heavenly officials inside their golden palaces jolted awake, every one of them running out to ask each other:

"Which new dignitary has ascended?"

"Such a grandiose entrance!"

Yet who knew? They had exclaimed in wonder the first second, but in the next, all the deities of heaven were thunderstruck.

Weren't you done?!

That infamous weirdo, the Laughingstock of the Three Realms, the legendary Royal Highness the Crown Prince, he...he...he... he fucking ascended again!

"**C**ONGRATULATIONS, Your Highness."

Hearing this, Xie Lian looked up, and he smiled before saying anything. "Thank you. But can I ask what you're congratulating me for?"

Ling Wen-zhenjun stood tall with her hands folded behind her back. "Congratulations, you have won first place on the chart of 'Heavenly Official Most Hoped to be Banished Down to the Mortal Realm' of this calendar cycle."

"Well, no matter what, first place is first place," Xie Lian said. "But since you're congratulating me, is there anything that's actually worth being happy about?"

"Yes," Ling Wen replied. "First place on this chart receives one hundred merits."

Xie Lian immediately said, "If there are any similar charts in the future, please absolutely call me up."

"Do you know who second place is?" Ling Wen asked.

Xie Lian pondered for a moment, then replied, "That's too hard to guess. After all, in terms of ability, I should be able to take the first three places myself."

"Pretty much," Ling Wen said. "There isn't a second place. You're so far ahead that you've left everyone in the dust."

"That's too great of an honor," Xie Lian replied. "Then who was first place for the previous calendar cycle?"

"There is no previous winner," Ling Wen said, "because this chart was first established today."

"Huh?" Xie Lian was taken aback. "You don't mean to say that this was a chart set up just for me?"

Ling Wen replied, "You can think of it as, you just so happened to make it in time and just so happened to steal first place."

Xie Lian grinned, his eyes squinting into crescents. "All right. I'll be happier if I think of it that way."

"Do you know why you got first place?" Ling Wen continued.

"By popular demand?" Xie Lian guessed.

"Let me explain the reason to you," Ling Wen said. "Please look at that bell."

Xie Lian turned his head to gaze toward where she pointed, and what he saw was an extremely beautiful sight. There were grand palace temples made of white jade, abundant towers, pavilions, and gazebos, with heavenly clouds lingering about as streams flowed and birds danced.

He took a good look for a while, then asked, "Did you perhaps point in the wrong direction? There's no bell anywhere."

"I didn't," Ling Wen said. "It's right there; don't you see it?"

Xie Lian looked again seriously, then answered honestly, "I don't."

Ling Wen replied, "It's all right if you don't. There used to be a bell there, but when you ascended, it fell because of the tremors."

"..."

"That bell is older than you, but it has a spirited character and enjoys a good spectacle. Whenever someone ascends, it tolls a few times in applause. When you ascended, the tremors were so strong that the bell tolled like mad and couldn't stop at all. In the end, it shook itself off the bell tower before it finally ceased. And when it fell, it crashed down onto one of the heavenly officials passing by."

"Um...is everything better now?" Xie Lian inquired.

"Not yet. It's still under repairs," Ling Wen replied.

"I meant that heavenly official who was hurt," Xie Lian clarified.

"The one it hit was a martial god," Ling Wen said. "A flick of his hand and the bell was chopped in two right then and there. Now, please look over at that golden palace. Do you see it?"

Again, Xie Lian looked to where she was pointing and saw amidst the haze of clouds the resplendent golden glazed roof. "Ah, this time I see it."

"It's not right if you see it," Ling Wen said. "There wasn't anything there before."

"..."

"When you ascended, the golden pillars of the golden palaces of a number of heavenly officials collapsed from the tremors, and their glazed roof tiles shattered. There are some that won't be so easily fixed, so the heavenly officials could only put together some last-minute palaces to make do for the time being."

"And I'm the one responsible?"

"You're the one responsible."

"Mm..." Xie Lian asked to confirm, "So I've offended many heavenly officials since the moment I arrived?"

"If you can make amends, maybe not," Ling Wen said.

"How do I make amends?"

"Easy. With eight million eight hundred and eighty thousand merits."

Xie Lian grinned again.

Ling Wen added, "Of course, I know you don't have even a tenth of that amount."

Xie Lian replied earnestly, "How do I say this? Even though I'm very sorry, if you want just a ten-thousandth of that amount, I don't have it."

The faith of mortal believers was converted into the spiritual power of a heavenly official. Every stick of incense they lit and every offering they gave were thus called "merits."

Xie Lian turned solemn in place of the smile and asked seriously, "Are you willing to kick me down from here and give me eight million eight hundred and eighty thousand merits for it?"

"I'm a civil god," Ling Wen said. "If you're looking for someone to kick you down under, you'll need to find a martial god to do it. The harder they kick, the more merits they'll give."

Xie Lian heaved a long sigh. "Please allow me to think about what I should do."

Ling Wen patted his shoulder. "Don't worry, there will always be a path when the carriage reaches the mountain."

"Boats always sink when they reach the pierhead for me, though,"[2] Xie Lian said.

If this were eight hundred years ago, when the Palace of Xianle was at its peak of prominence, eight million eight hundred and eighty thousand merits would be nothing; the crown prince could throw it out without batting an eye. But the present wasn't the same as the past, and all his temples in the Mortal Realm had long since been burned to the ground. He had no believers, no incense, and no offerings.

There was no need to say more on the subject. Either way he had nothing, nothing, absolutely nothing!

He crouched by himself on the side of the main street of the Heavenly Capital feeling distraught for a while before suddenly remembering: he'd ascended for almost three days now, but he still hadn't entered the communication array of the Upper Court. He'd forgotten to ask what the verbal password was.

---

2   "When the boat gets to the pierhead, it will go straight with the current" is a proverb that means "Everything will be all right."

The heavenly officials of the Upper Court had gotten together and set up an array that could instantaneously allow the consciousness to communicate and pass on messages. Once ascended, one must enter the array, but a password was required for the consciousness to find the designated channel. The last time Xie Lian had entered the array was eight hundred years ago, so he didn't remember the password at all. He let his consciousness scatter to search and saw a channel that seemed to be what he was looking for, so he went in randomly. The moment he entered, he was blasted by an outpouring of crazed yelling from all directions.

"Place your bets and no take-backs! Let's wager on how long our Royal Highness the Crown Prince can last before going down again!!"

"I bet one year!"

"One year is too long; last time it was only one incense time! It'll be three days this time, I think. I put my merits down on three days, three days!"

"Don't, you dimwit! Three days is almost over already; do you even know how to gamble?!"

...Xie Lian silently exited the array.

He'd entered the wrong one. That couldn't be it.

The heavenly officials of the Upper Court of Heaven were all big-wigs who guarded over a given region. They were widely known by every household and kept occupied by a myriad of state affairs. Since they were deities who ascended respectably, in keeping with their status, they were generally more reserved and often put on airs. Xie Lian himself had been the only one who dragged out every single heavenly official inside the communication array to greet them out of excitement the first time he ascended, incomparably earnest and exceedingly thorough in introducing himself from head to toe.

After he exited that array, he went on another random search and entered a different one. This time, he relaxed, thinking to himself, *How quiet—it's probably this one.*

Just then, he heard a voice say softly, "So, Your Highness is back?"

It was a very comfortable voice, the sound soft and gentle, the tone decorous. However, if one were to listen closely, one would discover that the voice was quite cool and indifferent, the same as the sentiment it carried, causing that soft gentleness to turn into something more malicious in intent.

Xie Lian had intended to enter the array in a proper manner, then lie low, but since the other party had already addressed him, he couldn't keep pretending to be deaf and mute. Besides, he was still delighted that there were actually heavenly officials in the Upper Court who would willingly start a conversation with a God of Misfortune like himself.

Thus, he quickly answered, "Yeah! Hello, everyone, I'm back again."

Yet little did he know, after this exchange, every single heavenly official who was currently inside the communication array perked up their ears.

That heavenly official said languidly, "Your Highness certainly ascended with tremendous force this time, huh?"

Within the Upper Court of Heaven, emperors, kings, generals, and chancellors were everywhere, and heroes flowed like water.

In order to become a deity, one must first achieve greatness. Within the Mortal Realm, those who had obtained accolades or ones in possession of great talent had always had a better chance at ascension. So it wasn't an exaggeration to say that rulers, princesses, princes, and generals weren't a rarity here. Everyone was a Darling of the Heavens. Everyone acted courteously with each other, so they would address one another as Your Majesty, Your Highness, Lord General, Alliance Chief, Head Chief, whatever, as long as the title was flattering. However, the words from this one heavenly official seemed to have something lurking beneath their tone.

Although he said "Your Highness" this, "Your Highness" that, Xie Lian couldn't sense a bit of respect from him at all. It was more like he was poking him with a needle. There were also several heavenly officials inside the communication array who were authentic crown princes, and they were feeling the hairs on their backs rise from such an address, incredibly uncomfortable. Xie Lian could tell that this other party didn't come with good intentions. But he didn't want to fight, so he chose to run instead.

He smiled. "It wasn't too bad."

However, that heavenly official wouldn't give him the chance to run. He said tepidly, "It's Your Highness, after all, so it wasn't too bad for you. But my luck doesn't seem to be as good."

Suddenly, Xie Lian heard a private message from Ling Wen.

She only said one word: "Bell."

Instantly, Xie Lian understood.

So this was the martial god who was hit by the bell!

If that was the case, then the other party wasn't angry without reason. Xie Lian had always been adept at apologizing, so he immediately said, "I've heard about the accident with the bell, and I'm dreadfully sorry. I do apologize."

The other party humphed, the meaning unclear.

There were a great number of renowned martial gods in the Heavenly Realm, and many of them were newly ascended dignitaries who came after Xie Lian's time. Xie Lian couldn't be sure who this person was by voice alone, but he couldn't stay ignorant of his name after apologizing either. So Xie Lian inquired, "Might I ask how I may address my lord?"

The other fell silent at this.

Not only did the other fall silent, it was like the entire communication array froze, and the air was assaulted with stagnation.

From the other end, Ling Wen sent him another message. "Your Highness, although I think you should have recognized him after talking for so long, I still want to give you a hint. That's Xuan Zhen."

"Xuan Zhen?" Xie Lian said.

He was stumped for a moment before he finally came around, then sent a voice message back in shock. "That's Mu Qing?"

General Xuan Zhen was the Martial God of the Southwest who possessed seven thousand temples; his name in the human world was considerably distinguished, and this General Xuan Zhen's real name was Mu Qing. Eight hundred years ago, he was a deputy general at the Xianle Palace of the Crown Prince.

Ling Wen was also quite shocked. "You really didn't recognize him?"

"I really didn't," Xie Lian replied. "He didn't talk to me like this back then. Besides, I can't even recall when we last met; it was either five or six centuries ago. I can barely remember what he looks like, so how can I possibly remember what his voice sounds like?"

The communication array was still deep in silence. Mu Qing didn't utter a sound. The other heavenly officials were pretending they weren't listening while waiting on the edge of their seats for whichever one would continue the conversation.

Things *were* rather awkward when it came to those two. The complicated plot had been spread in rumors for so many years, and everyone basically knew the story at this point. Back then, when Xie Lian was still the esteemed crown prince of Xianle, he trained at the

Royal Holy Temple. This Royal Holy Temple was a royal cultivation hall in the Kingdom of Xianle, with a very strict standard for selecting disciples. Mu Qing came from the slums, and his father was an executed criminal; someone like that didn't qualify for acceptance to the Royal Holy Temple, so he could only run errands. Within the temple grounds, he was someone who cleaned the Royal Highness's room and served tea and water.

Xie Lian saw how hard he was working, so he requested that the state preceptors make an exception and accept Mu Qing as a disciple. It was only by the golden mouth of the Royal Highness that Mu Qing could enter the temple to cultivate and be trained alongside the crown prince. Then, after ascension, Xie Lian appointed him his general and took him along to the Heavenly Capital.

However, when the Kingdom of Xianle fell and Xie Lian was banished to the mortal world, Mu Qing didn't follow him. Not only did he not follow, he never even spoke a word in Xie Lian's favor. Either way, the crown prince was gone, so he was free. He found a cave on a piece of auspicious land and trained arduously, and not a few years later, he passed a Heavenly Tribulation and ascended to heaven himself.

In the past, one was in the heavens and one on earth. Now, there was still one in the heavens and one on earth—it was simply that their positions had switched completely, that's all.

On this end, Ling Wen said, "He's very upset."

"I figured as much," Xie Lian said.

"I'll go start another topic of conversation; you'd best take the chance to leave," Ling Wen suggested.

"Nah, it's okay," Xie Lian replied. "It's fine as long as we pretend nothing's happened."

"Are you sure?" Ling Wen said. "I feel awkward just watching you two."

"It's not that bad!" Xie Lian replied.

For someone like Xie Lian, everything besides death really was okay; he didn't have a lot, and certainly not shame. He had done much, much more awkward things, so he genuinely felt that this was okay. Yet who knew that "okay" wasn't a word to be uttered lightly? He had only just said "it's okay" when a voice roared angrily.

"Who the fuck knocked down my golden palace?! SHOW YOURSELF!!"

This angry roar was going to make the heads of all the gods explode.

While they were already filled to the brim with surging complaints, still, each of them held their breaths, waiting soundlessly to hear how Xie Lian was going to answer this accusatory cry. Yet unexpectedly, things only got more exciting. Before Xie Lian had opened his mouth, Mu Qing spoke up first.

Or rather, he only snorted. "Heh."

The newcomer spat coldly, "*You* knocked it down? Good. Just you wait."

Mu Qing replied coolly, "I didn't say it was me; don't make false accusations."

The other said angrily, "Then what are you laughing about? Are you out of your mind?"

"No reason. You just sound funny, that's all," Mu Qing said. "The one who knocked down your golden palace is in the communication array right now. Go interrogate him yourself."

With things reaching this point, Xie Lian was too embarrassed to run away just like that.

He cleared his throat. "It was me. I'm sorry."

The moment he spoke, the one who came after also fell silent.

Next to his ear, Ling Wen messaged him again. "Your Highness, that's Nan Yang."

"This one I know," Xie Lian said. "But it seems he doesn't recognize me."

"He does," Ling Wen confirmed. "It's just that he spends most of his time roaming the Mortal Realm and rarely comes back to the Heavenly Capital. He didn't know you had ascended again, that's all."

Nan Yang-zhenjun was the Martial God of the Southeast. He possessed eight thousand temples and was incredibly loved by the people. His real name was Feng Xin, and eight hundred years ago, he was the number one heavenly general of the Xianle Palace of the Crown Prince.

Feng Xin was loyal to a fault, and he had been Xie Lian's imperial bodyguard since the crown prince was fourteen years old. He grew up with Xie Lian; they entered the heavens together, were banished together, and drifted together. Unfortunately, they couldn't endure all eight hundred years together. In the end, it was an unhappy separation as each went their own way, never to meet again.

The master of forgone days, fallen so low as to be the Laughingstock of the Three Realms with neither offerings, temples, nor believers. All the while, the two servants under him had both passed a Heavenly Tribulation and became great martial gods themselves who guarded their own domains.

Under these circumstances, it was impossible for anyone not to think too much. If Xie Lian had to choose between Feng Xin and Mu Qing and say who made him feel more awkward, he would answer "they're both fine!" But if bystanders had to choose whether they wanted to see Xie Lian brawl with Feng Xin or Mu Qing, then that would depend on the individual's taste. After all, all three had sufficient reasons to beat each other up, so it would be a hard pick.

Which was why everyone was severely disappointed when Feng Xin did not respond for the longest time. He didn't say a single word and instead went invisible. And so Xie Lian concluded the scene on his own, beating himself up voluntarily: "I didn't think things would get this out of hand. It wasn't intentional, and I do apologize to everyone for having caused trouble."

Mu Qing replied sarcastically, "Oh, what a coincidence."

Coincidence. Xie Lian also thought this was quite the coincidence. How did he so coincidentally hit Mu Qing and wreck Feng Xin's palace? From any bystander's perspective, this was practically intentional revenge. But the truth was thus: he was just the type who could pick up the single poisoned cup in a thousand cups of wine. It wasn't like one could do anything about what others thought, so Xie Lian could only reply, "I will do my utmost to compensate everyone for their golden palaces and any other damages. I pray you will all give me a little time."

It didn't take any brains to see how obvious it was that Mu Qing wanted to keep making snide remarks, but his golden palace didn't suffer any damage, and the bell that fell on him was also chopped in two. If he continued to be so overbearing, it'd be unseemly for someone of his status. Thus, he also fell silent and went invisible. When Xie Lian saw that the awful messes themselves were now gone, he quickly fled too.

He was still pondering deeply and seriously on where he could go to get his hands on eight million eight hundred and eighty thousand merits. The next day, Ling Wen invited him to the Palace of Ling Wen.

Ling Wen was a heavenly official who managed the affairs of celestial personnel and controlled the smooth sailing and rapid career promotion of humans. The entire palace was stacked full of official documents and scrolls from the ground to the ceiling, quite an astounding sight, enough to make one quake with fear. On the way over, every heavenly official who emerged from the Palace of Ling Wen was holding stacks of documents that were taller than the average person. Their complexions were ghastly pale, looking either like they were breaking down or numb.

After Xie Lian entered the great hall, Ling Wen turned around and got straight to the point. "Your Highness, the Heavenly Emperor has a request for you. Will you give him some assistance?"

There were plenty of Zhenjun and Yuanjun in the Heavenly Realm, but there was only one who could be addressed as Emperor. If this lord wanted something done, he needn't ask first, which was why Xie Lian was a little taken aback before he replied, "What is it?"

Ling Wen handed him a scroll. "Recently, there have been a large number of grand believers from the north making frequent prayers, so I imagine things must not be peaceful there."

The name "grand believer" usually referred to one of three types of people. The first type were the rich, those who paid for incense and religious services and built temples. The second type were missionaries, people who promoted the religion and gave sermons. The third type were believers who possessed absolute faith in both heart and body.

Among the three, the first type dominated. The richer someone was, the more they feared and respected gods and ghosts, and there were as many rich people as there were fish in the sea. The third type was the least common, because if someone could genuinely reach that level, then their spiritual state must be exceptional, and they wouldn't be far from ascension themselves.

The ones spoken of here were, obviously, the first type.

"The Heavenly Emperor cannot attend to the north right now," Ling Wen explained. "If you are willing to make a trip over on his behalf, then in the future, regardless of how many offerings these grand believers give as a gesture to pay off their vows, everything will be counted under your altar. What do you think?"

Xie Lian received the scroll with both hands and said, "Thank you."

This was clearly Jun Wu helping him, but the Heavenly Emperor made it sound like he was asking Xie Lian for help. Of course Xie Lian could tell, but he couldn't find the right words to express how he felt besides those two.

Ling Wen replied, "I'm only responsible for getting things done. If you wish to say thanks, wait until the Heavenly Emperor returns and go thank him directly yourself. By the way, do you need me to lend you any spiritual devices?"

"No," Xie Lian said. "Even if you give me a spiritual device, I won't have any spiritual power once I go down, so I couldn't use it anyway."

Having been banished twice, Xie Lian had lost all of his spiritual powers. Things were fine in the Heavenly Realm; the Heavenly Realm was the place where the divine palaces stood and spiritual qi was abundant, endless, and right at his fingertips for him to use. However, once back in the Mortal Realm, he was stunted. If he wanted to have a spiritual battle with anyone, he'd have to borrow said power from someone to make do—quite the inconvenience.

Ling Wen pondered for a moment. "Then it's best if we call a few martial officials over to lend you a hand."

The martial gods that were currently in office either didn't know him or loathed him. Xie Lian knew that much, at least. "Forget about that too. No one will come."

Ling Wen had her own considerations, however. "I'll give it a try."

It wouldn't matter whether she tried or not, but Xie Lian neither agreed nor protested and let her go off to try on her own. Thus, Ling Wen entered the communication array and clearly and loudly asked:

"Everyone, the Heavenly Emperor has an urgent matter in the north and is in dire need of capable hands. Is there any martial highness who can assign two martial officials from their palace?"

Just as the words were spoken, Mu Qing's voice popped up airily. "I hear the Heavenly Emperor is not in the north at the moment, so this is probably a call for assistance from His Highness the Crown Prince, am I right?"

Xie Lian thought to himself, *Are you just lurking inside the communication array at all times of the day...?*

Ling Wen thought the exact same thing and dearly wanted to slap Mu Qing out of the array for obstructing her work, but still she smiled outwardly. "Xuan Zhen, how come I keep seeing you inside the array these days? Seems like you've got free time on your hands lately. Congratulations."

Mu Qing replied coolly, "My hand is wounded. I'm currently nursing the injury."

Every heavenly official thought to themselves, *That hand of yours can chop the mountains and slash the seas without breaking a sweat. What could splitting a bell do to you?*

Ling Wen had wanted to wait until she had tricked two people into volunteering before saying anything at first, yet not only did Mu Qing figure it out easily, he had to say it out loud too. Now there surely wouldn't be anyone available. As expected, not a single soul responded, but Xie Lian didn't think anything of it. He turned to her.

"I told you no one would come."

"If Xuan Zhen didn't say anything, I would've succeeded," Ling Wen said.

Xie Lian chuckled. "You worded it like a pipa player with half her face covered, and within the fog, the flower looks three times more beautiful. If others thought it was to do work for the Emperor, of course they would've come. But if they came and discovered they'd be working with me, there would probably be a riot, and how could we cooperate under those conditions? Either way, I'm used to being alone; it's not like I lost any limbs during all these years, so we'll leave it as it is. Thanks for all the trouble, I'll be off now."

Ling Wen was out of ideas too, so she cupped her hands in salute. "All right. Wishing everything goes smoothly for Your Highness down below. May heaven officials give their blessings."

"No paths are bound!" Xie Lian replied, waved his hand, and left in a dashing manner.

Three days later, the Mortal Realm, in the north.

There was a tea shop by the side of a major street. Its storefront wasn't big, a small operation, but what was good about it was the scenery. There were mountains and waters, people and the city. It had it all, but not much; not much, but just right. If one was to have a chance meeting here in this landscape, it would definitely become a beautiful memory.

The tea master inside the shop was extremely idle. When there weren't any customers, he'd bring a stool out to sit by the entrance to watch the mountains and the waters, the people and the city, quite jolly as he looked on. Today, he saw a white-clad cultivator who had come down the road from a distance. The cultivator was travel-worn, as if he had walked for a long time.

When the man came close, he brushed past the small shop at first, but suddenly, he halted. Then, very slowly, he backed up. Lifting the tip of his bamboo hat, he looked up, glanced at the shop sign, and smiled. "'Little Shop of Chance Encounters,' what an interesting name."

While this man appeared somewhat tired, his expression was a cheerful one, so much so that the one watching him couldn't help but lift the corners of his lips too. The man then asked, "Excuse me, is Mount Yujun nearby?"

The tea master pointed in a direction for him. "It is indeed around here."

The man let out a sigh, managing not to let his entire soul out while he was at it. He thought to himself, *I've finally made it.*

This was indeed Xie Lian.

When he left the Heavenly Capital that day, he had originally set the desired landing location in the Mortal Realm to be somewhere near Mount Yujun. Yet who knew when he left in such a dashing manner, and jumped down dashingly, that his sleeve would be caught by a dashing cloud. Yes, it was caught by a cloud. He didn't know how his sleeve got caught, but either way, he tumbled across the million-meter-high sky, and by the time he tumbled down, he no longer knew where he was. After walking on foot for three days, he finally made it to the first intended landing point, and he sighed deeply with emotion.

Xie Lian entered the shop and picked a table next to the window, ordering tea and snacks. After he finally settled, there was suddenly the sound of weeping and gongs being played outside.

He gazed toward the main street and saw a group of men and women, both young and old, escorting a bright-red marriage sedan as it passed by.

The air surrounding this procession was downright odd. At first glance, it seemed like a marriage procession, but upon a closer look, there was solemnity, grief, fury, and terror on those faces. The only emotion missing was joy. It didn't look like they were festive at all, yet still they all wore red with flowers and made an ostentatious show. Such a scene truly was exceedingly peculiar. The tea master raised the copper teapot in his hand high and tipped it to pour tea. He also saw this scene play out, but he only shook his head before moving on.

Xie Lian watched as the bizarre procession disappeared into the distance, and he grew deep in thought for a moment. Just as he was about to take out the scroll Ling Wen had given him to read it over once more, he suddenly sensed something dazzling flit by.

When he looked up, a silver butterfly flew past his eyes.

That silver butterfly was glittering and translucent, and as it fluttered through the air, it left a sparkling bright trail in its wake. Xie Lian reached out toward it in spite of himself. This silver butterfly was incredibly intelligent; instead of being alarmed by the movement, it stopped on the tip of his finger. Its wings shimmered, beautiful and serene, and beneath the sunlight, it felt like the illusion of a dream that would shatter with a single touch. A moment later, it flew away.

Xie Lian waved at it as a farewell, and when he turned his head back around, there were two more people sitting at his table.

There were four sides to this table, and those two each took a side, one left, one right. They were both young men of eighteen or nineteen years of age. The one on the left side was taller, with deep brows and handsome features, and his eyes carried a sort of unbridled wildness. The one on the right was extremely fair, elegant, and poised. His expression was a bit overly distant and cold, making him look as if he was extremely displeased. Actually, neither of them looked pleasant.

Xie Lian blinked. "You two are?"

The one on the left replied, "Nan Feng."

The one on the right said, "Fu Yao."

I wasn't asking for your names... Xie Lian thought.

Just then, Ling Wen suddenly transmitted a message. "Your Highness, there are two junior martial officials from the Middle Court who have volunteered to go assist you. They've already descended to find you and should be there by now."

This Middle Court was naturally the opposite of the Upper Court. The heavenly officials of the Heavenly Realm could be crassly divided into two groups: those who had ascended and those who hadn't. The Upper Court consisted of heavenly officials who ascended on their own abilities. There were only about a hundred of them in the entire Heavenly Realm; extremely eminent. As for the ones in the Middle Court, they were brought up as "appointed generals." Strictly speaking, they should be addressed as "Peer Heavenly Officials," but when everyone addressed each other, they'd often take out "Peer" in the name.

One might ask, if there was an Upper Court and a Middle Court, was there a Lower Court?

No.

Actually, there had been one when Xie Lian first ascended. At the time, the division was still "Upper Court" and "Lower Court." However, later everyone discovered a problem: when one was introducing oneself, it sounded really bad to say "I am xxxx, from the Lower Court." With the word "lower," it felt like one was lower compared to the others. It must be known that there were definitely geniuses and outstanding figures with impressive spiritual power among them, and what they were missing was only that one Heavenly Tribulation before they could become real heavenly officials. And who knew if that day would arrive soon? Thus, it was proposed that one word be changed, and saying "I am xxxx, from the Middle Court," sounded so much better...even though they both meant the same thing. In any case, after it was changed, Xie Lian couldn't get used to it for the longest time.

Xie Lian stared at these two junior martial officials, each appearing more upset than the other, not looking at all like they had come "voluntarily."

He couldn't help but ask, "Ling Wen, they don't look like they're here to help me work, more like they're here for my good-for-nothing head. I hope they're not here because of your trickery."

Unfortunately, what he said didn't seem to be transmitted, and he couldn't hear Ling Wen's voice by his ears anymore either. He figured it was because he'd been away from the Heavenly Capital too far and too long, and his spiritual powers were depleted. Without any choice, Xie Lian first flashed a smile at the two junior martial officials, then said, "Nan Feng and Fu Yao, was it? Let me first thank you both for volunteering to come help."

The two only nodded, giving quite the attitude. It seemed they must've come from the retainment of distinguished martial gods. Xie Lian told the tea master to bring two more cups, then he raised his own teacup and scraped the tea leaves aside as he asked casually, "Which Highnesses are the two of you from?"

"The Palace of Nan Yang," replied Nan Feng.

"The Palace of Xuan Zhen," replied Fu Yao.

"..."

Well, this was certainly horrifying.

Xie Lian gulped down his mouthful of tea. "Did your generals tell you to come?"

The two answered in unison, "My general didn't know I was coming."

Xie Lian pondered for a moment before asking again, "Then, do you know who I am?"

If these two junior martial officials had come in blind because of Ling Wen's deception and helped him, then they would get scolded by their own generals upon their return. It wouldn't be worth it.

"You're His Royal Highness the Crown Prince," Nan Feng said.

"You're the justice of the Mortal Realm, the center of the world," Fu Yao said.

Xie Lian choked for a moment, then asked Nan Feng, uncertain, "Did he just roll his eyes?"

"Yes," Nan Feng replied. "Tell him to beat it."

It wasn't a secret that Nan Yang and Xuan Zhen didn't get along. When Xie Lian first heard of this, he wasn't surprised in the least, because Feng Xin and Mu Qing hadn't shared any great friendship in the past. What had kept things peaceful was that they were subordinates, so when the crown prince said "don't fight, you have to be good friends," everyone held back and didn't flip out. Back then, when they got really upset, they'd stab each other with words at most. But with the way things were now, faking it was no longer necessary.

This was also why the two heavenly officials' folk believers in the southeast and southwest regarded each other with contempt. Throughout the years, the Palace of Nan Yang and the Palace of Xuan Zhen had always seen each other as enemies. The two before him now were a classic example.

Fu Yao sneered. "Ling Wen-zhenjun said that all willing volunteers are welcome, so on what grounds are you telling me to scram?"

The word "willing," uttered using that expression of his, really wasn't persuasive. Xie Lian said, "Let me just confirm. You two really came as willing volunteers? If not, then please don't force yourselves."

The two answered in unison, "I'm willing."

Looking at those two grim and dispirited faces, Xie Lian thought inwardly, *You guys actually mean "I want to kill myself," right?*

"Well, in any case," Xie Lian continued, "let's talk business first. I'm sure you both know what we're doing here in the north, right? So I'm not explaining it from the top..."

"Nope," the two said in unison.

"..." Not having a choice, Xie Lian took out the scroll. "Then I guess I'll start from the very beginning for you two."

It was said that many years ago, at the foot of Mount Yujun, there was a couple about to get married.

This couple was deeply in love. That groom waited for the marriage procession to arrive, but he waited for a long time and still there was no sign of the bride. Anxious, the groom went to the bride's house, but his father- and mother-in-law told him that the bride had long since set out.

Both families reported this to the authorities, and they searched all over to no avail. If she was eaten by the beasts of the mountain, then at the very least there'd be a leftover arm or leg; how could she just vanish into thin air? Thus, of course there was suspicion that the bride wasn't willing to marry, so she colluded with the marriage procession and ran off. Yet who knew that many years later, when another couple was to marry, the same nightmare replayed?

Once again, the bride was gone. However, this time there was something left behind. On a small road, the search party found a foot that hadn't yet been fully eaten.

2

Three Clowns, Night Discussion on the Palace of Tremendous Masculinity

EVER SINCE THEN, things had gone out of control. Less than one hundred years after that first incident, there had been a total of seventeen brides who went missing in the Mount Yujun area. Sometimes there'd be a couple of decades of peace, and sometimes two would go missing in the short span of one month. A horrific legend quickly spread of a ghost groom who lived on Mount Yujun, and if a woman caught his eye, he would kidnap her on the road and devour the marriage procession.

Ordinarily, this affair wouldn't have been reported to the heavens. Although seventeen brides had gone missing, there were thousands more who were perfectly fine. Either way, the girls couldn't be found, and they couldn't be protected even if everyone wanted to do so; they could only make do with the status quo. Now there were fewer families willing to marry their daughters into this area, and the locals didn't dare make a fanfare of their weddings, that was all. But it just so happened that the father of the seventeenth bride was a lord official who doted on his daughter. When he heard of the local legend, he meticulously selected forty valiant and capable military officials to escort the marriage procession of his daughter. But the daughter was spirited off anyway.

This ghost groom had really stirred up the hornet's nest this time. No one this old lord official sought in the Mortal Realm could do anything about it, so in a fit of outrage, he assembled a group of government friends and conducted a wave of crazed religious services. He even followed the guidance of a great master and opened his stores to feed the poor, among other similar deeds. It was a huge uproar that shook the city, until finally this alerted a few heavenly officials above. Without going to such ends, it was practically impossible for the voices of insignificant mortals to reach the ears of gods in heaven.

"That's the gist of it," Xie Lian said.

Since those two still looked very uncooperative, he couldn't tell if they had actually been listening. If they didn't listen, he'd have to tell the story again. Nan Feng looked up, though, and frowned. "Are there any similarities between the missing brides?"

"There are those who are poor and those who are rich, those who are beautiful and those who are ugly, there are lawful wives and there are concubines. In short: there's no pattern," Xie Lian said. "We can't determine at all what this ghost groom's preference is."

Nan Feng *mn*-ed and picked up his teacup to take a sip, seeming to be thinking now. Fu Yao, on the other hand, never touched the tea Xie Lian had pushed in his direction and had been languidly cleaning his fingers with a white handkerchief this entire time.

He said coolly as he wiped, "Your Highness, how would you know that it must be a ghost groom? This can't be certain, since no one's ever seen it before. So how can we know if it's male or female, if it's old or young? Aren't you a little too quick to judge?"

Xie Lian grinned. "This scroll is a summary provided by a civil official from the Palace of Ling Wen. The ghost groom is just the common name for it. However, what you've said makes a lot of sense."

They spoke a bit more, and Xie Lian realized that these two junior martial officials' reasoning and logic were quite coherent. While they didn't appear very friendly, they weren't muddled at all when discussing important matters. Xie Lian felt relieved. Looking out the window, the hour was getting late, so the three left the small shop for the time being. Xie Lian put on his bamboo hat and walked for a bit before abruptly realizing the two behind him weren't following, so he looked back, puzzled. Turned out, the other two were also watching him in equal bemusement.

Nan Feng asked, "Where are you going?"

"To find some place to settle for the night," Xie Lian replied. "Fu Yao, why are you rolling your eyes again?"

Nan Feng continued his questions, still puzzled. "Then why are you heading to the wild bushes?"

Xie Lian often camped out in the wild and slept on the streets, and he could lay out a cloth on the ground and spend the night just like that. So naturally, he was ready to find some cave to start a campfire in as he'd always done. But it was with Nan Feng's reminder that he suddenly realized that Nan Feng and Fu Yao were both martial officials under a martial god; if there were any Nan Yang temples or Xuan Zhen temples around, then they could enter directly, so what need was there to sleep out in the wild?

A short while later, the three found a broken-down Tudi[3] shrine in an incredibly inconspicuous little corner that worshipped a round, small, stone Lord of the Soil and Ground. With incense residue and shattered platters, it looked exceedingly desolate. Xie Lian called out a few times. This Lord of the Soil and Ground hadn't been worshipped or called by anyone for years, so when he suddenly heard the call, he snapped open his eyes and saw three people standing before his shrine. The two on the left and right respectively were both enveloped in a sheen of spiritual light abundant like some nouveau riche, their faces barely visible. The deity jumped in alarm.

---

3   Tudigong, or Tudi, is a Daoist tutelary deity, a type of minor god that acts as patron or protector of a specific location, group of people, or thing.

His voice trembled. "Do the three heavenly officials have any-thing to command of this humble one?"

Xie Lian inclined his head. "No commands. I just wanted to ask if there are any local temples that worship either General Nan Yang or General Xuan Zhen?"

The Lord of Soil and Ground didn't dare to affront him and replied, "Um um um..." Then, in a quick divination with the pinch of his fingers, he answered, "There's a local town temple about two-and-a-half kilometers from here, and the one worshipped is...is...is the General Nan Yang."

Xie Lian put his hands together in prayer. "Many thanks."

However, that Lord of Soil and Ground was blinded by the two balls of spiritual power on both sides of Xie Lian, so he quickly van-ished. Xie Lian fumbled out a few coins and placed them in front of the altar shrine, and when he saw there were fallen remnants of burned incense sticks on the ground, he picked them up and relit them. Throughout the entire thing, Fu Yao was rolling his eyes so hard that Xie Lian almost wanted to ask if his eyes were tired.

About two-and-a-half kilometers later, they indeed spotted a local town temple standing fiery red by the roadside. While the temple was small, it had everything. People were going in and out, extraordinarily lively. The three concealed their forms and entered the temple. The one worshipped within the hall was a clay divine statue of the martial god Nan Yang, bedecked in armor with a bow in hand.

When Xie Lian saw this divine statue, he hummed inwardly.

In a small temple in the countryside, the craft and painting of divine statues could be expected to be rough. But on the whole, this statue was still significantly different from Xie Lian's own impres-sion of Feng Xin.

However, distorted divine statues were something that every heavenly official had long since gotten used to. Never mind that their own mothers wouldn't recognize them sometimes, there were heavenly officials who didn't even recognize themselves when they saw their own statues. After all, there weren't many artisan masters who had actually seen the real forms of the heavenly officials, so the statues were either distorted beautifully or hideously. One could only rely on the posture, spiritual apparatus, attire, and crown to determine which heavenly official it was.

Usually, the more affluent the area, the more the divine statue would please the heavenly official. The more impoverished a place, the worse the taste of the craftsmanship, and the more tragic the sculpture became. To speak of the present, there was only General Xuan Zhen whose divine statues were in a better situation. Why? Because for everyone else, if their statues were ugly, then whatever, leave it be. But when Mu Qing saw that his statues had been hideously sculpted, he would either secretly destroy them and make people start over, or appear in dreams to express his displeasure. This went on for a long time until the grand believers all learned that they had to find an artisan master who could sculpt beautifully!

All the temples of Xuan Zhen were exactly the same as their general: particular and tasteful. But after Fu Yao entered the Temple of Nan Yang, for two whole hours he thoroughly criticized the statue of Nan Yang from head to toe: how the design was deformed, the colors tacky, the craftsmanship crude, the taste bizarre. Xie Lian watched as the blue veins on Nan Feng's forehead slowly popped out, and thought he best quickly find another topic of conversation.

It just so happened that there was a girl who entered to pray, and she very sincerely knelt. Xie Lian said warmly, "Speaking of,

Nan Yang-zhenjun's main domain is in the southeast. I never imagined you guys would have such a following in the north too."

When people constructed temples, they were imitating the divine palaces of the Heavenly Realm, and divine statues were reflections of the heavenly officials' venerable selves. Temples attracted worship and were where believers gathered, becoming an important source of spiritual power for heavenly officials. And due to various reasons—such as geography, history, and customs—people of different regions often worshipped different gods. A heavenly official's spiritual power would be maximized on their own turf, and this was the main advantage of having a domain. Only to a heavenly official like the Heavenly Emperor, who had believers from all over the world and possessed temples everywhere, was the notion of a main domain meaningless. It was a good thing that the holy temple of Nan Feng's own general was so popular even outside his main domain. He should have been proud, but judging by his expression, this was very much not the case.

On the side, Fu Yao gave a light smirk. "Yes, yes, he's deeply loved."

Xie Lian said, "But I just have a question that I don't know if..."

"If you're going to say 'you don't know if it's appropriate,' then don't say anything," Nan Feng interrupted.

No, I was going to say "don't know if anyone has the answer," Xie Lian thought.

But he had a feeling that it'd be bad if he said it, so in the end, he decided to change the subject again.

Yet unexpectedly, Fu Yao languidly said, "I know what you want to ask. You must be wondering why there are so many female believers coming to worship?"

That was indeed the question Xie Lian had in mind.

There had always been fewer female believers than male in the martial gods' stream; only Xie Lian himself was an exception, eight hundred years ago. However, the reason for this exception was very simple, and it was also only two words: good-looking.

He knew very well that it wasn't because he was distinguished or because he had extraordinary spiritual powers. It was merely due to the fact that his divine statue was good-looking, and his palace temples were handsome too. Practically all of his palace temples were constructed by the royal family, and the highest-skilled experts and artisans of the kingdom were summoned to sculpt the divine statues exactly in accordance with his face. Besides, because of that phrase "Body in the abyss, heart in paradise," the artisans liked adding flowers to his divine statues and planting seas of flowering trees at his temples. Thus, at the time, he had another title: "The Flower-Crowned Martial God." The lady believers liked that his divine statues were good-looking and that his palace temples were filled with flowers, and due to that alone, they were willing to casually enter to pray.

The usual martial gods were too heavy in killing aura and often had their faces sculpted to be serious, savage, and cold, so when lady believers saw, they would rather pray to the bodhisattvas instead. While this statue of Nan Yang had none of the killing aura, it was far from good-looking, and yet there still seemed to be more female believers praying than male. Nan Feng obviously didn't want to answer this question either, which was making Xie Lian even more curious. It just so happened that right then, that girl finished her worship. She rose to her feet to reach for the incense, then spun around.

While she was turned away, Xie Lian nudged the other two. They were already very annoyed, and with his nudge, they looked, and *whoosh*, both their faces dropped.

"Too ugly!" Fu Yao exclaimed.

Xie Lian choked for a moment, then chided, "Fu Yao, you can't talk about girls like that."

If he had to be honest, what Fu Yao said was true. That girl's face was incomparably flat, looking exactly like someone had leveled it with a slap. It would almost be an insult to say her features were plain; if they must be described, then only "crooked nose and slanted eyes" could be used.

However, Xie Lian didn't register whether she was beautiful or ugly at all. The main thing was, when she spun around, there was an enormous tear on the back of her skirt, and he really couldn't pretend he didn't see it.

Fu Yao was startled at first, but he quickly regained himself. The popped veins on the corners of Nan Feng's forehead also instantly vanished.

Seeing his face change colors so drastically, Xie Lian quickly soothed, "Don't be nervous, don't be nervous."

The girl took incense and knelt down anew, and said as she prayed, "May General Nan Yang give his blessings. This believer Xiao-Ying prays for that ghost groom to be captured soon, so no other innocents will be harmed by him..."

She was sincere and devout in her prayers and didn't sense anything peculiar going on behind her at all, nor was she aware that there were three men crouching next to the foot of the divine statue she was praying to.

Xie Lian fretted. "What do we do? We can't let her walk out like this. Everyone on her way home will see."

Besides, judging by that tear on the back of her skirt, it was obvious someone had intentionally ripped it with a sharp object. She probably wouldn't just be seen by a crowd of onlookers, she would also be publicly laughed at, and that would truly be considerable humiliation.

Fu Yao was unconcerned. "Don't ask me. The one she's praying to isn't my General Xuan Zhen. 'Do not look at what is improper.' I saw nothing."

Meanwhile, blood was draining from Nan Feng's handsome face. He only knew to wave, not talk; a perfectly fine, unbridled, strapping young man was forcibly rendered mute, completely hopeless. And so Xie Lian had no choice but to take action himself, taking off his outer robe and throwing it down below. The outer robe flapped in the air for a moment and drifted down onto the body of that girl, blocking the very inelegant tear on the back of her skirt. The three sighed a breath in unison.

However, that breeze was strange, and it startled the girl. She looked around, took off the robe, and hesitated briefly before she placed it onto the altar. She was completely unaware, and after sticking the incense in the burner, she made her way out. If they let her out to walk around like that, the little maiden would probably not have the face to look at anyone ever again. The two on Xie Lian's right and left were either frozen or frozen, completely useless however you wanted them, and he sighed. Nan Feng and Fu Yao felt the space beside their bodies empty suddenly. Xie Lian had already taken form and jumped down.

The lamplight inside the temple was dim, and a small gust rose from his leap, causing the firelight to flicker. The girl Xiao-Ying only saw a blur before a man suddenly emerged from the darkness, reaching out to her with his upper body bare, and she was scared out of her wits right then and there.

As expected, she screamed. Just when Xie Lian was about to speak, the girl's slap already struck out in a flash, and she yelled *"harassment!"*

Thwack! And Xie Lian was slapped just like that.

The slap was clear and crisp, and the two crouching on top of the altar both felt the side of their faces twitch at the same time.

Xie Lian wasn't mad at the strike, however, and only forcefully stuffed the outer robe into her arms, swiftly whispering something. The girl was greatly alarmed, felt her behind, and suddenly flushed red in the face. Tears welled up in her eyes; who knew whether it was anger or indignation. She clutched the outer robe Xie Lian gave her and dashed out covering her face, leaving Xie Lian standing there half-bare. With the girl gone, the temple was now deserted. A cool breeze wafted through the hall, and it was suddenly a little chilly.

He rubbed his cheek, and with that red hand-mark on half of his face, he turned to the other two. "All right, everything's resolved."

Nan Feng pointed at him. "Did...you tear your wounds?"

Xie Lian looked down and *oh*-ed.

After undressing, what was revealed was a body smooth and fair like jade. Except his chest was heavily wrapped in layer after layer of white cloth, firmly bound. Even his neck and wrists were wrapped in bandages. Innumerable small cuts crawled out from the edges of the white bandages, truly a startling sight.

He figured his sprained neck was pretty much recovered by now, so Xie Lian started unbinding his bandages. Fu Yao glanced at him, then questioned, "Who was it?"

"What?" Xie Lian asked.

"Who fought you?" Fu Yao demanded.

"Fought?" Xie Lian was confused. "No one?"

"Then all those injuries on your body..." Nan Feng was hesitant.

Xie Lian looked at them blankly. "I fell on my own."

"..."

Those were indeed the injuries from when he tumbled down from heaven three days ago. If it were from a fight with another person, then he actually might not have been hurt so badly.

Fu Yao grumbled something, but it wasn't clear. Either way, it definitely wasn't praising him for his fortitude, so Xie Lian didn't bother to ask, focusing only on removing the heavy layer of bandages from his neck. The next second, Nan Feng and Fu Yao's gazes hardened as their eyes fell on his throat.

A black collar encircled his snow-white neck.

Sensing their stare, Xie Lian gave a light smile and turned around. "First time seeing a real cursed shackle?"

Cursed shackle. Like its name implied, it was a shackle formed by a particular curse.

Heavenly officials who were banished from heaven would have the mark of sin, forged by the wrath of heaven, branded onto their bodies. This brand formed a fetter that sealed spiritual powers away, never to be freed. Just like a brand on the face, or chains shackling hands and feet, this was a form of punishment, and a warning. It was both terrifying and humiliating.

As the Laughingstock of the Three Realms who was banished twice, of course Xie Lian had such a cursed shackle on his body. It was impossible for those two junior martial officials not to have heard of this before, but there was still a little difference between having heard and seeing it personally. Thus, Xie Lian could understand why they would react the way they did.

He figured this might be making the two junior officials wary and uncomfortable. After all, it wasn't like those shackles were a good thing.

At first, he used the excuse of going out to search for clothes in order to get a chance to step outside, but he was stopped in his tracks by Fu Yao's eyeroll and his comment: "It'd be incredibly indecent for you to go out in the street looking like that."

In the end, it was thanks to Nan Feng, who tossed him a temple attendant's robes that he'd grabbed from the back of the building, that Xie Lian was able to stop being so indecent. However, even after they'd settled back down, it felt like the incident earlier had caused the mood to become somewhat awkward. And so, Xie Lian took out the scroll given by the Palace of Ling Wen.

He said, "Do you guys want to take another look at this?"

Nan Feng raised his eyes and gave him a look. "I've looked through it already, I think *he's* the one who needs to take a better look at it."

"What do you mean I'm the one who needs to take a better look at it?" Fu Yao countered. "That scroll isn't detailed at all, completely worthless, and you think it's worth another look?"

Hearing him say the scroll was worthless, Xie Lian couldn't help but feel a little sad for the ashen-faced junior civil officials at the Palace of Ling Wen who put this together.

Fu Yao then continued, "Oh yeah, where were we? The Temple of Nan Yang—why does Nan Yang have so many female believers, right?"

All right. Xie Lian put the scroll away and rubbed his pulsing forehead. He understood now. No one would be able to look through it tonight!

If they weren't going to focus on the real business, then why not see what the side business was all about? Turned out, other than the Royal Highness who spent centuries collecting scraps in the Mortal Realm, every deity knew that there was a period of time when Nan Yang-zhenjun—Feng Xin—was called "Ju Yang-zhenjun." The man himself deeply detested this title, and everyone only had one word for his experience: injustice!

The original correct writing used the characters "Ju Yang," which meant "Perfect Sun." The incident that warped them happened many years ago. During that time, a king was constructing a great number of temples and palaces. To demonstrate his faith and sincerity, he personally drafted the titles for every temple or palace's establishment plaque. But when it came to the Palace of Ju Yang, for some reason, he used characters for "Ju Yang" that meant "Tremendous Masculinity."[4]

This gave the officials responsible for the construction much grief. They just couldn't figure out whether His Majesty changed it intentionally or if it was an accident. If it was intentional, why wasn't there a clear decree that indicated yes, this is what We want to change to? If it wasn't intentional, why would their king commit such a low-level mistake? It wasn't like they could say "Your Majesty, you're wrong." Who knew if His Majesty would mistake them for being sarcastic about his carelessness? That they were hinting that his knowledge was shallow? That his heart was insincere? This was His Majesty's royal writing; were they going to trash it if they weren't going to use it?

Divine beings had hearts most difficult to discern, and the officials were in pure agony. After much deliberation, instead of causing grief for His Majesty, they thought they might as well cause grief for Ju Yang-zhenjun.

It had to be said that they made the right decision. When the king discovered that Perfect Sun had become Tremendous Masculinity, he didn't make any statements, but instead invited a bunch of scholars to scour the ancient texts with great vigor to find countless minuscule reasons and compose many essays to painstakingly prove that it should've been Tremendous Masculinity in the first place, and that Perfect Sun was wrong. In any case, every Palace of Perfect

---

4 俱陽 "Perfect Sun" vs 巨陽 "Tremendous Masculinity"

Sun in the country became a Palace of Tremendous Masculinity overnight.

Feng Xin, whose divine title changed so randomly, didn't find this out until decades later. He basically had never bothered to look closely at the signs of his own temples, but one day, he suddenly felt rather baffled. Why were there so many women coming to pray in his temples, each of them flushed with shyness on her cheeks? And what in the world were they praying for when offering incense?!

After he figured it out, he charged up to the peak of the ninth sky and shouted his curses to the scorching sun and the vast skies.

He shocked every heavenly official.

After he was done cursing, there was nothing he could do, so he could only relent. It wasn't like he could pick on those women who were praying so sincerely, so he forced himself to listen for many years. It wasn't until a decent ruler came along who thought Tremendous Masculinity was horribly obscene that it was changed to "Nan Yang," for "Southern Sun." Nonetheless, no one forgot what else he could grant beyond his duties as a martial god. However, everyone also upheld an unspoken rule: never call him by that name. At the same time, they also upheld a general consensus: How to evaluate this Nan Yang-zhenjun? With one word: good!

Don't let him open his mouth to yell at people and everything should be good!

Nan Feng's face was already as dark as the bottom of an aged wok, yet Fu Yao was suddenly feeling poetic, and he recited demurely:

"Friend of women
A trusty companion;
Ask for a son
Most powerful is he,

The secret formula
To bolster masculinity,
A son in your prayers
Nan Yang delivers.
Aha ha, aha ha, aha ha ha ha ha ha..."

Xie Lian very kindly held back his laugh, leaving a bit of face for Nan Yang in front of his divine statue. Nan Feng, however, was outraged. "Don't you act all sarcastic here! If you're really that bored, go sweep the floor!"

The moment those words were spat, Fu Yao's face also darkened to the color of a pot bottom. If the Palace of Nan Yang couldn't stand to hear the words Tremendous Masculinity, then the Palace of Xuan Zhen couldn't stand to hear people bring up the term "sweep." This was because, when Mu Qing was still an errand boy at the Royal Holy Temple, all he did all day was serve tea, deliver water, sweep, and change the sheets for Xie Lian at the Palace of the Crown Prince. One day, Xie Lian saw him silently reciting training incantations while sweeping. He was thus moved by his spirit for learning and hard work under such harsh and difficult circumstances, and persuaded the state preceptor to take him in as a disciple.

How to best describe this incident? It could be considered grand or insignificant, it could be humiliating or a compliment; it depended entirely on the individual in question. Obviously, the individual in question had taken it as the humiliation of his life, since Mu Qing and every martial warrior under his command would flip out whenever they heard the word "sweep."

Sure enough, Fu Yao steadied himself, then after throwing a look at Xie Lian—who was waving his hand, appearing fully innocent—he sneered.

"Listening to you, those who don't know would think your Palace of Nan Yang sides with the Palace of the Crown Prince and fights hard to right the injustices against him."

Nan Feng sneered too. "Your general certainly is the ungrateful one that bites the hand that feeds him, what more can I say?"

"Um..."

Xie Lian was just trying to intercept when Fu Yao *aha ha*-ed and said, "The kettle is calling the pot black, what right do you have to point fingers?"

"..."

Listening to them turn him into the mallet with which they took turns to beat the heavenly official standing right up there on the altar, Xie Lian finally couldn't take it any longer. "Wait, hold up. Stop, stop."

Of course no one paid him any mind, and they even started throwing fists. Who knew who threw the first punch, but either way, the altar was split in half just like that, and platters of fruit rolled all over the ground. Seeing how there was no way he could stop this fight anymore, Xie Lian sat himself in the corner and heaved a sigh.

"What a sin."

Then, he picked up a small steamed bun that had rolled to his feet. He dusted off its skin and was about to bite down when Nan Feng saw him from the corner of his eye and immediately slapped it away.

"DON'T EAT THAT!"

Fu Yao stopped too, and appeared shaken and disgusted. "How can you eat it when it's rolled in the dirt?!"

Xie Lian used this chance to raise his hand. "Stop, stop, stop. I have something to say."

He separated the two and said, looking amicable, "First, That Highness the Crown Prince you two speak of happens to be me.

This Highness hasn't even said anything, so don't sling me around like a weapon to attack each other." He paused for a moment, then added, "I don't think your generals would ever behave like this. If you two act so indecorously, you'll ruin their reputations."

When those words were spoken, the faces of the other two changed to something indiscernible. Xie Lian continued, "Second, you two are here to help me, right? So is it you who listens to me, or is it me who listens to you?"

It was a moment before the two replied, "We listen to you."

While their faces looked like they were saying "Listen to you? Dream on," Xie Lian was already very satisfied. Then, *pah!* He put his hands together in prayer.

"Good. Now thirdly, the most important thing: if you must throw something, then please throw me instead of food."

Nan Feng finally pried away the steamed bun that Xie Lian had clutched in his grip hoping for a chance to eat it. He said, looking like he couldn't take it anymore, "If it's fallen to the ground, don't eat it!"

The next day, back at the Little Shop of Chance Encounters.

The tea master was once again by the entrance relaxing with his leg up when he saw the three approaching from a distance. The cultivator in light, simple white robes with a bamboo hat hung on his back led the way, while two tall, black-clad youths trailed behind him.

That cultivator strolled up languidly with crossed arms, and he spoke equally languidly, sounding more idle than the old man. "Shopkeeper, three cups of tea, please."

The tea master smiled. "Coming!"

Then he thought to himself, *Those three silly guys are here again. What a shame, each looks sightlier than the other, but each of their brains is more damaged than the next. What god, what ghost, what heavens? When you're crazy, what good is a decent face?*

Xie Lian still picked the spot next to the window, and after they settled, Nan Feng spoke up. "Why do we have to come here to discuss things? You sure there won't be people listening in?"

Xie Lian replied warmly, "It's fine. Even if other people hear us, they won't care, they'll only think we're insane."

"..."

"In order to avoid the three of us continuing to waste each other's time like this, let's lay it all out," Xie Lian said. "Now that we've calmed down overnight, have you guys thought of any ideas?"

Fu Yao's eyes flashed, and he said coldly, "Kill it!"

"No shit!" Nan Feng said.

"Nan Feng, don't be so rude. Fu Yao didn't say anything wrong," Xie Lian said. "The way to solve this problem is to kill the creature, but the bigger issue is, where do we go? What are we killing? How do we kill it? I suggest..."

At that moment, the sound of gongs and drums came from the main street, and the three looked out the window.

It was that bleak and tragic wedding procession again. This party of men and horses blew their instruments to the utmost, hollering and cheering as if they were afraid people couldn't hear what they were about.

Nan Feng frowned. "Isn't it said that the people around Mount Yujun don't make spectacles of these rituals anymore?"

This procession consisted of large, strong, buff men. Their expressions and muscles were both taut, and cold sweat oozed from their foreheads. It was like they weren't carrying a festive and cheery bridal sedan but rather a guillotine that'd end their lives early. It made one wonder just what sort of person was seated in that sedan.

After hesitating for a moment, just as Xie Lian was thinking of going to check things out, a sinister wind blew past, raising one of the curtains on the side of the sedan.

The figure behind the curtain was lying slumped in a very strange position inside. Her head was bent in an awkward angle, and underneath the bridal veil there were bright red lips curled in an overly exaggerated smile. The sedan tipped and the covering fell, exposing a pair of bulging eyes staring their way.

From the looks of it, this was clearly a woman who'd had her neck wrung, and who was now laughing at them uproariously but soundlessly.

Perhaps it was because the sedan carriers were shaking too hard, but that bridal sedan wasn't steady in the least, so the woman's head bounced along with the bumps. They bumped and bumped, and *THUD*, the head fell off and rolled onto the street.

The headless body sitting inside the sedan also fell forward with a bang, and the whole person crashed out of the sedan.

ONE OF THE SEDAN carriers wasn't paying attention and stepped on an arm. He screamed without thinking, and then immediately the entire wedding procession was in an uproar. Good lord, that band of men whipped out their shining broadswords!

They yelled, "What's the matter?! Has it come?!"

Commotion had broken out in the street. When Xie Lian looked closely, the body with its head severed wasn't a real person but a wooden puppet.

"Too ugly!" Fu Yao commented again.

The tea master just happened to be coming over with the copper teapot. Xie Lian recalled his attitude yesterday, so he asked, "Shopkeeper, I saw that group of people banging drums and gongs yesterday, and I see them doing the same again today. What are they doing?"

"Seeking their own ruin," the tea master said.

"Ha ha ha..." Xie Lian wasn't surprised. "Are they trying to lure out that ghost groom?"

"What do you think?" the tea master replied. "The father of a missing bride will award a great sum of money to whoever finds his daughter and captures that ghost groom, so that group has been messing around, all day every day, creating a foul atmosphere."

The father who was awarding the bounty must be the lord official. Xie Lian took another glance at that crassly built head of a woman, knowing the men were attempting to disguise the puppet as the bride.

Fu Yao commented in disgust, "If I were the ghost groom, I'd wipe out this entire troupe for sending such an ugly thing to me."

"Fu Yao, you're not speaking as an immortal should," Xie Lian said. "And can you fix that eye-rolling habit of yours? Why don't you set a small target for yourself first and roll only five times a day or something like that?"

"Set it at fifty times a day and it still won't be enough!" Nan Feng added.

Just then, a young man suddenly poked out from the procession, spunky and spirited. Judging by sight, he was the leader. He raised his arm and hollered, "Listen to me, LISTEN TO ME! It's completely useless to keep this up! How many times have we made this trip in the past few days? Has the ghost groom ever shown itself?!"

The group of men agreed and started to grumble while that youth continued, "I think, since we started this, we should just do it and charge right up Mount Yujun. We'll search the mountain and drag that ugly freak out to kill it! I'll lead the way. Any good, brave men can follow me, kill the ugly freak, and we'll split the bounty!"

There were only a small and scattered number of men at first who answered his call, but the voices gradually grew bigger and louder. In the end, everyone was roaring in agreement, surprisingly sounding rather immense in strength.

Xie Lian wondered, "Ugly freak? Shopkeeper, what's the ugly freak they're talking about?"

The tea master replied, "Apparently the ghost groom is an ugly creature living on Mount Yujun, and because it's so ugly, no woman loves it. That's why it grew hate in its heart and began robbing others of their brides to ruin their happy occasions."

The scroll from the Palace of Ling Wen didn't record this. Xie Lian wondered, "Is that explanation true? Is it not speculation?"

"Who knows," the tea master replied. "Apparently quite a few people have seen it; its entire face is wrapped in bandages, with savage eyes peering out. It doesn't know how to talk and can only growl like a wolfhound. The rumors are quite bizarre."

"Just because its face is wrapped in bandages doesn't mean it's ugly. There's also the possibility that it's so beautiful that it doesn't want others to see," Fu Yao said.

The tea master was speechless for a moment. "Who knows. Either way, I've never seen it."

Right then, a young girl's voice came from the street. "Don't...don't listen to him, don't go. Mount Yujun is a very dangerous place..."

The one who spoke while hiding at a street corner was the girl who was praying for blessings at the Temple of Nan Yang last night, Xiao-Ying. When Xie Lian saw her face, he could feel his own aching and subconsciously rubbed his cheek.

That youth appeared grim when he saw her, and he shoved her. "What's a little woman doing, interrupting when the big men are talking?"

Xiao-Ying cowered a little when she was shoved, but then she gathered her courage and said in a small voice, "Don't listen to him. Whether it's faking a wedding procession or searching the mountain, aren't you all seeking your own deaths by doing something so dangerous?"

"Well, don't you make it sound nice," the youth rebuked. "Us guys are putting our lives on the line to exterminate evil for the people, but what about you? Selfish and greedy, refusing to play the role of the fake bride and get on the sedan; you don't have half the courage of the people here, but now you're here to obstruct us? What are you scheming?"

He shoved her with every word, making everyone inside the shop frown at the sight. Xie Lian looked down and unwrapped the bandage on his wrist as he heard the tea master speak. "That Xiao-Pengtou wanted to coax that girl into playing the fake bride before, his words sweet like honey. But the girl refused, so now he's changed face."

On the street, the group of burly men also exclaimed, "Stop standing there blocking our way, move aside!"

When Xiao-Ying saw this, her flat face was flushed bright red, tears rolling in her eyes. "Why...why must you talk like this?"

That youth, Xiao-Pengtou, continued, "Was I wrong? I told you to play the fake bride, and did you not refuse?"

Xiao-Ying replied, "It's true that I didn't dare do it, but you didn't have to slash...slash my dress..."

The moment she mentioned this, Xiao-Pengtou instantly jumped as if he stubbed his toe. He pointed at her face and yelled, "You ugly freak, don't slander people around here! Me? Slash your dress? Are you taking me for blind?! Who knows if you didn't do it yourself because you want to flash people! As if anyone would want to see an ugly face like yours even with a ripped dress! Don't blame this on me!"

Nan Feng couldn't bear to listen anymore, and the teacup shattered in his hand with a crack. Just as he was about to stand up, however, a white silhouette drifted past. At the same time, Xiao-Pengtou, who was jumping a foot high, yelped and fell on his butt on the ground, holding his face while blood dripped from between the cracks of his fingers.

No one in the crowd had a chance to see what exactly happened before the boy was already sitting on the ground. At first, they thought it was Xiao-Ying who went berserk. Yet when they looked at her, they couldn't actually see her. A white-clad cultivator had come and shielded her.

Xie Lian tucked his hands in his sleeves, not bothering to look back. He grinned happily at Xiao-Ying, bending slightly at the waist to meet her eyes. "Miss, I was wondering if I might have the pleasure of inviting you inside for a cup of tea?"

Xiao-Pengtou was sprawled on the ground. His mouth and nose were in excruciating pain; his entire face was in agony, as if he had just been cracked brutally by a steel whip. Yet this cultivator clearly didn't carry any weapons, nor did Xiao-Pengtou see how the man had struck or what he had used to strike.

He scrambled to crawl up, then brandished his blade and yelled, "This man used wicked magic!"

When the group of burly men behind him heard "wicked magic," they all brandished their broadswords. Yet unexpectedly, Nan Feng suddenly struck with his hand from behind, and *crack!* A pillar snapped and broke.

Having witnessed such godly strength, the group of burly men instantly lost color in their faces. Although stricken with fear, Xiao-Pengtou still remained stubborn and shouted at them as he ran away. "I'll concede defeat today—where did you fellow good men come from? Leave your names, and we'll meet again someday…"

Nan Feng didn't even care to answer him, but next to him, Fu Yao replied, "Very kind, very kind, this one is from the Temple of Ju…"

Nan Feng struck out another hand, and those two began to spar soundlessly. Xie Lian wanted to invite the little maiden in to sit for a bit at first, order some fruit tea or something, yet before he could, she walked off on her own while wiping away tears. He sighed, watching that retreating back, then went inside by himself.

When he entered the tea shop, the tea master chided, "Remember to pay for that pillar."

Thus, when Xie Lian sat down, he turned to Nan Feng. "Remember to pay for that pillar."

"..." replied Nan Feng.

"Before that, let's focus on proper business," Xie Lian said. "Who can lend me some spiritual powers? I need to enter the communication array to verify some information."

Nan Feng raised his hand, and the two clapped palms as an oath, counting it as binding an extremely simple contract. Thus, Xie Lian could finally enter the communication array once more.

The moment he entered, he heard Ling Wen say, "Your Highness finally managed to borrow some spiritual powers? Is everything in the north going well? Were the two junior martial officials who volunteered themselves any help?"

Xie Lian looked up and glanced at the pillar Nan Feng snapped with his palm earlier. Then he glanced at Fu Yao, who was currently resting with his eyes closed, wearing a cold and distant expression. He then replied, "The two junior martial officials both have their own values, and they are both talents worth nurturing."

Ling Wen chuckled. "Then we must congratulate General Nan Yang and General Xuan Zhen. On Your Highness's words, the future of those junior martial officials must be infinite, and they will soon ascend themselves."

It wasn't long before Mu Qing's voice surfaced coolly. "He didn't inform me of this outing, so let him be. Either way, I don't know anything."

You really are lurking in the communication array all day... Xie Lian thought.

"Your Highness," Ling Wen said. "Where have you settled? The north is guarded by General Pei; his worshippers are abundant. If Your Highness has any need, you can stay temporarily at his Temples of Ming Guang."

"There's no need for the trouble," Xie Lian replied. "We didn't find any Temple of Ming Guang nearby, so we settled in a Temple of Nan Yang. A quick question, Ling Wen, about this ghost groom: Do you have any more information?"

"Yes," Ling Wen replied. "The result of its rank evaluation was just processed by my palace. It's a wrath."

A wrath!

In regard to the monsters, demons, and ghosts that caused great turmoil within the Mortal Realm, the Palace of Ling Wen had categorized them based on their abilities. The ranks were as follows: fierce, malice, wrath, and supreme.

A "fierce" murdered one, a "malice" could murder a sect, a "wrath" could slaughter an entire city. As for the most fearsome "supremes," once they were born into this world, they were destined to bring ruin to nations and people and complete disorder everywhere.

This ghost groom that had been holing up in Mount Yujun was ranked a wrath, only one level lower than a supreme. That meant no one who saw it could escape unharmed.

Thus, after Xie Lian exited the communication array and informed the other two of this, Nan Feng said, "Then the 'ugly bandaged male' is probably just a rumor. Or they saw something else."

"There's another possibility," Xie Lian said. "Like for example, under certain circumstances this ghost groom will not or cannot cause harm."

Fu Yao said disapprovingly, "The Palace of Ling Wen is so inefficient, taking this long only to come up with a rank. What's the use?!"

"At the very least, we have an understanding of the enemy's strength," Xie Lian said. "But since this is a wrath, the ghost groom's spiritual powers must be very strong, and a fake puppet will not be able to deceive it at all. If we want to lure it out, then we can't cast a camouflage spell on puppets for the wedding procession, and we can't carry weapons either. The most important thing is: the bride must be a living person."

"We'll just find a woman on the street to use as bait," Fu Yao said.

Nan Feng, however, rejected the idea. "No."

"Why not?" Fu Yao said. "Think they'll be unwilling? Give them a sum of money, and they'll be willing then."

"Fu Yao, even if there are women who are willing, it's best if we don't employ this method," Xie Lian said. "This ghost groom is a wrath. If there are any mishaps, nothing will happen to us. But if the bride is kidnapped, a meek woman won't be able to escape or fight back, so it's certain death for her."

"If we can't use women, then we have to use men," Fu Yao said.

Nan Feng said, "Where are we going to find a man who's willing to..."

He trailed off, and the two gazed over.

Xie Lian was still sitting there, smiling. "???"

Nighttime, the Temple of Nan Yang.

Xie Lian emerged from behind the back of the temple with his hair down and flowing, looking disheveled. The two standing guard by the temple entrance looked, and Nan Feng swore "Fuck!!" right on the spot before charging out.

Xie Lian was speechless for a moment, then said, "Was that necessary?"

No matter who looked, they could tell with one glance that this was a handsome man with gentle brows. But this was precisely the reason why many would be unable to stand the image of a perfectly good, handsome man wearing a woman's wedding dress. Nan Feng,

for example, couldn't bear it at all, which was why his reaction was so extreme.

Xie Lian saw Fu Yao was still standing there, scanning him up and down with a complicated look.

He asked, "Is there anything you wish to say?"

Fu Yao nodded. "If I were the ghost groom and someone sent a woman like this to me..."

"You'd wipe out the entire town, was it?" Xie Lian finished for him.

Fu Yao replied frigidly, "No, I'd kill the woman."

Xie Lian smiled. "Then I can only say: thank goodness I'm not a woman."

Fu Yao said, "I think... Why don't you go ask in the communication array now to see if there is any heavenly official who is willing to teach you transformation magic? That would be more practical."

There certainly were several heavenly officials who, on account of their own unique needs, knew transformation magic. However, it was probably too late to learn now. Over on the other side, Nan Feng came back in with a gloomy face. He was much calmer after having sworn; a trait that was truly entirely the same as the general he served.

Seeing it was getting late, Xie Lian said, "Whatever, it's all the same when the veil goes on."

He was about to put the covering on when Fu Yao raised a hand and stopped him.

"Hang on, you don't know how that ghost groom harms people. If he raises the veil and feels deceived, wouldn't that just provoke unnecessary trouble? Rage is unpredictable, and events can take unexpected turns."

Xie Lian thought that made sense, but when he took a step, he heard a *rrrrrip*.

This red wedding dress Fu Yao got him really didn't fit that well.

A woman's form was much daintier. After he put on the dress, while the waist was surprisingly just fine, he was severely restricted in raising his arms and lifting his feet. When the movement was too wide, the robes ripped. Just as he was looking everywhere to see where the fabric was torn, a voice came from the entrance of the temple.

"Excuse me..."

The three looked to the source of the sound and saw Xiao-Ying, holding a properly folded white robe in her hands while standing at the entrance of the temple. She was watching them with trepidation.

"I remember it was here where I met you, so I wanted to come over to see if I'd run into you again..." Xiao-Ying said. "I've washed these clothes; I'll put them here. Thanks so much for yesterday and today."

Xie Lian was just going to smile in response when he suddenly remembered his own appearance and decided it was best if he didn't speak to scare people.

Yet unexpectedly, not only was Xiao-Ying not frightened, she took another step forward. "Are you... If you like, I can help?"

"...No, Miss, please don't misunderstand, this isn't a hobby of mine," Xie Lian explained.

Xiao-Ying quickly replied, "I know, I know. What I meant was I can help you, if you don't mind. You guys...you guys are going to go catch the ghost groom, right?"

Her voice and her expression both lifted instantly. "I-I know how to tailor clothes, I've got needles and thread on me at all times, I can help fix anywhere that doesn't fit, and I can even help with make-overs—let me help you!"

"..."

Two incense time passed, and Xie Lian once again emerged from the back of the temple with his head down. This time, the bridal veil was already in place. Nan Feng and Fu Yao had wanted to take a look at first, but in the end they decided to cherish their eyes. The sedan they called over was already waiting by the entrance of the temple, and the carefully selected sedan carriers had also been waiting for a long time.

It was a night when the moon was obscured, and the winds raised. Adorned in a brand-new wedding dress, the crown prince thus mounted the bright red bridal sedan.

The entire body of that bridal sedan was dressed in bright red satin, which was embroidered with colored threads spelling the words "Blooming Flowers and Full Moon" and "Dragon and Phoenix Bring Prosperity," idioms meaning "perfect happiness" and "extremely good fortune." Nan Feng and Fu Yao were on the right and left respectively, escorting the bridal sedan on either side. Xie Lian sat poised within the sedan, swaying along with the movement of the sedan carriers.

The eight sedan carriers carrying the large palanquin were all outstanding military officers. In order to find expertly skilled sedan carriers to play the part of the wedding procession, Nan Feng and Fu Yao went directly to that lord official's residence and demonstrated their power, then revealed that they planned to probe Mount Yujun that night. Without a word, the official summoned a squad of big, tall military officers. However, it wasn't in the hope of extra help that the expertly skilled were chosen. Rather, it was so that when the wrath ghost launched attacks, they could run away and protect themselves.

But in truth, it was actually those eight military officers who were secretly looking down on them. They were the top, number one experts at the government office, and leaders of outstanding heroes wherever they went. Yet those two pretty boys were riding over their heads and had ordered them to be sedan carriers? It wouldn't be wrong to say they were quite upset. The master's orders had to be followed, so they forcibly suppressed the disdain in their hearts. Nonetheless, it was difficult to avoid the frustration flaring up, so every so often they'd purposely jerk their legs or shake their hands, making the sedan ride quite bumpy. Others might not be able to tell, but if the one sitting inside the sedan was just a bit weaker and more delicate, they would have probably puked their guts out.

The sedan bumped and bumped, and sure enough, they heard Xie Lian inside the sedan let out a low sigh. The military officials couldn't help but feel rather proud inwardly.

Outside, Fu Yao said coolly, "What's the matter, Miss? Tears of joy at finally marrying at your old age?"

Indeed, when a bride left home for the first time, many teared up and wept in the bridal sedan. Xie Lian didn't know whether to laugh or cry, but when he spoke, his voice was calm and natural, revealing nothing of the discomfort from the bumpy ride.

"No. It's just...I suddenly realized that this wedding procession is missing something very important."

"Missing what?" Nan Feng asked. "We've prepared all that we need."

Xie Lian smiled. "Two accompanying maids."

"..."

The two outside exchanged a look, then they both shuddered violently, seeming to have imagined something.

Fu Yao replied, "Just pretend that the family's poor, that there's no money to buy maids, and deal with it."

"All right," Xie Lian said.

When the sedan-carrying military officers heard all this gag, they couldn't help but chuckle. With this, the displeasure did indeed disperse quite a bit, and a bit more camaraderie developed, making the sedan much steadier. Thus, Xie Lian leaned back into a proper sitting position and closed his eyes to rest his mind.

Unexpectedly, not long after, a child's laughter abruptly sounded by his ears.

Hee hee ha ha, kee kee chee chee.

The laughter rippled across the mountain, ethereal and peculiar. However, the bridal sedan neither paused nor stopped, continuing steadily on its way. Not even Nan Feng or Fu Yao made a noise, seeming to not have noticed anything amiss.

Xie Lian opened his eyes and called in a low voice, "Nan Feng, Fu Yao."

From the left side of the bridal sedan, Nan Feng answered, "What is it?"

"Something's come," Xie Lian replied.

By that time, this "wedding procession" had gradually entered the deeper parts of Mount Yujun.

Quiet blanketed the wilderness, and the creaking of the wooden sedan, the crackling of broken leaves and branches when stepped on, the breathing of the sedan carriers, all seemed to sound louder in this silence.

And that child's laughter still hadn't died. It was sometimes distant, as if it came from deeper within the woods, and sometimes close, as if it was leaning over on the edge of the sedan.

Nan Feng grew serious. "I don't hear anything."

Fu Yao also said coldly, "Me neither."

In that case, it was even more impossible for the sedan carriers to have heard anything.

"That means it's purposely letting only me hear," Xie Lian said.

The eight military officers considered themselves experts in martial arts, and also felt there was no pattern to the ghost groom taking brides, so they were confident they would go home empty-handed tonight and weren't frightened in the least. Yet for some reason, the forty-some military officers from before who mysteriously went missing delivering the bride suddenly came to mind, and cold sweat appeared on some of their foreheads.

Xie Lian sensed that some had stalled in their steps and said, "Don't stop. Pretend nothing is the matter."

Nan Feng waved, gesturing for them to keep going.

Xie Lian then said, "It's singing."

"What's it singing?" Fu Yao asked.

Xie Lian listened carefully to that child's voice, then repeated verse by verse, a pause after each one. "New bride, new bride, new bride in the red bridal sedan..."

In the quiet of the night, his somewhat slow voice was clear. But while he was clearly the one reciting, it was as if those eight military officers were hearing the voice of a young infant singing this odd little nursery rhyme along with Xie Lian, making their blood run cold.

Xie Lian continued, "Brimming tears, past the hills, smile not... under the bridal veil...the ghost g... Is it the ghost groom? Or what is it?"

After a pause, Xie Lian said, "No. It keeps laughing. I can't hear clearly anymore."

Nan Feng frowned. "What did that mean?"

"It means exactly what you heard," Xie Lian said. "It's to tell the bride inside the sedan to only cry and not smile."

"I meant, what's the meaning of this creature running over to give you hints like this?" Nan Feng said.

Always having the opposite opinion, Fu Yao said, "It might not be giving hints. It's also possible that it's purposely trying to encourage the opposite, and only smiling can keep one safe and sound, but its objective is to trick people into crying. It's hard to say if the brides from the past were deceived like this."

"Oh, Fu Yao, when hearing such a voice on the road, any normal bride would be scared to death. How could they smile?" Xie Lian said. "Besides, what's the worst that can happen whether I cry or smile?"

"Getting kidnapped," Fu Yao said.

"And isn't that our objective for tonight's outing?" Xie Lian asked.

A hard sniff came out of Fu Yao's nose, but he stopped his rebuttals.

Xie Lian continued, "And there's another thing I feel I must tell you both."

"What?" Nan Feng asked.

"I've been smiling ever since I mounted the bridal sedan," Xie Lian said.

"..."

Just as he spoke, the body of the sedan abruptly dipped.

There was suddenly a commotion outside among the eight military officers, and the bridal sedan came to a complete stop.

Nan Feng shouted, "DON'T PANIC!"

Xie Lian raised his head slightly. "What's going on?"

Fu Yao replied coolly, "Nothing. We've run into a bunch of beasts, that's all."

Just as he answered, Xie Lian heard the sharp howl of wolves pierce the night sky.

A pack of wolves was blocking the way!

This didn't feel normal no matter how Xie Lian thought about it.

"Quick question. Are there often wolves running about on Mount Yujun?"

One of the military officers carrying the sedan answered, "It's unheard of before! How is this Mount Yujun?!"

Xie Lian raised his brows. "Mn, then we've come to the right place."

These were only wild wolves of the mountains; they couldn't do anything to Nan Feng and Fu Yao, nor could they do anything to those military officers who spent years rolling around the edge of danger. It was just that they were all focused earlier on deciphering that bizarre and eerie nursery rhyme, which was why they were so taken by surprise.

From deep within the woods in the dark of the night, pairs and pairs of haunting green wolf eyes lit up. One starving wolf after another slowly emerged from within the forest, surrounding them. However, it was so much better to face beasts one could see and hit than to face a creature one could neither hear nor touch. And so, the group started rubbing their hands and clenching their fists, ready to get down to slaying.

However, the good part was yet to come. What followed closely behind the wolves was the sound of rustling and crackling, a series of odd noises that sounded like beasts but not quite, and like humans but not.

A military officer exclaimed in alarm, "What...what's that?! *What is that thing?!*"

Nan Feng also cursed. Xie Lian knew that something unexpected had happened and tried to stand. "What's happened now?"

Nan Feng immediately replied, "Don't come out!"

Xie Lian had only just raised his hand when the sedan violently jolted as if something had pressed against the sedan door. He didn't lower his head, but he dropped his eyes slightly, and from beneath the bridal veil, he saw the back of the head of something black.

It had actually climbed into the sedan!

That creature crashed headfirst through the sedan door but was then forcefully dragged out by the man outside. Nan Feng swore in front of the sedan. "Fuck, it's a binu!"

Xie Lian knew this was going to be downright troublesome the moment he heard it was a binu.

Based on the evaluation of the Palace of Ling Wen, binu were creatures that didn't even deserve to be ranked fierce. Allegedly, binu were once humans. But by the looks of them now, even if they were considered humans, they'd be deformed humans. They had heads and faces, but the features were smeared and unclear. They had arms and legs but were too weak to walk. They had mouths and teeth, but they couldn't bite anyone to death no matter how much they tried.

But, if there was a choice, everyone would rather run into the scarier fierce- or malice-ranked ghosts than these creatures.

This was because binu often appeared at the same time as other monsters, demons, and ghosts. While the prey was distracted battling with the enemy, they'd suddenly pop out and use their untiring, pestering limbs, their sticky and gooey bodily fluids, and their endless reinforcements of companions to tangle up the prey like sticky candy. Even though their combat power was extremely low, because their vitality was exceedingly tenacious and they often appeared in large groups, it was impossible to shake them off and also very difficult to kill them all quickly. Gradually, they would drain your strength and you'd get tripped up. That instance of carelessness, the opportunity for which your enemy was waiting, would spell your end.

And when the prey was killed by the other monsters, demons,

and ghosts, the binu would pick at the remnant broken limbs the stronger beings left over after eating. They'd eat with keen pleasure and gnaw the bones full of holes and scraps.

This was truly a very disgusting creature. For any heavenly official in the Upper Court, all they needed to do was to release their spiritual light and summon their weapons, and those creatures would withdraw in fright. But to the junior officials of the Middle Court, those creatures were exceedingly vexing.

Fu Yao spat with disgust from a far distance, "I. *Hate.* Those. Things. Did the Palace of Ling Wen mention their presence here?"

"No," Xie Lian said.

"Then what do we need them for?!" Fu Yao exclaimed.

"How many have come?" Xie Lian asked.

"About a hundred, possibly more!" Nan Feng replied. "Don't come out!"

Creatures like binu were strong in numbers, and over a dozen were already very difficult to manage. Over a hundred? That was more than enough to drag them to their deaths. They usually preferred to stay in areas heavily populated with people; he had never imagined there'd be so many on Mount Yujun. Xie Lian pondered for a moment, then raised his arm slightly, revealing a wrist that was half-wrapped in bandages.

"Go on," he said.

The moment those two words were spoken, that white bandage suddenly slipped off his wrist on its own like it was alive and flew out of the curtain of the bridal sedan.

Xie Lian sat poised within the sedan and instructed gently, "Strangle them to death."

In the black of the night, it was as if the white silhouette of a viper suddenly slithered forth.

When that white silk band was pretending to be a bandage wrapped around Xie Lian's wrist, it looked like it was only several meters long. Yet when it was slaughtering with such devilish lightning speed, it was like it was endless. A seamless series of cracking sounds later, dozens of wild wolves and binu had their necks wrung in an instant!

The six binu wrapped around Nan Feng instantly fell to the ground dead. He sent a wild wolf flying with the strike of a hand, never dropping his guard once. He shouted with disbelief toward the sedan, "What was that thing?! Didn't you say you can't manipulate spiritual devices without spiritual powers?!"

Xie Lian replied, "There are always exceptions..."

Nan Feng was furious, and he slapped the sedan door. "Xie Lian! Explain properly right now what that thing was!! Was it...?"

His slap almost broke the entire sedan completely. Xie Lian had to quickly raise his hand to support himself against the door, slightly taken aback. The way Nan Feng spoke actually reminded him of how Feng Xin used to be when he was mad. Nan Feng was about to say more when suddenly, the wailing of military officers came from the distance.

Fu Yao said icily, "If there's anything to say, say it after fighting this wave off first!"

Without any choice, Nan Feng had to rush over to rescue the people.

Xie Lian swiftly snapped out of it and ordered, "Nan Feng, Fu Yao, you guys leave first."

Nan Feng whipped his head around. "What?!"

Xie Lian explained, "If you guys are around the sedan, the creatures will keep coming and the fight will never end. Take the men away first; I'll stay behind and meet this groom."

Nan Feng was about to swear again. "You'll be by yourself..."

However, Fu Yao said coldly, "He can control that silk band, so nothing will happen for the moment. If you've got the time to drag your feet, why don't you settle this group first, then come back and help? I'm off."

Well, he certainly was snappy and carefree, leaving without a thought, dragging not a single step. Nan Feng clenched his teeth, knowing what Fu Yao said was true, so he turned to the military officers who were there.

"Come with me first!"

Sure enough, after they left the bridal sedan, while that pack of wolves and binu were still pestering them, there weren't any new waves joining the fray. The two each escorted four military officers, and on the way, Fu Yao fought as he spat hatefully.

"I can't believe this. If I wasn't..."

He stopped mid-speech. The two met eyes, and the look was odd. Fu Yao swallowed his words and turned his head away, both temporarily stopping and not bringing it up. They then continued to hurry forward.

Around the bridal sedan, corpses were strewn all over the ground.

The silk band Ruoye had already strangled every wolf and binu that had lunged forward. It came flying back, gently wrapping itself back onto Xie Lian's wrist on its own. Xie Lian sat within the sedan quietly, surrounded by the infinite darkness and the rustling of the sea of trees.

All of a sudden, everything fell quiet.

The sound of wind, the sound of the sea of trees, the howling and roaring of demonic creatures, all sank into a deadly silence in an instant, as if they were afraid of something.

And then, he heard a very soft chuckle.

It sounded like a man, but also a youth.

Xie Lian sat poised and quiet.

The silk band Ruoye was quietly encircling his hand, ready to strike at a moment's notice. If whoever had come showed a trace of killing aura, it would instantly, wildly strike back with ten times the power.

Yet unexpectedly, what came wasn't the anticipated attack or any murderous intent but something else.

The curtain of the bridal sedan was lightly lifted, and from underneath the bright red veil, Xie Lian saw the person had extended a hand to him.

The fingers were well defined. A red string was tied on the third finger, and on that long, slender, fair hand, it looked like a bright and colorful affinity knot.

Should he give his hand, or no?

Xie Lian maintained his composure. He hadn't decided yet: Should he continue to sit tall and still, or pretend to be a bride who was frightened and at a loss, dodging back? The owner of that hand was rather patient, however, and incredibly well mannered. Xie Lian didn't move, and so that hand didn't move either, seeming to be waiting for his response.

A moment later, as if something had taken control of him, Xie Lian reached out.

He rose to his feet, ready to push aside the curtain to descend the sedan, but the man had already moved first, lifting the red curtain for him. This man who had come grasped his hand but didn't squeeze too hard, as if he was afraid of hurting him, somehow giving the impression of taking the utmost care.

Xie Lian had his head bowed and let the man guide him slowly out of the sedan. Below the veil, Xie Lian could see by his feet the dead body of a wolf that the silk band Ruoye had strangled. An idea came to him, and Xie Lian lightly tripped, falling forward with an alarmed gasp.

The man immediately reached out and caught him.

Xie Lian also twisted his hand to catch the man's helping arm and felt something cold. It turned out the man was wearing a pair of silver vambraces around his wrists.

The vambraces were exquisitely beautiful, with primitive decorative patterns. Maple leaves, butterflies, and savage beasts were engraved upon them, quite mysterious and quite unlike anything from the Central Plains, more akin to the ancient artifacts of foreign tribes. The vambraces appeared polished and refined, locked around the man's wrists.

Icy cold silver and fair white hands. Both were without a trace of life but carried an evil, killing aura.

Xie Lian's trip and fall earlier was a feint; he had a mind to test this man who'd come. Ruoye had been circling languidly inside the large, expansive sleeves of his wedding robes, ready to strike at a moment's notice. However, the man only took his hand and guided him forward.

Xie Lian purposely walked extremely slowly. This was because: one, he couldn't see the path clearly with the veil on, and two, he wanted to stall for time. Yet this other person matched his pace and walked slowly along with him, the other arm coming around to support him every now and then, as if afraid Xie Lian would trip again.

No matter how high on his guard Xie Lian was, to be treated this way, he couldn't help but think: *If he was a real groom, then he'd genuinely be a most gentle and considerate one.*

Then, he suddenly heard an exceedingly soft clinking sound. With every step the two took, that sound would ring crisply. Just as he was mulling over what that sound could be, there were suddenly the low, suppressed growls of wild beasts from all around.

Wild wolves!

Xie Lian jerked slightly, and the silk band Ruoye abruptly snapped tight around his wrist.

Yet unexpectedly, before he could do anything, the man who was holding his hand softly tapped the back of that hand like he was comforting him, telling him not to worry. The two taps were so soft they could practically be called gentle. Xie Lian was slightly taken aback, but the low growling was already suppressed. When Xie Lian listened closely, he suddenly realized that these wild wolves weren't growling but whimpering.

It was clearly the whimpering of beasts that had reached the peak of fear and could not move while they struggled before death.

Now his curiosity for who this man was grew even stronger. He wanted to lift the veil to look first and worry about everything else later, but he knew that wasn't the best course of action at the moment. So he could only peek through the crack below the red covering, his view limited, and miss the larger picture. The only thing he saw was the lower hem of a vividly red robe. Below the red robe were a pair of black leather boots, walking languidly.

Those black leather boots were wrapped tight around long, slender legs, looking mightily beautiful as they walked. On the sides of the black boots there dangled two fine silver chains, and with every step, the silver chains would sway, clinking and crinkling, sounding extremely pleasant to the ear.

The steps were nonchalant but sprightly, much like those of a youth. However, his every step was also confident, like there was nothing that could stand in his way. If anyone dared to block him, he'd rip them to pieces. Because of this, Xie Lian couldn't quite say just who exactly this character was.

Just as he was deep in thought, something hauntingly white on the ground suddenly intruded on his vision.

It was a skull.

Xie Lian's steps faltered for a moment.

He could immediately tell that the way the skull was placed was amiss. This was clearly a point in some magic formation, and if moved, the entire enchantment would probably attack this spot in an instant. But judging by that youth's steps, it was as if he didn't notice there was anything here at all. Xie Lian was just considering whether he should warn him when he heard the crisp sound of a tragic *crack!* The youth stepped down and instantly crushed the skull to dust.

And then, as if he sensed nothing, he walked over, stepping through that mound of dust indifferently.

Xie Lian was speechless. "..."

With just one step, he crushed the entire enchantment into a mound of wasted dust...

Just then, that youth's step paused. Xie Lian tensed, wondering if he was about to act, but the youth only stopped for a moment before continuing to guide Xie Lian along. After a couple of steps, suddenly there was pitter-patter from above, as if beads of raindrops were beating down on the surface of an umbrella. Turns out, that youth had opened an umbrella and raised it over both of their heads.

Although it wasn't the time for it, Xie Lian couldn't help but praise inwardly that he really was quite thoughtful. But at the same time, he was also very curious.

Is it raining?

On the mystic black mountain, within the vast wilderness, somewhere deep in the far distant ranges there came the long howls of the wolves. Perhaps it was because a slaughter had just occurred on the mountain, but the faint scent of blood was still permeating the cold, frigid air.

Everything about this situation was eerie to the extreme, but that youth held him in one hand and the umbrella in the other as he walked leisurely on, appearing for no reason to be bewitchingly romantic and deeply affectionate.

That strange shower came strangely and ended strangely as well; it wasn't long before the dripping sound of raindrops hitting the umbrella ended, and the youth also came to a stop. He seemed to have put away the umbrella while at the same time, he finally let go of Xie Lian's hand and moved one step closer.

The hand that had been holding his own this entire way softly folded a corner of the veil and slowly lifted it upward.

Xie Lian had been waiting for this moment the entire time. He stood still, watching as the clinging red curtain was slowly pulled up—

The silk band shot out!

It wasn't because the youth exuded a killing aura but rather because he must be apprehended: seize him first and talk later!

Yet unexpectedly, when the silk band Ruoye flew out and carried with it a blast of wind, that bright red veil left the youth's hand, fluttering up, then down. Before Xie Lian had the chance to see the remnant shadow of that red-robed youth, Ruoye had shot through him.

The youth shattered into thousands of silver butterflies, scattering into a breeze of silver twinkling stars.

While it wasn't the time for it, after Xie Lian had backed a couple of steps away, he couldn't help but sigh in awe. This sight truly was as beautiful as a fantastic dream.

Just then, one silver butterfly errantly flew past his eyes. When he tried to look closer, however, that single silver butterfly fluttered twice around him before joining the whirl of butterflies, melting into a part of the silver that enveloped the sky as they fluttered their wings to fly into the night.

It was a good while before Xie Lian came back around, and he wondered, *So was that youth the ghost groom?*

In his opinion, he didn't think so. If those wolves on Mount Yujun were his subordinates, why would they appear so terrified upon seeing him? And that enchanted array on the way must have been set up by the ghost groom, yet he so casually...crushed it.

The more he pondered, the stranger this was. But then Xie Lian tossed Ruoye over his shoulder and thought, *Well, whatever. He could also just be a passerby. I'll leave this for now and focus on the matter at hand.*

But after scanning around, he *eh*'d. It turned out there was a building not far away, standing there somberly.

Since that youth had brought him here and this building was so painstakingly hidden inside this enchantment array, Xie Lian decided he must go inside and take a look.

Xie Lian took a few steps, then halted abruptly. After some thought, he turned back and picked up the veil from the ground. He dusted it off and clutched it in his hand before continuing to make his way to the building.

This building was a tall structure with red walls, the bricks and wood appearing rather mottled, much like an aged local town temple. However, in Xie Lian's experience, this design was most likely a martial god temple. Sure enough, when he looked up, he saw the large, solidly metal words nailed on the top of the entrance:

"Temple of Ming Guang."

The Martial God of the North, General Ming Guang, was also the General Pei that Ling Wen spoke of in the communication array, whose worship was abundant in the north. No wonder they didn't find any Temples of Ming Guang nearby but found a Temple of Nan Yang. Turns out, the Temple of Ming Guang on

Mount Yujun had long since been locked away by an enchantment array. Could this ghost groom have anything to do with General Ming Guang?

However, this General Ming Guang was a mighty and unapproachable great heavenly official, flush with success. Additionally, his status in the north was very secure. Personally, Xie Lian didn't think a heavenly official like that would have any connection with a malicious creature like the ghost groom. It wasn't strange to have one's base be overtaken by a malicious creature without one's knowledge; he'd have to wait and see what the truth really was.

He walked up to the temple and the doors were closed but not locked, so when he pushed, they opened. After pushing the doors in, a strange smell assaulted his senses.

It wasn't the dusty air common to an unvisited place of many years but rather a faint stench of rot.

Xie Lian closed the doors behind him to make it seem like no one had entered, then crossed the threshold into the temple. At the center of the great hall was a martial god statue, naturally that of the Martial God of the North, General Ming Guang. Humanoid objects such as sculptures, puppets, and portraits were easily tainted by the aura of evil. Thus, the first thing Xie Lian did was to go up and look closely at this martial god statue.

After examining it for a while, his conclusion was: this divine statue was exquisitely sculpted. Wielding a sacred sword and wearing a jade belt, his appearance was handsome with an imposing bearing. There weren't any issues, and the rotting smell didn't come from this divine statue either. Thus, Xie Lian put it out of his mind and started to make his way to the back of the great hall.

When he turned around, Xie Lian froze completely, and his pupils shrank.

A group of women dressed in bright red wedding robes, their heads covered with veils, stood tall before him.

The faint stench of rot was exuding from these women.

Xie Lian quickly composed himself, then started counting. One, two, three, four...until he counted to seventeen.

They were the seventeen brides who went missing in the Mount Yujun area!

The red on some of the wedding dresses had faded, the robes looking exceedingly old and tattered, so he assumed they were the earliest brides who went missing. Some of the brides were still wearing brand-new wedding dresses, and the styles were new too. The smell of aged, rotting corpse was still very light on them, so they must be the ones who went missing recently. Xie Lian thought for a moment, then removed the veil of one of the brides.

There was a tragically pale face under the bright red veil, so white that it was faintly glowing green. With the soft light of the moon shining upon it, it was quite horrifying. But the most horrifying part was that, while the muscles of this woman's face were already contorted with death, on this face there hung a stiff smile.

Xie Lian pulled off the veil of the next woman, and there were the same curled lips.

An entire building full of dead people, and they were all dressed in wedding robes with smiles on their faces.

The strange nursery rhyme sung by that child seemed to be ringing in Xie Lian's ears again: *New bride, new bride, new bride in the red bridal sedan... Brimming tears, past the hills, smile not under the bridal veil...*

Suddenly, there was a strange sound coming from outside the temple.

It truly was a strange sound. So strange that it was hard to describe: like two rods wrapped in heavy cloth were violently thumping on the forest floor, but also like something heavy was being pulled with difficulty along the ground. That sound traveled far and came close very quickly. It was merely an instant before it reached the entrance of the Temple of Ming Guang. *Creeeak*, the doors of the Temple of Ming Guang opened.

Whatever had come, whether it be human or creature, was most likely that ghost groom. And now, it had returned!

There was nowhere to escape at the back of the hall, nor anywhere to hide. Xie Lian's mind spun for a second. Seeing the row of brides, he instantly put on his own veil, joining the line and standing still.

If there were only five to six corpses standing there, then of course it'd be easy to see that the numbers weren't correct. But there were seventeen bride corpses here, and unless each one was counted like he did earlier, it'd be difficult to notice someone was mixed in.

He'd only just joined the line before he heard that strange *THUMP THUMP, THUMP THUMP* "walk" in.

Xie Lian remained still while he pondered. *What exactly is this sound? By the length and pauses, it's a bit like the sound of footsteps, but what creature's footsteps sound like this? It's definitely not the youth who brought me here. He was extremely at ease, and when he walked, he clinked.*

Suddenly, he realized something, and his heart jumped to his throat.

Oh no, my height is wrong!

These corpses were all women, but he was very much a man, and was born a notch taller than women. While an extra person couldn't be noticed with a glance, if there was someone particularly tall in the group of corpses, then that was very noticeable!

But then again, Xie Lian's mind turned, and he quickly collected himself once more. He certainly was taller than these brides, but the girl Xiao-Ying had only bound his hair simply and didn't do much else with it. The brides here were all dressed to the nines, their hairdos shooting for the skies. There were even some who were wearing phoenix crowns, a giant piece rising high on their heads, so they might not be shorter than him, considering. Even if he was taller, he shouldn't be that conspicuous.

Just as he was thinking this, he heard a *sshhhh* sound that was about six meters away from him.

A moment later, there was another *sshhhh*, and this time, it was a bit closer.

Xie Lian realized what the ghost groom was doing now.

It was pulling off the veil of each one of the brides and checking the faces of the corpses one by one!

WHAM!

If he didn't strike now, when would there be a better time? The silk band Ruoye shot out and hit the ghost groom squarely.

There was a loud rumble, and black mist assaulted his face. Xie Lian didn't know whether that evil mist was toxic or not, but since he had no spiritual light to shield his body, he immediately covered his nose and mouth. At the same time, he prompted Ruoye to whirl widely to vent the air, dispersing the black mist. There was another *THUMP THUMP, THUMP THUMP*, and when Xie Lian cracked open his eyes, he saw a small, short form by the entrance of the temple flash past. The entrance was thrown open, and a ball of black mist bolted for the forest.

Xie Lian made the decision on the spot and chased after it

immediately. Yet who knew he hadn't gone far before he saw fires blazing within the woods. The screams and shouts of a rampage came from the distance.

"Charge—!"

The voice of a youth was particularly loud and clear. "Catch the ugly freak and exterminate evil for the people! Catch the ugly freak and exterminate evil for the people! We'll split the bounty evenly!"

It was indeed Xiao-Pengtou. Xie Lian inwardly let out a frustrated cry; this group had said they were going to come to the mountain, and they actually did. There was originally an enchanted array concealing the area, but that array had been crushed to smithereens by the youth earlier. And this group, with their blind luck, actually found the place. Upon a second look, the direction the noise came from just so happened to be the direction in which the ghost groom had fled!

Xie Lian grabbed Ruoye and charged out, shouting, "Don't move!"

The group froze for a moment. He was about to say more when he heard Xiao-Pengtou inquire enthusiastically, "Miss! You were kidnapped by the ghost groom, right? What's your name? We're here to rescue you; you can relax now!"

Xie Lian was taken aback, finding this hilarious before remembering that he was still dressed in women's attire. There were no mirrors inside the Temple of Nan Yang, so he had no idea how he looked right now, but from their reaction, Miss Xiao-Ying's hands must be adept. In their shock, the group actually took him for a real bride, and this Xiao-Pengtou was probably hoping Xie Lian would be that seventeenth bride so he could go collect the reward money. However, given the situation, he could not allow these villagers to run amok under any circumstance. Moreover, he couldn't guarantee that the ghost groom had continued to flee.

Coincidentally, right then, two black-clad youths came rushing over. Xie Lian immediately called, "Nan Feng, Fu Yao, come aid me, quick!"

Yet who knew, when those two heard and looked over, they were both taken aback, then backed a couple of steps away in unison. Xie Lian had to ask many times before they came around.

Xie Lian asked, "Did you two come from that direction? Did you run into anything on the way?"

"No!" Nan Feng replied.

"Good," Xie Lian said. "Fu Yao, follow this path immediately and search the surrounding area. Make sure the ghost groom hasn't escaped."

Fu Yao turned and left when he heard the instructions.

Xie Lian then said, "Nan Feng, you stay and guard this place, and make sure not a single person leaves. If Fu Yao doesn't find the ghost groom on the mountain, then it must be in that crowd right now!"

Upon hearing this, commotion erupted within the crowd. Xiao-Pengtou had realized he wasn't a woman by now, and he was the first to jump.

"Not a single one can leave? ON WHAT GROUNDS?! Are there no laws in this land?! Guys, don't listen to them..."

He hadn't yet landed from his jump when Nan Feng struck out a palm, and a large tree, as wide as a man's hug, snapped and collapsed. The crowd instantly remembered that this young man chopped things whenever there was a disagreement. If he chopped them like that pillar, then any form of monetary repayment would be useless, so they all shut up.

Xiao-Pengtou exclaimed, "You said the ghost groom is among us? Every single one of us has a proper name and family. If you don't believe me, use a torch to light up everyone's face and check individually!"

"Nan Feng," Xie Lian called.

Nan Feng took the torch from Xiao-Pengtou and went around to shine it over every single person. Each face was covered in sweat, or nervous, or at a loss, or excited, all extremely spirited.

Xie Lian couldn't discern anything, and he came before the crowd. "Everyone, I apologize for any offense earlier, but I injured the ghost groom and it escaped. It definitely couldn't have gone far. My two young friends here didn't run into it on the way here, so I'm afraid this creature is mixed within the group. Will you please take a good look at each other, see each other's faces clearly, and check if there's anyone you don't recognize in the crowd."

When the crowd heard that the ghost groom could be mixed within their own group of people, their blood ran cold. They didn't dare to be careless. They peered at each other, you looking at me and me looking at you. They had looked for a while when there was a sudden yell.

"Why are you here?!"

Xie Lian's brows shot up, and he rushed over. "Who is it?"

Xiao-Pengtou snatched someone else's torch and shined it at the corner of the crowd. "THIS UGLY FREAK!"

The one he was pointing at was Xiao-Ying. Xiao-Ying's slanted eyes and crooked nose appeared somewhat contorted under the firelight, and she had her arms raised to block her face, looking like she couldn't bear to be exposed under the firelight's glare.

"I...I was worried, so I wanted to come up and look..."

Seeing how alarmed she appeared, Xie Lian took away the torch in Xiao-Pengtou's hand and turned to the others. "How is it, everyone?"

The group all shook their heads.

"There isn't anyone we don't know."

"We've seen everyone here."

"Could it be possessing someone?" Nan Feng asked.

Xie Lian hummed for a moment. "It's doubtful. That was a solid body."

"Since it's a wrath, it's hard to say whether it can change shape," Nan Feng said.

While the two were hesitating, Xiao-Pengtou was again the first to shout, "The ghost groom isn't among us, do you see? If you see, then why won't you let us go?!"

Scattered voices agreed here and there, and Xie Lian gave them a sweeping look.

"Will everyone please stay here in front of this Temple of Ming Guang and not move even half a step away."

The group was about to complain again, but when they saw Nan Feng's cold glare, they didn't dare.

Just then, Fu Yao also returned. He reported, "There's nothing nearby."

Gazing at this heavily packed crowd before the Temple of Ming Guang, Xie Lian slowly said, "Then it must be one of these people."

FU YAO NOTICED that Xiao-Ying had shrunk into the crowd, and he frowned. "Why is there a woman here?"

While his tone wasn't furious, it didn't mean well either. When Xiao-Ying heard him, she bowed her head. Xie Lian explained, "She was worried, so she came here to look."

Fu Yao questioned the others, "Did you all come up with her?"

The crowd was a little uncertain at first, but then they replied:

"Don't remember."

"Can't tell."

"No, when we came up she wasn't here, right?!"

"Either way, I didn't see her."

"Me neither."

Xiao-Ying quickly said, "It's because I was following secretly..."

Xiao-Pengtou immediately cut her off. "Why did you follow in secret? Are you guilty of something? Are you the ghost groom in disguise?"

With such an accusation, the space near Xiao-Ying immediately cleared out, and she waved in a fluster, "No...no, I'm Xiao-Ying, I'm real!" She turned to Xie Lian. "Young master, we just saw each other! I helped you put on rouge, did your hair and your whole makeover..."

Xie Lian could not find the words to reply to that. "..."

Everyone turned their eyes on him, and some started to whisper among themselves. He vaguely heard the words "hobby," "abnormal," "unbelievable," and he cleared his throat.

"This was a mission requirement. Mission requirement. Nan Feng, Fu Yao, you..."

Xie Lian looked around, and only then did he notice that Nan Feng and Fu Yao had been staring at him oddly the entire time. They very rigidly pulled some distance away from him.

The way they were staring at him gave him goosebumps from head to toe. "...Is there something you wish to say to me?"

How could he have known that this girl's makeover work was so gifted that his brows were shaped elegantly, his face was fair as jade powder, and his lips were touched with rouge? If he didn't open his mouth, then he was entirely a gentle, demure, and beautiful young lady. This gave the two a huge shock and mired them in disbelief, making them question their lives and feel uncomfortable all over. The face was still the same face, but they no longer knew who they were talking to.

Fu Yao turned to Nan Feng. "Was there something you wanted to say?"

Nan Feng immediately shook his head. "There's nothing I want to say."

"...Why don't you guys just say something?" Xie Lian asked.

Just then, some men from the crowd spoke up:

"Hm? This is the Temple of Ming Guang?"

"There's a Temple of Ming Guang on this mountain? Amazing, I've never seen it before."

The crowd looked over in wonder. Xie Lian, however, suddenly said, "That's right, the Temple of Ming Guang."

Nan Feng could tell something was off about his tone. "What is it?"

Xie Lian replied, "The north is clearly General Ming Guang's territory. It's not like his worship isn't flourishing, so how come there is only the one Temple of Nan Yang at the foot of Mount Yujun?"

It was easy to understand why the lord official had prayed to the Heavenly Emperor. The Heavenly Emperor was the number one martial god of the past thousand years, and his status was higher than General Ming Guang; naturally, the higher up you prayed, the more guarantee there was. However, General Ming Guang and General Nan Yang were equal in status, with not much difference. If it must be debated, then General Ming Guang possessed nine thousand temples, over a thousand more than Nan Yang. So it was really hard to imagine why they would seek from afar and forgo what lay close at hand.

Xie Lian wondered, "Technically, even if this Temple of Ming Guang on Mount Yujun was overtaken and people couldn't find it, they could've simply built another Temple of Ming Guang. Why build the martial temple of another god?"

Fu Yao could understand. "There must be another reason."

"Right, there must be another reason that would make the people in the Mount Yujun area never build another Temple of Ming Guang," Xie Lian said. "Can either one of you lend me a bit more spiritual power? I'm afraid I'll have to go ask..."

Just then, someone made a commotion. "Whoa, there's so many brides!"

That voice had come from inside the temple, and Xie Lian whipped around. He told that group to properly stay in the open ground in front of the temple, but they ignored him completely and went in!

Nan Feng shouted, "The situation's dangerous, don't run around!"

However, Xiao-Pengtou rebuked him. "Don't listen to him, guys, they won't dare to do anything to us! We're good citizens, as if they'd actually dare kill us! Get up everyone, get up, get up!"

He was certain Xie Lian and company wouldn't actually do anything to them, so he started to riot. Nan Feng cracked his knuckles, looking like he was holding back his curses. As a martial officer of the Palace of Nan Yang, how could he break the limbs of mortals whenever he wished? If any supervisory heavenly officials were to report him, it wouldn't be funny.

Xiao-Pengtou sneered. "Don't think I don't know what you guys are thinking. Aren't you just tricking us into not moving so you can steal the credit and go claim the reward for yourselves?"

With him egging people on, over half of the group actually started to move, and they ran into the temple along with him.

Fu Yao waved dismissively and said apathetically, "Let them be, those unruly people." He sounded extremely disgusted, not wanting to care anymore.

However, there came a shriek from inside the Temple of Ming Guang.

"They're all dead!"

Xiao-Pengtou was also alarmed. "All dead?!"

"ALL DEAD!"

"What is this wickedness? This one looks like she's been dead for decades, but she still hasn't rotted?!" He quickly got over it, however. "Doesn't matter if they're dead. Transport all the corpses of the brides down the mountain; their families will still have to pay up anyway."

Xie Lian's eyes slowly darkened. The group gave the idea a thought, and it certainly made sense. Some sighed, some grumbled, and there were those who were cheerful again.

Xie Lian stood at the temple entrance. "Why doesn't everyone come outside first? The air in the back of this temple is heavy with death. Without any ventilation for years, there'll be issues if you folks were to breathe it in."

This sounded very logical, and the group didn't know whether they should listen. Xiao-Ying begged in a small voice, "Everyone, let's not be this way? It's so dangerous here, why don't we listen to this young master first and go out to sit..."

But this group didn't even bother to listen to Xie Lian, so why would they listen to her? No one paid attention. Xiao-Ying didn't give up, however, and repeated herself a few times.

Xiao-Pengtou directed them: "Go for the fresh corpses, guys. Who knows if the families of the ones that are too old are still alive; don't waste your energy hauling those."

There were even those who praised him for being clever and able. Xie Lian really didn't know whether to laugh or cry at this, and when he saw there were people touching where they shouldn't, he warned aloud.

"Don't remove the veils! That veil can separate the qi of the corpse and the qi of the living. There's a lot of you, and the living qi is too abundant; if they suck it in, it's hard to know what will happen."

However, in order to pick out the freshest corpses, the group of men had already pulled off pretty much all the veils. Xie Lian exchanged a look with Nan Feng, who had come to the door, and shook his head, knowing they couldn't stop them. After all, it wasn't like they could beat the men to a bloody pulp and render them immobile; otherwise, if something happened, wouldn't they lose the ability to run? A very hopeless situation.

Just then, one of the burly men removed the veil of one of the brides and exclaimed, "My god, this little hussy is super cute!"

The men all came to surround the corpse.

"She wasn't even married yet, right? What a waste to just die like that."

"Her clothes are a bit tattered, but she's the prettiest!"

This bride probably hadn't been dead for too long; the skin of her face was still rather supple. Someone said, "I dare you to feel her up."

"What's there to be scared of?" Xiao-Pengtou said.

Then he pinched the corpse's face a couple of times. It was so silky-smooth that it made his heart itch, and he reached out, ready to touch her again. Xie Lian couldn't bear to watch anymore and was about to stop him when Xiao-Ying rushed over.

"Don't do this!" she exclaimed.

Xiao-Pengtou gave her a backhanded shove and yelled, "Don't get in men's way!"

But Xiao-Ying climbed to her feet again and cried, "You're going to incur Heaven's wrath like this!"

Xiao-Pengtou was furious now, and he cursed. "Goddammit! You ugly freak, you're so nosy!"

He swore as he moved to kick her, but Xie Lian easily lifted the back of Xiao-Ying's collar with one hand and pulled her away. Unexpectedly, however, they heard a *THUD*.

Xiao-Pengtou yelled, "WHO HIT ME?!"

Xie Lian looked back. Xiao-Pengtou was bleeding from a gaping wound on the head after having been hit, and there was a blood-stained rock on the ground.

Xiao-Ying was stunned for a moment before quickly apologizing. "Sorry, sorry... I was scared and accidentally threw it..."

However, even if she was eager to take the blame for it, no one would believe her, because the direction was completely wrong. This rock was hurled from a window behind Xiao-Pengtou. When Xiao-Pengtou yelled, everyone had turned to look in that direction, just in time to see a flash of a shadow outside the window.

Xiao-Pengtou hollered, "IT'S HIM! That ugly freak with bandages on his face!"

Xie Lian stuffed Xiao-Ying into Nan Feng's hands and strode a couple steps forward. Propping his right hand on the window lattice, he hopped over and ran toward the forest in pursuit. A few of the bolder ones who had their eyes on the bounty followed him and leapt out the window as well. However, when Xie Lian reached the edge of the forest, he suddenly caught a whiff of blood. Sensing something off, and with alarm bells ringing in his head, he came to a sudden halt.

He warned, "Don't go in!"

He had shouted his warning, but those people thought, *I'll give chase even if you won't,* and charged into the forest without stopping. The others who had originally gathered in the temple swarmed out too, and when they saw that Xie Lian stopped at the edge of the woods, those who weren't as bold crowded around to watch. Before long, they heard screams, and a few shadows stumbled out from the forest. They were the few who had barged in first earlier, and now they were staggering out. When the crowd saw them after they stepped under the moonlight, they were instantly scared out of their wits.

They were still living humans when they had entered, how did they become blood-soaked humans when they came out?

From their faces to the clothes on their bodies, these people were stained with red, the blood gushing forth like a spring. If someone bled this much, it meant certain death. However, those men were still making their way toward them, step by step. Terrified, everyone retreated uniformly until they were behind Xie Lian.

Xie Lian raised his hand. "Calm down. The blood isn't theirs."

Sure enough, those men said, "Yeah! The blood isn't ours. It's...it's..."

Even when drenched in blood, the horror on their faces could not be concealed. The group followed the eyes of those men and looked into the forest; it was pitch-black, so they could not see exactly what lay within. Xie Lian took over a torch, took a few steps forward, and then raised it to probe ahead. Something in the darkness dripped onto the torch, giving off a sizzling sound. He glanced at the torch before looking up. After composing himself for a moment, he raised his hand and then tossed the torch up.

Although the hurled torch only illuminated the area overhead for an instant, everyone still got a clear look of what had been above the trees.

Long black hair, deathly pale faces, tattered military officers' uniforms, and arms dangling in the air.

The swinging corpses of more than forty men were suspended upside down at varying heights on the trees. No one knew how long their blood had flowed, but they had yet to dry up. They dripped and dripped, forming a terrifying scene: a forest of hanging corpses amidst a falling rain of blood.

This group of people outside the forest were all strong, burly men, but they had never seen such a sight before. They were petrified into silence. When Nan Feng and Fu Yao came over and saw this scene, their expressions froze.

After a moment, Nan Feng said, "Green Ghost."

"Indeed," Fu Yao agreed. "It's his favorite trick."

Nan Feng turned to Xie Lian. "Don't go over there. It'll be a bit of a problem if it's him."

Xie Lian looked back and asked, "Who are you talking about?"

"A 'near-supreme.'" Nan Feng replied. Xie Lian asked, puzzled, "'Near-supreme'? You mean, close to the power level of a supreme?"

"That's right," Fu Yao said. "The 'near-supreme' Green Ghost is a malicious creature who has been evaluated by the Palace of Ling Wen as close to the level of a supreme. He adores games like this forest of hanging corpses. You could say he's infamous."

Xie Lian thought, *That's really unnecessary. If you're a supreme, you're a supreme. If you aren't, then you aren't. Just like there's only "ascended" and "not ascended," there's no "nearly ascended" or "about to ascend." Adding a "near" only makes it awkward for everyone.*

He recalled when that young man led him all the way here; there had been the sound of rain pitter-pattering on the surface of his umbrella. Could he have held it up to shield him from the blood rain of this corpse forest?

He let out a soft "ah," and the other two immediately asked, "What's the matter?"

He thus gave a brief account of how he had met a young man while he was in the sedan and how that young man had brought him here. When he was done, Fu Yao said skeptically, "I noticed the enchanted array on this mountain when I came up. It was immensely tough, but he broke it so handily?"

Xie Lian thought, *Rather, he crushed it under his heel without even noticing the feat.* He said, "That's right. This 'near-supreme' Green Ghost you speak of, could that be him?"

Nan Feng considered it briefly, "I've never seen the Green Ghost before, so I can't say. Does that young man you saw have any distinctive features?"

"Silver butterflies," Xie Lian said.

Earlier, when Nan Feng and Fu Yao saw the forest of hanging corpses, they remained considerably composed. But the instant those two words left Xie Lian's mouth, he could clearly see the drop in their faces.

Fu Yao exclaimed in disbelief, "What did you say? Silver butterflies? What kind of silver butterflies?"

Xie Lian realized that he had probably said something significant and explained, "They're like silver, yet also like crystal. They don't seem to be living creatures. But they look quite pretty."

He saw Nan Feng and Fu Yao exchange looks with expressions so grim their faces were almost green.

After a while, Fu Yao said darkly, "Leave. Right now."

"We haven't settled the case of the ghost groom yet, how can I leave?" Xie Lian said.

"Settle?" Fu Yao said. He turned back and sneered. "Seems like you have really tarried too long in the Human Realm. This ghost groom is merely a wrath. Even the Green Ghost of this hanging-corpses forest is merely a 'near-supreme,' as pesky as he might be."

After another pause, he suddenly said in a stern voice, "Do you know who the master of those silver butterflies is?"

Xie Lian replied honestly, "I don't."

"...Even if you don't, there isn't time for me to explain now," Fu Yao said stiffly. "In short, he isn't someone you can handle. You'd better hurry back to the Heavenly Realm and ask for reinforcements."

"Then you head back first," Xie Lian said.

"You—"

"The master of those silver butterflies never showed any hint of malice," Xie Lian said. "If he does harbor malice, if he really is as terrifying as you claim, then no one within the perimeter of Mount Yujun would be able to escape his clutches. All the more reason someone has to stand guard here right now. So why don't you go back first and help me seek reinforcements?" He could tell Fu Yao didn't want to remain here and deal with so many troublesome matters. If that was the case, then Xie Lian wouldn't force the issue. Fu Yao was a straightforward person, so he really did leave on his own with a toss of his sleeves. Xie Lian turned toward Nan Feng and was about to inquire further about that young man when there was another commotion in the crowd.

Someone shouted, "We caught him! We caught him!"

Now Xie Lian didn't have the time to ask anything anymore either. "Who did you catch?"

Two more bloody figures emerged from the forest. One was a burly fellow who had charged into the forest earlier, and who was one of the few who was not scared off by the blood rain in the corpse forest. The other one was a young boy being dragged along by him in a firm grip, his head and face messily wrapped with bandages.

Xie Lian still remembered what the tea master he had met earlier in the little shop had said: *"Apparently, the ghost groom is an ugly creature living on Mount Yujun, and because it's so ugly, no woman loves it. Which is why it grew hate in its heart and began robbing others of their brides to ruin their happy occasions."*

They thought that might have been a rumor at the time. Who would have guessed that there was really such a person?

Be that as it may, whether he was the ghost groom was a different matter altogether. Xie Lian was just about to take a closer look at the bandaged boy when Xiao-Ying rushed over.

She yelled, "You've got the wrong person! This isn't the ghost groom. He isn't!"

Xiao-Pengtou shouted back, "He was caught red-handed, and you still say he isn't? I..." He paused, as if something had suddenly dawned on him, then he continued, "Oooh, I was wondering why you're always acting so strange, always insisting 'he isn't, he isn't.' So you're in cahoots with this ghost groom?!"

Stunned, Xiao-Ying hurriedly waved her hands. "No, no, I'm not. He's not, either. He hasn't done anything. He's just an ordinary... ordinary..."

Xiao-Pengtou pressed on aggressively, "Ordinary what? Ordinary ugly freak?" He yanked at the bandaged boy's hair a couple of times and said, "Then why don't we take a look at how this 'ordinary' ghost groom looks, since he loves stealing others' women so much?!"

His random grabbing made a mess of a few strips of the bandages, and the bandaged boy instantly held his head and screamed. His cries were full of fear, incredibly mournful and pitiful.

Xie Lian seized Xiao-Pengtou's arm. "Enough."

When Xiao-Ying heard that young boy's screams, her tears tumbled down, and when she saw Xie Lian stopping Xiao-Pengtou, it was akin to seeing hope. She hurriedly grabbed his sleeves and begged, "Young...young master, help me, help him."

Xie Lian cast her a look, and Xiao-Ying let go of his sleeve in embarrassment, as if afraid he would scorn her touchy-feely hands and would not want to help her anymore.

Xie Lian comforted her, "It's fine."

He took another look at the bloody-headed, bandaged boy, and realized that he was also peeking at Xie Lian with wide, bloodshot eyes through the gaps in the bandages under his hands. The boy only stole a glance before quickly lowering his eyes, and he hurriedly secured the bandages again. Although he did not reveal his face, a patch of skin was exposed, and that bit was already horrifying, as if it had been burned by fire. It was not hard to imagine how scary the face that laid under the bandages was, and the others sucked in a breath while the boy shrank even more.

Xie Lian noticed that the way those two cowered was exactly the same. It was as if they were afraid to step into the light, afraid to see other people. He sighed inwardly.

Next to them, Xiao-Pengtou was alarmed. "What are you scheming? We are the ones who caught the ghost groom."

Xie Lian let go of him. "I'm afraid the ghost groom won't let you catch him so easily. My friend searched around here earlier, but he didn't find him. It's possible this boy came much later. The real ghost groom should still be here."

Xiao-Ying also mustered up her courage. "You want the reward money…but you can't just catch anyone at random to make up the numbers…"

Xiao-Pengtou clearly wanted to hit her again after hearing this. He had been causing trouble since earlier, and Xie Lian finally couldn't endure it anymore. He waved his hand and Ruoye flew out to give Xiao-Pengtou a slap with a *THWACK* that knocked him over. Nan Feng seemed to have reached his limit too and immediately followed up with a kick. The youth finally toppled to the ground and remained still. This person was the lead instigator, so once he became immobile, the crowd didn't know who to take aim at and settled down. There were a few scattered outcries here and there, but the commotion was over.

Xie Lian thought, *Finally, we can get down to business.*

He sized up the young boy on the ground for a moment, then asked, "Were you the one who threw the rock in the window earlier?"

His voice was gentle. The bandaged boy, who was trembling uncontrollably, peeked at him again and nodded.

Xiao-Ying explained, "He doesn't want to harm anyone. He just wanted to help me when it looked like Xiao-Pengtou was going to hit me…"

Xie Lian asked the boy again, "Do you know what's with all those corpses hanging in the forest?"

Xiao-Ying answered, "I don't know what's going on, but he's definitely not the one who hung them up…"

The bandaged boy trembled nonstop, but all he did was shake his head repeatedly. Nan Feng, who had been staring at him, suddenly said, "Who is the Green Ghost Qi Rong to you?"

Xie Lian gave a slight start on hearing this name. The bandaged boy, however, just looked blank. He showed no reaction when the name was uttered, and he was too scared to reply to Nan Feng.

"He...he's too scared to talk..." Xiao-Ying explained.

All this while, she had been trying her best to protect this strange boy. Xie Lian implored gently, "Miss Xiao-Ying, what exactly is the matter with this child? Tell me everything you know."

Xiao-Ying seemed to summon up a little courage at the sight of Xie Lian. Firelight shone brightly on her face, but she was no longer avoiding it.

Wringing her hands, she said, "He really didn't do anything bad. This child simply lives on Mount Yujun. Sometimes, when he's too hungry, he'll run down the mountain to steal some food. There was once when he happened to steal from my house... I saw that he couldn't really talk and there were injuries on his face, so I found some cloth for him to bandage himself with. I'd also give him food sometimes..."

Xie Lian had initially thought them to be a couple, but now that he learned of all this, Xiao-Ying's reciprocal protectiveness was more like that of an older sister, or even an elder taking care of him.

She added, "Later, there were many who thought he was the ghost groom. I couldn't convince them, so I could only hope that the real culprit would be quickly captured... I thought, since you're so capable, prepared to act as a bride to catch the ghost groom and everything, then at the very least you wouldn't catch the wrong person, because he would never ever hijack the wedding sedan. But the moment I headed out, I heard that Xiao-Pengtou and the rest wanted to search the mountain today too. I was really worried, so I secretly came up to take a look."

She stood as a shield before the boy like she was afraid the others would hit him again, and defended him further. "He really isn't the ghost groom. Look at him, it's taken so few to beat him like this. How in the world could he defeat so many military officers escorting the bride's sedan...?"

Xie Lian and Nan Feng exchanged glances, both equally finding this to be a headache.

If it was as she said, then wasn't the boy completely unrelated to this incident?

The bandaged boy, the "wrath" ghost groom, the "near-supreme" Green Ghost, and that powerful, influential master of the silver butterflies, who made all heavenly officials turn pale at the mere mention of his name. To think this small Mount Yujun would see a never-ending flow of strange guests. This was truly a tough case to deal with. Who was who? What was the relationship between who and who? Xie Lian felt his headache intensify several times over. He rubbed his forehead and temporarily stopped thinking about how much truth there was in Xiao-Ying's words.

Something else suddenly came to mind that he'd been meaning to ask, and he said, "Miss Xiao-Ying, have you always lived near Mount Yujun?"

Xiao-Ying replied, "Yes. I've always lived here. I can guarantee that he has never done anything bad here."

"No, I wanted to ask you something else," Xie Lian said. "Are there no other Temples of Ming Guang built in the vicinity of Mount Yujun, other than the one on this mountain?"

Xiao-Ying was taken aback. "Um..." She thought about it, then said, "There should have been others, I think."

At her response, Xie Lian suddenly had the vague feeling that he'd grasped something important. He asked, "Then why did I only see a Temple of Nan Yang at the foot of the mountain but not a Temple of Ming Guang?"

Xiao-Ying scratched her head. "They tried to build one before, but I heard that every time construction of a Temple of Ming Guang was in the works, there would always be a fire for some reason half-way through... Some people said that it probably meant General Ming Guang could not protect this place for some reason, so they switched to General Nan Yang..."

Nan Feng noticed Xie Lian's frozen expression and asked, "What's the matter with you?"

Xie Lian suddenly realized that it was all too simple.

The brides who could not smile, the temple that caught fire for no reason, the temple of Ming Guang locked away by the enchanted array in the mountain, the majestic Martial God statue of General Pei, the ghost groom who had disappeared into thin air after being wounded by Ruoye—

All too simple!

It was only because there was always something else interfering and diverting his attention that he hadn't realized such a simple truth right from the start!

He forcefully seized hold of Nan Feng and exclaimed, "Lend me some spiritual powers!"

Nan Feng was startled but hurriedly struck a palm with him in midair. He asked, "What's the matter?"

Xie Lian dragged him and ran. "I'll explain later. Think of a way to subdue the corpses of those eighteen brides first!"

Nan Feng said, "Have you lost your senses? There are only seven-teen brides' corpses. You are the eighteenth!"

Xie Lian said, "No, no, no."

He explained: "There were only seventeen before, but now there are eighteen. Among the eighteen brides' corpses, one is fake: the ghost groom is hiding among them!"

The two dashed back to the Temple of Ming Guang, however the back of the great hall was already completely empty. There was only a pile of messily strewn red veils where the brides stood earlier.

Seeing this sight, Xie Lian cried mentally, *This is bad, this is bad, darn it, darn it.*

He quickly picked up the veils on the ground. After he did so, he heard alarmed cries coming from outside the temple. The two looked out the window and saw that a mob of women in scarlet wedding dresses had formed a circle and were slowly closing in on the group of villagers.

Each of the women had a pale, greenish face wearing a smile, her arms raised straight out. They were the corpses of the brides from earlier!

No one could remain calm while watching helplessly as they slowly closed in. The crowd didn't care to accost that bandaged boy anymore and fled. Xiao-Ying immediately rushed over to support him.

Xie Lian called out helplessly, "Don't run!"

He had lost count how many times he'd said that tonight. Whenever something happened, he'd have to say it at least thirty to forty times, yet there was always someone ignoring him. What a helpless affair.

He waved his hand, and the silk band Ruoye flew out toward the sky. He made a casual hand sign, and Ruoye began whirling in the air on its own like the mad dance of a celestial being, incredibly eye-catching. When those brides saw that there was something over this way, lively and spinning rapidly with its tail whipping at them, a good number of them were lured over. There were also seven that were attracted to the scent of blood in the deep of the forest, so they slowly hopped in that direction.

Xie Lian exclaimed, "Follow them, Nan Feng! Don't let them go down the mountain!"

He didn't need to worry; Nan Feng had already gone off to chase them. Two of the brides came and attacked in Xie Lian's direction, their fingers bright red, their nails sharp. Xie Lian took out the red veils he had collected off the ground earlier and hurled them out with both hands. Two of the veils spun as they shot out, squarely covering the heads of those two brides. Instantly, their movements stalled.

As expected, when the heavy, bright red veils covered the eyes and the noses of those corpses, they could no longer see the shadows of mortals nor smell their scent. And since their dead bodies were stiff, they couldn't bend their own arms to remove the veils; they could only grab randomly at the air with their extended arms as if they were playing blind man's bluff. This was truly both a horrifying and silly sight. Xie Lian stood in front of them and tentatively waved his hand in front of the two brides' eyes, and when he saw they were grabbing cluelessly in another direction, he contemplated for a moment. But, in the end, he still couldn't help but say, "Please forgive my impropriety," before seizing their arms and placing their claws on each other's necks.

When the two brides suddenly felt something in their hands, their bodies shook, and since they couldn't see anything, they started strangling each other viciously. Xie Lian then quickly ran off with a wide wave of his hand, and Ruoye followed him like a streak of white rainbow before landing on the ground to form a large white circle.

Xie Lian called after the people who were fleeing in all directions, "Everyone, get into the circle!"

The group hesitated as they ran, but Xiao-Ying immediately helped the bandaged boy over to stand inside. After some thought, she ran out again and dragged Xiao-Pengtou, who was passed out on the ground, into the circle as well. Right then, one of the brides hopped to the edge of the white circle, and her claws shot out to grab for them, yet it was as if there were a transparent wall that forcibly divided the space.

Xiao-Ying noticed the bride couldn't hop in no matter how she tried and quickly shouted, "Everyone, come in, quick! They can't enter this circle!"

When the men saw this, they hurried back like a swarm of bees. Thankfully, Xie Lian had Ruoye burst to a great length beforehand, and the circle was big enough, otherwise he would be worried there would be people squeezed out because it was too cramped. The brides couldn't hop into the circle and knew they couldn't do anything to this group, so they uniformly spun around and, shrieking, lunged in Xie Lian's direction.

However, Xie Lian was already waiting for them, and from his sleeve he pulled out a large bundle of veils. The many red cloths in his hands spun, up, down, left, right, flying in all directions, both his hands and feet moving nonstop, covering each one as they came, swift and precise. With every bride veiled, the bride would begin to slow and feel around like a blind person. The veils in his hands were spun to blurs as they were thrown with ease, forming countless red silhouettes flying through the air. The people inside the circle actually started cheering in spite of themselves.

"NICE!"

"Amazing, so amazing!"

"You trained for this, right?!"

When Xie Lian heard them, he blurted out of habit, "Thank you, thank you. Please support my act with money if you have the means, or with applause if you haven't... Wait?!"

He only noticed something wrong after the words left his lips. He'd gotten caught up and let slip the speech he used to say when he busked and hurriedly stopped himself. While he was talking, several more brides jumped up; jumps that were surprisingly over two meters high and ten meters long, and in the span of a second, the stench of rot came before his nose.

Xie Lian pushed off with the tip of his foot, his body sweeping past them, and while in the air, he mentally chanted the verbal password to a certain private communication array.

"Ling Wen, Ling Wen the all-knowing! I have a question: Do you know if the Martial God of the North, General Ming Guang, had any intimate female friends?"

Ling Wen's voice rang in his ear. "Your Highness, why do you ask?"

"I've got a bit of a situation here right now, kind of urgent," Xie Lian said. "Not gonna lie, there are a dozen dead people chasing me right now."

"Huh? That awful?!" Ling Wen was shocked.

"Not too horrible," Xie Lian said. "So, did he? I know this question is more personal in nature and it's not easy to answer, which was why I didn't ask in the general communication array. It's necessary for the mission, and the information will never be divulged."

"You've misunderstood, Your Highness," Ling Wen replied. "It's not that this question isn't easy to answer, but it's that Ol' Pei really has had *too* many intimate female friends. Your question is so sudden, I don't know which one you're referring to at the moment."

Xie Lian almost slipped in his step. "All right. Then, among General Pei's female friends, is there one who is possessive, extremely jealous, and has some form of disability?"

"Now that you've mentioned it, I do recall someone," Ling Wen replied.

Xie Lian sent two more veils flying, causing another round of applause, and he spun around, cupping his hands at the audience in thanks. "Tell me!"

Ling Wen began, "Before Ol' Pei ascended, he was a general. He became involved with the female general of an enemy state on the battlefield, someone extremely beautiful and fierce in character. Her name was Xuan Ji."

"Okay, Xuan Ji," Xie Lian acknowledged.

Ling Wen continued, "General Pei is someone who, hmm...when he sees a beautiful woman, he'll have to go and entangle himself even if there's a blade to his throat. This woman led an army and crossed swords with him, and she was defeated."

Xuan Ji became a prisoner of war and was taken to the enemy camp. While the guards weren't paying attention, she was planning to end her life on the spot. But she did not succeed: a general cut her verdant sword in half with one swing of his blade and saved her. And this dashing General Pei of the enemy state was the General Ming Guang who later ascended.

As for this General Pei, one, he was always someone who cherished beauties, and two, the result of the war was already determined, so even if the fighting dragged on, the situation was already impossible to flip. And so, Xuan Ji was released. However, with all this frequent contact and back and forth, it was easy to imagine what would come of it.

Just then, one of the brides caught Xie Lian's leg and dug her fingers in, almost sinking her claws into his flesh. He wanted to kick out at first but realized at this angle he could only kick her face.

Well, you can't hit a lady's face, Xie Lian thought, so he changed his position and kicked her shoulder instead while sending another veil flying. "Sounds like a beautiful tale."

"It *was* a beautiful tale at first," Ling Wen said. "But what killed it was that Xuan Ji was adamant about being General Pei's lover for the rest of his life."

Xie Lian ran a couple of steps and leapt, scaling up the roof, then looked down at the five or six brides who continued to close in on him down below.

He wiped away his sweat. "There isn't anything wrong for a woman to want to be the only lover in a lifetime."

"There isn't," Ling Wen said. "But when two countries clash, the battlefield is heartless. Those two had originally agreed willingly that it was going to be a short-lived affair, that today would exist but not tomorrow, and to speak only of romance and not of war. But with someone like Ol' Pei, I'll be honest, it's already pretty good if he doesn't cheat on you."

" ... "

"However, Xuan Ji was a dignified lady general and intense in temperament. If it was something she wanted, she'd clutch on firmly without ever letting go..."

"Hold on, hold on!" Xie Lian interrupted. "Tell me first, is Xuan Ji disabled? And how so?"

"It's her..." Ling Wen's voice abruptly came to a stop.

For goodness' sake! Every time, when he got to the most important part, the bit of spiritual power he'd borrowed would run out. It seemed next time he'd have to get straight to the point right from the start. In between flying and jumping, Xie Lian rapidly reorganized his thoughts. If the bandaged boy wasn't the ghost groom, and this group of villagers had also confirmed that the ghost groom wasn't among them, then the only place left to hide was among the seventeen brides!

When Xie Lian snuck into the fold, the ghost groom couldn't immediately tell that the numbers were wrong. On the flip side, when the ghost groom mixed in with the brides, Xie Lian also couldn't tell there was an extra corpse at a single glance. Now that he thought about it closely, after the silk band Ruoye had injured the ghost groom, he only saw a ball of black mist stealing for the forest, but he couldn't say for sure that the ball of black mist contained a person. What probably actually happened was that when he rushed out the temple entrance to give chase, the ghost groom remained in the temple full of black mist, brushing past him and returning to the back of the hall—hiding itself like a leaf among the trees and mixing in with the corpses of the brides.

Then the "ghost groom" wasn't a groom but a bride: a woman dressed in a wedding dress!

Since it was a woman, many things could now be explained. For example, why there was no Temple of Ming Guang on or around Mount Yujun. It wasn't that the locals didn't want to build the temples, it was because they couldn't. Xiao-Ying had said, *"I heard that every time construction of a Temple of Ming Guang was in the works, there would always be a fire for some reason halfway through..."* This didn't sound like a coincidence at all and could be nothing but arson. Why set fires to burn temples? Under normal circumstances it would happen because of hatred. So then why would there be a Temple of Ming Guang on Mount Yujun that was locked within an enchantment to keep out visitors, yet the maintenance and the craftwork of the divine statue within the temple were so exquisite?

Why was the ghost bride all decked out in a wedding dress herself but couldn't bear to see other brides in wedding dresses smile when passing through Mount Yujun?

When every dot was connected, Xie Lian couldn't think of any answer besides jealousy and possessiveness. And that odd sound, like cloth-covered rods dragging something heavy—if it was truly the sound of footsteps, then Xie Lian could only think of one possibility!

Every bride that was chasing him had been veiled. Xie Lian finally landed back on the ground, let out a light sigh, steadied himself, and then straightened up to count.

One, two, three, four...ten.

Seven brides had hopped into the forest and Nan Feng had gone to chase them. He veiled ten brides and they were all here. That meant there was one more who hadn't shown her face.

Right then, he heard that familiar sound of *THUMP THUMP, THUMP THUMP*, coming from behind him.

Xie Lian slowly turned around, and an extremely short, small form entered his field of vision.

He drew in a small breath and thought, *I knew it.*

This short, small woman before his eyes was dressed in red wedding robes, but there was no air of joy, only sorrow. The reason she was short wasn't because that was her natural stature but because she was kneeling on the ground.

The bones of both her legs were broken, but the legs remained, and she had been using her knees to walk all this time. The odd *THUMP THUMP* sound he heard was the sound of her dragging her two broken legs to hop across the ground.

That female ghost bore a handsome oval face, her brows high and arching; she was truly exceedingly beautiful. No wonder the men had spoken of her so much before. While her beauty was initially laced with three parts heroism, it was now stormy with resentment, as if she had been trapped in a small, confined space for years, barred from the light of the sun. She was kneeling on the ground, and the bridal robe was tattered and frayed below the knees.

Xie Lian and the ghost stared at each other unyieldingly for a while before he spoke up. "Xuan Ji?"

It seemed it had been many years since anyone called her by that name. It was a long time before the resentment on her face quietly faded some, and a flash of light shone in her eyes.

"...Was it he who sent you to find me?" she asked.

Xie Lian supposed that this "he" naturally referred to General Pei.

Xuan Ji then pressed on, "What about the man himself? Why won't he come see me?"

That passionate expression and hopeful tone while she spoke made Xie Lian feel that he'd best not say "he didn't." Seeing that he hesitated to respond, Xuan Ji slumped onto the ground.

Her back leaned against that handsome, tall martial god statue. Her bright red bridal robe spread about her on the ground like a giant flower of blood. Her hair was disheveled, and her face filled with agonizing torment, as if she was suffering from extreme misery.

"...Why won't he come see me?"

Xie Lian couldn't answer this question either, so he could only remain silent. Xuan Ji raised her head to gaze upon that divine statue and moaned sorrowfully.

"Pei dear, oh Pei dear, I've betrayed my kingdom for you, abandoned my everything and become like this. Why won't you come see me anymore?"

She pulled at her own hair, demanding, "Could your heart be made of iron?"

Xie Lian didn't react to any of this, but when he heard her, he silently pondered. Xuan Ji said she betrayed her kingdom for General Pei. Could that mean that this General Pei she spoke of cajoled her into divulging enemy secrets while the two were in the heat of their passion, causing Xuan Ji's kingdom to fall into a disadvantage on the battlefield? She also said that it was because of General Pei that she'd become this, and by "this" she naturally meant this tragic, broken-legged form. Xuan Ji was a female general; upon the battlefield, there was no way she would be disabled, so those legs of hers could only have been broken later. Could that have something to do with General Pei too? Was it General Pei deserting what he started that led to such deep and severe resentment?

Xie Lian felt everything he thought of was rather vulgar. However, with Xuan Ji having such profound resentment to the point where she was harming innocent lives, as vulgar as it was, Xie Lian could only force himself to think in that direction. Just then, the sound of a girl screaming suddenly came from outside the temple.

"Help! Help!"

Xie Lian and Xuan Ji both looked out of the window at the same time. Where Ruoye had formed the white circle, a man was trying to drag that bandaged boy out while Xiao-Ying clung to the man's leg, not letting go.

The man started yelling curses; it was Xiao-Pengtou. "Fuck off! You dumbass, what if you call that female ghost over?!"

Xiao-Ying shouted, "If she comes, she comes; you're scarier than any ghosts! I...I'd rather see a female ghost instead!"

Turned out that Xiao-Pengtou, whom Xie Lian had knocked out with one whip of his silk band, had come to. When he saw the sluggishly fumbling brides all around, he first jumped in surprise, but soon realized none of them could detect humans. He was exceedingly gutsy, hotheaded, and foolhardy, and he planned to drag the bandaged boy down the mountain to collect his bounty while no one else dared to move. He didn't care at all whether or not this boy was really the ghost groom; everyone down the mountain said he was, so he was. Yet unexpectedly, Xiao-Ying pounced over screaming and shouting, alerting all the drifting brides in the surrounding area, including Xuan Ji inside the Temple of Ming Guang.

Xie Lian saw that it was him again and mentally grumbled that he should have whipped harder earlier; best if the man was whipped so hard he didn't wake for three days and three nights.

He shouted, "Go back into the circle!"

Xiao-Pengtou saw that a stream of black mist had come lunging at him and hastily retreated. However, the bandaged boy was still in his grip, and Xiao-Ying was still clinging onto his leg, so in the end, he was still too slow by a beat. Instantly, the black mist enveloped him, and he was then sucked back to Xuan Ji's hand. He turned his head to look; wasn't this disheveled, long-haired, haunting, chilling woman the beautiful corpse he had touched among all those brides lying on the ground earlier?

It wasn't until that moment that he finally learned what fear meant. He shrieked at the top of his lungs while Xuan Ji curled her five fingers, digging them deep into the back of his head. In an instant, his skull was pulled out through the heavy layer of flesh on his scalp.

The skull that was just pulled out was still steaming hot, its mouth still wide open and screaming. "AAAAAAAAAAHH—!!!!"

The people within the white circle also had their mouths open wide and screaming, so terrified that their souls had left their bodies. "AAAAAAAAAAHH—!!!!"

Xiao-Ying was also thoroughly terrified, pulling the bandaged boy into the circle as she screamed. Xuan Ji reached her fingers out at them again, but Xie Lian dashed over and blocked her.

"General, please refrain from committing further murderous sins."

He called her "General" in hopes of reminding her that she was once a heroine who fought bravely on the front lines to protect her kingdom. Yet Xuan Ji crushed the head that was screaming in terror in her grip, that gorgeous face now seven parts twisted.

She sneered. "Is he too scared to see me?"

Xie Lian couldn't think of any other way, so he wondered if he should pretend to be someone sent by General Pei to smooth things over first. But Xuan Ji didn't need his response at all. She laughed heartily and whipped around, pointing at the divine statue.

"I burned your temples and caused havoc in your land, just so you'd come to take one look at me! I've waited for you for years!"

She stared at that martial god statue in a long trance, then suddenly leapt up, strangling its neck and shaking it like mad.

"But you still won't come to see me! Is it because you know you wronged me? Won't you look at my legs?! Look at how I am now! This is all for you! For you!! Is your heart made of iron?!"

As a bystander, Xie Lian didn't want to comment on who was right or wrong, but in his opinion, he really couldn't help but think, *If you wanted to see him, could you not have used a saner method? In any case, if someone did all this because they wanted to see me, I would have zero desire to show up.*

On the other end, Xiao-Ying and that bandaged boy finally returned to the circle anew. Looking his way, she whispered in concern, "Young master..."

Hearing her, Xie Lian gave her a smile, indicating that she needn't worry. Yet unexpectedly, the moment he smiled, Xuan Ji's face instantly contorted, and she lunged over from the divine statue.

"Since you won't look at me and prefer to look at those girls who love smiling, I'll let you look to your heart's content!"

Although the one she was strangling was Xie Lian, her words were directed at General Pei. At first, Xie Lian had thought that Xuan Ji's heart was full of jealousy for those happily smiling brides in their sedans because she herself couldn't marry the one she loved. He hadn't expected that it was because this General Pei liked girls who smiled, so she, in her distorted mind, connected that to brides who were about to marry their lovers. No wonder she burned all the Ming Guang temples around the mountain. Now that he thought about it, it was probably because she couldn't stand having to share this one divine statue with all those women who'd visit Ming Guang temples day in and day out.

This female ghost was indeed a wrath. Even with both legs broken, her movements were fast as a devil's, and even after being beaten by Ruoye, her strength was still formidable. Xie Lian couldn't keep going with her strangling him like this, but just as he was about to summon Ruoye, there was a loud cry.

"AAAAAAAAAAAAAAAH—!"

That girl Xiao-Ying saw that he couldn't hang on anymore, so she picked up a branch and came charging over; she was yelling as she charged, seeming to pump up courage for herself. But Xuan Ji didn't even need to lift a finger. She only gave a chilling look, and before Xiao-Ying had even gotten close, she was sent flying meters away and crashed heavily onto the ground headfirst.

The bandaged boy croaked out a loud "AAAH!" as he ran over. Xie Lian was shocked too, but right as he sat up, he felt a chill on the back of his head. Xuan Ji's five fingers were already in place, like she was going to yank his skull from his skin just like earlier. In this dire situation, Xie Lian's right hand shot out and grabbed her wrist.

He shouted, "Bind!"

A sharp *WHOOSH* sound echoed through the air, and the white silk bandage heeded the command, circling and twisting about Xuan Ji, trussing her up. Xuan Ji's legs were broken, so she couldn't dodge in time. Thus, with a heavy thud, she fell to her knees and started rolling on the ground, trying to break free of the white silk band. Yet the more she struggled, the tighter the bindings became. The instant he was set free, Xie Lian didn't even take a moment to catch his breath before he immediately got to his feet and ran to where Xiao-Ying landed.

Even with Ruoye having been recalled, most of the crowd still didn't dare to move rashly, but there were also a number of daring villagers who had gotten used to those fumbling brides and went circling. The bandaged boy was kneeling next to Xiao-Ying's sprawled form, not knowing what to do, so anxious he was like a small insect on the rim of a boiling pot. No one dared touch her, afraid that she had broken something critical and if she should struggle the injury would worsen. Xie Lian gave a quick once-over and knew that no matter how careful he was it'd be pointless. There was no way she'd survive after such a fall.

While he hadn't interacted much with this girl Xiao-Ying, hadn't even spoken with her much, Xie Lian still knew that she was a kind-hearted girl despite her ugly appearance. Such an ending for her truly made the heart heavy.

At least Xuan Ji shouldn't be able to struggle free of Ruoye. Xie Lian thought, *Even if it's pointless, Xiao-Ying shouldn't be left in this position right before her death.*

And so, he very carefully flipped her over.

Xiao-Ying's face was covered in blood, and the crowd around clicked their tongues and sighed as they watched.

However, she still had breath left, and she whispered, "Young master...have I made things worse...?"

Although she didn't make anything worse, she didn't actually help either. Xie Lian was already going to summon Ruoye at the time and didn't require anyone else's help. Besides, with that single branch of hers, even if she had managed to hit Xuan Ji, it wouldn't have done anything, never mind that she wouldn't have been able to get near the female ghost's body in the first place. With all that, this could be said to be a completely meaningless death.

Xie Lian answered, "No. You've been a great help. You see, the moment you came over, the female ghost's attention was diverted, which was how I had the chance to subdue her. Thank you so very much. But you can't do that again next time, all right? If you're going to help, you have to tell me first. Otherwise, if I don't pick up on it, things will go downhill fast."

Xiao-Ying chuckled. "*Hahhh*, young master, you don't need to comfort me anymore. I know I wasn't any help, and that there won't be a next time."

Her words were jumbled and unclear, and when she spat out a mouthful of blood, there were even a few broken front teeth mixed in. That bandaged boy was shaking with panic, *woo woo*-ing, trying to speak.

Xiao-Ying turned to him. "In the future, don't go down the mountain to steal food anymore. If you're discovered, you'll be beaten to death."

"If he ever gets hungry, he can come to me," Xie Lian said.

Xiao-Ying's eyes lit up hearing this. "...Really? Then, thanks so much..."

She smiled and smiled, until suddenly, two lines of tears streamed down from that pair of tiny eyes.

She whispered, "I feel I haven't lived through many good days in all my life here in this world."

Xie Lian didn't know what to say, so he gently patted her hand.

Xiao-Ying then sighed. "Never mind. Maybe I'm just...born unlucky."

Her jumbled words certainly did sound a little odd. With a bent nose and slanted eyes and an appearance so ugly it was silly, her bloodied, tear-streaked face was almost funny to behold.

With tears still rolling down, she choked, "But, even then, I still...I still..."

Her breathing stopped, and she passed with those words. The bandaged boy saw that she had died and started to weep quietly while hugging her dead body. His face was buried in her belly, like he had lost his only pillar of support, and he didn't dare to raise his head no matter what.

As for Xie Lian, he reached out and helped close her eyes. He spoke to her mentally, *You're stronger than me.*

Right then, the sound of a bizarre bell tolled.

CLANG!

CLANG!

CLANG!

Three booming tolls, and all of a sudden Xie Lian felt his head go dizzy. He wondered out loud, "What's going on?"

Then he looked all around. All the brides had collapsed to the ground, only their arms still up and reaching toward the sky. The crowd of villagers had also slumped, as if they were all knocked out by the sound of the deafening bells. Xie Lian himself felt his head become rather heavy, and though he forced himself to stand with his hand supporting his forehead, his legs went weak and he fell with one knee to the ground. Fortunately, someone helped support him. When Xie Lian looked up, it was Nan Feng.

Turned out, the moment those seven brides entered the forest, they immediately spread out. Nan Feng had run all over almost the entirety of Mount Yujun before he managed to capture all of them, and had only just returned.

Seeing him quite calm, Xie Lian immediately asked, "What's with that bell?"

"Don't worry, it's reinforcements," Nan Feng replied.

Xie Lian looked over, following his gaze. Only then did he notice that, before the Temple of Ming Guang, a row of soldiers had appeared, standing there since who knew when.

These soldiers were outfitted in armor, emitting sharp and awe-inspiring auras, and their bodies were enveloped in a thin sheen of spiritual light. In front of the soldiers there stood a poised, elegant, and tall young military general, obviously not a mortal. That military general approached with his hands clasped behind his back and came before Xie Lian, bending slightly at the waist, giving a quick bow.

"Your Highness."

Xie Lian hadn't yet opened his mouth to make inquiries before Nan Feng whispered next to him.

"This is General Pei."

Xie Lian instantly took a glance at Xuan Ji, who was on the ground. "General Pei?"

This General Pei didn't quite match what he had imagined and was also grossly different from the divine statues. That divine statue's heroic form was vivacious, its eyes spirited and energetic, with a handsomeness that was aggressive and invasive. While this young military general was also handsome, his complexion was pale, and his countenance was as calm as cool jade. There was no sense of a murderous aura, only an unrippled tranquility. He was a military general, but he could also be said to be a tactician.

General Pei noticed Xuan Ji on the ground and spoke: "The Palace of Ling Wen informed us that this incident at Mount Yujun might be related to our Palace of Ming Guang, and so this servant has come. I didn't expect that it really did have something to do with us. We have troubled Your Highness."

Xie Lian thanked Ling Wen mentally. He wondered, how in the world was the Palace of Ling Wen inefficient?

He replied, "General Pei is working hard too."

Xuan Ji, who was still vaguely struggling, heard the words "General Pei" and suddenly looked up. She demanded enthusiastically, "Pei dear, Pei dear! Is that you? Have you come? Have you finally come?!"

She was bound by Ruoye, and as overjoyed as she was, she could only rise into a kneel. Yet unexpectedly, her face immediately blanched the moment she saw that military general.

"Who are you?!"

On his end, Xie Lian had already given Nan Feng a general account of just what the ghost groom affair was about. When he heard her, he wondered, "Isn't this General Pei? Could she have waited for too long and doesn't recognize him anymore?"

"This is General Pei," Nan Feng answered. "But it's not the one she's waiting for."

Xie Lian was confused. "And there are two Generals Pei?"

Yet Nan Feng replied, "That's correct. There are indeed two of them!"

Turned out, the General Pei this female ghost Xuan Ji was waiting for was the main god of the Temple of Ming Guang. The one before them now was the deputy god of the Palace of Ming Guang, a descendant of the senior General Pei. In order to differentiate the two, everyone addressed this one as "General Pei Junior." In legitimate Ming Guang temples, both must be worshipped, one facing the front and one facing the back. General Pei was the principal god of the main hall, so his divine statue faced the entrance of the temple hall, whereas General Pei Junior's divine statue was set up behind. While he was of a later generation than his ancestor, by looks they appeared no different than brothers. Two ascendees from one household was certainly considered a beautiful tale.

Xuan Ji scanned the area and didn't see the one she wanted to see among the soldiers either. She cried bitterly, "Where's Pei Ming? Why hasn't he come? Why won't he come and see me?"

General Pei Junior inclined his head and replied, "General Pei has important business to tend to."

Xuan Ji muttered, "Important business?"

Tears streamed beneath the long hair draping over her face. "I've waited for him for hundreds of years, what important business could he have? Back then, in order to see me, he would cross half the border in one night, so what important business could he have now? So important that he can't even come down to spare me a glance? Is there something important? I don't think there is!"

"General Xuan Ji, please be on your way," General Pei Junior said.

From the troop, two soldiers of the Palace of Ming Guang approached and pulled Ruoye from Xuan Ji's person. After it affectionately wrapped itself back around Xie Lian's wrist, he gently patted it twice to comfort it. Xuan Ji allowed herself to be grabbed by those two soldiers, briefly dazed before she suddenly started struggling with force, cursing while pointing to the heavens.

"Pei Ming! I curse you!"

This screech was sharp, and Xie Lian was taken aback, thinking to himself, *Isn't this cursing the ancestor in front of the descendant?*

General Pei Junior, however, didn't react at all. He said impassively, "Please excuse us."

Xuan Ji screamed until she went hoarse. "I CURSE YOU! You'd best never fall in love with anyone, otherwise if that day should come, I'll curse you to be just like me: to burn with the fire of love unceasingly, forever and ever! The fire of love will burn your body, scorch your heart and your insides!"

Right then, General Pei Junior greeted Xie Lian and the others, "Excuse us. Please wait a moment."

Then he raised his middle and index fingers and lightly pressed them against his temple. This was the spell to activate the spiritual communication array, so he had to be communicating with someone. A moment later, he *enn*'d and dropped his hand, clasping it behind him again, and turned to Xuan Ji.

"General Pei wants me to tell you: 'That's impossible.'"

Xuan Ji screeched, *"I curse you—!!!"*

General Pei Junior waved his hand slightly and ordered, "Take her away."

The two soldiers carried Xuan Ji, who was struggling like crazy, and dragged her off.

Xie Lian spoke up. "General Pei Junior, might I ask, how will Xuan Ji be handled?"

"Sealed under a mountain," General Pei Junior replied.

To use a mountain as a seal was certainly the usual way the Heavenly Realm dealt with monsters and ghosts. After a brief moment of hesitation, Xie Lian continued. "General Xuan Ji's resentment is quite strong; she couldn't let go of the hatred that stemmed from betraying her kingdom for General Pei. Perhaps sealing isn't the right long-term solution."

General Pei Junior, however, only inclined his head. "She said she betrayed her kingdom because of General Pei?"

"She certainly did say so," Xie Lian said. "And that it was because of General Pei that she became like this. Whether that's the truth, though, I don't know."

"If it must be said that way, it's not altogether wrong," General Pei Junior said. "She did betray her kingdom for General Pei. However, the details might be different from what bystanders might imagine. After she and General Pei separated, in order to keep him, General Xuan Ji offered up military intelligence of her own volition. General Pei was unwilling to win unfairly, so he didn't take the offer."

...Well now, he never expected that the whole "I betrayed my kingdom for you" thing was actually something like that.

Xie Lian replied, "Then when she said both her legs being broken was also because of General Pei, it was...?"

"She broke those legs herself," General Pei Junior answered.

...Broke them herself?

General Pei Junior replied emotionlessly, "General Pei doesn't like forceful women, but General Xuan Ji has a strong character, which was why they couldn't be together for long. General Xuan Ji couldn't accept it and told General Pei that she was willing to sacrifice for him and change herself. Thus, she ruined her own martial skills and broke her own legs.

"With that, she basically destroyed her own wings to tie herself to General Pei's side. General Pei didn't abandon her to her own devices and kept her around to take care of her, but he never intended to marry her. General Xuan Ji's wish was never fulfilled, and so she killed herself out of resentment. Not for anything else, but just so

General Pei would be sad. However, pardon my bluntness..." The way he spoke had always been polite and overly calm. "...That would never happen."

Xie Lian rubbed his forehead and didn't speak, thinking to himself, *Who the heck are these people?*

General Pei Junior continued, "I don't know the right and wrong of all this either. I only know that if General Xuan Ji was willing to let go, things wouldn't have to be this way. Your Highness, I will take my leave now."

Xie Lian also cupped his hands and sent them off.

Nan Feng commented, "Weirdos."

Xie Lian thought, he himself was the Laughingstock of the Three Realms, an infamous weirdo, so he'd best not comment on anyone else. This was something between General Pei and Xuan Ji, so for bystanders, there was no point in discussing who was right or wrong. Their sympathies only went out to all seventeen of those innocent brides, and the military officials and sedan drivers who escorted them but suffered a terrible fate for no reason.

Having brought up the subject of the brides, Xie Lian instantly turned his gaze to look and saw that the seventeen corpses of the brides had started to show various stages of deterioration. Some had already dissolved into white bones, while some were starting to rot, emitting waves of foul odor. The stench roused the people lying on the ground and they gradually came to, but when they saw the scene, they jumped in shock and terror once more.

Xie Lian used this opportunity to nag at them to spread the philosophy of good and bad karma, advising them to pray a lot for each of the brides once they went back down the mountain, and to think of a way to contact the families of those brides to come and collect their corpses. He also cautioned that they must never commit the same deeds as those corpse-sellers, and they shouldn't commit any wrongdoings either. After such a thrilling night, and with the lead instigator gone, no one else dared to speak against Xie Lian. They each acknowledged him apprehensively, all of them feeling like they'd just had a nightmare. Only then did they realize they had acted as if possessed. Why were their minds filled only with money when there were so many dead people around? Thinking back, they all found it horrifying. The night before, everyone was doing the same thing, relying on the fact that their numbers were great and they had a leader, and they all rushed in without thinking. Now that they harbored fear in their minds, they very earnestly repented and prayed for blessings.

The day hadn't yet broken. Fearing that there might be wolves and others stirring up trouble, even though Nan Feng had just run a huge circle around the whole mountain, he now had to lead this large group of people back down. He didn't complain, however, and arranged with Xie Lian to discuss afterward what was to be done with that Forest of Upside-Down Corpses.

When the bandaged boy woke up, he sat next to Xiao-Ying's corpse once more, hugging her, not saying a word. And so, Xie Lian also sat down next to him. He spent a while coming up with a script, but just as he was about to speak to comfort him, Xie Lian suddenly noticed that the boy's head was bleeding.

If it was blood from the Corpse Forest then it would've dried, but this blood was still dripping, so it could only be from an injury.

Right then, Xie Lian told him, "Your head is wounded, take off your bandages and let me have a look."

That boy slowly looked up, and those bloodshot eyes glanced at him like he was scared and hesitant. Xie Lian smiled gently.

"Don't be afraid. If there's a wound, then it must be dressed. I promise I won't be scared off by you."

The boy hesitated for a moment, then turned around, and circle by circle he slowly unwrapped the bandages. His movements were very slow, but Xie Lian waited for him patiently and was already pondering the issues that would come after.

This boy for sure can't stay on Mount Yujun anymore, but where can he go? He can't come back to the heavens with me, and I don't even know where my next meal is coming from. I'll have to think of a reliable way to settle him. And the Green Ghost Qi Rong...

Just then, the boy finished removing the bandages and turned around.

And just as Xie Lian saw that face in its entirety, he felt like all the blood in his veins had drained completely.

5
Red-Clad Ghost, the Burning of the Martial and Civil Temples

O N THE FACE OF THE BOY, as Xie Lian had first suspected, there was a field of serious burn scars. Except, beneath the bloody scars, there were traces of three or four tiny faces.

Those faces were no bigger than the palms of a baby, and they were scattered crookedly across his cheeks and forehead. After being burned, the features on each tiny face were shriveled in pain, as if screaming in agony. The sight of these weird, screaming faces squeezing and squirming on a regular human face was indeed more horrifying than any demon!

Xie Lian felt as though he were plunged into a nightmare the instant he saw this boy's face. A fear so immense paralyzed him until he couldn't recall standing up, nor tell what the expression on his face was, but it must've been intimidating. The boy was already on tenterhooks when he removed his bandages at that hesitant, slow pace. After seeing Xie Lian's reaction, he took a couple of steps back, as if aware of Xie Lian's inability to accept that face of his. He suddenly covered his horrifying face and leapt up from the ground, then let out a shout and fled into the deep woods.

Xie Lian finally came around and shouted, "Wait!" He called out as he chased after him, "Wait! Come back!"

But Xie Lian had been dumbstruck for a good moment before he came around. The boy was obviously familiar with the

mountain paths and used to escaping in the dark, so it took him no time to vanish completely. No matter how Xie Lian yelled for him, he wouldn't show himself. There was no one around to help Xie Lian search and his powers had to be exhausted by now, so there was no way he could contact the others through the array. He ran all over the mountain, searching for a good part of an hour to no avail.

A cold breeze blew past and cleared his mind a little. Knowing that running around aimlessly like a headless fly served no purpose, Xie Lian forced himself to calm down. *Maybe he'll go back to take Xiao-Ying's body,* Xie Lian thought as he returned to the Ming Guang temple. But then, he stopped in his tracks.

Many men dressed in black with grave expressions had gathered in the woods at the back of the temple, and they were in the midst of carefully unloading those forty-something upside-down corpses. A tall man with folded arms was standing before the woods, overseeing the operation. When he turned his head around, it was the exquisite-yet-cold face of a youth. It was Fu Yao. It looked like he had made a trip back and brought a number of helping hands along from the Palace of Xuan Zhen.

Xie Lian was about to speak but was interrupted by the sound of footfalls behind him. Nan Feng had returned from sending the villagers away. Upon seeing the situation at hand, Nan Feng glanced at Fu Yao and said, "Didn't you run away?"

The comment was not pleasant to the ears, and Fu Yao raised his eyebrows in displeasure. Xie Lian didn't want them to start another argument at a time like this, so he said, "I asked him to find reinforcements."

Nan Feng sneered. "Well, where are they? I thought you could at least ask your general to come personally?"

Fu Yao replied coolly, "When I went back, I heard General Pei Junior had already come to the scene, so I didn't bother our general. Even if I had, he's probably too busy to come anyway."

Actually, based on Xie Lian's understanding of Mu Qing, Xie Lian was pretty sure that he wouldn't come even if he had the time. But under the present circumstances, there wasn't time to dwell on that. He said tiredly, "Stop your fighting for a moment and help me find the bandaged boy."

Nan Feng frowned. "Wasn't he guarding that girl's body with you earlier?"

"I scared him off after asking him to remove his bandages," Xie Lian replied.

Fu Yao smirked. "Please, your cross-dressing isn't that terrifying."

Xie Lian sighed. "It's my fault for being in a stupor. Miss Xiao-Ying's death was already a big shock to him. He probably couldn't take the blow of thinking that I was scared of his face, so he ran off."

Fu Yao wrinkled his nose. "Is he really that ugly?"

"It's not a matter of ugliness," Xie Lian replied. "He...has the Human Face Disease."

Hearing those three words, both Nan Feng and Fu Yao froze.

They finally understood why Xie Lian was shocked.

Eight hundred years ago, a plague swept through the Kingdom of Xianle, and it wiped out the nation. Those who caught the plague would first develop small warts all over their bodies, then as the warts swelled, the skin would grow rough. The swollen parts would slowly grow more uneven, with three indentations and one protrusion, just like...eyes, mouths, noses. The facial features would then metamorphize until the warts eventually took on the shape of a human face. If they were left alone, more and more human faces would grow on their bodies. It was said that some of these human faces, once fully formed, could speak and even scream.

They called this the Human Face Disease!

Fu Yao's expression went through a myriad of changes as he dropped his folded arms. "That's impossible! It was exterminated hundreds of years ago! There's no way it could reappear!"

"I'm not mistaken," Xie Lian only said.

Nan Feng and Fu Yao couldn't refute him. No one could refute this if it came from Xie Lian.

Xie Lian continued, "There are many burn scars on his face, probably from self-inflicted burning to get rid of the faces."

The first reaction of those who contracted the disease was usually to slice off the faces with knives or burn them away with fire; they would use any means possible to rid themselves of those lesions.

Nan Feng's voice turned solemn. "The boy is probably not a normal human being, then. He has to be at least a few hundred years old. All else aside, is he contagious?"

Even though this was a severe headache, it was a question Xie Lian considered calmly and logically, so he replied with conviction, "No, the Human Face Disease is highly contagious. If he were still contagious, then the entire mountain would've been infected by now, considering how long he has been hiding here. His condition should already be...cured. Only the scars remain."

They couldn't afford to be careless. Fu Yao seemed to have some real influence in the Palace of Xuan Zhen and was able to call forth capable hands to help with the search. But no matter how deep they dug or how far they looked, they could not find any traces of the bandaged boy. Perhaps he had already fled Mount Yujun and vanished into the sea of people. The best they could do now was to return to the heavens, request that the Palace of Ling Wen conduct a search, and wait for news. Fortunately, the boy was not contagious, but Xie Lian thought of how horrifying he looked. If he was discovered after he left the mountains, he might end up hunted as a monster. It was best that they find him soon.

Without further delay, Xie Lian picked up Xiao-Ying's body and descended the mountain. Since he was slightly out of it, he didn't realize he brought the body into the tea shop until the tea master yelled at him. Xie Lian immediately apologized and went back out to entrust Xiao-Ying's burial to someone else before reentering the tea shop. After settling everything, he sat down and heaved a soundless sigh.

This case was finally over, but Xie Lian thought that the few days since he ascended felt longer than an entire year of collecting scraps in the Mortal Realm. Climbing, jumping, flying, screaming, tumbling, disguising, and performing...his bones were going to collapse. Even then, there were still many mysteries and aftermaths left for him to deal with. Maybe he'd raise a bard banner and roam the world telling tales of how collecting scraps was better than ascension.

Fu Yao lifted the hem of his robe and sat down next to him. Alas, he could no longer keep it in and rolled his eyes. "How much longer are you gonna wear that thing?"

It felt incredibly endearing, somehow, to see his eyes roll. Xie Lian finally took off the wedding dress, wiped away his makeup, and then realized dejectedly, "Was I talking to General Pei Junior in this dress the whole time? Nan Feng, why didn't you remind me?"

"Probably because you looked so obviously happy in it," Fu Yao replied.

After running errands all day, Nan Feng finally sat down for a rest too. "Don't worry about it. General Pei Junior won't care. You can dress ten times weirder and he won't tell anyone when he goes back."

Xie Lian was grateful for all the errands this junior official had run and poured him some tea. He thought about how coolheaded General Pei Junior was in the face of Xuan Ji's madness and commented, "General Pei Junior is certainly calm and collected, very composed."

Nan Feng took a sip of the tea and said, "He may look well mannered, but he's like his ancestor, difficult to deal with."

That was something Xie Lian could of course see. Unbelievably enough, Fu Yao agreed too. "General Pei Junior is a nouveau ascendent of the last couple hundred years, but he's got a strong tailwind and climbs the ladder pretty fast. When he was appointed Deputy General by General Pei, he was barely twenty years old. Do you know what he did?"

"What?" Xie Lian asked.

"He slaughtered an entire city," Fu Yao replied coldly.

Xie Lian looked thoughtful on hearing this, but he wasn't surprised. In the Upper Court, kings and generals roamed. Regarding fighting for and protecting of one's land, it was said that the success of a general is built on the bones of millions. To reach godhood, one must first become a hero, but the path a hero walked was always bloody.

Fu Yao concluded, "In the Upper Court, there aren't many who are trustworthy and worth meeting."

Xie Lian thought it funny that Fu Yao sounded like he was speaking from experience and cautioning a newcomer. He wondered if Fu Yao only spoke because he had been bullied in the Heavenly Realm himself, and the experience had affected him deeply. But then again, even though Xie Lian had ascended three times, he never stuck around for long. So when it came to understanding the gods, he might actually know less than these two junior officials.

Nan Feng, on the other hand, seemed to strongly disagree. "Don't listen to such inflammatory statements, there's good and bad every-where. There are still a number of trustworthy officials in the heavens."

"Hah! Trustworthy officials? Do you mean your general?" Fu Yao sneered.

Nan Feng responded, "I don't know about my general, but defi-nitely not yours!"

Xie Lian was long used to this kind of situation. And with other things on his mind, he didn't have the energy to pull them apart.

The case in the north had concluded. The first thing Xie Lian did upon returning to the heavens was to report the bandaged boy to the Palace of Ling Wen and place a request to search for him.

Ling Wen took the request with a grave expression. "I will do my utmost to find him. Truly, I did not think this journey to the north would open such a giant can of worms. Thank you for your hard work, Your Highness."

Xie Lian replied, "I have the two junior officials who volunteered to help to thank, and General Pei Junior as well. I am sincerely grateful."

"This all came from relationship trouble caused by Ol' Pei himself, so of course Junior has to take care of it. He's used to it, so there's no need to thank him," Ling Wen said. "If Your Highness is not busy, please enter the communication array. We are to have a meeting regarding what has transpired."

Xie Lian also had many questions he'd like answers to. After leav-ing the Palace of Ling Wen, he wandered about and found a small stone bridge. The stone bridge crossed a small gurgling stream with crystal clear waters. He could see the clouds drifting under the water, and through the flowing waters and clouds, there stood the rising and falling mountain ranges as well as the vast, squarely erected cities of the Mortal Realm.

This is a good place, Xie Lian thought. And so he sat on the head of the bridge, mouthed the password, and entered the communication array.

It was one of those rare times when the communication array was bursting with liveliness, with voices echoing and reverberating from all directions. The first thing he heard was Feng Xin swearing.

"Holy fuck! Have you all picked a mountain for the sealing yet?! That Xuan Ji is a madwoman; no matter what we ask, she only screams to see General Pei and tells us nothing useful about the location of the Green Ghost Qi Rong!"

General Pei Junior responded, "General Xuan Ji has always been stubborn and intense."

Feng Xin yelled angrily, "General Pei Junior, is your General Pei back yet? Let her meet him. Then get the Green Ghost Qi Rong's location out of her and get rid of her!"

Feng Xin had never been good with women, and Xie Lian felt sorry that he was the one given the task of interrogation. General Pei Junior replied, "It doesn't matter even if they meet. She'll just become more insane."

A voice came through, "Another round of upside-down corpses... Qi Rong really is too crass. Disgusting."

"Even the Ghost Realm thinks he's vulgar; that means he truly is very much so!"

Words between the officials flew seamlessly around in the array, and it was clear that they were all on familiar terms with one another. As a newcomer who'd only just ascended again after an eight-hundred-year absence, Xie Lian should have laid low and remained silent, but after a while, he couldn't resist and asked, "Everyone, what was with the upside-down corpses? Was Green Ghost Qi Rong in the area too?"

Xie Lian rarely spoke in the communication array, so his voice was foreign to many, and the officials did not know whether to respond. Surprisingly enough, the first to answer him was Feng Xin.

"Green Ghost Qi Rong wasn't at Mount Yujun. However, the upside-down corpses were offerings Xuan Ji presented to him, as per his order."

"Xuan Ji is a subordinate of the Green Ghost?" Xie Lian asked.

"Correct," General Pei Junior replied. "Xuan Ji passed away many hundreds of years ago. She held a grudge but was too powerless to stir up havoc until just over a hundred years ago, when Green Ghost Qi Rong took a liking to her and took her under his wing. Only then did her spiritual powers improve by leaps and bounds."

What he really meant was that the chaos Xuan Ji caused was not General Pei's fault, because she wasn't originally this strong. All blame should go to Green Ghost Qi Rong instead, since he was the one who took her under his command and gave her the power to cause harm. Everyone was already of the opinion that this sin was all General Pei's to bear, though no one said it out loud. Yet he noticed, and spoke of it so openly in this reminder that it shut everyone up and made them hide their real thoughts deeper within.

Xie Lian then spoke up again. "Has Mount Yujun been thoroughly inspected? What about the child spirit?"

This time, Mu Qing's voice rang out. He said in an inscrutable tone, "Child spirit? What child spirit?"

Xie Lian realized Fu Yao must not have reported every detail—maybe his volunteering to help was even done in secret. So, without mentioning Fu Yao to spare him any unnecessary problems, Xie Lian explained. "When I was in the wedding sedan, I heard the giggles of a child who sang nursery rhymes as a word of caution. The two junior officials next to me didn't notice, which means that this child spirit must have remarkable powers."

"There were no child spirits found on Mount Yujun," Mu Qing stated.

Xie Lian was confused. Perhaps the child spirit had come specially just to warn him? Thinking of this, Xie Lian was suddenly reminded of another matter that had been on his mind all this time. He asked, "Speaking of which, I met a young man who can control silver butterflies at Mount Yujun. Does anyone know who he is?"

The noisy communication array suddenly fell completely silent. Xie Lian was expecting this reaction, so he simply waited patiently.

A moment later, Ling Wen asked, "Your Highness, what did you say just now?"

Mu Qing said coldly, "He just said that he met Hua Cheng."

Upon finally learning the name of that young man in red, Xie Lian felt his spirits lift inexplicably. He smiled. "So he's called Hua Cheng? Hm, it's a fitting name for him."

The tone of Xie Lian's voice rendered all the officials even more speechless. Another moment passed before Ling Wen cleared her throat. "Um... Your Highness, have you ever heard of the Four Calamities?"

Much ashamed, I only know of the Four Famous Tales, Xie Lian thought to himself.

The so-called Four Famous Tales referred to the extravagant stories of the deeds of four gods prior to their ascension: The Young Lord Who Poured Wine, The Prince Who Pleased God, The General Who Snapped His Sword, and The Princess Who Slit Her Throat. Of course, "The Prince Who Pleased God" alluded to the awe-inspiring display of the crown prince of Xianle upon the Grand Avenue of Divine Might.

Having one's name among the Four Famous Tales did not necessarily indicate that those four were the strongest of the gods; the
Four Famous Tales were as such simply because they were the most
well known and most spoken of. Xie Lian had always been slow on
the uptake when it came to news from the outside world; he could
even be said to be out of touch with the outside world and ignorant
of its affairs. He only knew about the Four Famous Tales because he
was one of the four. The Four Calamities was probably something
that grew popular later, but Xie Lian had never heard of the term
before. Since it included the word "Calamity," it couldn't be anything good.

"Much ashamed, but I've never heard of them," Xie Lian said.
"Who are the Four Calamities?"

Mu Qing responded coolly, "Your Highness walked the Mortal
Realm for hundreds of years, and yet you are still so ill-informed. I'm
really curious to know what you've been doing all this time."

Eating, sleeping, busking, collecting junk, duh?

Xie Lian smiled. "It's not easy being mortal. There are plenty of
things to busy myself with, and they're all complicated. It's not easier
than being a heavenly official."

"Please remember well, Your Highness," Ling Wen said. "The Four
Calamities are: Ship-Sinking Black Water, Night-Touring Green
Lantern, White-Clothed Calamity, and Crimson Rain Sought
Flower. They are the four Ghost Kings of the Ghost Realm, who
cause endless headaches for all in the Heavenly Realm."

Humans become gods when they ascend, ghosts when they fall.

The gods created heaven to reside in, drawing a clear boundary between themselves and mortals. They watched from above and ruled
from beyond reach. The Ghost Realm, on the other hand, was not
separated from the Mortal Realm. Monsters, demons, ghosts, and

mortals all shared one earth. Some ghosts hid in the darkness, and some pretended to be humans as they walked among the people and roamed the Mortal Realm in disguise.

Ling Wen continued, "Ship-Sinking Black Water refers to a water ghost. Although he has reached supreme status, he's fairly low-key and rarely starts trouble. Not many have seen him before, so we won't mind him for now.

"Night-Touring Green Lantern refers to that vulgar, corpse-hanging Green Ghost Qi Rong. He's the only one in the four not yet a supreme. He is likely included because he's always causing trouble and is really quite annoying. Or maybe because four names are easier to remember, so he's just there to pad the numbers. We'll skip him too.

"White-Clothed Calamity should be someone Your Highness is familiar with. He's also known as White No-Face."

Hearing the name, Xie Lian, who was sitting on the stone bridge, suddenly felt a stab of pain in his heart that spread all over his body. His hands began to shake, and he unconsciously clenched them into fists.

Of course he was familiar.

They say that when a supreme is born, it can destroy an entire nation and throw the world into chaos. The first country White No-Face destroyed was Xianle.

Xie Lian remained silent, and Ling Wen continued.

"In any case, White No-Face is already defeated. Even if he still exists somewhere in this world, it's now past his time in the limelight.

"Your Highness, the silver butterflies you saw at Mount Yujun are also called wraith butterflies. Their master is the last of the four, and one the world does not want to incur the wrath of: Crimson Rain Sought Flower, Hua Cheng."

In the heavens, "notorious" was the word to describe the Heavenly Emperor and the crown prince of Xianle. Although the meaning of "notoriety" was completely different between the two, the word still resonated equally. However, in the Ghost Realm, there was only one worthy of being called "notorious," and that was Hua Cheng.

If you wanted to learn about a god, simply walk into his temple and take a look at the way he was dressed and the weapons he wielded, and you'd more or less understand him. If you wanted to know more, simply listen to folktales, plays, and stories passed down by word of mouth. A god's mortal past and deeds were well documented. Ghosts, on the other hand, not so much. The kind of person they were while still alive, and their appearance at present, were all a mystery.

The name Hua Cheng[5] was very obviously fake, and his appearance was most likely fake too. In the rumors, he was sometimes a twisted boy given to capricious mood changes, sometimes a gentle and mannered handsome young man, sometimes a gorgeous seductress with a venomous heart, anything goes! As for his true self, the only thing that one could be sure of was that he dressed in red and often appeared alongside a bloodbath with silver butterflies flitting between his sleeves. And when it came to Hua Cheng's backstory, there were endless different versions. Some say he was born without a right eye and was bullied and humiliated for it since birth, so he was filled with hatred for the world. Some say he was a young soldier who died in a lost battle for his country and later came to walk the earth in resentment. Some say he was a fool who was tormented by the death of his love; some even say he was a monster. In the most outrageous version, supposedly—only supposedly!—Hua Cheng ascended and became a god but immediately jumped back down on

5   "Hua Cheng" means "Flower City."

his own and became a ghost. But that version wasn't widespread. No one knew if it was true or false, and not many believed it. It had to be false, though; even if it were true, it'd be a complete embarrassment for the heavens if someone ditched a heavenly official role to become a ghost. Either way, the more diverse the stories were, the more mystery he was shrouded in.

There were also many reasons for the gods to fear Hua Cheng. For example, his behavior was unpredictable: sometimes he would carry out a massacre in cold blood, and sometimes he would do odd acts of kindness. He also wielded a great deal of influence in the Mortal Realm and had legions of followers.

That's right. Mortals worshipped gods to ask for blessings and protection so that they could escape the evils from the Ghost Realm, and that was how the gods came to gain so many followers. Yet, Hua Cheng, a ghost, had such a large following on earth that he could influence the world single-handedly.

Here is a story that must be told. When Hua Cheng first appeared, he did something notorious.

He openly challenged thirty-five heavenly officials. The challenge was to spar with the martial gods and to debate with the civil gods.

Thirty-three of the thirty-five thought it hilarious but were also infuriated enough to take up his challenge, thinking they could join forces to teach this little devil a thing or two.

The first to step up to the plate were the martial gods.

The martial gods were the strongest of the heavenly officials; each had plenty of believers, and they were all-powerful. In the face of a newborn ghost, it was a sure win. Yet unexpectedly, it turned out to be a complete annihilation after one battle. Even their weapons were completely smashed to pieces by Hua Cheng's freakish scimitar.

It was only after the battle that they found out Hua Cheng was born of Mount Tonglu.

Mount Tonglu was a volcano, and within its mountainous domain there was a city called Gu. The City of Gu wasn't a place where people cultivated poison, but rather the city itself was a great venom.

Every few hundred years, tens of thousands of ghosts descended upon the City of Gu to butcher one another until at last only one remained, and thus was the venom brewed. It usually ended in complete elimination, but those few who were capable enough to make it out alive would emerge as the devil incarnate. Only two such ghosts had ever made it out of the City of Gu in the past several centuries, and as expected, those two both became well-known ghost kings.

Hua Cheng was one.

After the defeat of the martial gods, it came time for the civil gods to rise to the challenge. Surely Hua Cheng could fight, but not debate?

Unfortunately for the civil gods, they could not defeat him. Hua Cheng could recite the classics and debate the contemporaries. He was sometimes polite, sometimes vicious, sometimes unyielding, sometimes incisive, and sometimes quibbling. He was impenetrably sharp, his arguments flawless. He verbally abused the civil gods from top to bottom, past to present, and infuriated them so much that they puked blood and washed the skies red.

Hua Cheng gained fame overnight.

However, that alone wasn't enough to call him scary. What was scary was that after the challenge, Hua Cheng demanded all thirty-three officials make good on their word.

Before the challenge, it was decided that if Hua Cheng were to lose, he would offer up his own ashes. If the officials were to lose, they must descend from the heavens and return to being mortals.

If it weren't for his arrogant attitude and his decisive stake, and the conviction of the thirty-three officials that they would not lose, they never would have accepted such terms.

However, not a single heavenly official voluntarily honored the terms. It was humiliating to renege on their bet, but when they thought about it, if only one of them was defeated it'd be an embarrassment, but if all of them were defeated and humiliated, then no one would lose face. They could even turn around and mock the other party! So they all came to a tacit understanding that they'd pretend nothing had happened. Mortals were forgetful anyway. They would forget all about this in fifty years or so.

They were not wrong about the mortals, but they were wrong about Hua Cheng.

The gods refused to fulfill their promise? That was fine, he would give them a hand.

Thus, Hua Cheng burned every single temple and shrine of all thirty-three gods.

This was the stuff of nightmares for all the gods in the heavens: the red-clad ghost's burning of the thirty-three martial and civil gods' temples.

Temples and followers were the main source of power for heavenly officials. Where would followers go to pray if there were no temples? If they didn't pray, there wouldn't be merits. The massive loss of temples and merits greatly injured the heavens. To rebuild would take at least a hundred years, and even then, they wouldn't be the same as before. This was a catastrophe greater than failing in transcending Tribulations. The number of temples and shrines of these heavenly officials combined was at least in the tens of thousands, but Hua Cheng managed to burn them all in a single night. How? No one knew, but he did it. Pure madness.

The gods cried foul to the Heavenly Emperor, but there was nothing he could do. The heavenly officials themselves accepted the challenge and the terms, and Hua Cheng was cunning enough to only destroy temples without hurting anyone. It was as if he dug a hole and asked the gods to jump, and the gods themselves dug the hole bigger and dove in. With the way things were, what more could they have done?

At first, the thirty-three heavenly officials had wanted to show the world the defeat of this crazed little devil, so they broadcast the challenge into the dreams of many royals and nobles to display their strength and might before their most devout believers. But all the royals and nobles saw was their miserable defeat. When the mortals woke up, they switched from worshipping heavenly officials to worshipping that ghost. The heavenly officials who lost both their temples and believers soon grew weaker and weaker, until they were erased from existence. It wasn't until a new wave of ascensions that those empty positions were filled again.

Ever since then, the name Hua Cheng was feared in the heavens. Even just hearing a mention of red robes or silver butterflies brought cold sweat to many. Some feared he would challenge them and burn their temples if they were to incur his displeasure, some were blackmailed into silence and inaction because he had them by the balls, and some even oddly respected him because of how wide his reach was in the Mortal Realm. Sometimes, they even had to ask him for help paving the way for them while they carried out their duties. This went on for a long time, and many heavenly officials developed a peculiar sort of admiration for him.

Thus, the heavens feared, hated, and respected this ghost king.

Among the thirty-five gods who were challenged, the two who declined were General Xuan Zhen, Mu Qing, and General Nan Yang, Feng Xin.

They thought the challenge was beneath them and didn't care to take it. Turned out, that was the right decision to make. But even then, Hua Cheng hadn't forgotten about those two. Many Zhongyuan Festival patrols ended in fists and blood when both parties crossed paths with each other, and those crazy, maniacal silver butterflies left an everlasting impression on both men. Hearing this, Xie Lian thought of that fluttering silver butterfly that sparkled and danced adorably around him in delight. He couldn't picture it as described in the rumors.

Was that little silver butterfly really that scary? Xie Lian wondered. *It wasn't that bad... It was kind of cute.*

6
Clothes Redder than Maple, Skin White as Snow

F COURSE, those were words he would never say out loud. But no wonder Nan Feng and Fu Yao's faces changed when they heard about the silver butterflies. They must've had a hard time at the hands of the silver butterflies' master, together with the two generals they served.

"Your Highness, d-d-d-did Hua Cheng do anything to you?" an official asked, as if Xie Lian should be missing an arm or a leg.

"He didn't really do anything, just..." Xie Lian stopped, at a loss for words.

Just what? He couldn't possibly say that Hua Cheng just hijacked his sedan, held his hand, and strolled with him in the woods?

Stumped for a moment, Xie Lian finally said, "He broke Xuan Ji's enchantment array at Mount Yujun and took me inside."

The heavenly officials all grumbled inwardly but remained in uneasy silence. After a while, an official finally asked, "What do you all think of this?"

From the voice alone, Xie Lian could imagine how the various officials looked as they shook their heads and shrugged.

"Who knows?! Completely no idea!"

"No one knows what he wants, how scary!"

"What on earth is he thinking? No one can read that Hua Cheng..."

Although Hua Cheng had been ubiquitously known as the devil incarnate, Xie Lian didn't think he was that scary. And all things considered, Xie Lian had Hua Cheng to thank for his help in the northern case this time around. Either way, his first mission after ascension was complete.

It was predetermined that all merits from the northern case would be counted under Xie Lian's name, but that old lord official was so overwhelmed with grief over the death of his daughter that he didn't actually remember to fulfill the promises of his prayers until much later, and the merits were discounted because he did so mournfully. Yet somehow, with a little bit here, a little bit there, and a lot of oversight everywhere, Xie Lian was finally able to repay most of the eight million eight hundred and eighty thousand merits.

Xie Lian was at last debt-free! Feeling light with that weight off his shoulders, happy and high-spirited, Xie Lian decided he'd now focus on being a good god, and it would be great if he could become acquaintances or friends with other heavenly officials. Even though the Upper Court communication array was generally peaceful, it would turn boisterous once things got busy. Sometimes if an official was feeling good or had encountered something interesting, they'd share in the array, and there'd be merriment. Although Xie Lian didn't recognize most of the voices, he would listen silently. But he couldn't always remain invisible! After a while, he'd randomly join the conversation:

"That really is quite interesting."

"I read this pleasant verse in passing and thought I'd share with everyone."

"Here's an effective little cure for back and leg pains; thought I'd share with everyone."

Unfortunately, every time he'd share these mindfully selected, physically and mentally beneficial tips, the communication array would go silent.

Finally, Ling Wen couldn't take it anymore and told him privately:

"Your Highness, what you're sharing in the communication array is nice, but even those who are hundreds of years older than you wouldn't share those kinds of things."

Xie Lian felt a little depressed. He wasn't even that old, so how did he end up becoming the senior among the heavenly officials, who couldn't keep up with the trending topics of the youngsters? Probably because he'd been away for too long and always lived a solitary life without a care for the outside world. Alas, it couldn't be helped, so whatever. He gave up, and became less depressed.

But there was another problem: there were still no new shrines built for him in the Mortal Realm. Maybe there were, but the heavens hadn't found them, so there weren't any records. Even old Lords of the Ground and Soil had shrines. As a formally ascended official, one of three times at that, having neither shrine nor temple nor followers was pretty awkward. But, as awkward as it was, it was only other heavenly officials feeling awkward for him. Xie Lian personally thought it wasn't that bad.

And one day, on a whim, he suddenly thought: *If no one worships me, I'll worship myself!*

None of the heavenly officials knew how to respond to that.

Who had ever fucking heard of a god worshipping himself?! To reach such tragic heights, what was the point?!

However, Xie Lian was used to receiving nothing but awkward silence the moment he spoke and thought amusing himself could be fun. Once he made up his mind, he jumped back down to the Mortal Realm.

This time, he landed in a small village in the mountains. It was known as Puqi, named for the water chestnut.

Rather than a village, it was more like a hillside hamlet. With green trees and clear waters, it was a pleasant country landscape with continuous stretches of rice paddies. With such beautiful scenery, Xie Lian thought he'd landed in a really good place this time.

When he looked further, he saw there was a small, dilapidated shack on a hill, and upon asking around, the villagers told him: "That house is decrepit, there's no owner, and vagrants sleep a night in there every once in a while, so you can go make yourself at home."

Well, wasn't that just perfect for him? Xie Lian walked toward the shack.

As Xie Lian walked closer, he realized that the shack looked decrepit from afar, but on closer inspection, it was literally crumbling. Two of the four columns that held up the rectangle-shaped shack were probably rotted through. When the wind blew, the entire shack would shake and creak, possibly ready to collapse at any time. But it was still within Xie Lian's range of acceptable. He went in for a look and began to tidy up the place.

The villagers were quite surprised to see that someone was actually going to settle in that shack, and all came to check Xie Lian out. They gave Xie Lian a huge, warm welcome. Not only did they donate a broom to help with cleaning and watch as he swept until he was covered in dust, they even gave him a basket of freshly picked water chestnuts. With their skin peeled off, the water chestnuts were white and crisp, fresh and juicy. Xie Lian squatted on the doorstep and ate them. He then put his hands together, and feeling thankful for this blessing, he decided to call this place "Puqi Shrine."

Puqi Shrine already had a table inside that could be used as the altar—after a couple of wipe-downs. Xie Lian busied himself with cleaning this and that, and the onlooking villagers soon realized that this young man was building a shrine of sorts. Curiosity overtook them, and they questioned him.

"Which god are you going to worship?"

Xie Lian cleared his throat and said, "Yes. Um. This shrine will be for the Prince of Xianle."

Everyone's face went blank. "Who's that?"

Xie Lian replied, "Um...I don't know either? He's a prince. I think."

"Ooh. What does he do?"

"Probably watches over you and keeps you safe."

While collecting scraps in passing.

The villagers asked excitedly, "Then, does this prince oversee the blessing of wealth?"

It'd already be pretty good if you don't get blessed into debt, Xie Lian thought to himself and gently replied, "I'm afraid not."

The crowd started throwing suggestions at him.

"Why not worship the Water Master? For wealth! It'll bring in good money for the temple!"

"What about Ling Wen-zhenjun? Then maybe our village will produce a scholar!"

A girl shyly offered, "Um...what about...what about..."

Xie Lian maintained his smile. "What about?"

"General Ju Yang."

"..."

If Xie Lian really built a Ju Yang Shrine, Feng Xin would probably shoot him dead on the spot with an arrow!

After roughly tidying his shrine, all that was left that Xie Lian needed were an incense burner, some fortune shakers, and other miscellaneous sundries. But Xie Lian forgot the most important thing: the statue of a god.

He carried his bamboo hat on his back and stepped out the door— oh yeah, there was no door either. He pondered for a moment. This shack definitely had to be repaired. And so Xie Lian wrote and put a sign out front: *"Please kindly donate to the renovation of this broken shrine for the accumulation of good merits."*

Xie Lian left, walked for three to four kilometers, and entered town. To do what? To get a life of course, so he went to do what he did best.

In fairy tales, gods didn't need to eat. But in truth, it was hard to say. The almighty could certainly extract and absorb the necessary spiritual energy directly from sunshine and rain dew, but the problem was: it wasn't a matter of ability, but rather, why would you?

Some gods, due to their cultivation methods, required clean internal organs and could not touch even a drop of mortal grease. If they were to ingest mortal sustenance, it would be as if they had been struck with food poisoning and they would get diarrhea. Thus, they would only ingest cleanly-grown spiritual fruits or magical beasts that had life-prolonging and power-strengthening effects.

Xie Lian didn't have those problems. With the cursed collar on, he was no different than a mortal. He could eat anything, and through experience, nothing he ate could kill him either. Even if it was a bun that had been set aside for over a month, or a cake that had gone moldy, he could eat it all without harm. With such a body, he could pretty much get by just collecting scraps. To compare them, building a shrine cost him money, while collecting scraps made him money, so ultimately, truly, collecting scraps was better than ascension.

Xie Lian had the looks and grace of a saint, so he had the upper hand when collecting scraps, and it took him almost no time to collect a giant bag. On the way back, he saw an old ox cart that was piled high with hay. The cart looked like one he'd seen before in Puqi Village, so it should be going the same way. He asked for a ride, and the cart driver tilted his chin to signal for him to get on. Carrying his big bundle of junk, Xie Lian climbed on to take a seat. It was only when he settled down that he realized there was someone else lying on the other side of the tall stack of hay.

This person, whose upper body was hidden behind the hay, had his left leg crossed over his right. It appeared that he was lying there with his arms pillowed behind his head, taking a rest. He looked so carefree and at ease that it made Xie Lian a little envious. That tight pair of black boots on a pair of long legs was a sight pleasing to the eyes, and it reminded Xie Lian of a different pair that walked with him at Mount Yujun. Xie Lian could not help but sneak several more looks to confirm that there were no silver chains on those boots, which seemed to be made of animal pelt.

This is probably a young master coming out to play, he thought.

The cart shook as it drove languidly. Xie Lian pushed back his bamboo hat and took out a scroll to read. He didn't really care for worldly affairs, but after having created too many awkward situations, he figured he'd better do some studying. The cart rattled and time passed. Looking up, they were traversing a maple grove, a sea of flaming red in a field of green. The rustic charm of the mountainous countryside, with fresh grass that refreshed the mind, was extremely intoxicating. But Xie Lian could not help but be slightly taken aback.

A long time ago, in his youth, when he cultivated at the Royal Holy Temple, the entire mountain of maple was like this, shimmering like gold, intense like fire. The unforgettable sight before him now inevitably took him on a trip down memory lane. Xie Lian watched for a long time before looking down at the scroll.

The first few lines on the scroll were thus:

The Prince of Xianle, ascended thrice as: a Martial God, a Misfortune God, a Rubbish God.

"...Well, all right," Xie Lian said out loud. "If you think about it, a martial god is no different than a rubbish god. All gods are equal. All beings are equal."

A snicker came from behind, and a voice said, "Is that right?"

The youth on the other side of the cart lazily continued in a drawl, "People naturally love saying that all gods are equal and all beings are equal, but if that were true, then pretty much all those different gods wouldn't exist."

Xie Lian looked at the boy, who was still lying there idly without showing any intention of getting up. He had likely interrupted out of boredom.

"You're probably right," Xie Lian said and smiled.

Xie Lian returned to his scroll and continued reading.

Further down the line read: *Many believe that, as the God of Misfortune, any paintings or writings of the Prince of Xianle have the powers of a curse. If placed on the back of a person, or on the main entrance of a household, then the cursed person or household will run into all sorts of bad luck...*

...It was hard to tell whether this was a description of a god or a ghost.

Xie Lian shook his head. He couldn't bear to read any more about himself. It was probably better to read about other prominent gods of today, so he wouldn't be discourteous if he ran into them and ended up not being able to tell them apart. A villager had mentioned the Water Master earlier, so Xie Lian moved on to find the description of the Water Master.

The Water Master Wudu: controls water and simultaneously wealth. Most merchants have a Water Master shrine in their stores and homes to guarantee their wealth.

Xie Lian thought this was strange. "Why would a God of Water control wealth?"

The youth behind the hay responded, "When merchants transport goods, their cargo is mainly sent on the waterways, so they always go to the Water Master Temple and light up a tall incense to pray for a safe journey, promising this or that when they return. After a while, the Water Master gradually came to control wealth."

The youth was actually answering his questions specially for him. Xie Lian turned around. "Really? Interesting. The Water Master must be a very powerful major god, then."

The youth sneered. "Yeah, he's the 'Water Tyrant,' after all."

Judging by tone, Xie Lian didn't think the boy took that particular heavenly official all that seriously. It didn't sound like he was complimenting him either. "What's the 'Water Tyrant'?"

The youth replied leisurely, "When a ship travels down a major river, it all depends on him whether the ship can set sail. No offerings means capsizing. Pretty tyrannical, so that's how he received the nickname. Kinda like General Ju Yang and the Sweeping General."

Famous gods usually had a nickname or two between all the realms. For example, Xie Lian was known as the Laughingstock of the Three Realms, the Infamous Freak, the Jinx, the Loser, ahem, ahem, etcetera. Usually, it was fairly disrespectful to use those nicknames on heavenly officials, like if anyone were to call Mu Qing the Sweeping General, he'd surely fly into a rage.

Xie Lian made a note to himself on what *not* to call the Water Master and said, "I see. Thanks so much for enlightening me." He paused briefly, and, thinking this youth to be a rather intriguing conversationalist, he continued, "My friend, you look young, but you know a lot."

The youth replied, "Nah. Just bored. I read whatever when I'm free, that's all."

In the Mortal Realm, it was easy to find books on lore that spoke of the stories of gods and ghosts, the subjects ranging from their kindnesses and grudges to trivialities. Some were real and some fake. It wasn't odd that the youth knew so much.

Xie Lian put down his scroll. "Then, my friend, you know about gods, but do you know about ghosts too?"

"Which ghost?" the youth asked.

Xie Lian replied, "Crimson Rain Sought Flower, Hua Cheng."

The youth chuckled and finally sat up when he heard that name. He turned around, and Xie Lian's eyes suddenly lit up.

The youth was about sixteen or seventeen years old. His tunic was redder than maple leaves, and his skin was white like snow. With eyes as bright as stars, he looked askance at him with a smile. He was exceptionally handsome, but there was an inexplicable hint of wildness in his looks. His hair was tied in a loose ponytail, crooked and carefree.

The cart was driving through the forest of flaming red maples, where maple leaves danced their way to the ground. A leaf playfully landed on the shoulder of the youth, and he blew it off softly, then looked up at Xie Lian, speaking with a shadow of a smile.

"What do you want to know? Ask away."

He looked teasing, yet somehow possessed the perfect composure of omniscience. Though he sounded youthful, his voice was deeper than was typical for his age and was pleasant to the ears.

Sitting upright on the cart, Xie Lian watched him thoughtfully for a moment, then said, "'Crimson Rain Sought Flower' evokes quite the imagery. Do you know where it came from, my friend?"

Out of respect, Xie Lian didn't say "my *little* friend." The youth sat up casually, propped an arm up on a raised knee, and fixed his sleeves.

He replied, unconcerned, "Nothing major, really. Just that, there was once an incident where he cleaned out the nest of another ghost, and a shower of blood rain poured down from the skies. He saw a flower was getting battered by the bloody rain, so he tilted his umbrella and shielded it."

Xie Lian pictured it in his head, imagining such an act of elegance under the rancid shower. He then thought about the burning of those thirty-three temples and laughed. "Does Hua Cheng pick fights often?"

The youth answered, "Not often. Depends on his mood."

"What was he like before his death?" Xie Lian asked.

"Definitely not a good person," the youth replied.

"What does he look like?"

The youth raised his eyes to look at him when he heard the question, tilted his head, and stood up before sitting down next to Xie Lian.

"What do you think he looks like?" He turned the question on Xie Lian.

Seeing the youth up close, Xie Lian thought he was too handsome for words. But his beauty was deadly like a sword, sharp and mesmerizing, making it hard to stare head-on. Xie Lian only met his eyes for a moment, then lowered his eyes in defeat.

He turned his head slightly and continued to ask, "If Hua Cheng is a big-shot ghost, I'm sure he has many forms and changes often."

The youth arched his brows at Xie Lian turning away and replied, "Yeah, but there are still times when he would use his real face. Of course, we're talking about his true form."

It might have been his imagination, but Xie Lian thought the distance between the two of them seemed to be a little wide, so he turned his face back around. "Then, I feel his true form is probably a youth like you."

The youth lifted his lips slightly. "Why do you say that?"

Xie Lian replied, "No reason. You say whatever and I think whatever, everything is whatever, that's all."

The youth laughed. "Who knows? But he's blind in one eye." He pointed to his right eye. "This one."

That was nothing outrageous. Xie Lian recalled one of the many backstory versions where Hua Cheng wore a black eyepatch to hide that missing eye and asked, "Do you know what happened to his eye?"

"That's a question everyone wants the answer to," the youth replied.

Others asked because they wanted to know what Hua Cheng's weakness was, but Xie Lian asked purely out of curiosity. He didn't say anything, and the youth continued. "He dug it out himself."

Xie Lian was taken aback. "Why?"

"A moment of madness," the youth answered.

...He could dig out his own eye when struck by madness. Xie Lian was now more curious than ever about this Crimson Ghost King. It couldn't have been something as simple as a moment of madness, but there were probably no more details about that story.

Xie Lian pressed on, "Does Hua Cheng have any kind of weakness?"

He wasn't expecting the youth to have the answer; it was just a casual question. If Hua Cheng's weakness was so easily known, then whatever the rumored weakness was couldn't possibly be true.

But the youth answered immediately, "His ashes."

If one got ahold of a ghost's ashes, one could take command of said ghost. If the ghost disobeyed, then by getting rid of the ashes, the ghost would dissolve and its soul disintegrate. This was common knowledge, but using it on Hua Cheng seemed fruitless.

Xie Lian smiled. "There's probably no one who can obtain his ashes, so that weakness is the same as having no weakness."

"You never know," the youth said. "There are circumstances where a ghost would voluntarily give away his ashes."

"Like the bet he had with those thirty-three heavenly officials?"

"Yeah, right," the youth scoffed.

He didn't need to say the words for Xie Lian to understand that he meant there was no way Hua Cheng would have lost. He continued, "There's a custom in the Ghost Realm where if a ghost has a special someone, they entrust their ashes to that person."

That was akin to handing over one's life to another person. Such passion, what a charming tale that would be. Xie Lian commented, interested, "I didn't know the Ghost Realm had such a romantic practice."

"They do," the youth said. "But not many dare to practice it."

Xie Lian thought as much. It wasn't only ghosts who deceived humans, there were humans who deceived ghosts too. There must be endless tales of manipulation and betrayal.

Xie Lian sighed. "It certainly is painful to think about, to have given everything for love and lose everything in return."

The youth laughed out loud. "What's there to be afraid of? If it were me, I'd have no regrets giving away my ashes. Who cares if they want me to disintegrate or just scatter the ashes for fun!"

Xie Lian grinned, then suddenly realized that they still didn't know each other's names despite having chatted for so long. "My friend, what's your name?"

CLOTHES REDDER THAN MAPLE

The youth raised one hand over his forehead to block out the rays of the blood-red sunset and squinted his eyes as if loathing the sun. "Me? I'm third in my family. They call me San Lang."[6] He didn't say his full name, and it wasn't Xie Lian's place to ask.

"My family name is Xie, given name is Lian. Are you heading to Puqi Village too?"

San Lang lay back into the hay, put his arms behind his head, and crossed his legs. "Dunno. I've no destination in mind."

It sounded as if there was a story to his words, so Xie Lian gently asked, "What's the matter?"

San Lang sighed. "My parents were quarrelling and kicked me out. I walked for a long time but had nowhere to go. I almost passed out from hunger on the streets before finding somewhere at random to lie down."

The clothes on the boy's back looked casual, but the material was of high quality. With the knowledgeable way he spoke and how carefree he appeared, Xie Lian had long since thought he was a boy from a wealthy family. It must be quite difficult for a respectable young man to wander so long on his own. Xie Lian understood that feeling. Hearing he was hungry, Xie Lian searched through his sack but only found a small steamed bun. Good thing it hadn't turned hard yet.

"Want it?"

The youth nodded, and Xie Lian gave him the bun. San Lang took a look at Xie Lian.

"What about you?"

"I'm all right. Not hungry yet," Xie Lian replied.

6   *San Lang means "third youth." It is common for peasants to name their children in numbers, while those of higher status would use the same naming conventions for familiar nicknames. Lang means "man" but also becomes a term of endearment when attached to a name; it is used by women to address their husbands or lovers, akin to "dear."*

San Lang pushed the bun back. "Then I'm all right too."

Xie Lian looked at him, then split the bun in half and gave him half. "You can have half, and I'll have the other half."

Seeing this, San Lang accepted the steamed bun and started munching. Watching him sit and eat a simple bun obediently, Xie Lian felt like he was abusing the boy.

The ox cart drove slowly over the rugged hills as the sun gradually set and the two chatted in the back. The more they spoke, the more Xie Lian thought San Lang to be an extraordinary youth. At such a young age, his diction and behavior were already mature and intelligent, calm and collected, as if there was nothing in this world he didn't know and nothing could stump him. Xie Lian thought he was wise beyond his years, but sometimes he would still reveal the folly of youth.

Xie Lian said he was the Shrine Master of Puqi Shrine, and San Lang asked, "Puqi Shrine? Sounds like there are plenty of water chestnuts to eat; I like them. Which god is it for?"

Having been asked that troublesome question again, Xie Lian cleared his throat and said, "The Prince of Xianle. You probably don't know him."

The youth smiled, but before he could say anything, the ox cart suddenly shook violently.

The two jerked with the cart, and Xie Lian reached to grab San Lang, fearing he might fall. But just when his hand touched San Lang, the youth shook off his hand as if burned. There was only a slight change in his expression, but Xie Lian saw it and thought, maybe this boy actually disliked him? They'd had such a good time chatting all this way, though, hadn't they? But now wasn't the time to ponder.

Xie Lian stood up and looked around. "What's going on?"

The old driver responded, "I don't know! Old Huang, why aren't you moving? Go on, now!"

The sun had set, and the ox cart was still in the deep woods, now filled with darkness. Old Huang the ox just stood there, stubbornly refusing to move no matter how the old driver urged it. It kept mooing, wanting to dig its head into the earth, and flicking its tail like a whip. This didn't feel right. Xie Lian was about to jump off the cart when suddenly, the old driver pointed straight ahead and screamed.

Farther up the road, a number of hovering balls of green flames were popping up, here and there. They gathered and burned, floating through the woods. A group of white-clad figures slowly made their way toward them, carrying their own severed heads.

Seeing this, Xie Lian cried, "Protect!"

Ruoye flew out from his sleeve and wrapped itself in a circle around the ox cart from above, protecting the three plus the one beast.

Xie Lian turned back and demanded, "What day is it today?"

The old driver didn't respond before the youth spoke up from behind.

"It's Zhongyuan."

The middle of the seventh month, when the gates to the underworld opened. He didn't check his calendar before coming out today, and it just happened to be the Zhongyuan Festival!

Xie Lian's voice dropped. "Stay close to me. We've run into evil tonight. If we go down the wrong path at the fork, we'll never return."

The figures were dressed in white prisoner garb and had no heads. It appeared they were newly executed criminals, and every one of them held a head in their hands. They wobbled slowly toward the ox cart as their heads buzzed in those bony arms.

Xie Lian instructed the other two on the cart in a low voice, "In a moment, when they approach, do not make a sound."

San Lang tilted his head. "Gege, I can't believe you're a man with superpowers!" He sounded greatly interested, and Xie Lian replied, "Not really superpowers, I only know a few tricks. They can't see us now, but it's hard to say whether they will when they get close."

That old cart driver's eyes were already wide with fear after seeing the flight of the silk cloth, and now that there were headless walkers, his eyes were about to roll back in terror. He shook his head repeatedly. "No no no no, I don't think I can hold my voice in! Daozhang, what should I do?!"

"...Then, there's another way. I apologize in advance."

Xie Lian swiftly swung his hand and tapped a point on the old man's back, and instantly the man slumped and passed out. Xie Lian caught him lightly and laid him down flat on the ox cart while he himself assumed the driver's seat. Suddenly, he sensed a strange movement behind him, and when he turned back to look, he saw that the youth had followed after him and settled right behind him.

Xie Lian asked, "Are you all right?"

San Lang propped up his chin. "Of course not. I'm scared."

Although there wasn't a single trace of fright detectable in his voice, Xie Lian still comforted him. "Don't be scared. You're behind me, nothing will harm you."

The youth smiled, not saying a word. Xie Lian suddenly realized the youth was staring at him. Then, quickly, it dawned on him that what this youth was staring at was actually the cursed shackle around his neck.

This cursed shackle was like a black collar bound to his neck, completely unconcealable. It could easily cause one to assume the worst. Xie Lian pulled at his collar lightly, even though it couldn't hide anything.

The skies had darkened, and that youth's expression could no longer be seen. Xie Lian picked up the reins to gently urge the onward. The group of ghosts in criminal garb walked over wan to pass, but they kept sensing that there was something blockin middle of the road, so they all cursed up and down.

"What the hell's going on? Why can't we pass?!"

"Yeah! What the hell! Is it haunted?"

"Fucking hell, we're the ones doing the haunting, all

Xie Lian finally soothed the ox, and the cart sile d by this band of headless criminal ghosts. Listening t banter, Xie Lian thought them rather hilarious. They w tty woes:

"Um, did you make a mistake? How c like the one holding your head is my body?"

"You're the one whose body grabbe ng head!"

"Hurry and switch back then, you ..."

"How come the cut around your ain't clean?"

"*Hahhh*, the executioner was a bie. It took him five or six tries before he managed to chop m d off. Made me think he did it on purpose!"

"Your family probably tip him well enough. Next time, don't forget to pay the gu he'll give you one clean chop!"

"There is no next tim The fifteenth day of the seventh month was the Zho an val, the biggest festival for the Ghost Realm. On th gates to the underworld opened, and all manner of spi sts, monsters, and demons swarmed out to celebrate with . Mortals needed to avoid them at all costs, and especially on a night like this, it was best to stay home with every door and window shut. But Xie Lian had always had rotten luck. He could drink only water and the water would get stuck between his teeth, and he could be wearing holy repellant gear and ghosts would appear, like was happening now. Ghost fires flared all around them and several were chasing after the fires, and some dressed in funeral garb were expressionlessly mumbling to themselves in front of a circle, trying to catch the offerings and joss paper money burned for the afterlife by mortals. A scene like this certainly epitomized the word "pandemonium." Xie Lian crossed through the middle, thinking that from now on he must pay more attention to the calendar when going out. Suddenly, a screech that sounded like a chicken being butchered rang out.

"Oh no! Oh no! Ghosts are being murdered!"

This scream made all the ghosts anxious.

"Where, where? Where are they murdering ghosts?!"

The ghost that screeched answered, "I'm scared out of my wits! I found so many shattered ghost fires over there, and they were all brutally crushed! What hostility!"

"All shattered? Then they're truly broken beyond saving! That really is too much!"

"Who did it? Could it be... Have we been infiltrated by monks and cultivators?!"

That band of headless people started shouting.

"Ah! Now that you mention it, weren't we just blocked by something on the road with no way of passing? Could that have been..."

"Where, where?"

"Right there!"

Xie Lian cried *oh no!* mentally. The next second, a large group of nefarious beings surrounded the ox cart, each of their faces savage.

They threatened maliciously, "I smell the steaming scent of the living…"

They couldn't hide any longer!

It was already unreasonable for a live human to crash in on a band of ghosts on Zhongyuan Festival, as if Xie Lian actually wanted to fight such a large mob of creatures. He urged the cart onward and shouted, "Go!"

The ox was terrified and was already stomping its hooves anxiously while it stood. Once it heard the shout, it didn't need to be ordered twice before it pulled the cart into a mad dash.

Xie Lian didn't forget to grab at the youth sitting behind him. "Sit tight!"

He withdrew Ruoye and conveniently whipped out the path of escape. An ox cart suddenly revealed itself amidst a circle of ghost fires and dashed out of the siege. Those green-faced, teeth-baring, missing-limbed ghosts screeched behind the cart.

"There really is a cultivator!! Damn cultivator is tired of living!!"

"A live human actually dared to crash our Zhongyuan gathering, you can't blame us for anything!"

"GET THEM!"

Xie Lian was gripping onto the reins with one hand as his other hand fumbled out a large handful of paper talismans and threw them to the ground.

"Hinder!"

Those were stumbling talismans, excellent tools for escape. A series of small rumbling noises could be heard; with every rumble, an obstacle was set up for that band of ghosts. It would stall them for a short time, but only a short one. Despite using up so many talismans, it wouldn't even be half an incense time before they caught up. Xie Lian was driving the cart down the mountain path in an escape like his rear was on fire when he suddenly called out.

"Stop—!"

Turns out that old ox had pulled the cart to a fork in the road. Xie Lian saw there were two pitch-black mountain paths ahead and immediately pulled on the reins.

Now, he had to be extra careful here!

On the night of the Zhongyuan Festival, sometimes when people strolled, they might discover a road that had never existed before. Such a road should never be taken, because if they walked the wrong one, they would enter the Ghost Realm and never return.

Xie Lian had only just arrived in the area and didn't know which path was the right one to take. Then he remembered that besides the large bag of junk he'd collected, he'd also purchased some miscellaneous items, including a fortune shaker. So he thought, why not shake out a fortune to decide? Thus, he fumbled for the fortune shaker and shook it in his hands with a clattering sound, mumbling as he shook. "'By the heaven official's blessing, no paths are bound! The great road leads to heaven; one to each side, may we go our separate ways!' The first stick left, the second stick right! We'll take the path with the best fortune!"

Just as the words left his lips, *clack, clack,* two sticks fell out of the shaker. But when he picked them up and looked, he fell silent.

The worst of bad luck!

Both sticks were the worst of bad luck; both roads were perilous, so didn't this mean they were going to die no matter what?

Xie Lian felt a little exasperated and shook the shaker furiously once more with both hands. "Dear fortune shaker, this is our first meeting, why are you so heartless? I'm going to try again. Please let me save face this time."

Clack, clack. Two sticks again, and when he picked them up, they were both still the worst of bad luck!

"Let me try?" San Lang spoke up suddenly.

It couldn't go any worse than his anyway, so Xie Lian passed the fortune shaker over. San Lang received it with a single hand and casually gave it a shake. Out fell two fortune sticks, and he picked them up and handed them to Xie Lian without even so much as a glance. Xie Lian gave them a look, and they were both, amazingly, the best of good luck. He couldn't help but be awed. Since he first reached such a state of misery, it seemed that oftentimes those around him would also have their fortunes affected by his crummy luck. Who knew if that was actually true, but either way it was a complaint he'd heard frequently. Yet this youth wasn't affected in the least if a casual shake could let him shake out two of the best of fortunes!

Since both fortune sticks showed the best of good luck, Xie Lian picked a path randomly and drove the cart as he praised sincerely. "My friend, your luck is really quite good."

San Lang casually tossed the fortune shaker in the back and smiled. "Really? I think my luck is pretty good too. It's always been so."

Having heard him say "it's always been so," Xie Lian thought that the difference between people truly was as great as heaven and earth.

After running for a while, wails and hollers could suddenly be heard from all around.

"Caught him! He's here!"

"Everyone come here! That damn cultivator is here!!"

Ghost head after ghost head popped out. Xie Lian spoke up, "Ah, I can't believe we still picked the wrong path."

The effect of the stumbling talismans was over; they were still surrounded after all!

There were at least a hundred in this mob of nefarious beings, surrounding them in wave after wave, and the numbers were still increasing. Xie Lian really didn't know why there were so many inhuman creatures gathered here, but there wasn't any time to wonder.

Xie Lian said warmly, "It wasn't my intent to disturb everyone, I pray you will show us mercy."

A headless ghost spoke up, "Tch! Stinkin' cultivator. Why didn't you show mercy first? The one who broke and dispersed a bunch of ghost fires over there was you, wasn't it?!"

Xie Lian replied innocently, "It wasn't us. Truth be told, I'm but a lowly scrap collector."

"Don't try to argue!! What kind of scrap collector looks like you? You're clearly a cultivator! And besides you, the *cultivator*, who here could do such a cruel thing?!"

"It doesn't take a cultivator to break and disperse ghost fires," Xie Lian reasoned.

"Then who could it be? Ghosts?"

Xie Lian quietly tucked his hands into his sleeves. "That's not impossible."

"*Ha ha ha ha* ha ha ha ha ha...damn cultivator! You...you...you..."

The band of ghosts who were roaring with mockery suddenly stopped in their tracks.

Xie Lian wondered aloud, "What about me?"

He might've asked a question, but they weren't just stopped in their tracks now. They all stared at Xie Lian as if they were seeing something exceedingly terrifying. Their mouths were either gaping open or shut tight, and a number of the heads held in the felons' hands were even dropped onto the ground.

Xie Lian ventured again, "Everyone? Are you all...?"

Yet unexpectedly, before he finished his question, the band of ghosts all fled the scene, like the wind blowing away remnants of clouds.

Xie Lian was baffled. "What the—?!"

He hadn't even taken out that bundle of talismans he clutched in his hand inside his sleeve yet, and he was found out? Were they really that sharp? And they weren't even particularly powerful talismans either. Xie Lian felt incredulous. Was it really him they saw?

Or something behind him?

Having thought this, he turned his head back and looked behind him.

But there was only the passed-out ox cart owner and that carefree, red-clad youth who was still propping up his cheek.

Seeing him look over, San Lang smiled and dropped his hand. "Daozhang, you're amazing! You scared all those ghosts away."

"..." Xie Lian smiled back. "Really? I didn't realize I was actually this amazing."

Then he pulled at the reins a couple of times, and the wheels of the ox cart began to roll slowly once more. The road after that was smooth, and it wasn't even an hour before the ox cart slowly pulled out of the forest and came to an open mountain path. Down below the hills, the warm glow of lights illuminated Puqi Village.

That really was the path of "the best of luck," with a close call but no actual danger.

A night breeze brushed by, and Xie Lian turned his head back once more. San Lang seemed to be in a very good mood and had lain down, watching the moon with his hands pillowed behind his head. Beneath the faint moonlight, the youth's complexion looked surreal.

After a moment of hesitation, Xie Lian smiled. "My friend."

"What is it?" San Lang replied.

"Have you ever had your fortune told?" Xie Lian asked.

"No?" San Lang replied, turning to face Xie Lian.

"Do you want me to give you a session?"

San Lang looked at him and smiled. "Do you want to give me a session?"

"A little bit," Xie Lian said.

San Lang gave a slight nod. "Sure."

He sat up, his body leaning slightly toward Xie Lian. "How do you want to read my fortune?"

"How about palm reading?" Xie Lian suggested.

Hearing this, the corners of San Lang's lips curled. It was hard to tell what that smile meant, but he only replied with, "Sure."

Then, he extended his left hand to Xie Lian.

This left hand was long and shapely, clean and elegant, a beautiful hand. It wasn't a soft and meek kind of beauty, rather, there was strength hidden beneath the muscles. It was a hand that one wouldn't want to have choking their throat. Xie Lian was careful not to touch San Lang due to the slight change in the latter's expression the last time they touched, so he simply looked down to study the hand up close.

The moon above was bright, but not too bright; even in the midst of night, it wasn't too dark. Xie Lian thoroughly scrutinized the hand before him as the ox cart languidly climbed the hills. The wheels and the wooden shafts creaked as they rolled.

"So?" San Lang asked.

Xie Lian took his time, then slowly said, "You've got a good hand."

"Oh yeah? How so?" San Lang asked.

Xie Lian raised his head and said warmly, "You have a strong character, extremely stubborn, but whenever you run into obstacles you remain true to yourself and manage to transform the bad to good. You have a limitless well of good fortune, my friend. Your future is bright and full of success."

All of that was complete bullshit, made up on the spot. Xie Lian had never learned palmistry. Once upon a time, when he was still banished, he often regretted not learning palmistry or face-reading from the state preceptors at the Royal Holy Temple. If he had such skills, then earning pennies on the streets wouldn't have been so hard, and he wouldn't have to busk or shatter boulders on his chest. What he really wanted to see wasn't the fortune of this youth but rather whether his hands had fingerprints and palm prints.

Normal ghosts and monsters could fabricate fake bodies and pretend to be human, but their craft was rough and often overlooked minute details, such as fingerprints and palm prints. However, the body of this youth appeared altogether normal, with clear palm prints, and there was no sign of magic undulation around him. If he was a ghost in disguise, then he had to be of a caliber greater than a wrath to create such a flawless disguise. But why would a ghost king of such special status spend his time traveling with Xie Lian on an ox cart to visit Puqi Village? Just as heavenly officials were always busily working like machines, ghost kings should have their hands full too!

Xie Lian pretended to be confident in his fortune-telling and sweated through his bold-faced lies until he couldn't come up with anything else. San Lang watched him unblinkingly the whole time, sitting through his nonsense with an intrigued smile, chuckling under his breath.

"Got any more? Hm?" San Lang asked.

No way, what more did he want Xie Lian to make up? "Is there something else you want me to look at?"

"Don't fortune-tellers always talk about love and marriage?" San Lang asked.

Xie Lian cleared his throat and replied solemnly, "To be honest, I'm actually not that great at fortune-telling, so I don't know how to predict relationships. But I don't imagine you have anything to worry about."

San Lang arched his brows. "Why do you say that?"

Xie Lian grinned. "There must be tons of girls with crushes on you."

"And why do you suppose so many girls must like me?" San Lang asked.

Xie Lian was about to go with the flow and answer before he realized that this kid was manipulating him into praising him. Helpless and amused, Xie Lian didn't know what to say and rubbed his forehead.

"San Lang..."

This was the first time Xie Lian ever called San Lang by name, and the youth laughed in delight, letting Xie Lian off the hook.

The ox cart had finally laboriously pulled into the village, and Xie Lian turned around and hurriedly got off the cart with his hand lightly supporting his forehead. San Lang followed behind and jumped off. Xie Lian finally looked up and realized that San Lang was actually a head taller than him! It wasn't obvious when the youth was lazily lying in the hay, but standing tall, the two couldn't see eye to eye on even ground.

San Lang stood before the cart and stretched, and Xie Lian asked, "San Lang, where will you go now?"

"Don't know. Maybe sleep on the streets. Or a cave will do," San Lang sighed.

"That won't do..." Xie Lian said, concerned.

San Lang shrugged. "Can't be helped. I've no place to go." Then he grinned. "Thanks for telling my fortune. I'll rely on your good words. See ya later."

Xie Lian sweated in embarrassment at the mention of his fortune-telling. Seeing that the youth turned to leave, he quickly called after him. "Wait! Why don't you come to my shrine, if you don't mind?"

San Lang stopped in his tracks and turned halfway around. "Is that okay?"

Xie Lian explained, "The place wasn't originally mine anyway, and I heard it housed a number of passersby before. But it's probably much shabbier than what you're used to. I'm afraid you wouldn't be comfortable."

If this youth really was a runaway young master, Xie Lian couldn't possibly let him run around the streets aimlessly. He strongly suspected that half a steamed bun was the only thing San Lang had eaten all day today, and youth or not, he would collapse somewhere if he kept that up. Hearing Xie Lian, San Lang turned fully around and said nothing, but walked up close to Xie Lian and leaned forward. Xie Lian didn't understand what he was up to, only that the distance between them had closed too fast. He suddenly didn't know what to do.

Then the youth straightened back up, lifting the giant bag of junk Xie Lian had brought back in his hand.

He said, "Then let's go."

Xie Lian blanked on the spot. He watched as the tall and slender youth walked away with his giant bag of junk as if it were the most natural thing in the world to do, and it made him mutter inwardly, *Forgive my sins.* San Lang strode a few steps out and started walking. Xie Lian was about to follow him, but he remembered at the last second that the old driver was still asleep in the ox cart, so he went back around and woke the old man, advising him to keep the incident tonight a secret. After witnessing his powers, the old man didn't dare to say no and hurriedly dragged his Old Huang home.

Only his rolled-up straw mat was left on the cart. Xie Lian hoisted it onto his back, turned around, and saw that San Lang had already started climbing the hill toward Puqi Shrine with his bag of random scraps.

Nearing the crooked, shaky shack that was Puqi Shrine, San Lang lowered his head and puffed out a laugh, as if seeing something amusing. Xie Lian approached, saw that he was looking at his sign requesting donations, and cleared his throat.

"As you see, that's it really. That's why I said you might not be comfortable here."

"It's not too bad," San Lang said.

In the past, it had always been Xie Lian who told others "It's all right, it's not too bad." Hearing it from someone else for the first time gave him complicated feelings. The Puqi Shrine door had gone rotten long ago, so Xie Lian had torn it down and replaced it with some curtains.

He lifted the drapes and invited, "Come on in."

And San Lang entered the shrine with him.

There wasn't much in the small shrine, only a long altar table, two small stools, a small cushion, and a donation box. Xie Lian reached for the bag in San Lang's hands, took out the fortune shaker, incense burner, and some paper and miscellaneous stationery, and placed them on the altar table. Then he lit a used red candle someone had stuffed into his hand while he was collecting scraps, and the shrine brightened instantly.

San Lang picked up the fortune shaker, playfully gave it a shake, and then put it down. "So. Is there a bed?"

Xie Lian silently took the straw mat from his back and unrolled it to show him.

San Lang quirked a brow. "There's only one?"

Xie Lian only met the youth on his way back from town, so of course he didn't think he needed to buy more than one. "If you don't mind, we can squeeze a bit for the night."

"That works," San Lang agreed.

Xie Lian then reached for the broom and swept the floor while San Lang looked around some more.

"Daozhang-gege, aren't you missing something in this shrine?"

Xie Lian had just finished sweeping and was kneeling on the ground laying out the mat when he heard him. He answered as he patted their bedding, "Other than followers, I don't think there's anything missing."

San Lang crouched down too, a hand propping up his chin. "What about a divine statue of the god?"

His words reminded Xie Lian. How did he forget the most important thing for a shrine: a god's statue?!

A shrine without its idol is no shrine. Although one could say the god himself was present, he couldn't possibly just sit up on the altar all day every day. Xie Lian contemplated for a moment and came up with a solution.

"I bought some paper and ink today. I'll paint a portrait tomorrow."

Painting a portrait of himself to be hung in the shrine he built for himself to pray to himself. If the Heavenly Realm caught wind of this, they'd probably laugh at him for another ten years. But the cost of commissioning a sculpture was rather hefty, and it took time too, so Xie Lian would rather be laughed at for ten years and save the money.

Unexpectedly, San Lang spoke up, "A portrait? I know how to paint one. Need my help?"

Startled, Xie Lian smiled. "Thanks, but I'm afraid you don't know how to paint the Prince of Xianle, am I right?"

After all, most of his portraits had been burned and destroyed eight hundred years ago. No matter how many were left now, not many people would have seen them before.

San Lang replied, "Of course I do. Weren't we talking about him earlier on the cart?"

Xie Lian remembered the conversation. That was indeed the case. Earlier, he had said, "You probably don't know him," but San Lang did not respond. Hearing him speak now, Xie Lian was amazed. He finished with the bedding and sat up straight.

"San Lang, don't tell me you really do know him?"

San Lang sat down on the mat and replied, "I do."

The expression and tone of voice of this youth when he spoke were both very interesting. He was always smiling, but one could never tell whether his smiles were genuine or if he was actually mocking the other party for being too slow to keep up with the conversation. Having listened to him chat on the way back, Xie Lian was rather interested in San Lang's appraisal of him.

Xie Lian moved to sit next to him and asked, "So what do you think about this Prince of Xianle?"

Both men looked at each other under the lamp. The flame of the red candle flickered slightly. San Lang had his back to the candlelight, and it was hard to see his exact expression with his eyes immersed in shadows.

After a moment, he replied, "I think Jun Wu must really dislike him."

Xie Lian wasn't expecting this answer and was taken aback. "Why do you think that?"

"Why else would he have banished the prince twice?" San Lang replied.

Xie Lian smiled a little and thought, *Indeed the thinking of a child.*

He lowered his head and slowly removed his belt. "I don't think it has anything to do with likes or dislikes. There are many things in this world that can't be explained that way."

"Hmm."

Xie Lian turned around, removed his white boots, and continued, "Besides, one needs to be punished for making mistakes. The Heavenly Emperor was simply doing his duty both times."

"Perhaps," San Lang responded noncommittally.

Xie Lian took off his outer jacket, folded it, and was ready to place it on the altar table. Wanting to say more, he turned around, only to see San Lang's eyes staring at his feet.

It was hard to describe that gaze; it was icy but searing, scorching but with a hint of chill. Xie Lian looked down and immediately understood. On his right ankle was a black cursed shackle.

The first curse was firmly locked around his neck, and the second was tightly fettered around his ankle. Both curses were placed in areas not easily concealed. In the past, if anyone asked, Xie Lian would lie and say they were for training purposes, but San Lang probably wouldn't be so easily placated.

However, San Lang only stared at his ankle for a while without saying anything. So Xie Lian lay down on the mat, not worrying over the issue anymore. The youth also obediently lay down next to him, but he didn't remove a single article of clothing. Xie Lian figured San Lang was probably not used to sleeping on the floor like this and thought perhaps he should find a way to get a bed after all.

"Let's rest."

Xie Lian softly blew out the candle and all became dark once more.

◇ ◈ ◇

Early next morning, when Xie Lian opened his eyes, San Lang wasn't next to him. He looked up and stopped, stunned. On top of the altar, there hung a portrait.

It was a portrait of a man with a golden mask, dressed glamorously in extravagant attire. There was a sword in one hand, a flower in the other. It was a beautifully and vividly painted portrait of the God-Pleasing Prince of Xianle.

It had been years since Xie Lian saw such a painting, and he stared at it stunned for a long time before getting up. He got dressed, then pulled back the curtain. San Lang was just outside, hiding in the shadows alongside the shrine, twirling the broom in his hand and watching the sky with a bored expression.

It seemed this youth really didn't like sunlight. The way he was watching the sky looked as if he wanted to pluck the sun and stomp it into pieces. All the fallen leaves around the shrine had been swept into a pile next to the entrance.

Xie Lian went out the door and asked, "Did you sleep well last night?"

San Lang was still leaning against the wall but turned his head and said, "Not bad."

Xie Lian walked over, took the broom from his hands, and asked, "San Lang, did you paint that portrait in the shrine?"

San Lang replied, "Uh-huh."

"It's really well done," Xie Lian praised.

San Lang's lips lifted, but he didn't say anything. Maybe it was because he'd slept all over the place last night, but his ponytail this morning seemed to be even more crooked, loose and casual. It actually looked quite nice: casual but not messy, rather playful.

Xie Lian pointed at his own hair and asked, "Want me to help you with that?"

San Lang nodded and headed back inside with Xie Lian. When San Lang sat down, Xie Lian let down his black hair and quietly started examining it.

Even if the palm prints and fingerprints were perfectly detailed, ghosts always had one flaw in their body creation. The hair of a living person was uncountable, and it came in individual strands that were intricate and distinct. The fake bodies created by ghosts had hair that was either a black blur or a pasted mass like long strips of fabric. Sometimes...they just went for a bald look.

Xie Lian had checked his palm prints and fingerprints the night before, and he had already lowered his guard. But seeing the portrait this morning raised his suspicions again.

How would an ordinary person know how to paint this portrait?

Yet when he combed his fingers gently through San Lang's hair, Xie Lian couldn't find anything amiss. After a while, San Lang let out a laugh as if he was ticklish from the touch. He turned his head slightly and looked at him out of the corner of his eye.

He said, "Gege, are you helping tie my hair? Or are you thinking of doing something else?"

With his hair down, San Lang still looked handsome, but there was an added air of wickedness. His question sounded like a tease, and Xie Lian grinned.

"All right, all right," Xie Lian said and quickly finished doing San Lang's hair.

But after that was done, when San Lang looked at his own reflection in the bucket of water in the corner, he turned back to Xie Lian with quirked brows. Xie Lian took a look and quietly cleared his throat.

The ponytail had been lopsided before. After Xie Lian retied it, it was still crooked.

Although San Lang didn't say anything and merely stared at him, Xie Lian hadn't felt this embarrassed in centuries. He lowered his hands and was just about to suggest they try again when suddenly there was a commotion outside. Sounds of footfalls approached, and several loud bellows rang out.

"Great Immortal!!"

Bewildered, Xie Lian ran to the door just in time to see his shrine surrounded by a large crowd, everyone's faces red and excited. The village chief sped ahead toward Xie Lian and grabbed his hand.

"Great Immortal! A living god has descended upon our small village! We are so thankful!!!"

"????" said Xie Lian.

The rest of the villagers also followed the chief and surrounded Xie Lian.

"Welcome to Puqi Village, Great Immortal!"

"Great Immortal! Can you bless me with a wife?"

"Great Immortal! Can you bless my wife with a child?"

"Great Immortal! We have fresh water chestnuts for you! Do you want water chestnuts?! After eating, can you conveniently bless me with a good harvest this year?!"

The villagers were so enthusiastic and passionate that Xie Lian had to take a few steps back, and he broke into a sweat. It seemed that the old driver from the night before had a big mouth! Xie Lian clearly told him not to tell, but the instant morning arrived, news had already traveled around the entire village!

The villagers had no clue what kind of god was worshipped in Puqi Shrine, but still they all crowded in, wishing to light incense in prayer. It didn't matter who it was, a god was a god, and prayers do no harm. Xie Lian had initially expected tumbleweeds and crows at the shrine, with only a few coming to offer prayers, so he didn't think to prepare a lot of incense. Who knew that with such hubbub, all the incense would be gone in a second? The little incense burner was filled to the brim, and its heavy smoke enveloped the shrine. Since Xie Lian had not smelled that scent in a long time, he even choked on it a few times.

He said as he coughed, "*Cough cough*, everyone, this shrine doesn't bless you with wealth, really, *cough*, please stop wishing for wealth! The result is unpredictable...

"I'm sorry, this shrine doesn't bless you with a good marriage either...

"No, no, no, it doesn't grant pregnancies either..."

San Lang stopped caring about his sloppy hair and sat next to the donation box, one hand propping up his chin, the other grabbing water chestnuts to eat. Many village girls saw him and blushed.

They turned to Xie Lian. "Um, do you grant..."

Xie Lian didn't know what they were going to ask, but felt instinctively that it must be stopped immediately, and cried, "No!"

When the crowd finally dispersed, the altar was filled with fruits and vegetables, even rice and noodles. No matter how this had happened, it was still an abundance of offerings. Xie Lian swept the floor and took out the trash, and San Lang followed him out.

"The shrine is doing pretty well."

Xie Lian shook his head and kept sweeping. "This was an unexpected turnout. Normally, there shouldn't be more than one or two passersby a month."

"How can that be?" San Lang asked.

Xie Lian glanced at him and smiled. "This was probably thanks to your good luck."

Saying so, he recalled that he wanted to change the door curtains, so he took out a new curtain to drape over the front entrance.

He stepped back to look at his work and noticed that San Lang stood still before it.

"What's wrong?"

San Lang stared at the curtains thoughtfully. Following his gaze, Xie Lian realized he was looking more at the seal drawn onto the fabric.

It was a seal that Xie Lian had drafted in passing before, one that was complex and imposingly well knit. Originally, it was for warding off evil and shielding from intrusions, but since it was Xie Lian himself who drew it, who knew if it might attract bad luck instead. Since there was no door, though, it was still safer to have a protection ward just in case.

Seeing the boy fixed in place before the curtain with the seal, Xie Lian's mind stirred.

He called out, "San Lang?"

Could it be that the seal had blocked San Lang out of the door, preventing him from entering the shrine?

7
Puqi Shrine Talks, Guileful Tales of Banyue Pass

S AN LANG GLANCED at him and flashed a smile. "I'm gonna head out for a bit."

He turned and left after casually tossing those words out. Xie Lian should have chased after him to ask, but he had a strange feeling that since San Lang had said he would leave for "a bit," then for sure he wouldn't be gone for too long, and he would definitely return. Thus, Xie Lian went back inside the shrine.

Xie Lian started rummaging through the junk he'd collected the night before when walking the streets and dug out a wok with his left hand and a butcher knife with his right. He eyed the vegetables on the altar and stood up.

After about one incense time, there was the sound of footfalls approaching the shrine, as expected. One could imagine from those unhurried footsteps that it was a particular young man, strolling leisurely. The two items in Xie Lian's hands had now transformed into two plates of food. He looked over them and heaved a long sigh, unable to bear the sight of such a tragedy. He set the plates down and went outside for a look. Sure enough, he saw San Lang again.

Outside the shrine, perhaps because of the blazing sun, San Lang had his red tunic peeled and tied around his waist. It revealed his white undershirt, and with the sleeves pulled back, he looked rather neat and tidy. His right foot stepped on top of a large wooden board, and he had a hatchet in his left hand. The hatchet was probably borrowed from one of the neighbors. It looked blunt and heavy, but he wielded it as easily as if it were a very sharp blade. San Lang nonchalantly hacked at the board, shaving off wood like dough. He peered from the corner of his eyes and saw Xie Lian come out.

"Just making something," he said.

Xie Lian walked over to watch and realized he was making a door! It was the perfect size, clean and beautiful, the surface smooth— surprisingly, an exquisite specimen of craft. Xie Lian thought that, since he must've come from a wealthy background, San Lang wouldn't be the manual labor type. Yet who would've known he was quite deft with his hands.

"Thanks for your hard work, San Lang," Xie Lian said.

San Lang simply smiled but didn't respond. He casually threw down the hatchet, installed the door, and then knocked on it twice. He said, "If you're going to draw a seal, at least draw it on a proper door. Works better."

Then he swept aside the curtain and entered the shrine.

It seemed that the strong seal on the curtains had no effect on him, and he didn't care about it in the slightest.

Xie Lian closed the new door behind him yet couldn't help but open it again, then close it. He opened and closed it again. Then again. Amazed by how well it was made, Xie Lian opened and closed the door several more times before suddenly realizing how silly he was being. San Lang had already sat down inside, and Xie Lian left the door to bring out the steamed buns the villagers had offered earlier in the morning and put them on the altar table.

San Lang looked at the buns and didn't say anything. He merely chuckled softly as if he'd seen through something, but Xie Lian poured two bowls of water like nothing was the matter. Just as he was about to sit down, he saw San Lang rolling up his sleeves. There was a small line of a tattoo on his arm, something written in strange characters.

San Lang noticed his gaze and pulled down his sleeves, then smiled. "It was done when I was young."

It was obvious San Lang didn't want to speak more on the subject, so Xie Lian didn't pursue it. He sat down and looked up at the portrait again.

"San Lang, you paint so well," Xie Lian said. "Did someone at home teach you?"

"No, I just do it for fun." San Lang poked at the buns with his chopsticks.

"How did you even know how to paint the Prince of Xianle?" Xie Lian asked.

"Didn't you say I know everything? Of course I know how to paint him too," San Lang laughed.

That was a cheating kind of answer, but San Lang was forthright in giving it. He evidently didn't care if his answers made Xie Lian suspicious, nor was he afraid of being questioned, so Xie Lian grinned and dropped the subject.

Just then, there was a loud commotion outside the shrine. Both of them raised their heads at the same time and exchanged looks. Someone started knocking on the door urgently, shouting.

"Great Immortal! Something's happened! Great Immortal, help!"

Xie Lian opened the door and saw a number of villagers crowding his doorway. The chief saw the door open and called out in relief.

"Great Immortal! This man looks like he's dying! Please save him!"

Hearing this, Xie Lian rushed to the group of villagers standing in a circle around what appeared to be a cultivator. He was unkempt and disheveled with sand all over him, and his robes and shoes were tattered. It seemed he had been running for his life for a long time before collapsing and passing out in the village, where the villagers brought him to Puqi Shrine in a hurry.

Xie Lian told the crowd, "Don't panic, he's not dead."

He bent down and tapped a few of the cultivator's acupoints, and in the process, Xie Lian found a few spiritual accessories: an eight trigrams map, a steel sword, and so on. This man didn't appear to be an ordinary cultivator, and Xie Lian couldn't help but grow grim.

Not long later, the cultivator slowly opened his eyes and asked in a croaking voice, "...Where am I?"

The chief exclaimed, "This is the village of Puqi!"

The man mumbled to himself, "...I'm out, I'm out... I've finally escaped..." He looked around him, and his eyes grew wide as he screamed in fear, "S-save me! *Help!*"

Xie Lian had expected this reaction and gently asked, "My friend, what's going on? What are you running from? Don't be afraid, take your time to speak clearly..."

"Yeah, don't be scared! We've got a Great Immortal on our side; he'll definitely solve all your problems!"

"???"

None of these villagers had actually seen him perform any miracles, but they had certainly taken him for a real god, and Xie Lian didn't know what to say to that. *Solve all problems? I definitely can't guarantee that...*

"Where did you come from?" Xie Lian asked the cultivator.

"I...I've come from Banyue[7] Pass!" the cultivator replied. The villagers looked at each other.

"Where's that?"

"Never heard of it before!"

7　"Banyue" means half-moon.

Xie Lian explained, "Banyue Pass is in the northwest, a fair distance away. How did you make it out here?"

"I...I've finally escaped and came here..."

His words were incoherent and his mood unstable. In such a situation, the more people around, the harder it was to speak with everyone talking at the same time.

So Xie Lian said, "Let's talk inside."

Xie Lian easily lifted the cultivator up from the ground and helped him into the shrine. He turned to say to the villagers, "Everyone, please leave. Don't stand here and watch."

The villagers, however, were very warmhearted. "Great Immortal, what's happened to him?"

"Yeah, what's going on?"

"If there's anything we can do to help..."

The more enthusiastic they were, the less help they were. Left with no choice, Xie Lian told them solemnly, "He...may be bewitched."

The villagers were alarmed at hearing this. Bewitchment was no joke! Better not stick around. The crowd broke up, and everyone hurried away. Xie Lian didn't know whether to laugh or cry, so he shook his head. He closed the door. San Lang was still at the table playing with his chopsticks, and he eyed the cultivator askance.

"Don't worry about him. Keep eating," Xie Lian told him. He then set the man down on the other stool while he stood. "My cultivator friend, I'm the Shrine Master here and also something of a cultivator myself. Don't be nervous, you can tell us anything. I can perhaps offer you my meager assistance if there's anything I can help with. You mentioned Banyue Pass?"

The cultivator took a few gasps of air. After coming to a place with fewer people and listening to Xie Lian's comforting words, the man finally calmed down. "Have you ever heard of Banyue Pass?"

"I have," Xie Lian said. "Banyue Pass is located within an oasis in the Gobi Desert. On nights of the half-moon, the scenery was beautiful to behold, hence the name."

"Oasis? Beauty?" The cultivator shook his head. "That's all from over two hundred years ago! 'Half-Moon'? More like Half-Dead!"

"What do you mean?" Xie Lian asked.

The man was upset, terrifyingly so. "Because at least half of those who pass through its gates disappear! How is that not the Half-Dead Pass?"

Well, Xie Lian had certainly never heard that before. "Who did you hear this from?"

"I didn't hear it from anyone! I saw with my own two eyes!" The man sat up straight. "There was a merchant group needing to cross the desert. They knew that place wasn't safe, so they hired my entire sect to protect them on their journey. But..." He cried angrily, "But in the end, I'm the only one left!"

Xie Lian raised his hand, gesturing for him to sit back down, no need to get so excited. "How many were you?"

"With my sect plus the merchant group, we were about sixty people!"

Sixty. According to Ling Wen's records, in the one hundred years Xuan Ji wreaked havoc, only two hundred or so people lost their lives. But from what this cultivator said, this had been happening for over a hundred years. If so many people went missing every time over the course of a couple centuries, the numbers would be significant once they added up.

"When did 'Half-Moon' Pass become 'Half-Dead' Pass?" Xie Lian asked.

The cultivator replied, "Maybe about a hundred and fifty years ago? It was right after it became the territory of an evil cultivator."

Xie Lian wanted to ask for more details about the murders and this "evil cultivator" he spoke of. However, he couldn't help feeling that something wasn't right, and it didn't sit well with him. At that point, there was no way to hide that strange feeling, and he furrowed his brows and became silent.

Suddenly, San Lang spoke up, "You've run all this way from Banyue Pass?"

"Yeah! Barely survived!" The cultivator sighed.

"Really." San Lang stopped talking, but Xie Lian already understood what was amiss.

He turned around and said warmly, "You must be thirsty, having run all this way?"

The man paused, but Xie Lian had already placed a bowl of water in front of him. "Here's some water, my cultivator friend. Have a drink."

Hesitation flashed across the man's face at the sight of the water. Xie Lian stood next to him, hands crossed in his sleeves, waiting patiently.

This man had traveled far from the northwest, and was running for his life, no less. He should be starving and parched. From the looks of him, it didn't seem like he ate or drank anything the entire way. Yet when he woke, all he did was talk and never once asked for a single drop of water or a bite to eat. He had no visible cravings when faced with the food and water on the altar after entering the shrine. Heck, he didn't even spare any of it a look.

Truly...it was entirely unlike the living.

Under Xie Lian and San Lang's gaze, the cultivator held the water bowl up to his lips and bent over to slowly gulp the water down. He did not look as if he was satisfying his thirst; instead, he looked cautious and guarded.

As he drank, Xie Lian could hear sloshing sounds, as if water was being poured into an empty bottle.

At that moment, Xie Lian knew what he was. He seized the man's arm. "You don't have to drink any more."

The cultivator's hand jerked as he looked at Xie Lian in bewilderment.

"Drinking wouldn't help anyway, right?" Xie Lian smiled.

The man's face instantly changed upon hearing this. He unsheathed his steel sword with his other hand and swung it toward Xie Lian. Without changing his stance, Xie Lian raised his hand and easily flicked the sword aside with a loud *clang*. Seeing that Xie Lian was still tightly gripping his hand, the cultivator gritted his teeth and pulled with force. Xie Lian felt the arm in his grip suddenly go limp like a ball deflating as it slipped away from his palm. The moment the cultivator broke free, he ran toward the door, but Xie Lian wasn't concerned. In this undisturbed space without people around, Ruoye could drag him back immediately even if he fled a good thirty meters away. But just as he raised his other hand, a sharp blast of air whipped by.

It was as if someone shot an arrow from behind him. It pierced the man through his stomach and nailed him to the door. Xie Lian looked closer, and it turned out to be a chopstick! He looked back and saw San Lang, unruffled, stand up from the altar and walk past him to pull out the chopstick.

San Lang waved the chopstick at Xie Lian. "This got dirty. I'll throw it out later."

Even with such a serious wound, the cultivator did not groan in pain, he simply silently slithered down from the door. Fluid flowed from his abdomen; it wasn't blood but rather the water he just drank.

Xie Lian and San Lang knelt next to the body, and Xie Lian felt around the wound, which seemed like a pricked hole in a blown-up balloon. Cold air was leaking out of it, and the cultivator's "corpse" gradually changed. He was clearly a buff man earlier, but now he'd shrunk a size down, and his face and limbs shriveled as he continued to shrink. He looked more like a little old man now.

"It's an empty shell," Xie Lian noted.

Some nefarious beings, if they could not transform into a perfect human shape, would create these empty shells. They would use realistic components to meticulously fabricate a fake skin bag. These skin bags often used real, living humans as references. Sometimes they would even use human skin directly to make the skin bags; naturally, that way their palm prints, fingerprints, and hair would all be flawless. And if the ghosts themselves did not wear these skins, there wouldn't be any evil aura stuck to them, so they would not be subdued by evil-repelling spells and talismans. That was why the seal on the door did not block the cultivator from coming inside.

However, these kinds of empty shells could easily be seen through. After all, they were hollow on the inside. If there was no one wearing the skin, it could only follow the instructions of the manipulator like a puppet. The instructions couldn't be overly complicated either; they had to be simple, repetitive, and set up beforehand. Therefore, the expressions and behavior of these skin bags were lifeless and sluggish, unlike real humans. For example, they could only repeat certain phrases, do certain repetitive things, or finish certain thoughts. If one asked too many questions, they wouldn't be able to answer and would end up exposing themselves.

Of course, Xie Lian had more practical ways of exposing these skin bags: just let them drink some water or eat something. After all, skin bags were hollow, without any organs. If they ate or drank, it would be like throwing something or pouring water into an empty can. The echo could be clearly heard, and it was a sound very different from that of a human consuming food and water.

The corpse had completely deflated into a pile of withered skin. San Lang poked at it with his chopstick and threw it away.

"This shell is rather interesting."

Xie Lian knew what he was talking about. This cultivator's expressions and movements were more than realistic. He had conversed with them animatedly, gestured wildly, and responded emotionally, very much like a real person. Whoever was controlling it had to be quite powerful.

Xie Lian glanced at San Lang. "Looks like you're quite knowledgeable about the wicked arts too, San Lang."

San Lang smiled. "Not really."

This empty shell sought Xie Lian out specifically to tell him about Banyue Pass. Whether it was fake or real, its intention was obviously to lure him there. To play it safe, he would have to inquire about it in the communication array. Xie Lian pinched his fingers and calculated the amount of power he had left; there should still be enough to use it a few more times. So he formed a seal with his hands to enter.

The communication array was livelier than usual, and not because of deities bustling around on official duties. Rather, it seemed everyone was playing some sort of a game, laughing and shouting. Xie Lian was rather amazed.

Just then, Ling Wen reached out to him. "Your Highness is back? How were your days down in the Mortal Realm?"

"It's all right, not too bad. What's everyone doing? They seem so happy!" Xie Lian asked.

Ling Wen replied, "The Wind Master has just returned and is giving away merits. Why don't you go and see if you can grab any?"

Sure enough, Xie Lian could hear the many officials cheerfully shouting.

"I grabbed a hundred merits!"

"How come I only managed to get one...?"

"A thousand! A *thousand*! Thanks, Wind Master! Ha ha ha ha ha..."

It was like catching money raining down from the skies, Xie Lian thought. His donation box was empty, but first of all, he didn't know how to make a grab for those merits, and second, the officials must be very familiar with each other to play this sort of casual game. Xie Lian wasn't on good terms with many and didn't think it was appropriate for him to join, so he paid it no mind and called out to the crowd.

"Does anyone know of Banyue Pass?"

The laughing and shouting came to a sudden stop, and silence ensued.

Once again, Xie Lian felt depressed.

It was fine if no one responded to his little snippets if they were odd or awkward; the other officials didn't share those, and he indeed seemed to be out of tune with them when he did so. But this was official business. The communication array was a place where heavenly officials often made requests for information on ghosts or mystic issues. If something came up or someone asked for assistance, everyone pitched in, giving suggestions or lending a hand. Those without anything to add would say "I'll ask around when I'm free." Banyue was work, so there was no good reason for no one to respond.

Just then, someone shouted, "Wind Master just threw out ten thousand merits!!!"

The communication array came alive again, and the officials went away to grab for more merits, thoroughly ignoring Xie Lian. That made him realize there was probably more to this than there appeared, and he probably wouldn't get his answers within the array. This Wind Master was certainly quite affluent, Xie Lian thought, giving away tens of thousands of merits like that, so amazing. He was about to exit the communication array when Ling Wen called out to him privately.

"Your Highness, why did you mention Banyue Pass?" Ling Wen asked.

Xie Lian recounted his encounter with the skin bag. "That empty shell pretended to be a survivor from Banyue Pass, and it has to have a motive. I wasn't sure whether his words were true, so I came in to ask. What's going on with that place?"

Ling Wen was quiet for a moment before she said gravely, "Your Highness, I advise you to stay away from this matter."

Xie Lian had thought she might say something similar. Otherwise, something like this wouldn't have lasted for over a hundred and fifty years without any questions, and make the entire court go silent just because he asked.

"Is it true that half the people go missing every time a group traverses Banyue?"

It was a long time before Ling Wen answered. "It's not easy for us to speak on this matter."

Xie Lian heard the deliberation in her words. There might've been something putting her on the spot, so he said, "All right, I understand. If it's inconvenient, then we shall not speak of it again, and we have never spoken in private on this subject either."

Xie Lian withdrew his consciousness and left the communication array. He rose to his feet and used the broom to sweep the fake skin to the side. After mulling over Ling Wen's words for a moment, he looked up at San Lang.

"San Lang, I'm afraid I will be going on a long journey."

Ling Wen's attitude was enough to show that this matter implicated a lot of important beings. Since this empty shell came to him on its own, then it must have wanted to lure him there. It was definitely not a good place to be.

Yet San Lang said, "Sure thing. Gege, bring me along too, if you don't mind!"

Xie Lian wondered curiously, "It's going to be a long and difficult journey, so why do you want to come?"

San Lang smiled. "Do you want to know about the evil cultivator of Banyue?"

Xie Lian paused, then said, "You know about that too?"

San Lang crossed his arms and replied leisurely, "Banyue Pass was originally not known as Banyue Pass. Banyue Pass is where the Kingdom of Banyue used to be located two hundred years ago."

He sat up straight, eyes going bright. "The evil cultivator of Banyue was..."

Xie Lian placed the broom against the wall and was about to sit down to listen when a knock on the door came.

It was already evening, and the villagers were hiding in their homes after hearing there was bewitchment about, so who was knocking? Xie Lian stood by the door and held his breath briefly, but he didn't see the seal reacting. Another knock came. It sounded like there were two people outside.

Xie Lian contemplated for a moment, then opened the door. Sure enough, two young men dressed in black stood at his door, one handsome, one elegant. It was Nan Feng and Fu Yao.

"You two..."

Fu Yao rolled his eyes, and Nan Feng blurted, "You're going to Banyue Pass, aren't you?"

"Where did you guys hear that?" Xie Lian wondered.

Nan Feng said, "Some officials were talking about it. I heard that you asked about Banyue Pass in the communication array today."

Xie Lian understood their intentions and crossed his hands in his sleeves. "I see. 'I volunteer,' right?"

Both junior officials' expressions contorted as though they had toothaches. "...Yes."

Xie Lian couldn't help but smile and said, "I get it, I get it. But I want you two to understand that, should there be any issues or crises enroute, you're welcome to run away at any time."

Xie Lian stepped aside to invite them in to discuss the journey in detail. But when the two saw the carefree teen sitting inside, their initially grim faces instantly turned dark.

Nan Feng charged in, pushed Xie Lian behind him, and shouted, "Stand back!!"

"What's wrong?" Xie Lian asked.

San Lang stayed in his seat and shrugged in reply. Then he also asked, "What's wrong?"

Fu Yao furrowed his brows and demanded, "Who are you?"

"He's a friend of mine. Do you know each other?" Xie Lian answered instead.

San Lang, looking completely innocent, asked, "Gege, who are those two?"

Hearing San Lang call Xie Lian "gege" made Nan Feng's lips twitch and Fu Yao's brows spasm.

Xie Lian raised his hand and said to San Lang, "It's nothing, don't worry."

But next to him Nan Feng shouted, "Don't speak to him!"

"What? Do you know each other?" Xie Lian asked again.

"..."

"No," Fu Yao said coldly.

"If you don't, then what are you..."

Before Xie Lian could finish, he sensed lights flashing next to him. Casually, he looked back and found that the other two had produced balls of divine energy in their palms at the same time. An ill sense of foreboding overcame Xie Lian, and he grabbed at them in alarm.

"Stop! Stop! Don't act rashly!"

The bulbs of divine energy were pulsing, staticky and dangerous, definitely not something a normal person could make.

San Lang clapped a couple times in polite appreciation. "Amazing! Absolutely magical." It was truly the most insincere compliment.

Xie Lian finally caught Nan Feng and Fu Yao's arms to stop them from firing. Nan Feng turned to him angrily and questioned, "Where did you meet him? What's his name? Where does he live? Where is he from? Why is he with you?"

Xie Lian answered, "We met on the road. His name is San Lang. I don't know anything else, only that he has nowhere to go, so I let him stay. Will you two please stop?"

"You—!" Nan Feng couldn't speak. It was as if he wanted to scream at Xie Lian but forcibly swallowed his words. "You let him in despite knowing nothing?! What if he has ulterior motives?"

Xie Lian wondered why Nan Feng's tone made him sound like his father. Any other heavenly official or just any person, if they heard someone younger say anything in such a manner, they would've been displeased. But first, Xie Lian was already used to all kinds of rebukes and taunts, so he felt nothing. And second, he knew that those two meant well and were only saying those things out of worry, so he didn't mind.

At that time, San Lang cut in. "Gege, are they your servants?"

Xie Lian replied gently, "The term 'servants' isn't quite right. To be more precise, they're helpers, I guess?"

San Lang smiled back. "Really?" The youth stood up, grabbed an item, and threw it at Fu Yao. "Then why don't you help out?"

Fu Yao caught the thing without sparing it a look. Once it was in his hand and he saw what it was, his temper surged straight to his head.

The youth threw him a broom!!

Fu Yao looked as if he wanted to crush both the broom and the teen into powder, and Xie Lian hurriedly took the broom from Fu Yao's hands.

"Calm down. Calm down. I only have one broom—"

Before Xie Lian could finish his words, he was cut off by a burst of white energy that shot out from Fu Yao's hand as he bellowed, "Reveal yourself!!"

San Lang stayed where he was, arms still crossed in a relaxed posture, but he tilted his head just slightly as the beam of energy narrowly missed him and smashed one of the altar table's legs. The table collapsed with a loud crack and all the plates crashed onto the floor in a heap. Xie Lian rubbed his temple and thought this had to stop. With a wave of his hand, he released Ruoye and bound Nan Feng and Fu Yao's arms. Both men struggled but failed to break free.

"What are you doing?!" Nan Feng shouted.

Xie Lian made a gesture for a time-out. "We'll talk outside. *Outside.*"

Then he waved his hand and Ruoye flew out, dragging the two in tow.

"I'll be right back," Xie Lian said to San Lang, then closed the door behind him.

At the front of the shrine, Xie Lian called Ruoye back, took the sign at the entrance, and set it down in front of the two. "Read this. Then tell me what it says."

Fu Yao read aloud, "Please kindly donate to the renovation of this broken shrine for accumulation of good merits." He looked up at Xie Lian. "Donations for renovations? You wrote this?! You are at the very least an ascended heavenly official, how could you write such a thing? Where's your dignity?"

Xie Lian nodded. "That's right, I wrote it. If you guys keep fighting inside, then I will be asking for donations for construction, not renovation. And then I would have even less dignity."

Nan Feng pointed to the shrine. "You don't think that boy is at least somewhat *odd*?"

"Of course I do," Xie Lian said.

"You know he's dangerous, but still you keep him by your side?" Nan Feng demanded.

Seeing they had no intention to donate, Xie Lian placed the sign back by the door and replied, "Nan Feng, that's where you're wrong. There are all kinds of people with various temperaments and mannerisms in the world; odd doesn't mean dangerous. Look at me. I'm odd in everyone's eyes, but do you think I'm dangerous?"

"..."

Well, that was undeniable logic. Xie Lian clearly possessed transcendent grace, and yet he still collected scraps all day; was that not the very definition of odd?!

Fu Yao demanded, "Aren't you afraid he has ulterior motives?"

Xie Lian asked, "Do you think I have anything worth enough for him to scheme for?"

Nan Feng and Fu Yao were stumped.

Indeed, schemes against another were often designed because a person coveted another's treasure. Tragically, they honestly couldn't think of anything belonging to Xie Lian that was worth scheming for. He had no money and no treasures. The boy couldn't be eyeing that junk he collected every day, could he?

Xie Lian continued, "Besides, it's not like I haven't tested him."

The two stared at him.

"How did you test him?"

"How did it go?"

Xie Lian explained his previous attempts. "The results are inconclusive. I've already done so much. If he isn't a mortal, then there's only one other possibility."

A supreme!

Fu Yao sneered, "Who knows. Maybe he *is* a supreme."

Xie Lian said softly, "Do you think ghost kings are as idle as we are, such that they'd come to a small village to collect scraps with me?"

"We aren't idle!"

"Okay, okay, okay..."

On top of the small hill, outside the shrine, the three heavenly officials could hear that youth moving about easily without worry within, as if he wasn't the least bit concerned about anything.

Nan Feng said in a low voice, "No. We still have to think of a way to test whether he's a supreme."

Xie Lian rubbed his forehead. "Go ahead and try, but don't go overboard. What if he really does turn out to be a runaway young noble? I get along pretty well with this kid, so be nice. Don't bully him."

The "don't bully him" made Nan Feng screw up his face, and Fu Yao's eyes rolled to the back of his head. Xie Lian nagged a bit more before reopening the door. San Lang was checking out the broken table leg, and Xie Lian cleared his throat to get his attention.

"Are you all right?"

"I'm all right." San Lang smiled. "Just checking to see if we can fix this table leg."

"Everything just now was a misunderstanding, please don't mind them," Xie Lian said warmly.

"Since you say so, I won't mind. Maybe they thought I looked familiar."

Fu Yao said frostily, "Yeah. Quite familiar. Probably why I was mistaken."

San Lang laughed. "What a coincidence! I think you two look rather familiar too!"

"..."

Although still on high alert, Nan Feng and Fu Yao were no longer reacting violently. Nan Feng said gloomily, "Make some room, I'm going to conjure a teleportation array."

The teleportation array was a spell that could compress thousands of kilometers into one step, infinitely convenient. However, each use consumed a considerable amount of spiritual power.

Xie Lian rolled up the straw bedding mat on the ground and said, "Why don't you draw it here?"

With all the commotion earlier, Fu Yao didn't have the chance to look at the shrine properly. Now that he had spent some time in the dilapidated shack, he looked around, feeling immensely uncomfortable. He wrinkled his brows. "You live in a place like this?"

Xie Lian grabbed a stool for him to sit on and replied, "I always live in places like this."

Nan Feng paused briefly when he heard that, then went back to drawing the array. Fu Yao didn't sit down, but his expression also turned complicated. He mostly looked shocked, but there was a tiny part that looked to be cheered at his misery.

He quickly neutralized his expression, however. "Where's the bed?"

"This is it," Xie Lian replied, hugging his straw mat.

Nan Feng looked up to glance at the mat, then lowered his head again. Fu Yao side-eyed San Lang, who was standing aside.

"You two are sleeping next to each other?"

"Is there a problem?" Xie Lian asked pointedly.

Alas, the two couldn't squeeze out anything more to say, so no more problems.

Xie Lian turned to San Lang. "You were interrupted before, San Lang. Who is that evil cultivator of Banyue? Do continue."

San Lang had been staring at them earlier, looking to be deep in thought, his eyes dark. He only snapped out of it when he heard Xie Lian call to him. He gave Xie Lian a small smile. "All right."

He paused for a moment, then began, "That evil cultivator of Banyue was the state preceptor of the ancient Kingdom of Banyue, one of the Dual Evil Masters."

"'Dual' means there's two of them. Who's the other one?" Xie Lian asked.

San Lang, having all the answers, replied, "Another evil cultivator from the Central Plains named Fangxin. He has nothing to do with the Kingdom of Banyue."

Xie Lian widened his eyes and continued to listen.

Turned out, the people of Banyue were a brutish warrior race who frequently enjoyed invading nearby lands. They seized an important checkpoint between the Central Plains and the Western Region, and the two countries constantly fought over the border. Battles, skirmishes; the conflicts were never-ending. Their state preceptor was learned in the demonic arts, and the soldiers of Banyue trusted in them with all their hearts, willing to follow the state preceptor to the ends of the earth.

However, two hundred years ago, a dynasty from the Central Plains finally dispatched an army to invade, and it leveled the Kingdom of Banyue.

Although the Kingdom of Banyue was annihilated, the resentment of the state preceptor and the soldiers would not disperse and remained behind to haunt the place. The Kingdom of Banyue was built upon an oasis, but after its fall and its eventual metamorphosis into Banyue Pass, it was as if the aura of evil permeated the land; the oasis was soon swallowed by the surrounding Gobi. Some said they still saw shadows of Banyue warriors, giant and terrifying, with maces in hand, patrolling back and forth, hunting. Thousands of civilians who used to live there gradually migrated, unable to make a living in a dying oasis. That was when the rumors of disappearing travelers started to spread. All those who came from the Central Plains wishing to pass through must leave behind half their assets as "toll": those assets being human lives!

Fu Yao smiled without mirth. "This young master sure knows a lot."

San Lang smiled back. "It's nothing. You just don't know very much, that's all."

"..."

Xie Lian smiled in spite of himself, amused by San Lang's sharp tongue.

San Lang continued lazily, "This is just based on unofficial history and ancient records of strange, supernatural occurrences. Who knows if the State Preceptor of Banyue is real. Maybe the Kingdom of Banyue didn't even exist."

"**E**VEN THOUGH it's rogue records and rumors you read, the Kingdom of Banyue certainly existed," Xie Lian explained.

"Oh?" San Lang said.

Just then, Nan Feng completed an interweaving array on the ground and called out to the others in the room. "It's done. When shall we go?"

Xie Lian quickly packed a small bag and came to the door. "Let's go now."

He placed his hand on the door and recited: "By the heaven official's blessings, no paths are bound!" Then he pushed gently.

When the door was pushed open, it was no longer a small hillside village outside. What replaced it was a wide city avenue.

As wide as the streets were, there was barely anyone on the road, maybe one or two pedestrians every now and then. This wasn't only because it was late in the evening but because the population in the far northwest was already small, on top of being this close to the Gobi. Even in broad daylight, there wouldn't be many walking about. Xie Lian closed the door behind him, and it was no longer Puqi Shrine on the inside but a small inn. That one step certainly was thousands of miles, the miracle of the teleportation array.

A couple of pedestrians walked by, grumbling as they stared at them, appearing quite guarded.

San Lang spoke up from behind Xie Lian. "According to historical records, when the moon sinks in the sky, follow the North Star and you will come upon the Kingdom of Banyue. Gege, look." San Lang pointed to the sky. "There's the North Star."

Xie Lian looked up and smiled. "It's so bright."

San Lang stepped closer to stand beside Xie Lian. He cast a glance at him, then looked up too. "Yeah. It seems the night sky in the northwest is somehow more uplifting than in the Central Plains."

Xie Lian agreed, and the two became immersed in a serious discussion on stars and the night sky. Meanwhile, the two junior officials behind them watched in disbelief.

Nan Feng questioned, "Why is he here too?"

"The door you created looked so magical, I followed along to check it out," San Lang replied innocently.

"Check it out?! Do you think this is a fun tour?!" Nan Feng shouted angrily.

Xie Lian rubbed his forehead and said, "Let it go. Since he's here, he's here. He won't eat your rations, I should have enough. San Lang, stay close to me, don't get lost."

"Okay," San Lang responded, looking obedient and good.

"This isn't a question of rations!!"

Xie Lian sighed. "Nan Feng, please keep it down. It's the middle of the night; everyone is sleeping. Let's just focus on the task at hand and stop sweating the small stuff. Let's go, let's go."

The four followed the North Star and traveled northward. After walking nonstop for an entire night, the towns and greenery along the way became more and more sparse, and the ground slowly gave way to sand. Finally, they reached the Gobi Desert. Although the teleportation array could cross over five hundred kilometers in one step, it used an exhaustive amount of spiritual power. The farther one went, the more spiritual power it sapped, and the time it took to restore that spiritual power also lengthened. This one step Nan Feng helped them take would require at least several hours to recover from. To conserve strength in case of an unforeseen battle, Xie Lian decided not to have Fu Yao perform the same conjuring. For a journey such as this, someone must have their spiritual powers at full strength.

In a desert climate, the difference between night and day was extreme. The nights were freezing to the bone but not too bad. However, when it became day, it was another story. The sky was clear and cloudless, giving way to a scorching sun. It was as if they were walking in a steaming oven, cooking them alive from the ground.

Xie Lian led the way, using the direction of the wind and small vegetation growing under rocks to find their path. After a while, he looked back, worried that someone may not be able to keep up. Nan Fen and Fu Yao were obviously fine, being immortal and all. Seeing San Lang, though, made him laugh.

Under the blazing sun, the youth had peeled off his outer red tunic and was using it to lazily block the sun, looking tired and cranky. His skin was pearl white, his hair coal black, and with the red tunic covering his face, his features seemed even more accentuated.

Xie Lian removed his bamboo hat and put it on San Lang's head. "Here, I'll lend it to you."

San Lang blinked, then a moment later, he smiled. "It's all right," he said and returned the hat to him.

Xie Lian didn't argue; if the boy didn't need it, there was no need to push.

"Let me know if you need it, then." Xie Lian straightened the hat on his head and continued walking.

After a while, the group noticed a small gray building in the midst of all the sand. Upon closer inspection, it appeared to be an abandoned inn. Xie Lian looked to the sky and saw that it was just past noon and time for the worst of the heat. They had walked all night; it was time for a break. Xie Lian led the group inside, and they found a table to sit and settle at.

Xie Lian took out a water bottle from his bag and handed it to San Lang. "Do you want some?"

San Lang nodded. He reached for the water bottle and drank from it before Xie Lian took it back to drink himself. He gulped down the water, his Adam's apple rolling up and down as he drank. He felt the coolness pass down his throat, incredibly refreshing.

Next to him, San Lang had his arm propping up his chin, stealing glances as Xie Lian drank. A moment later, he asked, "Is there any more?"

Xie Lian wiped away the bit of water that was caught on his moistened lips, then nodded and passed over the water bottle again. San Lang was about to reach for it when another hand blocked him from the water bottle in Xie Lian's grip.

"Hang on," Fu Yao said.

He retrieved his own water bottle from his sack and put it on the table, pushing it toward San Lang. "I have one too. Go ahead."

Xie Lian immediately knew what he was planning.

Knowing Fu Yao's personality, there was no way he would ever share his water bottle. He and Nan Feng had talked about testing San Lang the night before, so the liquid in the bottle must be Unmasking Water.

If a normal human was to drink a potion such as this, nothing would happen. However, if they were anything but human, the Unmasking Water would force its drinker to reveal their true form. Since Nan Feng and Fu Yao wanted to test to see if this youth was a supreme, the effects of the potion had to be considerable.

San Lang smiled. "Gege and I can share one bottle, it's fine."

Fu Yao and Nan Feng eyed Xie Lian, and he thought, *What are you both looking at me for?*

Fu Yao said coldly, "His is almost empty, don't worry, help yourself."

"Really? Then you two go ahead first," San Lang said, politely declining.

"..."

Those two both fell silent. A moment later, Fu Yao tried again, "You're a guest, you go first."

Fu Yao sounded polite and well mannered, but Xie Lian thought he must've squeezed those words through his teeth.

San Lang also made a "please" gesture. "You two are followers of the host, please drink first, otherwise it'd be indecent of me."

Xie Lian watched the three of them play this silly game of false pleasantries and pitied the sad water bottle being roughly pushed around the table with barely hidden force. He shook his head; he could feel the poor table tremble from their power play and feared it might not have long to live.

The secret battle went back and forth for several rounds when finally, Fu Yao snapped and sneered, "You not accepting this water means you have a guilty conscience!"

San Lang replied with a smile, "You're unfriendly and refused to drink first. Who knows if you've poisoned the water? Maybe you're the one with the guilty conscience?"

Fu Yao pointed at Xie Lian. "You can very well ask him whether this water is poisoned!"

"Is this water poisoned, gege?" San Lang turned to Xie Lian.

It was quite the cunning question. Technically, Unmasking Water was a potion that exposed one's true form and didn't harm real people.

Xie Lian replied slowly, "It's not poisoned, but..."

Fu Yao and Nan Feng focused their glare on San Lang, and he surprisingly let go of his grip on the bottle.

"All right." San Lang grabbed the bottle and shook it playfully in his hand. "If gege says it's okay, I'll take a drink."

He gulped down the contents of the bottle in one go. Xie Lian didn't think he'd be so straightforward and was shocked. Nan Feng and Fu Yao were stunned too and tensed immediately. Yet who knew, after San Lang drank all that Unmasking Water, he shook the bottle again, then threw it over his shoulder where it crashed and shattered.

"Tastes bad."

Bewilderment flashed across Fu Yao's face when he saw that the Unmasking Water did nothing to San Lang. A moment later, he replied coolly, "It's only water. Doesn't it all taste the same? What difference is there?"

San Lang reached for the water bottle next to Xie Lian's elbow again and replied, "Of course it's different. This one tastes much better."

Xie Lian smiled despite himself. San Lang really didn't care about any challenges being thrown his way, nor did he care about his true identity. So other than entertainment, this fight was meaningless. Xie Lian thought that would be the end of it, but Nan Feng stood up and dropped a sword onto the table with a loud clang.

With such a strong battle aura surrounding him, at first Xie Lian thought Nan Feng intended to end San Lang for good. It left him speechless for a moment.

"What are you doing?"

"The road ahead is dangerous," Nan Feng stated darkly. "This is my gift to our little buddy, for self-defense."

The sheath of the sword was ancient in design and bore wear and tear from the passing of ages. It was no ordinary sword. Xie Lian's eyes widened in recognition, and he put his hand over his forehead and turned away.

He muttered to himself, "It's Hongjing!"

The name of this sword was indeed "Hongjing," meaning "Red Mirror." It was a sacred sword. While it could not fight evil, no evil could escape its spiritual mirror. Should any non-human entities pull it from its sheath, the blade would turn red as if covered in blood, and the crimson blade would reflect the true form of that which unsheathed it. Whether wrath or supreme, none could escape!

There were no young men who would not be interested in swords or horses, so San Lang appeared rather intrigued. "Oh? Let me see!"

Sheath in one hand, hilt in the other, San Lang pulled at the sword. Nan Feng and Fu Yao stared intently. But when merely eight centimeters of the sword was pulled out, San Lang laughed.

"Gege, are your servants playing a joke on me?"

Xie Lian cleared his throat and turned back around. "San Lang, I already told you they're not servants." Then he spun back.

"Who's joking around with you?" Nan Feng demanded coldly.

"How can one defend oneself with a broken sword?" San Lang sheathed the sword and threw it back onto the table.

Nan Feng's face froze for a moment, then he immediately picked up the sword to check. He pulled it from the sheath and heard a clunk, and suddenly, in his hand was now a sharp and chilling... broken sword.

Hongjing's blade was broken eight centimeters down!

Nan Feng's face changed colors, and he turned the sheath upside down. There was the clattering sound of a mess of clinks and clanks; what was left of the blade within the sheath was now broken into bright, sharp little fragments.

The Hongjing sword was a powerful weapon that could expose its enemies, that wasn't a lie. But Nan Feng had never heard of any technique that could break it from within the sheath!

Nan Feng and Fu Yao both pointed at San Lang and cried, "You—!!"

San Lang snickered and leaned back in his chair, putting his black-booted feet up on the table. He tossed one of the broken pieces in his hand in the air to play with it. "I'm sure you guys didn't do this on purpose and just weren't careful enough with it on the road. Don't worry about me, I don't need some broken sword as protection. Keep it for yourselves."

As for Xie Lian, he simply couldn't look at Hongjing directly. The sacred sword used to be part of Jun Wu's collection. During his first ascension, Xie Lian once visited Jun Wu's palace and thought that, despite its lack of combat power, Hongjing was an interesting sword. So Jun Wu gifted it to him. After the first banishment, there was a time when things had gotten really hard, and Xie Lian gave the sword to Feng Xin to be pawned.

That's right. Pawned!

The money made from pawning Hongjing was enough to fill their stomachs for a few meals. Xie Lian had pawned off too many treasures during that time, and he had forced himself to forget every single one of them lest his heart bleed with regret. Feng Xin remembered the sword after his ascension and couldn't bear having a sacred object lost among mortals, so he managed to find it again. It was sharpened, cleaned, and hung in the Palace of Nan Yang, and

now it had been brought down by Nan Feng. In any case, whenever Xie Lian saw that sword his head would faintly ache, so he could only look away.

He could sense that the other three were about to start bickering again and shook his head. Instead, he carefully observed the weather outside. The wind was picking up, Xie Lian noted. There might be a sandstorm later. If they continued on their way, would they be able to find shelter?

Just then, over the golden sand, two shadows suddenly flashed by.

Xie Lian straightened up immediately.

Two silhouettes, one black, one white, sauntered unhurriedly but rapidly, as if they were gliding through clouds. The one dressed in black was slender and elegant. The one dressed in white, on the other hand, was a female cultivator, with a sword on her back and a whisk in hand. As they sped by the abandoned inn, the black figure didn't look back once, but the white figure glanced over and smiled. That smile was like their forms: gone in a flash but leaving a forebodingly strange feeling.

It was only because Xie Lian had been keeping an eye on the outside that he caught that scene, but the other three probably only saw their retreating backs.

Nan Feng rose instantly. "Who was that?"

Xie Lian stood up too. "Don't know, but they're definitely not ordinary people." After a moment's deliberation, he said, "The wind is picking up. Stop playing around, and let's go as far as we can."

Although the bickering trio constantly argued, they had nevertheless steeled their hearts to do what they came here to do. So they immediately stopped butting heads and cleaned up the pieces of Hongjing before heading out the door.

The four of them continued their trek, now against a blowing headwind. They walked for another four hours, wind howling in their ears, but the progress they made was nothing compared to the distance they were able to cover earlier in the day. The whipping gusts grew stronger, and the wind whipping the sand battered their faces and bodies, beating at any uncovered skin. The more they advanced, the more difficult it became. Gusts became deafening gales and whirling sand filled the air around them, obscuring their path.

Xie Lian, holding his bamboo hat down, called out, "This sudden sandstorm feels strange!"

No one answered him and Xie Lian looked back, afraid that someone might be lost. But all three were present and following, just no one had heard him. The gales were so strong that his voice was swallowed up. He wasn't particularly worried about Nan Feng and Fu Yao; even with crazed winds whipping, the two walked steadily, full of killing intent. San Lang, on the other hand, followed closely behind Xie Lian, never more than five steps away.

Even with so much sand blowing and thrashing about, San Lang remained calm and collected, hands clasped behind him as he walked. His red tunic and black hair danced wildly in the wind, as if he hadn't any care in the world. Xie Lian could feel how hard the sand was hitting his face and was worried by how little San Lang seemed to mind. He opened his mouth to tell the youth to watch out for sand getting in his eyes and sleeves but figured he wouldn't hear anything he'd say, so Xie Lian reached over directly to help fold in his sleeves, patting them down to make sure no sand would get in. San Lang was taken aback by the sudden gesture.

The other two behind them approached, and with everyone in better hearing range, Xie Lian tried talking again. "Be careful, everyone. This wind came out of nowhere, it's not right. There may be evil within."

"It's just a little sandstorm, how evil can it be?" Fu Yao said.

Xie Lian shook his head. "The wind is all right. It's what the sand might carry that I'm worried about."

Just then, a powerful gust whipped by, blowing off Xie Lian's bamboo hat. If it flew off, it would disappear into the desert forever! But San Lang reacted immediately and grabbed the hat just in time with an abnormally fast hand. He returned the bamboo hat to Xie Lian once more, and Xie Lian thanked him.

As he retied the hat onto his head, he said, "We should probably find shelter for the time being."

Fu Yao countered, "If there's evil in this storm trying to stop us from advancing, then we must continue!"

Before Xie Lian could say anything, San Lang burst out laughing. Fu Yao's head shot up, and he coldly demanded, "What are you laughing at?"

San Lang folded his arms and chuckled. "Does being contradictory give you the satisfaction of feeling unique and independent?"

Xie Lian had thought before that although this youth was always smiling, it was often difficult to discern whether it was genuine or purposely courteous as a form of mockery. This time, however, anyone could tell there was not a trace of sincerity in his smile. Fu Yao's eyes grew dark, and Xie Lian raised his hand.

"Stop right there, you two. If you've got things to say, you can say them later. It won't be funny if the wind gets any stronger."

"What? Think it'll blow you away?" Fu Yao mocked.

"Yes, that may very well ha—"

Xie Lian didn't finish before the three in front of him suddenly vanished.

Actually, they weren't the ones who vanished, he did: another powerful gust had carried him away for real!

A twister!

Xie Lian spun wildly in the sky. He threw out his arm and cried, "Ruoye! Grab hold of something dependably solid!!"

Ruoye shot out from within Xie Lian's sleeve. In the next moment, he could feel the other end of the white bandage sink as if it was tied to something, and it yanked him to a stop. After finally stabilizing himself in the crazed wind, Xie Lian realized that he had been blown over thirty meters above the ground!

Xie Lian was now like a kite, attached to the ground by only a single thread. With sand whipping at his face, he held fast and tried to see what exactly Ruoye had tied itself to. Squinting and blinking, Xie Lian finally recognized a red silhouette. The other end of Ruoye seemed to be wrapped around the wrist of the youth in red.

Xie Lian told Ruoye to grab hold of something dependably solid, and it grabbed on to San Lang!

Xie Lian didn't know whether to laugh or cry. He was about to command Ruoye to grab on to something else when the pull on his arm suddenly grew lighter. Xie Lian's heart sank.

This wasn't the feeling of Ruoye being released but something much worse. Sure enough, the red silhouette suddenly grew closer and was soon within reach.

San Lang had been dragged into the windstorm too!

Xie Lian tried to shout "Don't panic!" to him, but the moment he opened his mouth, he got another mouthful of sand. At this point, Xie Lian had gotten used to eating sand. He wanted to tell San Lang not to panic, but in all honesty, he didn't think the boy would fret in the slightest. Ruoye continued to withdraw back to Xie Lian, closing the distance between him and the boy who had just been blown into the sky. As he suspected, San Lang didn't look the least bit anxious, appearing as if he could calmly open a book and read right then and there. Xie Lian wondered if San Lang had gotten dragged in on purpose.

Ruoye wrapped itself around the waists of the two to tie them together. Xie Lian hugged onto San Lang, then commanded, "Go, try again, but don't bring up any more people!"

The silk band shot out once again, but this time it grabbed on to… Nan Feng and Fu Yao!

Xie Lian felt drained. "Ruoye," he said tiredly. "I said no 'people,' but I didn't mean it so literally…all right."

Xie Lian twisted himself toward the ground and shouted, "Nan Feng, Fu Yao! Hang on! Hang on tight!"

Down below, of course Nan Feng and Fu Yao did their utmost to try to anchor themselves, but the winds were simply too strong. Soon, to no one's surprise, another two silhouettes joined them in the twister.

Now all four of them were swirling about in the air at high speed. Within the dark yellowness between the heavens and the earth, that twister was like a slanted sand pillar reaching the sky. Four silhouettes tied together by a white silk band were whirling nonstop within it, going faster and faster, higher and higher.

"How did you both get blown up here too?" Xie Lian shouted, enduring all the sand blowing into his mouth.

All they could see was sand, and all they could hear was wind. They had no choice but to use their loudest voices to shout to each other.

"Ask your dumb Ruoye!" Fu Yao yelled back, spitting out sand as quickly as he got mouthfuls of it.

Xie Lian seized his "dumb Ruoye" with both hands and said woefully, "Oh, Ruoye, all four of us are counting on you now. Please, absolutely do not grab the wrong thing again. Now go!"

With heroic solemnity, Xie Lian released Ruoye once more.

"Stop relying on that toy! Think of something else!" Nan Feng roared.

But just then, Xie Lian felt a tug from the other end of the silk band and lit up. "Wait! Give it one more chance! It's caught something!"

"It better not be a random passerby! Let the poor person go!" Fu Yao roared too.

Xie Lian was also afraid of the same thing. He tugged back at Ruoye, but it remained taut and firm, and Xie Lian let out a breath of relief.

"It's not! It's something solid, quite stable!" Then he commanded Ruoye: "Pull!"

Ruoye rapidly shortened against the force of the crazed twister. The four silhouettes were quickly pulled out of the wind pillar, and gradually, in the midst of boundless yellow sand, Xie Lian could make out the contours of something large, black, and half-round down below.

This landmark was extremely big, about the size of a small temple; it was what Ruoye had latched on to. When they came closer to the ground, Xie Lian could finally see clearly that this round structure was actually a giant boulder.

In a windstorm of such force, this boulder was like a solid, silent fortress, no doubt the perfect shelter. While on the road earlier, however, none of them had seen such a rock. Who knew how far that strange twister had taken them? When they landed, they immediately circled around to the back of the boulder to shelter from the wind.

The moment they went around, understanding dawned on Xie Lian. "Thank the heaven official's blessings!"

Turned out, in the back of this boulder there was an opening. The hole was as wide as two doors but only half the height of one. Although a bit low, it was still possible for a grown person to enter if they bent down. The hole's opening was jagged and slanted, but it appeared to be haphazardly man-made rather than naturally formed. When Xie Lian entered, he discovered that the inside of the boulder was hollowed out, and quite deep. It was dark further inside, so he didn't bother trying to look around and settled down where there was light. He brushed the sand off Ruoye and wrapped it back on his wrist.

Nan Feng and Fu Yao were both spitting out sand and covered in it from head to toe, from their eyes to their ears to their mouths and noses and all over their clothes. They peeled off their outer robes and shook them out; they were heavy with fine grains of sand. Of the four of them, only San Lang looked unruffled as he lazily dusted himself off and made himself proper again. Other than his lopsided ponytail, his carefree form remained unaffected. That ponytail had been tied by Xie Lian and was askew to begin with, so a little wind made no noticeable difference anyway.

Nan Feng wiped his face and started cursing while Xie Lian dumped sand from his bamboo hat. "*Hahhh*, I didn't think you two would get pulled in as well. Why didn't you use the Thousand-Pound Weight spell?"

"We did! It was useless!" Nan Feng spat angrily.

From the side, Fu Yao was still ferociously shaking sand out of his outer robe and said equally ferociously, "Where do you think we are? This is a desert in the northwest, not the main domain of my general."

Nan Feng continued, "The north is the territory of the two Generals Pei, and the west belongs to Quan Yizhen. You won't find a Nan Yang temple within a hundred-kilometer radius of this place."

There is a saying in the Mortal Realm that even a powerful dragon cannot win against the local snakes. As Nan Feng and Fu Yao were deputy generals of the southeast and southwest, it couldn't be helped that their powers were restricted when they tried to use them outside of their own territories. Seeing their incredibly sullen, frustrated faces, Xie Lian thought this was perhaps the first time they were sent flying by a huge wind to tumble in circles without any way to land.

"You two have worked very hard."

San Lang sat down next to him and propped up a cheek with his hand. "So are we just gonna sit here until the storm blows over?"

"Looks like we'll have to," Xie Lian turned to him and replied. "As strong as that twister is, it can't possibly blow a giant rock into the sky."

"You never know. Like you said, there's certainly something off about that wind."

A sudden thought came to Xie Lian. "San Lang, may I ask a question?"

"Ask away," San Lang replied.

"That State Preceptor of Banyue, is it a man or a woman?" Xie Lian asked.

"Did I not mention earlier? She's a woman."

Just as I suspected, Xie Lian thought. "Earlier, when we were resting at the abandoned inn, didn't we see two figures pass by? Their steps were graceful and strange, definitely not those of a mortal. And the one in white was a female cultivator."

Fu Yao looked doubtful. "It's not easy to identify whether they were a man or woman by the robes, and they looked taller than the average woman. Are you sure you saw right?"

"I'm absolutely sure," Xie Lian said. "So I thought she might be the State Preceptor of Banyue."

"It's possible," Nan Feng said. "But there was another black-clad figure traveling with her. Who could that be?"

"Hard to say, but that person was walking even faster than she was. Their strength is definitely no less than hers," Xie Lian said.

"Could it have been the other evil state preceptor, Fangxin?" Fu Yao wondered.

"I think, regarding that, the whole 'Dual Evil Masters' title was only given because, historically, their actions were similar. Both were equally evil, so people connected them together as a pair to remember them more easily. Like the 'Four Great Calamities' of the Ghost Realm; even if there aren't really four that fit, they are made four because it's simpler."

Hearing Xie Lian say this, San Lang burst out laughing. Xie Lian stared at him.

"It's nothing," San Lang said, "I just thought what you said made sense. One of the four in the Four Great Calamities is certainly only there for the headcount. Please continue."

Xie Lian continued: "In reality, the Dual Evil Masters have nothing to do with each other. I've heard of State Preceptor Fangxin: he was the State Preceptor of Yong'an, born at least a hundred years earlier than State Preceptor Banyue."

"You don't know of the Four Great Calamities in the Ghost Realm, but you know about State Preceptor Fangxin of Yong'an in the Mortal Realm?" Fu Yao asked in disbelief.

"I overhear things while collecting scraps in the Mortal Realm. It's not like I collect scraps in the Ghost Realm, so of course I don't learn anything about them," Xie Lian explained.

The wind outside the cave seemed to be dying down. Nan Feng approached the opening of their shelter, patting the rocky surface here and there, inspecting its material. He stared fixated at it for a moment, then lowered his head.

"Why would there be a hollow rock like this in the middle of a desert?"

He thought the boulder was rather suspicious, but Xie Lian wasn't surprised by it.

"Hollowed boulders like these aren't unusual. The people of Banyue used to build shelters like these to hide from sandstorms, or even for passing the nights while taking their livestock to graze. Some holes weren't dug but were rather blown out," Xie Lian said.

"How could they graze in a desert?" Nan Feng asked, confused.

Xie Lian smiled. "It wasn't all desert here two hundred years ago. There used to be an oasis."

"Gege," San Lang called.

"What is it?" Xie Lian turned his head.

San Lang raised his hand and pointed. "The rock you're sitting on seems to have writing on it."

"What?" Xie Lian looked down, then stood up and found that where he had been sitting was actually a stele, a carved stone monument.

After wiping off the layer of dust, there were indeed letters on its surface. However, the characters were carved rather shallowly, so the words weren't very clear. At least half the stele was still buried, and the words stretched from beneath the sand all the way up until they faded into blackness.

If there was writing here, it had to be examined!

"I don't have much power left. Can someone lend me a palm light? Thanks!" Xie Lian asked.

Nan Feng snapped his fingers, and a small burst of flame ignited in his palm. Xie Lian stole a glance at San Lang, but the youth didn't appear surprised. Xie Lian supposed that after seeing the teleportation array, there wasn't much more to be surprised about.

Nan Feng moved his palm to where Xie Lian directed him to brighten the writing on the stone stele. The characters were incredibly odd, slanting as if randomly scribbled by a toddler.

"What is this?" Nan Feng wondered.

"Banyue script, duh," San Lang replied.

"I'm sure Nan Feng asked the meaning of the words," Xie Lian said. "Let me see."

Xie Lian dusted more sand off the stone stele, revealing the first column of writing with the largest characters. That had to be the heading. The same characters also appeared repeatedly in various sections of the text.

Fu Yao approached and produced a palm torch. "You know how to read Banyue script?"

"Truth be told, I collected scraps in Banyue before that Evil Master of Banyue or whoever came about," Xie Lian replied.

"..."

"Is there something wrong?"

"Nothing," Fu Yao humphed. "Just wondering where you *haven't* collected junk."

Xie Lian flashed a smile, then looked down again at the characters. A moment later, he suddenly said, "General."

"What?" Nan Feng and Fu Yao answered at the same time.

Xie Lian looked up. "The first word on this stone stele is 'general.'" He paused for a moment. "But there's another character after it that I'm unsure the meaning of."

Nan Feng seemed to sigh in relief. "Then you'd best look some more."

Xie Lian nodded, and Nan Feng shifted his palm over further to light up the other words. Something didn't feel right, Xie Lian thought. There seemed to be something else on the periphery of his vision. With both hands pressed on the rock, Xie Lian slowly looked up.

Above the stone stele, the flickering flames illuminated a stiff human face. This face, with its bulging eyes, was staring straight at him.

"Aaaaaaaaaaaaaaaaaah!!"

The one who screamed wasn't Xie Lian or Nan Feng, but that stiff face.

Nan Feng immediately took out his other hand and ignited it as well. He put both hands together and grew the flames until they were bright enough to light up the entire cave.

The one whose face was revealed by the light was a person who had been hiding in the shadows the whole time. When the flames grew bigger, he scurried along the walls toward the back of the cave, and there Xie Lian saw seven or eight people huddled together and trembling in fear.

"Who are you?!" Nan Feng shouted.

Nan Feng's angry shout echoed in the cave, and Xie Lian, whose ears were still ringing from the scream earlier, covered his ears. Noise from the windstorms had deafened them, and anything spoken too softly wasn't heard. After they entered the cave, they had discussed the Evil Master of Banyue, then focused their attention on deciphering the stone stele, so no one had noticed there were others also hiding within their shelter.

The seven or eight people trembled. A moment later, an elder of fifty or so years stammered, "We're a merchant caravan passing through the area. Just ordinary merchants. The sandstorm is too fierce, so we're hiding in here for the time being."

He was the most composed in the group, and by the looks of it, the leader.

Nan Feng asked, "If you're just ordinary merchants, why are you sneaking around and hiding so furtively?"

The elder was about to respond when a youth of around seventeen years shouted, "We weren't planning on sneaking around! But you guys suddenly rushed in here; who knows whether you're good or evil? Then we heard you talk about the Evil Master of Banyue, then some Ghost Realm stuff, and you ignited fire in your palms. We thought you guys were Banyue soldiers out patrolling and hunting for flesh! No way we'd make a sound!"

"Stop talking, Tian Sheng," the old man hushed the boy, afraid that he might have offended the other party.

The youth had thick brows and large eyes, with the face and mind of a tiger. As soon as an elder spoke, he shut up immediately.

Xie Lian put down his hands, his ears no longer ringing, and said amiably, "It's nothing but a misunderstanding, just a misunderstanding. Let's all relax a bit; no need to be so nervous."

He paused for a moment before continuing to explain. "We're not Banyue soldiers. I am just a cultivator from a small shrine. These are...people...from my shrine. We only know a few tricks, nothing fancy. You're ordinary merchants, and we're ordinary cultivators without malicious intent. It just so happens that we all entered the same shelter to hide away from the same sandstorm."

His voice was soft and gentle, each word spoken slowly to calm everyone's nerves. After much explanation and reassurance, the merchant party finally relaxed.

Yet unexpectedly, San Lang suddenly laughed. "I think they're being way too humble. Those merchants aren't as simple as they say they are."

No one understood what he meant and looked at him in confusion.

"Don't at least half the travelers go missing when trekking through Banyue Pass? To cross this land while knowing that rumor; surely you're all extraordinarily brave. Nothing ordinary about you."

"That's not all true, young man," the elder responded. "Besides the fact that rumors are largely exaggerated, there are many caravans that have passed through without harm before!"

"Oh?" San Lang said.

"As long as you find the right guide and go around Banyue territory, all is well. So we sought out and found a local to lead us," the elder said.

"Yeah!" that youth Tian Sheng said. "It all depends on the guide! We owe everything to A-Zhao-ge! If not for him, we wouldn't have been able to avoid all those quicksand pits. When the sandstorm started, he knew exactly where to bring us to hide, otherwise we would be buried alive in sand by now!"

Xie Lian took a glance. This A-Zhao who guided them looked rather young, seemingly in his twenties, with an attractive, stony face. When he was praised by the other two, he didn't make a show of it.

His head was down, and he mumbled, "It's nothing. Just doing my duty. Hopefully when the wind dies down none of the camels or cargo will be damaged."

"They'll be fine for sure!"

The merchants were all very optimistic, but Xie Lian had a feeling things weren't as simple as they all thought.

If all trouble could be avoided by simply not crossing into Banyue territory, then did all the former travelers who lost their lives die because they didn't believe the rumors?

Xie Lian gave it some thought and said to Nan Feng and Fu Yao in a quiet voice, "This is too sudden. Once this storm passes, we'll need to make sure these people pass through safely before going to the Banyue ruins."

Then, Xie Lian looked back down to continue deciphering the Banyue writing on the stone stele. He recognized the word "general" earlier, but that was because it was a common word. It had been two hundred years since he last visited the Kingdom of Banyue. Even if he was fluent then, it had all been forgotten since. Shouldering the burden of translation really required time and patience.

Just then, San Lang said: "Tomb of the General."

Xie Lian remembered now. The last character was the one for "Tomb," "Grave," "Burial," and other similar terms. He turned to look at him, amazed.

"San Lang, do you know the Banyue script too?"

San Lang smiled. "Not much. I only know a few words because they're interesting."

Xie Lian was already used to him saying that. The word "tomb" was not one often used; if San Lang really only knew "not much," how could he just happen to know exactly what this one character meant? His "not much" probably meant the same as "ask away," and Xie Lian grinned immediately.

"Excellent! Maybe the characters you recognize happen to be the ones I don't know. Come closer and let's examine this together."

Xie Lian waved lightly to beckon, so San Lang went over. Nan Feng and Fu Yao stood next to them, lighting the tomb with their palm torches for them to read. Xie Lian lightly touched the words with his fingers, reviewing the writing in a low voice with San Lang, softly reading the words. The more they read, the more amazed they looked, before gradually growing glummer.

The merchant boy Tian Sheng was young, and youths were prone to curiosity. After the little chat earlier, it was as if they had become familiar, so he called out, "Gege, what does it say on the stele?"

Xie Lian snapped out of it and replied, "This stone stele is a memorial; it tells the story of the life of a general."

"A Banyue general?" Tian Sheng asked.

"No, a Central Plains general," San Lang answered.

"A Central Plains general?" Nan Feng was puzzled. "Why would the people of Banyue build a memorial for a Central Plains man? I thought the two nations were constantly at war with each other."

"This general was special," San Lang replied. "Although the memorial calls him a general, he was actually no more than a captain."

"Was he promoted to general later?"

"No. At the beginning, he led a troop of hundreds, but it dwindled to a troop of seventy, then to fifty."

"..."

"In other words, continued demotion."

The feeling of being demoted to the point of nothing was quite familiar to Xie Lian, and he could feel eyes on him. He pretended not to notice and continued to decipher the Banyue writing.

Tian Sheng couldn't understand and continued asking, "What kind of official gets demoted lower and lower in rank? As long as he didn't make any major mistakes, there should only be delays in promotion, not demotion, right? How much of a failure do you have to be?"

"..."

Xie Lian clenched his right hand in a fist and raised it to his lips. He faintly cleared his throat and replied in a stern voice. "Young man, receiving continuous demotion is not as rare as you think."

"Huh?"

San Lang chuckled. "It's true. It happens a lot." He paused before continuing. "This captain got demoted time and time again not because he was incapable or incompetent. It's because despite poor relations on both sides of this conflict, instead of winning battles on the battlefield, he kept getting in the way."

"What do you mean, 'getting in the way'?" Nan Feng asked.

"He prevented his enemies from killing civilians of the Central Plains, and he also blocked his own army from killing the people of Banyue. Every time he did this, he got demoted a rank."

San Lang spoke lightheartedly, and the seven or eight merchants sat closer to him like it was story time. Soon they got into it and started commentating.

"I don't think the captain did anything wrong!" Tian Sheng remarked. "It shouldn't be a problem to let soldiers kill each other but not civilians, right?"

"He's too blindly kind for a soldier, but overall, he didn't commit any crimes?"

"Yeah, he was saving lives, not killing people!"

Xie Lian smiled at all the comments.

These merchants before them had never lived a day at a battle-torn border; they were not the same people as those here two hundred years ago. The Kingdom of Banyue had long since perished. It was easy for them to say this, criticize that, even give compliments, but the actions of that captain weren't so easily forgiven back then, not with a simple remark like "he's too blindly kind." Within the group, only A-Zhao understood better—probably because he was a local.

"Now is now, two hundred years ago is two hundred years ago. To only receive demotions was a blessing for this captain."

Fu Yao, however, clicked his tongue. "How laughable."

Xie Lian could pretty much guess what he was about to say and rubbed his forehead.

Sure enough, the light of the flickering flames illuminated Fu Yao's glum look. "One must do the duty demanded by their position. If he became a soldier, then he must always remember to defend his country and kill enemies on the front lines. Casualties are inevitable in war. Such softheartedness has no place in war and will only drag down his fellow soldiers. His enemies will also think him foolish. No one will thank him in the end."

Fu Yao's words had irrefutable logic, and silence soon filled the cave.

He continued dryly, "People like that only have one end: death. They will either die in battle or at the hands of their own people."

After being struck speechless for a moment, Xie Lian broke the silence. "Yeah. You're right. He did die."

Tian Sheng was shocked. "Ah! How did he die? Was he really killed by his own people?"

After a moment of deliberation, Xie Lian still replied in the end. "Not really... Here it says that there was once a battle when both sides clashed, and as they fought, this man's boot laces came loose and he stepped on them, tripped, then..."

Everyone in the cave had assumed the death must have been tragic but heroic, so they were all taken aback at first, thinking what kind of death was that? Then, laughter exploded.

"Ha ha ha ha ha ha ha *ha ha ha ha!*"

"...He was trampled by the soldiers on both sides who were blinded by murderous rage and was cut down by a mess of random weapons."

"Ha ha ha ha ha ha ha ha ha..."

"Is it that funny?" San Lang quirked a brow.

Xie Lian also piped up. "Ahem. Yeah, it's rather tragic. Let's be more sympathetic and not laugh, okay? We're in his tomb, after all, let's give him some face."

"I don't mean anything malicious by laughing!" Tian Sheng immediately claimed. "But his death is just...so...ha ha..."

There was nothing Xie Lian could do. Reading the epitaph to this point, even *he* wanted to laugh. He didn't comment and continued to translate.

"In any case, even though this captain didn't have a good reputation in the army, some of the border citizens of both Banyue and Yong'an were very grateful for his efforts, so they called him 'General.' They built this simple stone tomb for him and erected a stone stele to remember him by."

"Later, the people of Banyue discovered another miraculous thing about this memorial: as long as one kowtows before this stone stele three times, one can transform all disasters met in the Gobi to good fortune," San Lang completed the translation.

He spoke so enigmatically that it was very convincing. His expression was also serious, so when the group heard, several of them immediately started prostrating, muttering that they'd rather believe it true than not. Xie Lian, however, was confused.

"Wha—? Is that written here? Is it really that magical?"

San Lang smiled softly and said in a lowered voice, "No. I made that up. But since they laughed earlier, their prostrating now should make up for it."

Xie Lian looked back at the stone stele and saw that it was indeed the end of the epitaph, and there were no more words. He had been feeling a bit woeful, but now he thought it funny.

He whispered back, "Why are you so mischievous?"

San Lang stuck out his tongue, and the two chuckled.

Just then, someone shrieked, "What's this?!"

The shriek echoed in the cave, sharply reverberating against the walls, and it caused all their hairs to stand up.

Xie Lian instantly turned toward where the shriek came from and demanded, "What happened?"

Where the merchants were once prostrating, everyone had jumped up in a flash and scurried away in fear and alarm.

"Snake!!"

Nan Feng and Fu Yao moved their palms toward the commotion and lit up the ground in that direction. Curled on the sandy floor was a slender, brilliantly colored snake!

"Why is there a snake?!" The crowd was growing increasingly anxious.

"How...how did this snake not make any noise?! We didn't hear when it slithered over at all!"

When the flames appeared near the snake, it instantly became alert and raised itself into an attack position. Nan Feng was about to torch it when someone leisurely strolled over. That person easily snatched the snake with his left hand, clutching it at its heart.

He brought it closer to observe it and said, "Isn't it normal to see snakes in the desert?"

Someone that fearlessly gutsy was, of course, San Lang. They say to fight a snake, seize it at the heart; if pressed there hard enough, no matter how venomous its fangs, it'll be helpless. The snake wrapped its long tail around San Lang's left arm meekly. At closer range, Xie Lian could see clearly: the snake had translucent skin, and its vivid red insides were visible and mixed with threads of black, resembling organs—rather disgusting. The tail was the color of flesh and segmented with layers of hard shell, unlike that of a snake, more like a scorpion.

Seeing this, Xie Lian's face changed, and he called out, "Watch out for its tail!"

Before Xie Lian finished speaking, the long snake body wrapped around San Lang's left arm suddenly let go. The tail snapped backward and tried to stab viciously toward San Lang.

Venomous as the tail was, San Lang's right hand was faster, and he easily caught it. Now holding both head and tail, San Lang showed off the snake to Xie Lian like it was an interesting toy, laughing.

"This tail is pretty interesting."

On the end of the tail there was a long, flesh-red needle. Xie Lian sighed in relief. "I'm glad you weren't stung. As I thought, this is a scorpion-snake."

Nan Feng and Fu Yao approached to observe the snake too. "Scorpion-snake?"

"That's right," Xie Lian said. "It's a kind of venomous vermin found only in Banyue; they're very rare. I've never seen one before, but I've heard of them. Body of a snake, tail of a scorpion, its venom has the strength of both combined, and if bitten or stung..."

Xie Lian trailed off. He watched San Lang twisting the snake, pulling and squeezing it as if it were a towel, stopping just short of tying it into a bow.

Xie Lian was speechless for a moment, then gently chided, "San Lang, stop playing with the poor thing, it's dangerous."

San Lang laughed. "Don't worry, gege, it's nothing. The scorpion-snake is the totem of the Banyue state preceptor, gotta take this rare chance to examine it!"

Xie Lian blinked. "The totem of the Banyue state preceptor?"

"That's right," San Lang said. "Apparently, it was because the state preceptor could control these scorpion-snakes that the people of Banyue believed in her infinite powers and worshipped her."

Hearing the word "control" alarmed Xie Lian. When it came to controlling anything, whatever it might be, they usually came in huge numbers. He immediately cried, "Everyone, leave this cave! There may be more than one scorpion-snake..."

Before he could finish there came a wail. "Aaaah!!!"

"Snake!" Other voices started yelling. "So many snakes!!!"

"Over here too!"

From the shadows, seven or eight scorpion-snakes soundlessly slithered into the cave. They came so swiftly and quietly from unknown crevices, but they didn't attack, only watched, judging. Soundless in both movement and attack, not even hissing, truly extremely dangerous. Nan Feng and Fu Yao released two fireballs and shot them toward the snakes, and a large ball of fire exploded inside the cave.

"Get out!" Xie Lian yelled.

No one needed to be told twice, and everyone ran outside. Luckily, it was still light out and the twister had long passed, the wind calmed. The group of them escaped into open ground and kept running.

As they ran, someone said, "That stone memorial is too scary! How come after we kowtowed three times we still ran into stuff like that?!"

Xie Lian was thankful that they didn't know those last words were fabricated by San Lang. But then, he heard someone else say, "Yeah! It's pretty much the same effect as worshipping the Scrap Immortal! The more you pray, the unluckier you become!"

"..."

Even when the issue was barely related to him, he still got shot. Xie Lian was speechless.

Suddenly, Tian Sheng yelped in alarm, "Uncle Zheng!"

That elder he had been assisting had collapsed. Xie Lian darted over.

"What happened?"

Pain filled the face of old man Zheng, and he raised a shaky hand. Xie Lian grabbed hold of his hand and frowned, his heart sinking. There was a growing, angry swelling spreading rapidly down his palm, and within the red and purple bruising, there were two small punctures, barely visible. A wound that tiny would not have otherwise been noticed until it was too late.

"Everyone, check and see if you have any wounds on your bodies!" Xie Lian called out immediately. "If you do, use a rope to stop the spread!"

Xie Lian turned the hand over to examine his meridians and saw that the red and purple swelling was visibly climbing up the veins of the arm. *What a formidable venom,* Xie Lian thought. He was just about to unravel Ruoye when, next to him, A-Zhao ripped a strip of fabric from his own clothing and promptly knotted it tightly around the old man's bicep to prevent the venom from progressing. Xie Lian mentally praised him. He looked up, and without needing him to say anything, Nan Feng had already taken out a medicine bottle and popped out a pill. Xie Lian helped the old man swallow it.

"Uncle! Are you okay?" Tian Sheng cried. "A-Zhao-ge, Uncle won't die, will he?"

A-Zhao shook his head. "To be bitten by the scorpion-snake means certain death within four hours."

Tian Sheng was shaken. "Then...what do we do?!"

Old man Zheng was the leader of the caravan, and the other merchants also started panicking. "Our friend here just gave him a pill, right?"

"That wasn't an antidote," Nan Feng said. "It's for temporary longevity. The most it can give him is twenty-four hours."

The crowd became even more distressed.

"Only twenty-four hours?"

"Does that mean we can only sit here and wait for death to come?"

"Is there no saving him from this venom?"

Right then, San Lang walked over slowly. "There is a way."

Everyone turned to stare at him. Tian Sheng turned his head joyously.

"Zhao-ge, if there's a way, why didn't you say so? Gave me a fright!"

However, A-Zhao stayed silent and shook his head.

"Of course it's not easy for him to say," San Lang said. "How could he possibly tell you that the bitten one can only be saved at the cost of everyone else's lives?"

"San Lang, what do you mean?" Xie Lian asked.

"Gege, do you know the story behind the scorpion-snake?" San Lang asked.

In the legends, many hundreds of years ago, there was once a king of Banyue who, while hunting, inadvertently caught two spirits borne from two venomous creatures: one snake and one scorpion.

The two venom spirits cultivated deep within the mountains, ignorant of the world and causing no afflictions. Nevertheless, the king considered their nature and believed they would cause evil sooner or later, so he decided to execute them. They begged and begged for their lives to be spared, but the king was cruel. He forced the two creatures to mate in front of him and his ministers to serve as entertainment at one of his many banquets, and after the feast, they were executed.

Only the queen pitied the two creatures. But she feared going against the will of the king, so all she could do was pick the leaf of a fragrant fern and cast it out to cover their corpses.

The snake and scorpion became vengeful spirits, immensely resentful, and they cursed the descendants borne from their mating to forever remain in the Kingdom of Banyue to destroy its people. Ever since then, scorpion-snakes were found only within Banyue territory. Should anyone be bitten or stung, the venom would spread through their body like wildfire, and they would die a miserable death.

However, thanks to that one act of kindness by the queen, the fern leaves used to cover their corpses became the antidote for their venom.

"That plant is called shanyue, and it only grows within the borders of Banyue," San Lang finished.

"Is...is the legend true? Can it be believed?" the merchants asked anxiously. "Buddy, this concerns life and death, don't joke around with us!"

San Lang smiled but said nothing, refusing to speak more after telling Xie Lian the tale.

Tian Sheng turned toward A-Zhao. "Zhao-ge, is what that red-clad gege said true?"

After a moment of hesitation, A-Zhao replied, "Whether the legend is true, I do not know. But the shanyue plant does grow within the walls of Banyue, and it is indeed the antidote for the scorpion-snake venom."

"Meaning the only way to live after getting bitten is to venture into the Kingdom of Banyue?" Xie Lian said.

No wonder so many caravans passed through Banyue territory despite knowing the deadly rumors. It wasn't that they were defiant and stubbornly went to seek their own deaths, but rather that if they didn't go, they would most certainly die!

The scorpion-snake was the totem of the Evil Master of Banyue, and she also controlled them. The appearance of these snakes was no mere coincidence. With only a few heavenly officials like them here, there was no way they could ensure the absolute safety of the entire merchant group, and there was no telling how many more snakes would show. Xie Lian raised two fingers and pressed them against his temple, trying to connect with the heavenly communication array to see if he could shamelessly borrow more junior officials. No dice. He couldn't connect to the array, couldn't reach out at all.

Xie Lian lowered his hand and wondered, *I didn't use up all my spiritual powers, did I? I calculated this morning, and there was still a little bit left.* He turned to Nan Feng and Fu Yao. "Can either of you try to enter the communication array? I'm getting no connection."

After a moment, the other two also looked grim.

"I can't get in either," Nan Feng said.

There were cases where the connection would become fuzzy near highly evil auras—auras potent enough to diminish the powers of various heavenly officials—and sometimes cut them off completely. It seemed that was the situation they were in now.

Xie Lian paced back and forth and wondered out loud: "It might be because we're too close to the Kingdom of Banyue, so the communication array is blocked..."

Just then, in the corner of his eye, there was a flash of red.

Nan Feng and Fu Yao were busy trying to reconnect with the communication array, and everyone else was occupied checking for wounds on their bodies. The boy Tian Sheng was anxiously holding tightly onto old man Zheng and didn't notice a wine-red scorpion-snake soundlessly climbing up his spine, curling near the neck, and opening its mouth. However, the fangs were not aiming at Tian Sheng's neck but at San Lang's arm right next to it!

The snake leaned back, then pounced!

In the speed of a second, before the snake had the chance to sink its fangs into San Lang, Xie Lian's hand shot out and snatched it right at the heart with blinding precision.

Given his strength, Xie Lian could crush the snake's heart if he wanted to, rupture its innards and spill its insides. But not knowing whether the snake's flesh was also poisonous, he didn't dare to press harder. Xie Lian raised his other hand to grab for the tail, but the snake was slippery and artful, making it difficult to catch. Xie Lian squeezed, but he only felt something soft and cold slither away from his fingers. The next moment, a sharp needle pain flared from the back of his hand.

The scorpion tail!

After the sting, Xie Lian snatched the tail and captured the snake properly, then squeezed down hard until it fell unconscious. Even having been stung, Xie Lian's face never changed, and he tossed the unconscious snake onto the ground indifferently.

"Everyone be careful, there may be more snakes around…"

He felt a tight grip on his wrist before he finished and looked to see that it was San Lang who caught hold of him.

"San Lang?" Xie Lian was slightly taken aback.

The reason he sounded confused was because, at that moment, the expression on the youth's face was *off*. It was unexplainable, frosty almost to the point of being frightening.

His eyes were focused intently on the tiny wounds on the back of Xie Lian's hand. The wounds themselves were originally the size of needle punctures, but the venom was vicious. The back of his hand had immediately swelled up angrily with a large patch of purply red, and those small puncture wounds had visibly enlarged to the size of knife cuts.

With a dark expression, San Lang wordlessly snatched Ruoye from Xie Lian's arm and immediately knotted it firmly on his wrist, preventing the venom from advancing. While Ruoye enjoyed snuggling up to Xie Lian, it wasn't normally that well behaved. And yet, in San Lang's hands it was so compliant it was like it was dead.

For all the time they'd known each other, Xie Lian had never seen San Lang look like this. He opened his mouth to speak, but San Lang turned to pull a dagger off the waist of one of the merchants. Nan Feng saw and knew instantly what San Lang was about to do, and he ignited a palm torch. Without sparing a look, San Lang burned the tip of the dagger to disinfect it before turning back to Xie Lian and drawing a cross over the puncture wound.

Just as he was about to lower his head to the hand, Xie Lian hurriedly said, "It's okay. The venom is aggressive, sucking it won't do much. I don't want you to get poisoned..."

San Lang ignored Xie Lian's protests, tightened his hold on Xie Lian's hand, and placed his lips upon it. Xie Lian felt his own arm tremble slightly, and he couldn't explain why.

Next to him, Fu Yao said in disdain, "I can't believe you went and got yourself stung. What were you doing, catching the snake when the kid might not have even been bitten? You're just causing unnecessary trouble."

That was true. Now that Xie Lian thought back to the airy way San Lang played with the snake in the cave, he probably wouldn't have even cared about an attack and would've easily avoided being bitten. But just in case. Just in case San Lang didn't notice the snake in time. Then wouldn't it be too late for regrets?

Xie Lian waved his good hand. "Don't worry. It's not like it hurts, and I won't die from it."

"You're really not in pain?" Fu Yao asked.

"Really. I don't feel pain anymore," Xie Lian answered honestly.

His words were true. Xie Lian was someone who possessed the worst of luck, so when he ventured deep into the mountains, eight times out of ten he would step on vipers or run into venomous insects and get bitten, stung, jabbed, or poisoned in thousands of ways.

However, he'd always been very stubborn at not dying, and at most he'd run a fever. After three days and three nights of fever, he'd wake up right as rain and continue on as if nothing had happened. He simply wasn't sensitive to pain. So as much as it hurt, he could live with it.

Right after he said this, San Lang finally looked up. The red swelling on the back of Xie Lian's hand had gone down, and San Lang's lips were stained with blood. His eyes were extremely cold, and he moved his glare to the unconscious snake on the ground. There was a loud *BOOM!* and the snake abruptly exploded into a purplish-red pool of blood and flesh.

The sudden blast surprised everyone, but no one knew who did it. Even if the blood didn't splatter onto anyone, there was still a feeling of unease blanketing the crowd.

Tian Sheng, remembering that Xie Lian had also been stung, asked worriedly, "Gege, you got stung too! What will you do?"

Xie Lian felt the bandage on his wrist and smiled. "Don't worry, little one. We'll still stick to the plan of going to the Banyue ruins and searching for the shanyue fern."

Another merchant asked, "You guys are going? What about us? Should we send someone to go with you?"

"You can all stay here. Banyue territory is dangerous; the more people there, the more mishaps can happen. We will find the fern and bring it back to you within twenty-four hours," Xie Lian said.

"Will...will you really? Thank you so much—!"

"How can we possibly ever..."

A number of the merchants started stuttering their thanks, but then their faces changed when Xie Lian continued to speak. "In order to reach Banyue as soon as possible, I want to borrow your guide temporarily, if that's all right."

Naturally, Xie Lian meant A-Zhao. The merchants went from grateful and relieved to largely hesitant. Xie Lian knew where they were coming from. They were afraid that Xie Lian might run off with their guide once he found the shanyue fern—or even if A-Zhao didn't run away, he would still be greatly delayed. Nevertheless, none of them wanted to venture into that wicked place where "at least half go missing," so it was a huge dilemma.

Their worries were perfectly normal, so Xie Lian quickly added: "And just in case anything else comes to attack you, Fu Yao will stay until we return."

With one man staying, the merchants finally agreed and nodded. "All right. As long as A-Zhao is willing to go with you."

Xie Lian turned to A-Zhao. "Are you open to lending us a hand, my friend? If not, that's okay too."

A-Zhao nodded and said, "Yes. But the Banyue ruins are actually not hard to get to. Just keep going in this direction and you'll reach them."

After bidding the merchants farewell, A-Zhao took the lead with Xie Lian, San Lang, and Nan Feng following right behind.

A while later, Xie Lian inquired, "A-Zhao, do the scorpion-snakes appear frequently in this area?"

"Not frequently. This was my first time seeing them too," A-Zhao replied.

Xie Lian nodded and had no more questions. Truthfully, he did live in the Banyue area for a number of years, and this was also his first time seeing a scorpion-snake. A-Zhao's answer was not surprising.

Nan Feng realized Xie Lian's intentions and asked in a low voice, "You're suspicious of this A-Zhao?"

Xie Lian responded in a whisper, "Either way, we've brought him out. Just keep an eye on him."

In the past, it was usually San Lang who would talk to him first. Xie Lian wasn't sure if it was because of the incident earlier, but the youth still looked rather upset, walking without speaking a word. Xie Lian couldn't figure out what was going on and didn't know how to talk to him, so he kept on walking as well.

The four continued to trek through the vast Gobi Desert for close to an hour. The windstorm had long since passed, and without any obstructions, they advanced quickly. Soon, they could see ragged weeds here and there, growing in cracks in the rock and sand. By the time the sun was setting, Xie Lian finally spotted an ancient walled city on the horizon.

The city was difficult to see because it was the color of sand, camouflaged by the yellow so it became one with the desert. Some parts of the city walls were caved in and buried in the sand. As they approached, they found that the walls were extremely high, towering over thirty meters. It wasn't hard to imagine the city's past magnificence, how grand it must've been.

Passing through the barbican, the four formally entered the Kingdom of Banyue.

Past the gates was a wide and empty city street, with dilapidated houses on each side and rotten beams and broken bricks strewn about. Perhaps out of habit, A-Zhao cautioned the others, "Please be careful and don't leave the group on your own."

The other three didn't need that reminder. The actual Banyue city was far different from what they'd imagined.

Nan Feng wondered, "This is the Kingdom of Banyue? It's smaller than a capital!"

"A desert country is only as big as the oasis it's built on," Xie Lian explained. "At its peak, the population was only about ten thousand. It was actually pretty lively in a small city like this."

Nan Feng continued to observe the surroundings. "It would probably only take a few days to siege a country of this size."

Xie Lian shook his head. "Not necessarily. Don't underestimate the people of Banyue, Nan Feng. Even if their population wasn't more than ten thousand, they kept the number of soldiers at an average of four thousand. There were more men than women; aside from the sick and old and the farmers, most men joined the army. Besides, the majority of those soldiers were over three meters tall, each more violent than the next. With maces in hand, they would keep fighting even with swords through their chests. They were very hard to fight."

A-Zhao seemed rather surprised and glanced at Xie Lian. "This young master seems to know a lot."

Xie Lian maintained his smile and was about to converse some more when Nan Feng posed a question.

"What's that wall?"

He was indicating a giant yellow earthen building in the far distance.

"Building" wasn't quite the right word to describe it. It was a giant enclosure formed by four massive mud-colored walls, with neither doors nor a roof. Each wall was over thirty meters, and on the very top there was a pole with something tattered attached, flying in the wind. It was a chilling image.

Xie Lian turned his head and glanced, then said simply, "That's the Sinner's Pit."

By the sound of the name alone, it was obvious it wasn't anything good.

"Sinner's Pit?" Nan Feng frowned.

Humming gravely, Xie Lian explained, "You can think of it as a jail. It was made specifically for imprisoning criminals."

"How does it imprison anyone if there isn't even a door? Throw them in from the top?" Nan Feng wondered.

Xie Lian was hesitating to answer when San Lang suddenly spoke up.

"They do get thrown in. And the pit is full of venomous snakes and starving beasts."

Xie Lian was relieved to finally hear him speak, but when he looked over to San Lang, the boy met his gaze and turned away.

Nan Feng swore. "That's no fuckin' jail! That's torture! How cruel! The people of Banyue were either sick in the head or savage psychos!"

Xie Lian rubbed his forehead. "Not all of them were like that. Some were quite endearing..." He paused suddenly, his brows furrowing. "Wait."

The other three stopped, and Xie Lian pointed upward.

"Look at that pole up above the pit. Is that a person hanging from it?"

In the dimming light of the setting sun and at such a distance, it was difficult to see what exactly was hanging from the pole. But going closer and scrutinizing the shape, it became obvious that it was a scrawny little person in black, their clothes unkempt, dangling in the wind like a ragdoll.

"It's a person," San Lang confirmed.

When A-Zhao saw the hanging person, his face paled. This was such a bizarre, anguishing display that even a calm individual like him couldn't bear the sight of it.

Just then, San Lang tilted his head and said in a low voice, "Someone's here."

He wasn't the only one who noticed. Xie Lian also heard feather-light footsteps approaching. The four immediately moved to hide in the many decaying houses on the roadside. Xie Lian and San Lang entered one house, and Nan Feng and A-Zhao hid in the one across the street. Soon after, at the end of the broken street, the female cultivator in white appeared.

The woman was dressed in a pale white robe with a whisk tucked in her arm, the garb of a Daoist priestess. She roamed along the street, peering here and there. Her eyes were bright and observant, as if she were in her own backyard garden and not the Banyue ruins. Strolling right behind her was another woman clad in black, her hands clasped behind her back.

The black-clad woman was beautiful yet cold. Her eyes were piercing, her raven hair long and free, and it was like she radiated chill from her very person. Although she was walking behind the female cultivator, no one would mistake her for a subordinate.

These were the same two they'd seen outside the abandoned inn at noon.

At that time, they had passed by too fast and Xie Lian couldn't make out the details of the lady in black, but he now saw clearly that she was indeed a woman. If the one in white was the State Preceptor of Banyue, who was the one in black?

The state preceptor swished her whisk leisurely and spoke, "Now where did they go? We were careless for one moment and they all disappeared. Do I have to dig them out and kill them one by one?"

Just as Xie Lian thought, they were being watched from the moment they stepped foot into the city.

The lady in black approached and stoically said, "You can call your friends to help you kill them."

By "friends," she must have meant the soldiers of Banyue.

The State Preceptor of Banyue laughed. "Ha! I don't like calling other people. I like calling you. Aren't you glad?"

The lady in black ignored her completely and said coolly, "There's nothing agreeable about being called out by the likes of you for something like this. Just go."

The State Preceptor of Banyue arched her brows but still sped away. Listening to them, it sounded as if they were close. They were no ordinary folks, so the lady in black must be someone of renown. Someone who would be close to the State Preceptor of Banyue? A mysterious fellow cultivator? Or was there a queen or general they didn't know about?

Xie Lian was trying to connect the dots rapidly in his mind, but he held his breath. Now wasn't the time to be discovered. It looked like the state preceptor had an unpredictable personality; if she should find them and excitedly summon her legendary, three-meter-tall, mace-wielding Banyue soldiers, more time would be wasted fighting them. Twenty-four hours. One hour wasted was another hour they'd sink deeper into danger. But there was no helping his bad luck; whatever he didn't want to happen would always happen. The lady in black was passing the house Xie Lian hid in, but stopped mid-step, and her piercing gaze swept over the decayed shelter.

The State Preceptor of Banyue was already farther ahead, but she noticed that her companion had stopped and came back around.

"Hey, are you coming?"

The lady in black didn't look at her. "You. Step back."

"All right," the state preceptor responded obediently and actually retreated. The lady in black was about to raise her hand when suddenly, a loud rumble blasted from across the street!

On the other side, the house Nan Feng and A-Zhao had hidden in had collapsed! The crumbling of one house led the entire row to cave in. Dust and sand rolled into the air and clouded the whole street. Within that cloud, a black shadow leapt out and shot a streaming flame toward the state preceptor, but the lady in black rushed forward and shielded her from harm. With her left hand still behind her, she flipped her right palm and easily absorbed the flames before reflecting them right back. The black shadow parried her while escaping and soon disappeared. The state preceptor immediately chased after that shadow, but the lady in black gave the house behind another sweeping look before following.

Bless you, Nan Feng, Xie Lian thanked mentally.

Everything happened so quickly but Nan Feng had no doubt known somehow that they were about to be in trouble and created a diversion to lead their enemies astray. He was the only one who leapt out, so A-Zhao must still be inside the collapsed house. After making sure the state preceptor and the lady in black were indeed gone, Xie Lian dragged San Lang out of their hiding spot and called out.

"A-Zhao, are you still alive? Are you hurt anywhere?"

A moment later, a muffled voice came from under the ruins. "...I'm fine."

Xie Lian was relieved. "Thank goodness."

Although Xie Lian trusted Nan Feng's ability to control the crash and that he would no doubt leave enough space for A-Zhao to stay safe, it was still more reassuring to see it with his own eyes. He raised one of the rotten beams with one hand, and after a moment, A-Zhao emerged from underneath, covered in dust from head to toe. He brushed himself off a bit and returned to his stoic expression.

"Now there are only three of us left," Xie Lian said. "Nan Feng is creating a diversion, so we must move faster. Do you know where we can find the shanyue fern, A-Zhao?"

The young man shook his head and said, "Sorry. I only know where the city is, but I've never been here before, so I don't know where the fern can be found."

San Lang spoke up. "They say the shanyue fern prefers shade. It is small, its roots thin, but its leaves are big, like a heart-shaped peach. Why not search near a large building?"

"A large building?" Xie Lian contemplated.

If they were talking big, there was no building larger than the palace. In the legend, it was after the festivities that the queen picked a shanyue leaf, which could mean the fern grew on the palace grounds.

The three moved their gaze afar, and in the center of the city there was indeed a palace built of brick and wood.

From a distance, the palace had a grandiose aura, but upon a closer look, it was not in much better shape than the dilapidated houses on the streets. Through the palace gates there was a massive garden; perhaps in the past it wasn't a garden but a palace square. With years of neglect, weeds had flourished and spread.

Indeed, it wasn't sand beneath their feet now but mud. This was most likely the last sign of the oasis that once was. And the shanyue fern could very well be growing among all the other plants.

"Let's not waste time," Xie Lian said. "We only have twenty-four hours. But keep an eye out for scorpion-snakes."

A-Zhao and San Lang both hummed in acknowledgment and lowered their heads to start searching through the plants. As they rummaged, it suddenly occurred to Xie Lian that, if the State Preceptor of Banyue could control scorpion-snakes, there should be an abundance of them slithering about in her territory. Ever since they entered the city, they had not seen a single snake.

He straightened up and was about to speak when one of his hands fell on a long object.

Looking down again, he found that it was a human leg.

"Waaaaaaaah!!"

Xie Lian withdrew his hand and was struck speechless.

It occurred to him that every time he was faced with some horrifying incident, or saw or touched anything frightening in the dark, it was always the other party who would scream before he could say anything. But shouldn't it be the other way around?

The plants in this garden were tall and thick, and whoever's leg Xie Lian had touched was someone who had already been hiding and crawling in the weeds. The moment they touched, the leg recoiled, and the weeds in front of him rustled.

Someone called out, "Don't hit me! Don't hit me! Gege, it's me!"

Xie Lian scrutinized the wild grass and saw that the one who emerged crying "don't hit me!" was thick-browed, large-eyed Tian Sheng. The boy in turn saw that Xie Lian recognized him and sighed a breath of relief. Xie Lian, on the other hand, wasn't relieved; rather, he became even more alarmed and raised his good arm in a defensive stance. In circumstances like these, it was more likely that this was an illusion created by something evil.

"Weren't you with the others back in the desert? How are you here? Are you really Tian Sheng?"

Tian Sheng explained hurriedly, "It's me! I'm the real thing! I'm not the only one; three other uncles also came. They're just inside. Look if you don't believe me!"

He pointed toward the inside of the palace, and sure enough, three men came running out; they were indeed the men from the caravan. When they saw Xie Lian, they froze in their dash and looked awkward.

Xie Lian puffed out a breath before finally rising to his feet and dusting off his white sleeves. "What's going on?"

The merchants looked at each other, and no one made any noise. It was Tian Sheng who spoke up after an awkward silence.

"...Gege, after you guys left, Uncle Zheng's pain flared up, and he was really miserable. We didn't know how much longer we should wait for you to return, and we were afraid that you guys might've gotten lost. A-Zhao-ge said to go straight to get to the Kingdom of Banyue, so we thought the more hands to help the better, so..."

So what he really meant was that the merchants regretted letting them go after all. They were afraid that Xie Lian and company would rob them of their guide after finding the shanyue fern for themselves, so they sent people to come follow them. Xie Lian imagined that Fu Yao couldn't persuade them otherwise and was probably also too lazy to hold them back. It was impossible to stop stubborn people who refused to listen to reason.

Xie Lian felt rather exasperated. "You're all too reckless. Who knows what there might be, and what might happen, in a place like this? And you still came?"

Tian Sheng himself knew that what they'd done made it obvious they didn't trust Xie Lian, and he felt bad. This was why he didn't make a sound while hiding in the weeds earlier, as awkward as it was.

"Sorry, this concerns a man's life, so we couldn't sit still..."

No matter. This was a life-or-death situation, and to be wary was entirely natural. To go so far into danger for an antidote also proved that they were worthy companions. Xie Lian couldn't continue to scold them for this and sighed.

"If you didn't bump into anything weird when entering the territory, then it's your good fortune. But how did you know to come to the palace to search for the shanyue fern?"

Tian Sheng scratched his head and replied, "We didn't know where to start, but in the story the red-clothed gege told, it was the queen who picked the leaves, right? The queen couldn't possibly leave the palace grounds, so I thought we'd come here and try our luck."

Well, this child's mind could certainly spin, and it spun right on target, Xie Lian thought.

Just then, San Lang spoke up from the side. "I found it."

Xie Lian turned to see San Lang striding with his long, lithe legs toward him. In his hands were a few turquoise-colored leaves with roots still attached at the stems.

The leaves were about the size of a baby's palm and in the shape of peaches, slightly pointy at the ends, with thin, tiny roots. Even without A-Zhao to confirm, Xie Lian knew without a doubt that this must be the shanyue fern. Without waiting for Xie Lian to say a word, San Lang grabbed his wounded hand and lifted it.

The hand that was stung was originally frighteningly swollen, but after San Lang sucked the poison from the wound, the swelling had gone down significantly despite it not being fully cleared of the venom. With Xie Lian's wrist in one hand and the shanyue fern in the other, San Lang closed his palm on the plant. After only a second, he reopened his palm and the fern was crushed into powder without him appearing to exert any force.

San Lang gently but firmly rubbed the powder onto Xie Lian's hand, and he could feel coolness and relief stinging on his skin.

"Thanks, San Lang," Xie Lian said.

San Lang didn't respond, however, and after applying the powder, he let go of Xie Lian's hand. Xie Lian couldn't help but think that the air between the two of them now was really strange, but he didn't know how to ask about it without sounding odd. This wasn't something anyone else would notice either, or something they could possibly understand.

"Gege, are you feeling better? Is the herb working?" Tian Sheng asked anxiously.

Xie Lian snapped out of it and replied, "Much better. It should be the right herb."

Hearing this, everyone became excited. "Hurry! Let's find more!"

Soon, A-Zhao also raised a handful of leaves, crying out, "There's more here!"

The shanyue leaves in A-Zhao's hands were much bigger and fuller than the small, pitiful one San Lang used earlier, but the shape and markings were all correct, so everyone crowded over and happily exclaimed:

"There's an entire field here!"

"So many!"

"Pick lots! Let's pick a bunch! Do you think we can sell this?"

Noisily, the merchants busied themselves picking the herbs. Xie Lian turned his head to examine his hand for a moment, then tried to start a conversation with San Lang.

"You also searched the same area they're in now, right? Didn't you find any there?"

It was obvious Xie Lian was trying to force a conversation, and after asking the question, he felt that he was rather pathetic. But San Lang shook his head.

"You shouldn't use the ferns over there."

"Why?" Xie Lian wondered curiously.

Before San Lang could answer, they heard someone scream. "Go away!"

Everyone stopped, their movements halting.

"Who said that? Who's screaming?"

"It wasn't me!"

"It wasn't me either..."

Then they heard that sharp voice again. "Go away! You're stepping on me..."

Only then did the group notice: the voice came from near their feet!

In a flash, the crowd retreated from that field of ferns. Seeing this,

Xie Lian walked over. He was used to being the one in the lead when it came to these things. He approached the bush where the shrieking had come from and stripped away the thick weeds. Everyone's breathing hitched.

Under the weeds, in the mud, there was a man's face.

In this field, there was unbelievably a live human being buried in the mud, with only his face showing above the surface!

It was a nightmarish sight, truly incomparably creepy. A couple of merchants screamed in fright, holding on to each other.

Xie Lian once again comforted them in a skilled and practiced manner: "Don't panic. Everyone calm down. It's only a face, nothing extraordinary. We all have faces, no?"

That face chuckled. "Oh, did I scare you? *Hahhh*, I frequently scare myself too."

After reassuring the others, Xie Lian half-crouched and examined this face in the mud.

It was a man's face, quite flat when he wasn't smiling but extremely wrinkled when he was. Xie Lian couldn't tell whether he was old or young and couldn't say whether he was handsome or not. He couldn't make much out of this face at all, so he simply asked directly: "Who are you?"

The face in the mud asked back, "Who are *you?*"

"We're merchants passing through," Xie Lian replied.

The mud face breathed a long sigh. "Merchant passersby. I used to be part of a caravan too, but that was fifty, maybe sixty years ago."

The situation just got freakier.

Was a man buried in the grounds of an old city ruin for fifty or sixty years still human?

One of the merchants shakily asked in trepidation, "Then...then... how did a senior like yourself...get...*here?*"

The mud face cleared his throat and screwed up his face. "I...I was captured by the Banyue soldiers. I accidentally entered the city. They caught me and buried me here, and made me the fertilizer for their shanyue ferns..."

No wonder the herbs in their hands were big and full! They were fed with live humans!

The merchants immediately dropped all the plants in their hands, feeling as though they were touching corpses.

Xie Lian couldn't help but glance at his hand too but heard San Lang say, "That one was fine."

No wonder that, even though San Lang had looked through that field earlier, he left it to pick a small, almost withered fern from elsewhere. He probably saw what was in the soil and guessed that the herbs were grown with human fertilizer. So he ignored the lot completely, and turned around and walked away until he found normally grown herbs in a remote area that was clean of corruption. Only after finding those herbs did he apply them to Xie Lian's hand.

"San Lang was considerate and careful. Thank you, truly," Xie Lian said.

San Lang nodded his head, but his face was still gloomy.

Ever since Xie Lian was stung by the scorpion-snake, San Lang had behaved like this. A couple of days ago it was all "gege this, gege that," but now he hardly called him gege anymore. Other than sucking poison and applying herbs, San Lang seemed to be avoiding bodily contact with him as much as possible, and this thoroughly puzzled Xie Lian. Xie Lian couldn't grasp what he was thinking, and it was making him feel unsettled.

Just then, the mud face began to speak again. "I haven't seen real people in so many years. Can...can you come closer and let me see you all properly?"

The merchants all looked at each other, everyone thinking they best not do what he asked. After a while, seeing no one stepped forward, the mud face muttered, "What? What. You don't want to? *Hahhh...* What a shame..."

"Why is it a shame?" Xie Lian turned and asked.

"There's something that's been bothering me ever since you all arrived," the mud face said. "So I wanted to confirm with my own two eyes, which is why I asked you to stand closer for me to see. I want to see each and every one of you clearly to make sure."

"To make sure of what?" Xie Lian pressed.

The mud face cackled, "Don't be scared if I tell you...there's someone among you I've met before, fifty years ago."

Hair raised on everyone's necks at that statement.

If someone met this mud face fifty years ago, they'd be at least sixty or seventy by now. But among the people present, the oldest definitely didn't look older than forty, so how was that possible?

Unless...that person wasn't really a person!

Xie Lian gave a sweeping look across everyone's faces, from A-Zhao to Tian Sheng. Some were in shock, some stricken with fear, some shaking with anxiety, some speechless and confused. Everyone's reaction was normal and within reason. If one had to pick the odd one out, it'd be San Lang. But for him, no reaction was probably the normal reaction.

Xie Lian turned back to the mud face. "Who is this person you speak of?"

The facial muscles of that mud face twitched, and it gave an exceedingly freaky smile, as if it was giving its all to make itself look more reliable, but it couldn't fully conceal the sinister smirk hiding beneath. He beckoned mysteriously.

"You...come closer, and I'll tell you."

Xie Lian believed him eighty percent the first time the mud face asked, but after this, only fifty percent.

Who knew if this monster was only luring them closer to commit some evil deed?

Of course Xie Lian wouldn't listen to him. He got to his feet and was about to walk away when the mud face raised his voice.

"Do you really not want to know who it is? He will kill all of you, the same way he killed us!"

9
Dallying HuaLian, Night Fall in Sinner's Pit

THE MORE ADAMANT the mud face was, the more alarmed Xie Lian became. "Everyone stand back, don't go near him, and don't listen to a single word he says."

The crowd dispersed in a panic. The mud face continued to chuckle.

"Don't leave—there's no need to be like this! I'm a human too; I won't hurt you!"

Oh, you're mistaken; you look nothing like a human! Xie Lian thought.

Just then, something unexpected happened. One of the merchants snuck back toward the field, probably thinking that he still had to bring back some herbs for the wounded. But when he bent down to pick up the ferns he had dropped in fright earlier, the mud face twisted and spotted him with a glint in its spinning eyes.

Oh no! Xie Lian thought, rushing toward the man. "Don't pick that up! Come back!"

But it was too late. The mud face opened its mouth, and a long, blood-red thing slithered out.

What a long tongue!

Xie Lian grabbed the merchant by his collar and hustled backward with him in tow. But the tongue that flew out was freakishly long and forced its way right into the merchant's ear!

Xie Lian felt the body in his grip convulse violently. The merchant's limbs writhed nonstop, and the man let out a short, agonizing scream before falling to the ground. That long tongue dug out a large chunk of something bloody from his ear and brought it back to the mud face's mouth. The mud face happily chewed and cackled, his laugh so disturbingly loud it filled the entire palace grounds.

"Ha ha ha ha ha ha ha *ha ha!!* So good, so good, so delicious, so delicious, so *delicious!!* I was so hungry, so hungry!!"

His voice was sharp and shrill, his eyes bloodshot, horrible and disgusting to the extreme!

This man, who had been buried for over fifty years in the ground of an evil-filled kingdom, had already been molded into its soil and became something other than human. Xie Lian loosened his grip on the deceased merchant, his entire arm shaking. He was about to strike the repulsive monster when the mud face screamed again.

"General! General! They're here! They're *here!!*"

A deafening cry, more savage than that of a beast's, echoed in the distance. A dark shadow dropped from the sky and landed heavily in front of Xie Lian.

The entire palace grounds quaked on its landing. When it slowly stood up, its enormous shadow enveloped the entire group.

This "man" was truly much too big.

His face was as grim as steel, his expression ferocious and turbulent like that of a beast. He was at least three meters tall, clad in leather armor on his shoulders and chest. Rather than a man, one could say he was more like a walking wolf. Behind him, more and more similar forms appeared. One, two, three...over ten of those "men" jumped off the roofs of the palace and surrounded them.

Each one of these "men" was as large as a horse, built like a beast, with a sharp, tooth-covered mace on his shoulder. They might as well have been werewolves. When they circled around the intruders in the garden, it was like a large steel cage had fallen upon them.

The soldiers of Banyue!

These soldiers emanated a dark aura and were undoubtedly no longer alive. Xie Lian was tense and held Ruoye in position, ready to attack.

However, when the Banyue soldiers saw them, they didn't rush in to kill. Instead, they raised their heads and roared with crazed laughter, howling in a foreign language. The sound of their words was ghastly, guttural and heavy with tongue-rolling. That was the language of Banyue.

Although it had been two hundred years and Xie Lian had pretty much forgotten the language, he did review it with San Lang earlier in the General's Tomb—and the words uttered by these soldiers were loud, simple, and vulgar, so they weren't difficult to understand.

He heard the soldiers call the first man "General." Their conversation was filled with phrases like "take them away" and "won't kill for now." Xie Lian took a deep breath to force himself to relax.

He said in a low voice, "Everyone, don't panic. These Banyue soldiers won't kill us for the time being. It seems they want to take us somewhere else. Don't do anything rash, I can't guarantee I can beat them in a fight. We'll figure this out as we go."

It was clear that these soldiers would be hard to fight, each of them rougher than the next. Even with Ruoye in hand, suffocating one would probably take a bit of time, never mind ten. With mortals with him, Xie Lian couldn't do anything bold and could only remain vigilant and protect them the best he could.

San Lang didn't say anything, and the others had already lost their nerve. Even if they wanted to do something rash, they wouldn't know how, so they could only nod tearfully.

Next to them, the mud face screamed again, "General! General! Please let me out! I detained your enemies, let me go home! I want to go home!"

Seeing the Banyue soldiers, the mud face became hysterical, screaming and crying, blabbering nonsense with some Banyue words mixed in, no doubt learned from the many years he spent buried here. The massive three-meter-tall man they called "General" seemed to find the squirming mud face deeply disgusting and swung his mace toward it. He smashed the face into a bloody mess, the teeth of his mace piercing the brain. When he pulled his mace up again, the entire body was pulled out with it, fulfilling his wish of "let me out!"

However, the body that was unearthed was not a full human body but a chilling skeleton!

The merchants screamed in terror. The mud face, bloody after crumpling off the mace, seemed to also freeze in fear after seeing his own body. He sucked in a sharp breath.

"What's this? What's *this?!*"

"It's your body," Xie Lian reminded him, seeing that the mud face was numb in disbelief.

It was easy to figure out. This man had been buried in the desert for more than fifty or sixty years. His body had fertilized the shanyue ferns until they cleaned him of his flesh and left only bones.

"How can this be?" the mud face cried. "My body isn't like this! This is *not* my body!!"

His voice was incomparably shrill, and he was a horrifying and tragic sight. Xie Lian shook his head, but San Lang sneered.

"*Now* you're not used to your own body? What was that thing that came out of your mouth earlier? You didn't think that was odd?"

The mud face countered immediately, "That wasn't odd! It was just...a tongue that's a bit longer than average!"

There was nothing but mockery on San Lang's face. "Yeah. Sure. Just a little longer, right. Ha ha."

"That's right!" the mud face cried. "It's only a little bit longer! It's just because I spent decades trying to live off insects, forcing my tongue to extend. That must be how it came to be like this!"

When he was first buried in the ground, perhaps he was still alive, and in order to survive, he had done his best to extend his tongue to eat flying insects and creepy-crawlies. Then, as he gradually became less and less human, his tongue also became longer and longer, and the "food" he ate also moved from insects to much more terrifying things.

However, because he had been buried underground for so many years, unable to see the state of his body, he was unable to accept the truth and refused to believe he was no longer human.

The mud face kept trying to argue, "There are plenty of people who have long tongues, not just me!"

San Lang smiled, and Xie Lian felt a chill watching him. This youth's smile really gave off a sense of cruelty, like he was on the verge of ripping off someone's face.

"Do you think you're still human?" San Lang questioned.

The mud face felt a sense of danger at the question and suddenly became agitated. "Of course I'm human! I'm human!"

The mud face screamed and tried to move his white, boney limbs all at once, as if trying to crawl away. Finally unearthed, he was mad with joy, cackling, "I'm going home! I can go home now! Ha ha ha ha ha h—"

Crack.

The Banyue "general" finally had enough of this monster's shrill cries. In a split second, he crushed the bones in one stomp, killing any more of his cries of "I'm human!"

After trampling the irritating mud face, the "general" roared at the soldiers. The Banyue soldiers all raised their maces and, growling at Xie Lian's group, started herding them out of the palace.

Xie Lian walked up front with San Lang still following close behind. Despite being ushered by ruthless Banyue soldiers, the youth's step was still light and casual, as if he were taking a stroll. Xie Lian had been hoping to find a chance to talk to him, and after a while, when the Banyue soldiers went back to conversing among themselves, he spoke to San Lang in a low voice.

"Those Banyue soldiers call their leader 'General.' I wonder who it is."

As expected, when he posed a question, San Lang still answered. "At the time when the Kingdom of Banyue fell, there was only one general. His name, translated, is Kemo."

"Kemo? As in 'Millstone'?" Xie Lian wondered at the odd name.

"That's right," San Lang said. "Apparently, it was because he was awfully weak when he was young and was often bullied. He rallied and built up his strength by training with large millstones, which is how he got his name."

Xie Lian couldn't resist thinking, *Then he could've just as easily been named Dali, for brawn...*

San Lang continued, "Legends have it that Kemo was the strongest warrior in the history of Banyue, three meters tall and extremely powerful. He was a loyal supporter of the state preceptor."

"Even after death? Is he taking us to the Banyue state preceptor now, then?" Xie Lian asked.

"Perhaps," San Lang replied.

If there were more Banyue soldiers there, how would they escape? Who knew how Nan Feng, who had lured the other two away, was doing? The shanyue fern was in their hands, but how were they going to deliver the ferns to the wounded within twenty-four hours?

Xie Lian contemplated as he walked and soon noticed that General Kemo was leading them to a remote place at the far end of the city. When they stopped and Xie Lian looked up, a colossal yellow earthen wall stood before him like a giant.

Their destination was the Sinner's Pit.

Although Xie Lian had lived in the Banyue area for a time, he'd rarely gone into town and had never gone near the Sinner's Pit. Seeing it this close, Xie Lian's heart started pounding for some reason.

The yellow-earthed walls had a set of stairs along the outside. While they slowly climbed the crude stairs, Xie Lian scrutinized the pit and tried to look with his human eyes into the depths until he finally understood why his heart was pounding.

It wasn't because of thoughts of how this was a place of torture and cruelty, and it wasn't his worry about everyone getting pushed in. He was feeling the palpitations of a very powerful array at work.

Someone had purposely set up an incredibly powerful array using the Sinner's Pit's surrounding terrain and structure. And this array only had one purpose: to prevent the fallen from ever resurfacing!

What that meant was, even if a rope or a ladder was sent down into the pit, whoever tried to climb from the bottom would get cut off halfway up and thrown right back down. Without outwardly showing his intent, Xie Lian used the wall as support to climb up the stairs. After walking for a stretch, he determined the material of the wall. He discovered that, while it looked like it was made of earth, it was actually incomparably hard stone, probably enforced with a layer of magic. It'd undoubtedly be very difficult to break.

When they reached the end of the stairs and came to the top of the pit, standing along the wall's eaves, the only word to describe the sight was awful. That is, it inspired awe.

The whole of the Sinner's Pit was formed by four great walls surrounding it. Each wall was over a hundred meters long, over sixty meters high, and over a meter thick, the structure standing solemnly tall. At the top of each wall there was nothing, neither gazebos nor railings.

Within the enclosure there was a deep abyss without a bottom in sight. With the growing night, there was only blackness and a chilling smell of blood wafting up from below.

No one dared look down while walking along the railing-less eaves tens of meters above the ground. After a while, they could see the pole that stood in the center. And attached to that pole was a hanging corpse, the same one they had spotted before. The corpse was a small, black-clad girl, her clothing tattered and head bowed.

Xie Lian knew that this pole had been used specifically for hanging criminals that deserved shame and humiliation. The prison guards would usually strip the criminals of their clothing and hang the bodies naked. The criminals would die from starvation or dehydration, and after death the corpse would be left to flail in the wind, scorch under the sun, and rot in the rain. When the corpse rotted completely through, it would fall into the pit itself. That sort of death was an exceedingly ugly sight.

The corpse of that girl didn't seem to be rotten, so it must not have been long since she died. Perhaps it was a local girl that the soldiers captured. What a cruel and vulgar thing to do to a young girl. A-Zhao, Tian Sheng, and the others' faces blanched at the sight and paused in their steps, afraid to go forward. Kemo didn't force them onward either but turned to the pit and let out a long cry.

Why is he yelling? Xie Lian wondered, but his question was soon answered.

From the bottom of the dark pit there came wave after wave of roars in response to the cry. Like predatory beasts, like monsters, like tsunamis, hundreds upon thousands, deafening to the ear. The walls trembled with the noise, making those standing on the eaves lose their balance. Xie Lian could clearly hear rocks and debris falling within.

Only criminals were thrown into the Sinner's Pit. Were those the souls of the criminals answering Kemo?

Kemo roared again, and Xie Lian paid more attention, listening. This time, Kemo wasn't making meaningless noise, and he wasn't cursing either. Instead, he was giving encouragement. Xie Lian was very sure he heard the words "my brothers."

After roaring, Kemo turned to the soldiers watching Xie Lian and the others and shouted another command.

Xie Lian understood. Kemo had said, "Just throw in two and detain the rest."

The others might not have understood what was being said, but the intent of those soldiers was not hard to guess. Everyone looked pale as ghosts. Xie Lian saw that a couple couldn't even stand upright anymore, shaking from fear.

He stepped forward and said in a small voice, "Don't worry. If anything happens, I will go forward first."

Xie Lian thought that if they all must fall, he might as well be the first one to check things out. It couldn't be worse than venomous snakes and beasts or menacing ghosts. He couldn't die from the fall, from getting beaten, from bites, or from poison. As long as it wasn't lava or fire, or some pool of corpse-dissolving water, it shouldn't be too terrible when he jumped down.

Besides, he had Ruoye with him. Even if he might not manage to escape the array, he could still use it to catch the others who fell after him. Kemo had said "detain the rest," meaning that most of the others should be safe temporarily. After all, it wasn't easy hunting for prey in the Gobi Desert, so they should savor them instead of eating everyone in one go.

Xie Lian's mind was clear. But who knew, there was someone next to him who couldn't wait any longer.

Ever since they reached the top of the Sinner's Pit, everyone—besides San Lang, who looked like nothing was out of the ordinary—was trembling, but especially A-Zhao.

He must've thought that if he was about to die, he might as well go down fighting. He clenched his fists and suddenly revolted. He went charging toward Kemo with his head down!

The charge looked like A-Zhao was ready to perish but wanted to take Kemo down with him by knocking them both into the pit. Even though Kemo was the bigger of the two, strong like a steel tower, he got pushed back three steps from A-Zhao's desperation. He roared in outrage and immediately threw the young man in.

Everyone started screaming when they saw A-Zhao plunge into the dark abyss, and Xie Lian called after him too.

"A-Zhao!"

From deep within the bottomless pit there came a roaring cheer and then sounds of the cruel ripping of flesh like fierce ghosts fighting over a meal. It was easy to understand from hearing those noises that the young man A-Zhao would never survive.

Xie Lian was dumbstruck by this development.

He had been suspicious that A-Zhao was a subordinate of the Banyue state preceptor, purposely leading travelers to the ruins. He also suspected that he was the one who was here "fifty or sixty years ago," but the young man ended up being the first killed. How could he possibly survive that jump?

Could he be faking his own death? But now that they were all captured by the Banyue soldiers, if A-Zhao really was the state preceptor's subordinate, he'd have the upper hand and could gloriously reveal his true identity. Certainly he didn't need to do anything extra, like faking his own death before their eyes. It was completely meaningless. But then, why did A-Zhao rush Kemo? Wasn't that an equally meaningless death?

Xie Lian's thoughts were in knots again, while the Banyue soldiers decided on the next human to push down. Kemo sized them up and pointed at Tian Sheng. Another Banyue soldier opened his large palm and reached out to capture the boy.

Tian Sheng screamed in terror, "Aah! Help! Don't take me! I'm..."

Without any more time to think, Xie Lian stepped forward. "Please wait, General."

Hearing him speak, and in the Banyue tongue no less, shock appeared on Kemo's dark-skinned face. "You know how to speak our tongue? Where are you from?"

"I'm from the Central Plains," Xie Lian replied.

He would've been fine with lying that he was also a citizen of Banyue, but that wouldn't have worked. With how rusty his Banyue dialect was, his lie would fall apart after conversing with Kemo for too long. Besides, it was also obvious from his appearance that he was a man of the Central Plains. The people of Banyue detested liars more than anything, so if Xie Lian was found out, the result would be much worse.

"Central Plains?" Kemo questioned. "Descendants of Yong'an?"

"No," Xie Lian replied. "The Kingdom of Yong'an has long since fallen. There's no more Yong'an now."

But to those of Banyue, all those who came from the Central Plains were pretty much the same: relatives of the descendants of Yong'an. The Banyue were annihilated by the army of Yong'an, so the moment he heard where Xie Lian was from, Kemo's dark expression flashed with rage. Many of the Banyue soldiers also started growling, cursing vulgarly at him. Xie Lian listened, but it wasn't much more than "despicable," "liar," and "throw him down." Xie Lian couldn't care less.

Kemo demanded, "Our kingdom disappeared in the Gobi over two hundred years ago. You are not of our people, why do you know our tongue? Who are you?"

Xie Lian couldn't help but steal a glance at the calm youth behind him, mentally hoping that if his lies fell apart later, maybe he could shamelessly ask San Lang to save him. He cleared his throat and was ready to start jabbering nonsense, when another series of enraged growls sounded from below.

It seemed that whatever was down in the pit had finished ripping A-Zhao apart, but they were still hungry for more and cried out to convey their thirst for fresh blood. Kemo waved his hand again, ready to have Tian Sheng thrown over, so Xie Lian spoke up.

"General, please take me first."

Kemo must have never heard anyone request to go first before, and his eyes bulged like balls. He demanded in disbelief, "You go first? Why?!"

Xie Lian couldn't tell him the truth and say it was because he wasn't scared. He thought for a second and came up with a logical answer. "General, they are innocent passing merchants. There's even a child among them."

Kemo sneered. "When your Yong'an army annihilated my kingdom, do you think we did not also have innocent merchants and children?"

The fall of the Kingdom of Banyue was over two hundred years ago, and since then, countless dynasties had come and gone. However, these were the dead for whom time had stopped. Hatred and grudges would not fade with the changing times.

Kemo continued, "You're very suspicious, I will need to question you. You are not going down. Throw in a different one!"

There was no helping it. Xie Lian was ready to jump if all else failed anyway. However, behind him, San Lang stepped forward.

Xie Lian's heart lurched, and he looked back.

With his arms crossed, the youth was nonchalantly looking down into the dark, bottomless Sinner's Pit with intrigued air.

This wasn't a good sign. Xie Lian called out, "San Lang?"

San Lang looked over at the sound of his call and smiled softly. "It's fine."

He took another step forward and was teetering dangerously on the brink. Both Xie Lian's head and heart started pounding.

He called again, "Wait, San Lang, don't move!"

At such a height, at the very edge of the pit, the hem of the youth's red clothes danced in the night breeze. San Lang glanced at him again with a smile.

"Don't be scared."

"You...come back here first. Come back here, and I won't be scared," Xie Lian said.

"Don't worry, I'm just going to leave for a bit. We'll see each other again soon," San Lang said.

"Don't—"

Before he finished, the boy took another step forward, his arms still crossed. Then with a light leap, he instantly vanished into the unfathomable darkness.

The moment he jumped, Ruoye shot out from Xie Lian's wrist and transformed into a streak of white, trying to grab hold of the youth's form. Yet the plunge was too fast, and the white silk band returned dispiritedly without even a sleeve corner.

Xie Lian fell to his knees at the edge of the wall and screamed, "San Lang!!"

Not a single sound.

After San Lang jumped, there was not a single sound!

Next to him, many of the Banyue soldiers started yelling instead, all dumbfounded and bewildered. What was wrong with today? In the past, they'd always had to catch their prey and throw them into the pit. But tonight, their prey took turns fighting to jump down on their own, and when held back, they jumped anyway?

General Kemo yelled for them to calm down. As for Xie Lian, when he saw that Ruoye didn't catch San Lang, he didn't waste any time thinking before pulling back the silk band and taking a leap off the wall himself. But when his body was still in midair, he felt his collar tighten, and he stayed in place.

Xie Lian looked back. It turned out that when General Kemo saw him jump, he reached out and nabbed Xie Lian by the collar, preventing his fall.

If you want to join me, that's fine too! Best if we go down together. Xie Lian urged with his mind, and like a snake, Ruoye shot out once more. It wrapped itself up Kemo's arm and roped his whole body.

Seeing that the white silk band was unpredictably deadly and spirited, Kemo's veins popped, and his muscles instantly swelled as if trying to forcibly rip the fabric tying him. Xie Lian was at an impasse with Kemo when he saw something peculiar out of the corner of his eye.

The corpse hanging on the pole suddenly jerked and raised her head slightly.

The band of Banyue soldiers also saw the corpse move and started yelling, swinging their maces to attack it. But the black-clad girl somehow untied herself and hopped off the pole before speeding toward them.

She was like a black wind blowing through the eaves, fast and wicked. The soldiers couldn't maintain their balance and were quickly swept into the Sinner's Pit one by one, screaming. Outraged, Kemo yelled extreme vulgarities at her, many of which were street slang that Xie Lian couldn't understand well.

But he did understand the first words: "It's that bitch again!"

The swearing ceased in the next moment because Xie Lian suddenly yanked Kemo over to fall into the Sinner's Pit with him.

Into the inescapable Sinner's Pit!

While falling, Kemo roared with such fury that it almost killed Xie Lian's eardrums. He had to recall Ruoye and give Kemo a kick while he was at it to get the general farther away from him, just to protect his ears. Soon after, he urged Ruoye to fly upward to try to grab hold of anything that could prevent him from falling deeper, or to slow him enough that when he hit ground it wouldn't be too painful.

However, the Sinner's Pit was formidably built and had an equally powerful array at work. So not only couldn't Ruoye reach higher, it also couldn't find anything to hold on to. Xie Lian thought he was going to crash and flatten like a pancake as he had many times before, when suddenly in the darkness there was a flash of silver.

The next moment, a pair of hands gently caught him.

Whoever it was caught him perfectly, as if they were waiting there at the bottom just to catch him. With a hand across his back to grasp his shoulders and another under his knees to support his weight, they easily dissolved the devastating force of the fall.

Xie Lian had just fallen from such a high place, and with such a forceful stop, that he was still somewhat dizzy and confused. He subconsciously reached out and held tightly onto the person's shoulders.

"San Lang?" he called out.

It was dark all around and nothing could be seen, including the person holding him. But still, he blurted out that name. The person didn't respond, so Xie Lian felt around their shoulders and chest, hoping to confirm.

"San Lang, is that you?"

Maybe it was because the stench of blood here at the bottom of the pit was heavy and disorienting. Who knew what was going through Xie Lian's head, but his hands continued to roam upward until he reached a strong, hard Adam's apple. He snapped out of it in shock and immediately reprimanded himself, withdrawing his hands.

"It's San Lang, right? Are you all right? Are you hurt?"

It took a moment before he heard the youth respond in a deep, low voice, from somewhere very close to him. "I'm fine."

For some reason, Xie Lian thought that his voice was curiously different from before.

"San Lang, are you really all right? Put me down," Xie Lian said.

"No," San Lang replied.

Xie Lian was taken aback by the response. What was going on? Was there something on the ground?

That pair of arms was still holding him tightly, without any intention of letting him go. Xie Lian raised his hand and was about to gently push himself away. However, just as he laid his hand on

San Lang's chest, he abruptly remembered how after he was caught from the fall, his hands had roamed and felt up that hard protrusion on the youth's neck. He quietly withdrew his hand again.

Xie Lian didn't know what was up. It had been hundreds of years since the last time Xie Lian cared about being "awkward," but now there was a voice in his head telling him that he'd better stay still and proper. To behave himself.

Just then, there was an enraged, sorrowful wail, and a sharp voice from the other end of the pit roared, "What happened to you?!"

Those words were shouted in the Banyue language, and from the voice, it was General Kemo that Xie Lian had dragged down with him. Since he was already dead, the fall wouldn't have killed him. It was a violent crash, however, so he probably blasted out a human-shaped crater in the ground with him embedded. And once he climbed out, he started yelling.

"What's going on? My brothers, *what happened to you*?!"

When he roared into the pit earlier from the top of the wall, there were hundreds and thousands of voices that answered his call, as if the pit was filled to the brim with angry, menacing ghosts. But right then and there, other than Kemo's cries, Xie Lian could only hear dead silence. There wasn't even any sound of breathing, or that of a heartbeat, from San Lang right next to him.

Xie Lian's breath hitched, suddenly realizing what was amiss.

That's right. Even though Xie Lian was pressed against San Lang, he couldn't detect the sounds of his beating heart, or of his breath!

Kemo roared, "Who killed you? Who was it?!"

When A-Zhao first fell, there were horrifying sounds of flesh being ripped apart. But after San Lang jumped, there was no more noise. Who else could have done it?

Kemo himself must have realized this, and he shouted toward them, "Killing my soldiers? You're dead! I'm gonna kill you!"

Although he couldn't see, Xie Lian could still sense danger rapidly approaching, and jerked.

"San Lang, watch out!"

"Don't worry about him," San Lang said, still holding Xie Lian tight. He made a small sidestep and spun around.

In the dark, Xie Lian heard a series of fine clinking sounds: pleasant to the ear, clear and intense, swishing here and there. Kemo pounced to capture them but missed the first time. He whirled around to lunge again, but San Lang easily sidestepped and dodged him again. Xie Lian's arms involuntarily climbed up San Lang's chest once more and held on tight to his shoulders, subconsciously clutching at his clothes.

But the arms carrying him were steady; even with all the spinning and sidestepping, the hold was still strong and secure. Xie Lian could feel something cold and hard on those arms that would poke at him every so often and was a little confused. In the endless blackness, streaks of shimmering silver flashed everywhere, and sounds of sharp metal slicing wounds into flesh were accompanied by Kemo's angry roars.

It was obvious that the Banyue general was heavily wounded by now, but as tough as he was, he refused to admit defeat and once again rushed toward them.

Xie Lian called out, "Ruoye!"

The silk band answered his call and shot out. A loud "snap" sounded above them. Kemo seemed to have been whipped high up in the air, then flipped and dropped to the ground.

This fall made Kemo roar angrily, "You two! Two against one! Despicable!"

You were gonna kill us! Who cares if it's two against one, or despicable or not? Saving my life is more important, and I'll kill you dead first, Xie Lian thought.

San Lang, on the other hand, only humphed a mirthless snort. "Even one-on-one, you won't win. You don't have to fight." The last line was directed to Xie Lian, and in speaking it, his voice was deeper, with none of the previous glib, mocking tone.

"All right," Xie Lian responded but also prompted him, "San Lang, why don't you put me down? I'll be in your way like this."

"You're not in the way. Don't get down," San Lang said.

"Why can't I get down?" Xie Lian asked in spite of himself. This guy couldn't possibly enjoy fighting while carrying someone, could he? He didn't need to go that far to look down on his opponent, did he?

San Lang's answer was only two words: "It's dirty."

"..."

Xie Lian had never imagined that would be the answer—and said with such seriousness too. He thought it was a little funny, but it also made him feel inexplicably strange, his chest growing slightly warm for some reason.

"You can't possibly keep holding me like this!"

"I could," San Lang replied.

Xie Lian was only joking, but San Lang's reply had no trace of humor. Suddenly, Xie Lian didn't know how to respond. While they were talking, Kemo never ceased attacking. Both of San Lang's hands were holding him firmly, but something else was keeping Kemo at bay, whipping him to his defeat.

While slowly backing off, he shouted, "That bitch made you two..."

He hadn't yet finished his words when a large boom sounded.

The massive man fell to the ground, beaten to the point where he could no longer stand.

Having heard this, Xie Lian said, "San Lang, don't kill him! We'll still need to question him if we want to get out of here."

San Lang indeed stopped his attacks and remained still. "I wasn't planning on killing him anyway. Otherwise, he wouldn't have lasted till now."

Dead silence returned anew to the bottom of Sinner's Pit.

After a moment, Xie Lian asked, "San Lang, were you the one who did all this down here?"

Even if nothing was visible in the dark, with such an overpowering stench of blood, such an aura of bloodlust, and Kemo's madness and rage, it was obvious what happened down here. There was another momentary silence before Xie Lian heard San Lang's response.

"Yes," he said.

It was the expected answer. Xie Lian sighed. "How should I say this..."

Xie Lian chewed on his words and organized his thoughts before continuing in an earnest tone. "San Lang, next time you see a pit like this, don't just jump in randomly. I couldn't even stop you. Really, I didn't know what to do."

San Lang didn't seem to expect that kind of response and was stumped for a moment. When he spoke again, he sounded a bit odd.

"You don't want to ask anything else?"

"What else do you want me to ask?" Xie Lian said.

"For example, whether I'm human," San Lang replied.

Xie Lian rubbed his forehead. "Hmm. I don't think that's necessary."

"Is it not?"

"Is it? It's not important whether you're human or not," Xie Lian said.

"Oh?"

Xie Lian crossed his own arms while being held in San Lang's and replied, "Forming a friendship should depend on how well two people hit it off and how well their personalities match, not their identities. If I like you, you could be a beggar and I'd still like you. If I dislike you, you could be the emperor and I'd still dislike you. Shouldn't it be like that? It's simple logic, so whether you're human or not is irrelevant."

San Lang laughed out loud. "Yeah. You're very right."

"Right?" Xie Lian said, laughing along too. But the more he laughed, the more he felt something was off, and it came to him suddenly.

He was still letting San Lang carry him. And the scary thing was, he had gotten used to being in this position without realizing it!

This was gonna be the death of him. Xie Lian cleared his throat quietly and said, "Um, San Lang. We can talk about that later. Why don't you put me down first?"

San Lang seemed to have flashed a smile and said, "Hold on."

He carried Xie Lian and walked on for a bit before gently setting him down. When Xie Lian was back on his own two feet, he could feel hard, flat ground.

"Thanks!"

San Lang made no gesture in response, and after thanking him, Xie Lian gazed upward.

In the deep blue sky there hung a brilliant crescent moon, exceptionally beautiful. It was just that it was framed by a squared-off sky that made him feel like a frog stargazing in a well.

Xie Lian tried urging Ruoye to reach for the top again, but as expected, it only leapt up halfway before it was stopped by something invisible and rebounded, unable to go higher.

"There's an array drawn around the Sinner's Pit," San Lang said.

"I know, I just wanted to give it a try," Xie Lian said. "I can't give up until I've tried, you know. I wonder how the others are doing up there. Will that girl in black also sweep them down?"

He recounted to San Lang how the girl who was hanged on the pole suddenly escaped and swept all the soldiers down into the pit. While talking, he stepped on something on the ground; it appeared to be an arm, and Xie Lian almost tripped. He steadied himself immediately, but San Lang still reached out and helped support him, chiding, "Be careful."

"I told you the ground was dirty," San Lang added casually.

Xie Lian now understood what "dirty" meant and said, "It's fine. I want to ignite a palm torch, see what's happened down here and go from there."

San Lang didn't respond. Just then, from afar, Kemo's cold voice bellowed again, "You two, doing the bidding of that bitch—the thousands of wronged souls of this kingdom will curse you!"

Xie Lian turned toward Kemo and asked using the Banyue tongue, "General Kemo, who is that...person you speak of?"

Kemo replied hatefully, "Why pretend to ask? That evil cultivator!"

"Is it the female cultivator who roams the city streets?"

Kemo spat angrily on the ground, and Xie Lian took that as a yes.

He continued to question, "Weren't you a loyal supporter of the Banyue state preceptor?"

Kemo was provoked by his words and yelled, "I, Kemo, will never again be loyal to her! I can never forgive that bitch!!"

A long string of curses followed. Kemo was hysterical and spoke rapidly, so fast that Xie Lian blanked out at the end, unable to follow. He quietly whispered, "San Lang, San Lang."

And so San Lang translated, "He's cursing. He says that woman betrayed his country, opened the city gates, and let the Yong'an army in to slaughter. She's got the blood of her people on her hands, and of his brothers who she pushed into this pit. He will hang her dead a thousand times. Ten thousand times."

"Wait, hold on!" Xie Lian quickly exclaimed.

How could this be? There were two things that didn't match!

First, "the woman cultivator roaming in the city streets" that Xie Lian spoke of earlier was supposed to be the lady in white. But now, Kemo was calling the Banyue state preceptor "bitch" and saying she pushed his brothers into the Sinner's Pit. Earlier, when the black-clad girl swept the soldiers into the pit, Kemo swore and cursed her with the same profanity. Plus the last bit, "hang her dead a thousand times"—Xie Lian suddenly realized they didn't seem to be talking about the same person.

Secondly, it was the Banyue state preceptor who betrayed the Kingdom of Banyue?!

Xie Lian interrupted Kemo. "General, the Banyue state preceptor you speak of, was it the girl in black hanging on the pole of the Sinner's Pit?"

"Who else could it be if not her?!" Kemo shouted.

"..."

The scrawny, corpse-like girl in black was the real State Preceptor of Banyue! But if that was the case, who were the lady cultivator and her black-clad companion, who strolled through the streets looking to kill them?

The girl in black had immeasurably strange powers and could easily sweep dozens of fierce, powerful Banyue soldiers off the wall. So how was she hanged above the Sinner's Pit?

The story was getting more and more bizarre, more and more convoluted, the more Xie Lian listened.

"General, I want to ask…"

"No more questions!" Kemo interrupted. "You killed my soldiers, what else could you want to know?! I won't answer. Now fight me!"

"I killed them. He didn't do anything," San Lang said. "You can answer his questions and fight me."

Well, that was irrefutable logic. Kemo yelled angrily, "You're both her helpers, there's no difference!"

Xie Lian immediately said, "General Kemo, I think you've misunderstood. The only reason we've come to the Gobi is to get rid of the State Preceptor of Banyue. How can we be the helpers she sent for?"

Hearing that Xie Lian was actually there to destroy the state preceptor, Kemo fell silent. After a while, he asked, "If you weren't helping her, then why did you kill my soldiers?"

"Because you were going to throw us into the pit and we had to defend ourselves?" Xie Lian explained.

"Nonsense!" Kemo argued. "I didn't throw a single one of you! I even caught you! You all jumped down yourselves!!"

"Yes, yes, yes, we all jumped into the pit ourselves," Xie Lian said. "General, we're all trapped at the bottom of this pit—let's just call it a truce for now, all right? Why did that Banyue state preceptor open the city gates to let the enemies in?"

As if Kemo would listen to reason. He said resentfully, "You two are despicable, fighting me two-on-one."

Xie Lian felt a little exasperated. "I really only smacked you once. I didn't do much."

He didn't mind being called despicable or sly or whatever. If the situation called for it, never mind two-on-one, he would bring a hundred to beat one down; who cared about fighting fair? But earlier, San Lang obviously had the upper hand even while carrying him, and he also told Xie Lian not to fight. Kemo seemed to think he could've won if it had been just him and San Lang, though, and Xie Lian felt bad for him. Still, it seemed Kemo was the type who could easily be made to spill the beans. Xie Lian would just have to go slow, not a problem.

San Lang, on the other hand, didn't have the same patience. He said leisurely, "You'd better answer his questions, for the sake of your soldiers."

"You already killed them," Kemo said. "It's pointless using them to threaten me."

"They are dead, but their corpses are still around," San Lang replied.

Kemo grew alarmed, unable to remain sprawled on the ground anymore. "What are you planning?"

"That depends on what *you* do," San Lang said.

Just by his voice, Xie Lian could imagine the way San Lang would narrow his eyes when he spoke. "Do you want their next lives to be fortuitous or for them to be reborn as a pool of blood?"

Kemo stopped but soon understood what San Lang meant. "You...!"

The people of Banyue took death and funerals very seriously. They believed that however the deceased looked at the time of their death, that was how they would be reborn. For instance, if the deceased was missing an arm, they would be reborn disabled. If the corpses in this pit were destroyed, what would their rebirths be like?

General Kemo was a purebred man of Banyue and couldn't help but be afraid. As expected, on the other side of the dark pit, Kemo gritted his teeth soundly in rage, then after a while he relented help-lessly. "Don't touch their bodies! They were good, brave soldiers. It was already a tragedy that they were trapped in this pit for so many years. I don't know if being killed by you is a blessing or not, but I will not have their corpses humiliated further."

He paused, then asked, "Are you really here to kill Banyue?"

Xie Lian replied warmly, "That is no lie. The more we know, the better chance we have of winning. Very little is known about the State Preceptor of Banyue in the outside world, so we have no idea how to fight her even if we want to. But you have worked under her before in the past, so perhaps you can enlighten us?"

Maybe it was because they shared the same enemy—the State Preceptor of Banyue—that a sort of bond was developed. Or per-haps in this inescapable abyss, atop the dead bodies of his soldiers, Kemo became disheartened. Whatever the case, Kemo seemed to have lost the will to attack them.

"You don't know why she opened the gates and let those Yong'an in? It's because she wanted revenge against us! She hates the King-dom of Banyue!"

"What do you mean she hates the Kingdom of Banyue? Isn't the Banyue state preceptor a person of Banyue?" Xie Lian asked.

"Yes, but not entirely," Kemo replied. "She's of mixed blood. And the other half is from Yong'an!"

"Ah..."

As it turned out, the Banyue state preceptor was born of a Banyue woman and a Yong'an man. Living on the border where the people of two nations shared mutual hatred of each other, things were dif-ficult for an interracial couple. After a few years, the Yong'an man had finally had enough and moved away from the border, back to affluent and peaceful Yong'an.

Although it was an amicable divorce, the Banyue woman soon passed away from heartache. They left behind a child, six or seven years of age. Without any guardians, the child grew up missing meals. The couple had received cold shoulders everywhere when they were around, and now their daughter also received contempt wherever she went. The people of Banyue were tall and brawny and saw beauty in strength and liveliness, but this girl was born of mixed blood and appeared small and scrawny among the Banyue children. She grew up bullied and became more and more sullen. The Banyue children wouldn't play with her, though there were some Yong'an children who did pay attention to her.

When this little mixed-blood girl was about ten, a riot broke out at the border and the two armies fought. That battle took many lives, and afterward, the little girl disappeared.

She had neither friends nor family in Banyue, so no one noticed or cared when she vanished. However, the next time she appeared, it was a different story.

In those years, she walked thousands of miles and single-handedly crossed the Gobi Desert to Yong'an. No one knew what kind of encounters she'd had, but when she returned, she had learned black magic and could control the venomous creature most feared by the citizens of Banyue: the scorpion-snakes.

Upon her return, though many were impressed, many were also afraid. That was because the girl's personality never changed, she was still gloomy and unsociable. There were also many who bullied her in the past, so if she were to enter the palace and become a high-ranking official, wouldn't she one day seek revenge against them and cause trouble?

"I'm sure there were many who spoke poorly of her," Xie Lian commented.

Kemo humphed. "It didn't stop at ill talk. They went straight to the palace to advise the king, saying she was an evil messenger sent forth from the scorpion-snake clan, here to bring ruin to the Kingdom of Banyue. But none of them succeeded."

"She got them hanged first?" Xie Lian guessed.

Kemo was even more disgusted. "You, man of Yong'an, why is your mind so full of depraved and vile developments? There was none of that! I protected her!"

Xie Lian was exasperated. "I already said I'm not from Yong'an... All right, whatever."

At the time, Kemo was already a distinguished, fierce warrior. There was an incident where he took his troops out to exterminate the nest of a band of desert bandits and brought the girl who had become the Palace Sorceress along.

That group of bandits was strong, and they had built their lair below the sand. In that battle, both sides suffered casualties, and while Kemo stole the victory, the battle caused the lair below the sand to collapse. Between that and the coming of windstorms, they couldn't stay. Kemo retreated with some soldiers, but the other group, which included the sorceress, didn't manage to escape.

Once they had retreated to a safe point and waited out the sandstorm, Kemo returned anew, hoping to dig out the soldiers to bury them properly. Yet who knew that when he got there, he found that the sorceress had, by her power alone, dug out a sizable hole and managed to drag all the surviving, wounded soldiers in to hide away from the winds.

All the bodies of the dead were dug up too and laid out in neat order. She had done this all by herself. When they got there, the sorceress's body was stained with blood, but still she guarded the entrance to that hole silently, hugging her knees and waiting for them like a little lone wolf.

"After that incident, I thought she was a good woman who acted on principle," Kemo said. "I believed that she never had any intention of harming the Kingdom of Banyue, so I became her guarantor with all my might and fought back against all those malicious voices."

In addition, Kemo himself had been bullied growing up and could understand her strife, so naturally, he paid more attention to her. The more attention he paid, the more he realized just how powerful this girl was. Thus, he endorsed her all the way, helping her reach the position of state preceptor while he became the one later recorded as the most loyal supporter of the State Preceptor of Banyue.

This lasted until another war broke out, and the Kingdom of Yong'an sent armies to annihilate the Kingdom of Banyue.

"With the two armies' conflict at a lengthy standstill, she conducted a grand ceremony to pray to the heavens, saying it was to bring blessings upon us Banyue soldiers," Kemo said.

Thus, the soldiers' will to kill was whipped up, their battle spirits inflamed, and they defended the city gates to the death. There were arrows, giant boulders, boiling oil, swords and blades; the slaughter was endless and massive.

Yet unexpectedly, just as the fighting was at its peak, this state preceptor suddenly opened the city gates.

With the gates opened wide, millions of enemy troops swarmed into the city like mad. As the iron cavalry trampled past, the entire walled city instantly became a ritual of blood!

Kemo, who was fighting hard against their enemies, went mad with rage when he heard that the state preceptor had opened the gates. But no matter how tough he was, one could not win alone against so many.

Kemo gritted his teeth. "I only learned right then that she had long been colluding with the enemy general and agreed to let their troops in at that moment. But even if I was destined to die in battle, before I died, I was going to kill that traitor no matter what!! So I sent a troop of soldiers to charge up the city tower, and we dragged her down and hung her dead over the Sinner's Pit. Hung on that pole!"

After the enemy troops passed, the Kingdom of Banyue became a dead realm. The state preceptor and the general who died in the battle also became trapped within the ruins, both keeping watch over the other in mutual grudge and hate.

"So," Xie Lian said, "General Kemo, you lead the Banyue soldiers under you to search for that shadow, the state preceptor, everywhere, and every time you capture her, you 'hang her dead' over the Sinner's Pit?"

"It won't be enough even if we hang her dead a thousand times, a million times!" Kemo exclaimed. "Because she's been apprehending all my soldiers who turned wrath and throwing them in the Sinner's Pit! She's set up a powerful array around the pit that only she herself can break. Once you fall, you can never climb back up. And those of us who have been betrayed by her, those soldiers who died wrongfully in battle, hold a deep resentment that only devouring the flesh and blood of those from Yong'an can appease and thus allow us to slowly pass from this earth with our hatred released. Otherwise, they can only howl into the long nights without absolution!"

"Is that why you keep capturing people to feed them?" Xie Lian asked.

"What else can we do?" Kemo replied. "Listen to them wail down below and do nothing?"

"The people you threw down, did you catch them yourselves, or...?"

"We can't stray too far from the Kingdom of Banyue. But thankfully, her snakes like to haunt the area and often crawl out of the ruins to bite people. And caravans who suffer bites come into the city to look for the shanyue fern."

"That mud face in the palace, was it you who buried him?"

"That's right. The man buried in the earth was originally planning on stealing the riches of the palace. But all the treasures our kingdom had were cleared out by those Yong'an men two hundred years ago."

"Why did you bury him instead of throwing him down here directly?" Xie Lian asked.

"There's gotta be fertilizer to grow the ferns, you know," Kemo replied. "Otherwise we wouldn't be able to hold the scorpion-snakes back. We don't want to run into those creatures either."

That's not right, Xie Lian thought.

If Kemo and his party consciously knew to grow and fertilize shanyue ferns, going as far as using live humans as fertilizer, then it was clear that even though they were no longer alive, their fear of those scorpion-snakes was still strong.

In that case, that fear must've been even greater while they were alive. If that Banyue state preceptor could control a murder weapon as great as those scorpion-snakes, then how was she so easily dragged down the city tower by a bunch of soldiers and hanged to death?

According to Kemo, in the past two hundred or so years, he had captured the state preceptor over and over and hanged her dead repeatedly. Either way, Xie Lian felt that if it were him, and he had such a killing weapon in his hands, he would never allow the enemy the chance to come near him.

And regarding the scorpion-snakes that would slither out of the ruins to bite people—was that an accident? Not likely. It was more likely that they were purposely trying to lure people into the pass.

Then was the state preceptor doing so intentionally? Wouldn't that only be helping Kemo catch live humans to feed his soldiers? "Mutual hatred" wouldn't make sense.

Were they pretending to be enemies, then? What was the point in that?

And in all of this mess, there was also the mysterious lady in white and her companion. Xie Lian decided to ask more questions. "General Kemo, when we first entered the city, we saw two ladies, one in white, and the other in black. Do you know who they are?"

Before there was a response, San Lang whispered, "Shhh."

Xie Lian didn't know what was going on, but he closed his mouth immediately. A strange hunch made him look up.

It was the same framed dark blue sky with a crescent moon. But next to the moon he saw a person: a small, black-clad silhouette was peering over the edge and looking down.

After watching them for a bit, the little form suddenly grew bigger—it had jumped down.

As the figure fell, Xie Lian could see clearly that it was the state preceptor who had been hanging from the pole earlier!

"Kemo, what's going on?" the state preceptor asked in the Banyue tongue as she landed.

The moment she spoke, Xie Lian thought her voice was very different from what he imagined. Although it certainly sounded somber, her voice was tiny. It was like the muttering of a sulky child, not cool or powerful at all. If not for his good hearing, Xie Lian might not have even heard her properly.

"What's going on?! They're all dead!" Kemo shouted.

"How did they die?" the state preceptor asked.

"Isn't it because you pushed them all down and trapped them in this godforsaken place?!"

"Who's here? There's another person," the state preceptor said.

There actually should've been two "people" at the bottom of the pit besides Kemo. But San Lang had neither breath nor heartbeat, so the state preceptor didn't detect his presence. It was also complete chaos on top of the walls earlier, and no one had kept track of who fell and who ran away, so she thought there was only Xie Lian.

"They're the ones who killed all my soldiers. Are you happy now? They're finally all dead!"

The state preceptor was silent. Suddenly a tiny burst of light flared, illuminating a small, black-clad girl conjuring a palm torch.

The girl surprisingly appeared to be only fifteen or sixteen. She was dressed in plain black cultivator robes, and her eyes were gloomily black as well. She was not unbeautiful, just unhappy. Her forehead and cheeks were covered with bruises, clear and distinct under the light.

If it hadn't been confirmed earlier, no one would believe that the State Preceptor of Banyue could be such a pale young girl.

The flames in her hand illuminated herself and her surroundings. At her feet were the armored corpses of Banyue soldiers.

Xie Lian couldn't help but sneak a glance beside him.

The palm torch in the state preceptor's hand was very small and did not light up the entire pit, so they were still immersed in darkness. But borrowing the small light, Xie Lian could still see the red-robed figure beside him.

Perhaps it was his imagination, but although San Lang had already been taller than him before, he now appeared even taller somehow. Xie Lian's gaze slowly moved upward and came to the youth's throat. He stopped for a moment, then continued upward, his eyes stopping at an elegantly shaped chin.

The features of San Lang's upper face were still hidden in the shadows, but Xie Lian thought the bottom half was subtly different from before. No less handsome, but the lines were much more defined. Feeling he was being watched, San Lang tilted his head, and his lips curled upward slightly.

Perhaps he wanted so much to get a better look, to get nearer, that without realizing it, Xie Lian took a step closer to him.

Just then, Kemo wailed in the distance, seemingly in shock after seeing the bloody tragedy before him. Xie Lian abruptly snapped out of it and turned to look, and saw Kemo clutching his own head. Despite the general's cries, the state preceptor's expression remained wooden, and she only nodded.

"Good."

In the midst of mourning, hearing those words made Kemo rage once more. "Good?! What's good?! What do you mean?!"

"'Good' means we're finally free," the state preceptor said.

She turned to Xie Lian, who was still shrouded in the dark. "Are you the one who killed them?"

"It was an accident," Xie Lian replied.

"You're lying through your teeth!" Kemo exclaimed.

Xie Lian responded bold-facedly, "Life is full of accidents!"

The state preceptor gave him a look, but her expression was unreadable. "Who are you?"

Her words were spoken in perfect Han dialect,[8] and weren't said in an interrogative tone.

"I'm a heavenly official. This one here is...my friend," Xie Lian replied.

Kemo couldn't understand their words but could tell they weren't fighting, and demanded, "What are you two saying?"

---

8   *Han was the dialect of Yong'an and the Central Plains, and is what most characters in the book speak.*

The state preceptor looked Xie Lian over and eyed San Lang for a moment before quickly looking away. "We've never had heavenly officials visit before. I thought you all already abandoned this place."

Xie Lian had expected that they would have to fight the State Preceptor of Banyue but was surprised to find her this despondent and devoid of any will to fight.

She continued, "Do you two want to leave?"

"Of course we do, but there's an array set in this pit, so we can't," Xie Lian said.

Hearing this, the state preceptor walked to one of the walls, raised her hand, and drew something. She then turned around and said, "There. I released the array. You two can leave now."

"..."

This was way too easy! Xie Lian really didn't know what to say.

Just then, a voice called from above, "Hey! Is anyone down there?! If not, I'm leaving!"

It was Fu Yao's voice.

Xie Lian heard San Lang *tsk* next to him and immediately looked up. There was a shadow of a man looking down into the pit.

Xie Lian shouted, "Fu Yao! There are people down here! I'm down here!"

He waved, and Fu Yao shouted back from above, "You're actually down there? What's at the bottom besides you?"

"Um...a lot of things. Why don't you come down and see for yourself?" Xie Lian said.

Fu Yao probably thought the same, and with a loud rumble, he hurled a large ball of fire into the pit.

In an instant, the entire Sinner's Pit was lit up, bright like day, and Xie Lian finally saw clearly the kind of place he'd been standing in.

All around him were mountains of bloody corpses piled high, innumerable bodies of Banyue soldiers stacked on top of each other, faces and limbs blackened, dark blood smearing their bright armor. The corner where Xie Lian stood was the only spot in the entire Sinner's Pit that did not have a dead body.

This was all done in a flash, in the dark, by San Lang after he jumped in.

Xie Lian turned to gaze at the youth next to him again.

Before, in the dark, he vaguely saw that San Lang looked taller and subtly different in certain features. But now, under the bright firelight, the one standing next to him was the same handsome youth he knew. When he saw Xie Lian looking over, he smiled.

Xie Lian looked down to check his wrists and boots, and both were also the same as before, having nothing that would cause any jingling sound.

Just then, Xie Lian heard a muffled noise. It was the sound of Fu Yao jumping down.

"Weren't you looking after the merchants?" Xie Lian asked.

Having just entered the pit, Fu Yao wasn't yet used to the stench of blood and fanned his hand to make the air flow. He replied indifferently, "We waited for over six hours and there was still no sign of you, so we figured something had happened. I drew a circle for them to wait in and came to check things out myself."

Xie Lian frowned. "The circle won't last long. With you gone, what if they leave the circle thinking you left them behind?"

Fu Yao shrugged. "Eight horses can't pull back a man who really wants to seek death. I can't stop stubborn people, so I won't try. What's with those two over there? Who's who?"

Fu Yao was on high alert, his guard raised against the two unknowns. But he soon discovered in astonishment that Kemo was already heavily wounded on the ground, barely able to stand, and the State Preceptor of Banyue was quiet with her head hung low.

"That one is the general of Banyue, and the other one is the State Preceptor of Banyue. Right now they're..."

Kemo suddenly leapt up before Xie Lian could finish. He had been lying on the ground gathering his strength and was finally able to jump up with a shout, aiming his fists at the State Preceptor of Banyue. A large, beefy warrior attacking a little girl—normally, Xie Lian would never allow that sort of thing to happen before him. But Kemo had every reason to hate the state preceptor, and she could defend herself perfectly well. However, she didn't, and allowed herself to be thrown around like a broken ragdoll.

Kemo shouted at the state preceptor, "Where are your scorpion-snakes? Come on! Let them bite me to death too! Give me that release!"

The state preceptor gloomily replied, "Kemo, my snakes don't listen to me anymore."

"Then why don't they kill you?!" he scoffed.

"...I'm sorry, Kemo," the state preceptor apologized softly.

"Do you really hate us that much?!"

The state preceptor shook her head, and Kemo became angrier. "You're going to be the death of me! If you don't hate us, why did you betray us?! You shameless spy, disgusting mole, traitor!!"

Fu Yao watched him strike harder and harder. The blows were all single-sided, and he couldn't help but frown. "What are they saying? Shouldn't we stop them?"

Xie Lian couldn't watch anymore either and rushed forward to stop Kemo. "General! General! Why don't you tell us who that Yong'an thug really is, and we'll—"

Suddenly, the state preceptor seized his wrist.

The grip was hard and came unexpectedly, and Xie Lian's heart dropped, thinking she was going to attack him. But when he looked back down at her, the state preceptor was on all fours on the ground. There was a small bruise at the corner of her mouth, and her head was raised, staring at him intently. She didn't say a single word, but her dark eyes were intense with the fire of life.

This demeanor overlapped with an image from a far-gone memory. After a pause, Xie Lian blurted, "It's you?"

The state preceptor also called. "General Hua?"

This back-and-forth stunned everyone in the pit.

Fu Yao rushed forward, knocked Kemo out with a punch, and demanded, "You two know each other?"

Xie Lian didn't have the time to answer him, however. He knelt down, gripped the shoulders of the state preceptor, and examined her face.

They'd been standing too far apart before, and he couldn't see clearly. Plus, it had been over two hundred years; this girl had matured in that time, and for many reasons, he didn't recognize her at first. But now that he looked again properly, it was the same face from his memories.

Xie Lian couldn't speak for the longest time, and it was a good moment before he sighed. "Banyue?"

The state preceptor quickly clutched at his sleeves, surprisingly a little excited. "It's me! General Hua, do you still remember me?"

"Of course I remember you. But..." Xie Lian gazed at her for a moment and sighed. "But what have you done to yourself?"

When she heard that, the state preceptor's eyes suddenly filled with pain.

"I'm sorry, Captain... I messed up," she muttered.

In that exchange, there was "General" this, "Captain" that, making it glaringly obvious to the bystanders. Fu Yao was dumbstruck.

"Captain? General? YOU? How did this happen? Then the Tomb of the General is...?"

Xie Lian nodded. "My tomb."

"Didn't you say you only came to collect scraps two hundred years ago?!" Fu Yao questioned.

"This...is a long story. That was originally the plan," Xie Lian answered.

Around two hundred years ago, due to certain reasons, Xie Lian couldn't muck around in the east anymore and decided to stay out of sight for a while. He had planned to cross the Qing Ridge and head to the south to start a brand-new life of scraps. Thus, he took up his compass and walked southward.

But the more he walked, the more he thought woefully, why was the scenery all wrong? There should have been an abundance of trees and greenery, cities and life, so how come his path was becoming more desolate?

However, Xie Lian pushed his suspicions aside and stubbornly continued. He walked and walked and came upon the Gobi Desert. It took a gust of wind blowing a fistful of sand into his face for Xie Lian to finally realize that his compass had long been broken.

The direction it guided him that entire journey was wrong!

Since there wasn't anything he could do about the whole thing, he thought that he might as well take this chance to visit the desert scenery, so he continued onward. The only difference was that he changed course slightly at the last minute for a destination to the northwest, and finally arrived at the border, where he temporarily settled near the Kingdom of Banyue.

"At first, I was just collecting junk or something in the area," Xie Lian said. "But the border was troubled, and with so many skirmishes, there were often runaway soldiers, so the army would draft anyone to make up the numbers."

"So you were forced into the army?" San Lang asked.

"Yeah," Xie Lian replied. "But doing anything was more or less the same, so it didn't matter to me. And then, after chasing away some bandits a couple of times, I somehow got promoted to Captain. The ones who gave me face would call me General too."

"Why did she call you General Hua?" Fu Yao questioned. "Your surname isn't Hua."

Xie Lian waved his hand and said dismissively, "Don't worry about it. I randomly made up a fake name at the time. I think it was 'Hua Xie.'"

Hearing the name, San Lang's face changed slightly, his lips faintly twitching. Xie Lian didn't notice and continued. "With a battle-torn border came many orphans. When I was free, I'd play with them sometimes. One of them...was named Banyue."

When there were bandits, Xie Lian was surely the bravest soldier, and no one dared block his way, nor even dared to stand beside him. But when there weren't, it was as if anyone could order him around.

One day he went and sat by a wall to start a campfire, using his own helmet to cook. As he cooked, the smell of it drifted out, and a few enraged soldiers came and kicked over whatever it was he was cooking. Xie Lian picked up his helmet with a broken heart, but when he looked back, he saw a small, disheveled, grimy child crouched behind him. She was picking up the stuff knocked to the ground with her hands and stuffing it into her mouth without caring whether it was too hot.

He was shocked. "Don't! Wait, little kid, you!"

As expected, that little kid scarfed down a few lumps of the stuff she had picked off the ground and then dry-heaved harshly, crying loudly. Xie Lian was so shaken that he picked her up upside down and ran laps until all the stuff she ate came back out. After that was done, he crouched down and wiped his sweat.

"Are you all right, little one...? I'm so sorry. But don't ever tell your parents about this, and next time, don't pick up any more random stuff off the ground to eat... Wait, what are you doing now?!"

That child's face was covered in tears, but she still went to pick food off the ground again, wanting to eat. It was only after Xie Lian grabbed her that he realized that the skin of this child's stomach was practically pressed to the back of her bones.

When people were starved to that point, anything could be eaten. Even if it was disgusting to the point of tears, she would still eat it.

Xie Lian had no choice and went to get her the last of his rations. After that incident, he would often see the child stalking him in the shadows nearby.

In his memories, the little girl Banyue was always gloomy. Her body and face were covered in bruises, and when she looked at him, she would clutch the hem of his clothes and stare at him just so from below. Because she was singled out by the children of the Banyue kingdom, besides Xie Lian, only a particular Yong'an boy living at the border would sometimes pay attention to her. She'd spend her days tagging along behind the two of them.

She rarely spoke, but she was fluent in the Han dialect, so Xie Lian didn't know where she came from. But she was a random wandering child, so he randomly took her in. When he was free, sometimes he'd teach her songs, sometimes wrestle, sometimes show off his busker move "Shattering Boulders on One's Chest," and other stuff, and they got along quite well.

Xie Lian shook his head. "I had thought the 'Banyue' in the state preceptor's title was the country. I didn't realize it was actually the name of the state preceptor."

"And then?" Fu Yao asked.

"And then...it's pretty much the same as what the memorial wrote," Xie Lian said.

After some silence, San Lang spoke up. "The memorial said you died."

As for that memorial, Xie Lian was extremely bummed out.

Weren't memorials usually full of praise and exaggerated good deeds to glorify the deceased? All those mentions of his demotions aside, why did it have to so seriously record the embarrassing way he died?!

While they were hiding away from the sandstorm and he read to this part, he could barely look at it straight on. If it wasn't for San Lang, who also understood Banyue script and was watching him, he would've pretended that section never existed. Having something like that written down, even *he* wanted to laugh at it, never mind other people. And he didn't even have the nerve to ask those seeking shelter in his memorial not to laugh as they commentated and joked about his epitaph. That made him feel really bummed.

Xie Lian's forehead was becoming red from all the rubbing. "Oh, that. Um. Of course I didn't die. I faked it."

Fu Yao had a face full of disbelief. Xie Lian explained himself. "I got trampled too hard and couldn't get up, so there wasn't any option besides faking my death."

Truthfully, Xie Lian couldn't quite remember exactly how he "died," nor why that battle broke out in the first place, only that it was over something petty. He really hadn't wanted to fight, and victory or defeat were meaningless. But by then his rank could go no lower, and no one would listen to him. In the midst of battle, everyone saw red, so when he rushed out and both sides saw it was him, for some reason all the blades and swords went after him and cut him down.

Fu Yao questioned, "You must have been standing in the middle being an eyesore, and that raised the ire of both sides, right? Otherwise, why would people cut you down on sight? Besides, I'm sure you knew there were many who hated you, so why didn't you avoid them? Why did you have to charge in? I'm sure you could've avoided the whole thing if you'd wanted to."

"I really don't remember, all right?!" Xie Lian said.

Even if nothing could kill him, he still couldn't endure that kind of butchering, so with the thought *"this can't go on!"* Xie Lian resolutely dropped to the ground to fake his death. But even in "death" he was trampled to the point of passing out. It was water choking him that roused him, because corpses were usually thrown into the rivers after battles. Xie Lian went with the river's flow and floated back to the Kingdom of Yong'an like a heap of junk. Afterward, he took several years to recover from his wounds, then picked up an unbroken compass to start off anew and finally made it to his original destination in the south. He then stopped paying attention to what went on in the Kingdom of Banyue.

"I'm sorry," Banyue muttered again.

Fu Yao furrowed his brow. "Why does she keep apologizing to you?"

San Lang suddenly spoke up, "Kemo stated that the State Preceptor of Banyue left for the Central Plains after a clash between the two armies. Were you involved in that?"

With that reminder, and recalling what was written on the memorial, some things were coming back to Xie Lian, though only in bits and pieces. "Ah, maybe..."

"It was to save me," Banyue said.

Everyone turned to look at her, and she said softly, "General Hua got flattened because he entered the fray to save me."

"..."

Xie Lian instantly remembered the agony of being trampled by thousands, and he hugged his body despite himself, but when he saw two others watching him with unreadable expressions, he pulled himself back in a hurry.

He said, "Not flat. Not too flat."

Who knew why Fu Yao was looking so smug? He said passive-aggressively, "Well, aren't you a saint."

Xie Lian waved dismissively. "Nothing of the sort. I don't remember the specifics anymore. But there were two children playing at the time, and I was just going to pick them up and run away immediately, but we didn't manage to retreat fast enough and got caught between the two armies..."

"If that's the case," Fu Yao demanded. "How can you not remember something like that?"

Xie Lian replied, "Do you not know how many hundreds of years old I am? So much can happen in just a decade, there's no way to remember everything in detail. Besides, some things are best forgotten. Rather than remembering how I was butchered and trampled hundreds of years ago, I'd prefer to remember that I ate a delicious meat bun yesterday, no?"

"I'm sorry," Banyue said.

Xie Lian sighed. "Oh, Banyue. Saving you was my own choice. You're not at fault. If you're going to apologize, perhaps it should be to others."

Banyue was taken aback and hung her head in silence.

Xie Lian continued, "But...maybe it's because my impression of you is from two hundred years ago, but I don't think you're the kind of child who'd seek revenge and betray others... Will you tell me what happened exactly? Why did you open the city gates?"

Banyue contemplated, shook her head, and remained silent.

"Then why did you let the snakes out to bite people?" Xie Lian asked.

This time, Banyue answered, "I didn't release the snakes."

Xie Lian was taken aback. "What?"

"I didn't release the snakes," Banyue repeated. "They ran off on their own. I don't know why, but they don't listen to me anymore."

Hearing this, Fu Yao grew impatient. Banyue pleaded, "General Hua, I'm not lying."

Before Xie Lian responded, Fu Yao cut in rudely. "Anyone would say that after being captured. Even if you say it wasn't intentional, I've heard all that before. All those people crossing the pass were clearly injured by your snakes. Show me your hands; you're under arrest."

Banyue shut up and extended both arms. Fu Yao immediately took out an Immortal-Binding Rope and apprehended both Banyue and Kemo, then he said, "All right. We've accomplished our goal for this trip. It's all over now."

Just then, San Lang spoke up. "She had no reason to lie."

Xie Lian also felt there was a need for further interrogation. He turned to Banyue. "Can you not control any of your snakes?"

Banyue answered, "I can control them, and they'll obey most of the time. But there are times when they won't. I don't know why."

After some thought, Xie Lian said, "Why don't you call them out and show us?"

Banyue was kneeling before him. Now, she finally rose to her feet and nodded. Soon, a wine-red scorpion-snake slithered out from underneath a corpse, raised its head, and curled itself on a pile of dead bodies. It soundlessly flicked its tongue at the group.

Xie Lian was about to take a closer look at the snake but saw Banyue widen her eyes, face strange. Xie Lian's heart dropped, and he thought, *Oh no.*

As that thought crossed his mind, the snake stopped flicking its tongue, opened its mouth, and pounced at him in attack.

It was a sudden lunge, but Xie Lian was ready. He was about to grab for it when *boom*, something exploded. When he opened his eyes again to see, the snake was already a splatter of guts on the ground, having been thoroughly blown apart. It was a calculated blast too, since none of the venom spilled.

Xie Lian immediately remembered another time when a snake died like that before they entered the Banyue ruins, but there was no need to say who did it at this point. He hadn't even had the chance to look at San Lang before a red sleeve flashed before him, barring and separating him from Banyue.

On the other side, Fu Yao said coldly, "I knew she was lying. Did you think that snake would manage to bite him under these circumstances? Foolish."

Banyue's face was already pale when she saw that snake, and when she heard him, her head shot up. "I didn't do it. I said there are some snakes that don't obey me, and that one was one of them just now."

Fu Yao didn't believe a single word. "Who knows whether it was disobeying or obeying you?"

"That one wasn't even called forth by me," Banyue said glumly.

Xie Lian was about to speak when another two wine-red scorpion-snakes poked out from under a different corpse, flicking their tongues and watching them intently. Then a third, a fourth, a fifth...from the mountains of dead bodies and every corner of the pit, there came innumerable scorpion-snakes!

Everyone stared at Banyue, who was kneeling on top of a pile of corpses, and Fu Yao started spinning a ball of spiritual energy in his palm and shouted at her.

"Make them go away! They can't all disobey!"

Banyue scrunched up her brows, looking as if she was trying to drive them out. Yet more and more scorpion-snakes appeared, curling and crawling, slithering ever closer. Bites from one or two snakes might not kill them, but from hundreds or thousands was harder to say. Even if they didn't die, it wouldn't be pretty. Xie Lian raised his wrist, about to call forth Ruoye, but saw that when the snakes slithered to a certain distance, they would stop and hesitate, forming a weird circle.

It dawned on Xie Lian, and he glanced at San Lang next to him. He was watching the snakes with condescension and immense contempt. The scorpion-snakes seemed to be able to read his eyes and didn't dare approach. They backed off bit by bit, lowering their heads as they did so, pressing their savage heads against the ground submissively like servants.

But there seemed to be another power controlling them, not allowing them to abandon their attacks and leave completely. Thus, many of the snakes turned around and slithered toward Fu Yao. Fu Yao swung his hand and a blast of flames burst from his sleeve, killing a circle of snakes and forcing back another.

That wouldn't last long, however. Xie Lian said, "Let's get out of here first!"

Whoosh! Ruoye shot out from Xie Lian's arm and flew upward. But a moment later, another whoosh and it was back on Xie Lian's arm. Xie Lian was slightly taken aback and raised his wrist, scolding the silk band now rewrapped around it.

"What are you doing back here? The array was released, there's nothing stopping you anymore, hurry and go!"

But Ruoye remained wrapped around his arm, trembling, as if it had bumped into something terrifying at the top. Xie Lian was about to coax it some more when suddenly, a long rope of something fell. *Plop*, it dropped on Fu Yao's shoulder. Fu Yao went to grab it, and his face changed the moment he brought it before his eyes. It was another scorpion-snake that fell from the sky!

This caught Fu Yao off guard, and after getting bitten, he hurled the snake toward Banyue. Even with her hands tied, she still reflexively tried to catch the snake, and after having caught it, the dark red snake curled itself up around her arm without attacking. Just then, another *plop* and a second scorpion-snake landed on the ground!

Xie Lian could guess why Ruoye refused to go up now. Borrowing the faint light of the moon, Xie Lian raised his head and only just barely saw this sight: hundreds of little wine-red dots were falling rapidly into the Sinner's Pit.

A snake deluge!

The red dots were coming closer. Xie Lian yelled, "Fu Yao! Fire! Shoot a stream of fire upward and get rid of them while they're still in the air!"

Fu Yao bit his palm to break the skin, swung his hand, and a series of blood drops shot out; an instant later they transformed into a screen of fire that jetted up through the pit. Those sweeping flames rose over thirty meters and hung in midair, disintegrating all scorpion-snakes that touched them, burning them to ash, dissolving the snake deluge.

Temporarily safe, Xie Lian let out a breath of relief. "That was good, Fu Yao! Thank goodness for you."

A spell like that evidently consumed an immense amount of spiritual power, and after one round, Fu Yao's face was pale. He turned around and ignited a ring of fire, dispelling the snakes on the ground, and shouted at Banyue, "And you say those snakes don't obey you? If you weren't controlling them, why wouldn't they attack you?"

San Lang laughed. "Maybe it's because of your bad luck? They didn't attack us either."

Fu Yao turned to look at him, his eyes sharp and narrowed. Xie Lian could sense trouble. He'd somewhat established a theory about the current situation but hadn't yet had time to sort through his thoughts, and Xie Lian didn't want to see the two of them start fighting now.

"Let's figure out what's going on with those snakes first," Xie Lian said. "Let's charge out."

Fu Yao sneered. "'What's going on'? Either the State Preceptor of Banyue is lying, or the one next to you is causing trouble."

Xie Lian glanced at Banyue, then at San Lang, and said, "I don't think it's either of them."

His tone was gentle but firm. It was the conclusion he came to after much thought. However, Fu Yao must have thought he was shielding them intentionally, and the face illuminated by the flames was unkind. Xie Lian couldn't tell if he was angry or laughing.

"Your Royal Highness," Fu Yao said. "Don't play pretend when you know the truth. Do you still remember your place? I'm sure you're already very aware of who exactly that cad next to you is. I refuse to believe you haven't realized it!"

XIE LIAN unconsciously stepped forward to stand in front of San Lang.

"I know better than anyone where my place is," Xie Lian replied.

"Then how dare you still stand next to him?!" Fu Yao shouted.

"Because...if I stand next to him, the snakes won't come," Xie Lian answered earnestly.

"..."

Hearing the response, San Lang *pfft*-ed and laughed out loud. Fu Yao grew grimmer.

"You—"

Grimmer and grimmer, his face suddenly turned completely black. It wasn't just his face but Xie Lian's entire view that dimmed into darkness.

The screen of flames and the ring of fire created by Fu Yao were suddenly completely extinguished!

Within the darkness, Xie Lian heard San Lang snicker and say "Useless trash!" Then he felt San Lang grip his shoulders to pull him close. Soon after, Xie Lian heard a sudden downpour of endless battering above them, like a thunderstorm hitting an umbrella.

Needless to say, now that the defense barrier was gone, the snake deluge came pouring down like mad. The open umbrella was blocking the downpour, and Xie Lian could smell the thick, foul stench of blood. He was about to fight, but San Lang stopped him.

"Don't move. No lowlifes will dare approach."

His tone was confident; the first sentence was soft and gentle, the second arrogant. Xie Lian wasn't worried, but hearing Fu Yao's angry roars across the pit, sounding like he was getting bombarded by snakes, he called out, "San Lang!"

"No," San Lang instantly replied.

Xie Lian didn't know whether to laugh or cry. "How did you know what I was going to say?"

"Don't worry so much, he can't die," San Lang said.

Just then, another roar came from ahead of them in the pit. "Banyue! If you want me to die, have them bite and kill me in one go! What the hell is this?!"

"It's not me!" Banyue cried.

It seemed that Kemo had awoken after the punch, discovered himself submerged in countless snakes, and believed it to be Banyue's doing.

"Fu Yao, can you light another fire? Do it again!" Xie Lian shouted.

Fu Yao gritted his teeth. "That cad next to you is restricting my powers, I can't light anything!"

Xie Lian felt dread, and San Lang said, "It's not me."

"I know it's not you," Xie Lian said. "But that's precisely what's wrong. Both Banyue and Kemo are bound by the Immortal-Binding Rope, so they can't use their powers. My powers are depleted, and you're not restricting anyone. Meaning there's a sixth person in this pit!"

"Have you lost your mind?" Fu Yao demanded. "What sixth person? No one else came down!"

"Who's there?" Banyue suddenly said.

"Banyue, what's happening? Is someone over there?" Xie Lian asked.

"Someone—" Banyue's voice cut off; whether her mouth was sealed shut or she lost consciousness they didn't know.

Xie Lian called out again, "Banyue?!"

Fu Yao was still fighting snakes, and brief flashes of white light blasted in waves in the darkness. "Be careful! She might be tricking you!"

"Not necessarily," Xie Lian shouted. "I'm going to save her first!"

Xie Lian was about to run into the snake deluge when he heard San Lang's voice next to his ear. "All right."

Xie Lian felt the hand gripping his shoulders tighten, and in a flash, they were dashing forward. Xie Lian realized in awe that the youth was advancing and attacking at the same time, but with an umbrella in one hand and him in the other. In the darkness, silver shimmers flashed about once more, clanking and clinking, when suddenly, the sharp sound of two swords clashing rang in everyone's ears.

"Oh?" San Lang said. "There really is a sixth person. Interesting."

Xie Lian had no idea how San Lang was controlling the weapon, or what kind of weapon it was. But whatever it was, it most certainly did crash head-to-head into another!

His opponent remained silent, and Xie Lian could only hear metal scraping metal as the fight intensified. From time to time there would be sparks flashing in the dark, but each flash was so short-lived it was hard to see the other's face.

Xie Lian listened to the fight while calling out, "Banyue, are you still conscious? Can you respond?"

No one responded. Fu Yao exclaimed, "Maybe the one fighting now is her!"

"No. That is definitely not Banyue!" Xie Lian said.

While both times were in the dark, when San Lang fought Kemo, he was light-footed and messing about, toying with the man. This fight, however, Xie Lian could tell San Lang was taking more seriously. The opponent was extremely skilled in martial arts and weaponry. Banyue was small and weak; from the look of her limbs alone, it was obvious that strength and weaponry were not her forte, so it was impossible for her to be the one fighting San Lang. But who was this sixth person? When did they appear?!

Fu Yao griped, "Someone who would betray her own country is no different from Xuan Ji. Why on earth do you still believe in her?"

"Fu Yao, can you not be so irritated all of a sudden?" Xie Lian said. "You...wait. What did you just say?"

Fu Yao struck out another palm and blew away a bunch of snakes. "I said, why on earth would you believe in her, like you believe in that cad next to you?!"

"No, not that—you said Xuan Ji. You mentioned Xuan Ji's name, didn't you?" Xie Lian said.

"Yeah, so what?! She's completely irrelevant!"

Xie Lian, however, held his breath. A moment later, he called out, "Stop fighting, there's no more need to hide. I know who you are!"

The sound of blades clashing never halted; the other was unmoved. But Xie Lian wasn't worried.

"Did you think I was bluffing when I said I already know who you are? General Pei Junior?"

"Who are you talking to?" Fu Yao was dumbstruck. "General Pei Junior? Don't be crazy. Who do you think he is? If he descended, everyone would know!"

"You're very right," Xie Lian said. "But what if it wasn't his true self that descended?"

In the darkness, the fighting weapons faltered for a split second, then picked up anew.

Xie Lian continued, "It took me too long to figure this out. I should've known from the beginning.

"I knew that for close to two hundred years there was something causing havoc, but none of the heavenly officials cared, and no one dared to speak of it. So there had to be someone no one wanted to offend keeping this scandal under wraps. Since I wasn't familiar with many of the officials, I didn't dare boldly pin this on anyone, and never tried to boldly deduce which heavenly official it could be."

It was Fu Yao's mention of Xuan Ji that reminded him.

It wasn't hard to connect the subject of Xuan Ji to the two Generals Pei, and the north was their territory. Fu Yao once said in passing that prior to his ascension, General Pei Junior slaughtered a city.

Which city?

It could very well be the Kingdom of Banyue!

The Upper Court wouldn't bat an eyelash at something like this; everyone needed to spill some blood if they wanted to do great things. But slaughtering a city wasn't anything glorious, after all. If the story spread too far, it would affect the number of new believers, so of course there would be some cover-ups after ascension. Thus, even if everyone knew something of the sort happened, they probably didn't know the details, or didn't care to know. Besides, unless someone possessed some sort of deep grudge, who would have had the time or motivation to dig up his past and offend the support behind his back?

Xie Lian spoke slowly, "That mud face said there was someone among us who visited this city fifty or sixty years ago. At first, I thought he was lying to deceive us into getting closer, but his words may very well have been true.

"Before, in that group of people, the one I was the most suspicious of was you. The caravan followed you, and you could take them anywhere. I had never seen a single scorpion-snake in the years I lived near Banyue, and now, while randomly seeking shelter from the sandstorm, they just happen to show up?

"I asked you to come search for the shanyue fern with us, but just before we left, you gave the directions to the ruins to the others so they could follow in our footsteps if they could no longer sit still. Earlier, on top of the walls, I already said that if anything were to happen, I would go forward first. You, who were always calm, suddenly jumped and died a meaningless death."

Xie Lian continued after a pause, "Your actions were strange and illogical at every turn. That it took me until now to realize who you are really is too late. Isn't that right, General Pei Junior? Or should I use your current name, A-Zhao?!"

Abruptly, everything became still.

It was a moment before a frigid voice spoke. "Did you not suspect that the mud face might have been talking about the red-clothed boy next to you?"

Just as he spoke, a stream of flames suddenly lit up across the Sinner's Pit.

Under the light, two bloody silhouettes were revealed. One was San Lang, dressed in red, standing properly and with his weapon already tucked away. The other was a plainly clothed young man with a sword tightly in hand, still brandished at the ready.

The plain-clothed young man was covered in blood, looking like he was also dressed in red. His expression was cold and reserved, and he was carrying someone over his shoulders. It was indeed A-Zhao.

To be fair, whether it was General Pei Junior himself or A-Zhao, that composed, calm, and collected aura never changed. Only Xie

Lian never thought in that direction, so he hadn't connected the two until now.

The one he was carrying over his shoulders was Banyue. It seemed he had called forth the snakes in order to steal her away during the chaos. Now that his identity was revealed, he no longer needed to create havoc, and the snake deluge ceased its bombardment. He sheathed his sword and gently laid Banyue on the ground.

On the side, Kemo was shocked. "Who are you? Didn't you fall to your death?!"

A-Zhao didn't spare a look at Kemo, instead staring intently at San Lang. "Kemo, you really haven't changed in hundreds of years," he said simply in the Banyue tongue.

Perhaps this maddeningly calm tone was overly familiar. Kemo's face immediately scrunched up in rage.

"...It's you!! Pei Xiu?!"

If not for the Immortal-Binding Rope solidly tying him down, Kemo would've lunged at him to fight to the death.

"General Pei Junior," Xie Lian said, "those scorpion-snakes listened to more than one command, didn't they? You controlled all the snakes that Banyue said no longer obeyed her, and took them out to do harm, correct?"

"Nn. It was me."

"Did Banyue teach you how to control the scorpion-snakes?" Xie Lian questioned.

"She didn't," Pei Xiu said. "But I easily learned for myself how she does it."

"General Pei Junior is exceedingly intelligent after all," Xie Lian commented.

After a pause, he then asked, "When did you two meet? *How* did you two meet?"

Pei Xiu, however, gave him a look. "General Hua."

Xie Lian was puzzled. "Why are you calling me by that title too?"

Pei Xiu asked quietly, "Do you not recognize me, General Hua?"

"..."

Now Xie Lian did.

The beginning was kind of blurry. Banyue was bullied and ignored by other Banyue children when she was younger, and only a young boy of Yong'an would sometimes pay attention to her. Like Banyue, that boy didn't talk very much. Quite a number of children living on the border were from military families, and many also enlisted in the army when they grew older. Could it be...

"It's you?!" Xie Lian was surprised. "I...I can't believe it took me this long to realize it was you."

Pei Xiu nodded. "It's me. I've only just recognized the general too."

No wonder. So it turned out Banyue and the enemy general had already known each other since childhood!

"Did Banyue really heed your order to open the city gates?" Xie Lian asked.

On the other side, Kemo spat and yelled, "Despicable Pei Xiu. Untie these ropes, let me fight him to the death!"

Pei Xiu said coolly, "First of all, we already had a battle to the death two hundred years ago, and you lost. Second of all, how am I despicable?"

Kemo exclaimed, "How could we have lost if you two hadn't colluded?!"

"Kemo, don't deny it," Pei Xiu said. "Even though I only had a troop of two thousand, for me, breaking through the city gates was only a matter of time."

Xie Lian couldn't help but interrupt. "Wait a sec, you only had two thousand under you, and you were sent to invade a country?

Why was that? Isn't that no different from sending you to your death? Were you, perhaps, even more elbowed-out in the army than I was?"

"..."

Pei Xiu stopped talking. It seemed Xie Lian had hit it on the head. Xie Lian then asked, "If you knew it was a sure win, why did you have Banyue open the city gates?"

"Because I needed to slaughter the city," Pei Xiu replied.

"What do you mean?" Xie Lian asked. "Since you were already going to win, why did you have to slaughter the city?"

It couldn't be his hobby!

"It was precisely because victory was at hand that we had to wipe out the city," Pei Xiu said. "And it had to be as soon as possible. Immediately. Leaving none behind."

That "leaving none behind" sounded ghastly.

Xie Lian pushed, "And the reason was?"

Pei Xiu answered, "On the night before the invasion, many of the leaders of Banyue's major clans gathered for a meeting and decided on a secret plot."

"What plot?"

"The people of Banyue were fierce in nature and hated Yong'an to the core," Pei Xiu said. "Even knowing they were about to be defeated, they wouldn't submit. So the entire population of the kingdom, the young and the old, the women and the men, all banded together to assemble something."

"What was that something?" Xie Lian could guess, but he wasn't sure. The word that came out of Pei Xiu's mouth confirmed his suspicions.

"Explosives!" Pei Xiu slowly enunciated each word: "They decided that if the kingdom was to fall, the citizens would all carry explosives on their bodies, escape to Yong'an, mix into large, crowded areas, and blow themselves up to cause riots. Meaning, if they had to die, then they would drag as many Yong'an people down with them as they could. If the kingdom should fall, then they would terrorize the country that brought their downfall!"

Which was why they had to be annihilated before those civilians had the time to flee...

Xie Lian instantly turned to Kemo, roughly summarized for him in the Banyue language and asked, "Is this true?"

Kemo looked dauntless and made no attempt to conceal the facts. "It's true!"

San Lang quirked his brow at this and commented, "How vile." He said those words in the Banyue tongue, though whether it was intentional was unknown.

Kemo replied angrily, "Vile? What right do you have to call us vile? If it wasn't for your assaults, we wouldn't have been forced to make that move. You ruined us, so we sought revenge. How is that wrong?!"

Pei Xiu responded, "Really now. How about we lay everything out in the open, then? How many times did Banyue citizens start riots near the border? How many caravans and travelers going to the Western Regions from Yong'an were ambushed by Banyue? You intentionally sheltered the bandits that terrorized Yong'an and killed our soldiers sent to exterminate them under the pretense of illegal border crossing. How is that not vile?"

Pei Xiu spoke unhurriedly, and his tone was calm, but each word was as sharp as a knife.

Kemo argued, "But it's because you forcibly occupied our land first that we had no choice but to retaliate."

"The border had always been ambiguous, so how can you say we forcibly occupied your land?" Pei Xiu countered.

"The lines were clearly drawn! It was you who didn't keep to the agreements!"

"The lines were drawn by Banyue, and Yong'an never agreed to them. Your so-called drawn border was nothing but pushing us into the desert and keeping the oasis all for yourselves, how ridiculous."

Kemo countered furiously, "The oasis was always ours! Our forefathers, generation after generation, the Banyue had always lived in the oasis!"

Both sides had their stories; just listening to them argue befuddled Xie Lian. This hostility was making him remember how badly he got beaten up, stuck in between both sides, and he could feel the pain on his face resurface.

Pei Xiu seemed to have had enough of quarreling with Kemo, and he turned to Xie Lian. "So you see, there are many things in the world that simply cannot be clearly defined or resolved. You can only fight."

Xie Lian sighed. "I'll agree to the first part."

San Lang, on the other hand, said, "Hm. I'll agree to the second part."

Kemo's anger was somewhat curbed, and he suddenly said, "The majority of Yong'an people were shameless, but you were the most shameless I'd ever met. Pei Xiu, you're a coldhearted man. You didn't kill us for your country, and it wasn't to save your people."

Pei Xiu fell silent at this.

Kemo continued, "You were the son of an exiled man, looked down on by all. You only wanted to secure your footing in the Yong'an army and keep climbing up, so you had to win that battle. So sad that Banyue still thought you were good and let you use her, and betrayed us for the likes of you."

"But isn't General Pei Junior a descendant of General Pei?" Xie Lian wondered. To have such a renowned ancestor watching over him, how could he have fallen so astray?

"He's not a direct descendant of General Pei," San Lang said. "He's from however many branches out."

So that was it. That meant that, had he not ascended, he probably wouldn't have had any chance of being blessed by the old ancestors.

Pei Xiu said quietly, "Banyue had always been my subordinate and only infiltrated the Kingdom of Banyue under my command. She is from both Banyue and Yong'an; once she chose her side, she had to be loyal to that side, and there was no such thing as betrayal. The Banyue people were evil; I have no regrets about killing them."

Suddenly, a voice came from above.

"No regrets about killing—well said! Will you say the same about all the travelers who you misled to this pass and who lost their lives in this pit?"

That voice had come from above everyone's heads, and Xie Lian instantly looked up. "Which great master is here among us?"

There wasn't a response, but a sudden strange noise. *Whoosh whoosh*, it was like the bellowing of wild winds. When that sound finally came near, Xie Lian could finally say with certainty: it definitely was the bellowing of wild winds!

This abrupt gale entered the Sinner's Pit from above, swept all the way to the bottom, and rolled everyone into the air!

Xie Lian immediately grabbed for San Lang, who was the closest to him, and cried, "Watch out!"

San Lang caught him too, face unchanging. Xie Lian only felt a spinning whirl, their bodies swiftly rising, and after a pause, they started plunging down. Xie Lian quickly tossed out Ruoye and coaxed in the midst of this chaos.

"All right, all right, everything's over. Hurry, my good Ruoye, come out and give us a hand!"

After a couple of pets, Ruoye finally flew out. However, with nothing in the air to grab on to and a giant Sinner's Pit below, Ruoye flew around once and shrank back. Feeling resigned, Xie Lian could only adjust his form for landing. If this was like previous incidents, he would've cratered headfirst a meter into the ground. But this time, just before they hit the ground, San Lang reached out and gave him a pull, and he actually landed with his feet flat on the ground! When his boots firmly touched down, he was even a little incredulous. But that feeling went away very quickly when a black-clad silhouette came stumbling before him.

Xie Lian saw who it was and called out in delight, "Nan Feng!"

It was Nan Feng indeed, but a disheveled Nan Feng. It looked as if he were rolled in dirt a dozen times before getting thrown into a rambunctious den of beasts to spend the night. His clothes were tattered and frayed, unkempt to the max. Hearing Xie Lian's call, he only waved and quietly wiped at his face, unable to even speak.

Xie Lian helped him to his feet. "What happened? Did those two ladies beat you up?"

Before he finished, two figures appeared behind Nan Feng and walked over. One of them was the female cultivator in white with a whisk in her arms, and she greeted Xie Lian cheerfully.

"How do you do, Your Royal Highness?"

Although Xie Lian didn't know who this was, proper etiquette must still be followed; but he didn't know how to address her, so he could only smile back and wave. "Greetings, fellow cultivator."

The lady in black standing to the side glanced coldly at Xie Lian but didn't seem to care about him. When her eyes moved on to

San Lang, however, she seemed to think he was a dubious figure and stopped for a moment.

The gusts earlier had blown everyone out of the pit, and the two ladies walked past Xie Lian, heading straight for Pei Xiu. He saw them approach and didn't appear surprised; after all, he had already seen them in town when he was still playing the part of A-Zhao. He knelt where he was, bowed his head to the lady cultivator in white, and greeted her quietly.

"Lord Wind Master."

Xie Lian was stunned hearing those words.

And here he'd thought she was some menacing ghost or monster—who knew she was actually a heavenly official? And she was the Wind Master, the one who was giving out ten thousand merits in one go in the communication array!

But now that he thought about it in detail, there wasn't anything out of place. At the time, she had said something along the lines of *"Now where did they go? Do I have to dig them out and kill them one by one?"* and made him think she was after them. In reality, this "they" might not have meant their group; she could have meant the Banyue soldiers. Xie Lian thought he was alone in this investigation, and thus naturally thought the lady cultivators were strange and wicked.

Xie Lian couldn't help but feel a nameless reverence toward a heavenly official who could easily hand out ten thousand merits. He turned to Nan Feng. "Why didn't you tell me this was the Wind Master sooner? And here I thought she might be some sort of snake or scorpion spirit. Such impropriety!"

Nan Feng's expression darkened. "I didn't know it was the Wind Master. I've never seen the Wind Master like this before. The Wind Master had always been...never mind."

Xie Lian understood. This was probably a fake appearance the Lord Wind Master donned, so he didn't dig into it. He asked, "Why did the Wind Master come to the Banyue Pass?"

"To help out," Nan Feng said. "When we saw them strolling in the streets earlier, they were actually looking for those Banyue soldiers."

Xie Lian recalled now the first time he asked about the Banyue Pass in the communication array. In the midst of that silent awkwardness, it was the Wind Master's sudden release of ten thousand merits that distracted everyone. The Wind Master had probably taken notice of his query then.

As Xie Lian mused, the Wind Master crouched down in front of Pei Xiu.

"Little Pei, I've heard everything, you know."

Pei Xiu hung his head.

The Wind Master demanded, "Do you admit that for the past two hundred years, you are the one who lured all those travelers into the Ancient Kingdom of Banyue?"

Since he was already caught, Pei Xiu didn't argue and only replied solemnly, "It was me."

"Why?" the Wind Master demanded.

After a pause, Pei Xiu asked, "Lord Wind Master has long been suspicious, can you not guess why?"

"Is it only because these souls of the dead are iron proof of the blood on your hands while you were a human and would become obstacles to your climbing higher in the future?" the Wind Master asked.

Pei Xiu neither agreed nor disagreed. Xie Lian, who was listening from the side, couldn't help but ask, "If anything, why didn't you just kill them directly? Why instead was your method feeding them the living to appease their resentment? How is that different from quenching the thirst of one by using another's flesh and blood?"

San Lang replied, "He couldn't."

That was true too. In the Upper Court, every move by a heavenly official like Pei Xiu was watched intently by countless eyes. There were many things he couldn't do directly: he couldn't use his true form to come down openly and kill off the resentful spirits of these soldiers, and he couldn't send troops to annihilate them either. This was already a concealed affair; if there was too much of a stir, wouldn't it attract everyone's gaze? At most, he could only send a clone like A-Zhao down quietly.

Using the scorpion-snakes that Banyue was a known expert in manipulating to go out and cause harm, attracting passersby to feed the resentful spirits and disperse their resentment; it was no doubt murder by proxy.

"Your General Pei wouldn't have ever done something like this," the Wind Master said. "This time, I'm afraid you've crossed the line."

The fact that he would release a clone to cause havoc at the Banyue Pass for almost two hundred years and lure innumerable passersby down the wrong path and into the ruins to die in the mouths of Banyue soldiers: for a heavenly official, this was no small issue whatsoever.

Pei Xiu had his head bowed low. "This junior knows."

The Wind Master swept her whisk. "As long as you understand. Reflect on yourself and think on it. We'll talk in the heavens."

"I understand," Pei Xiu said quietly.

Having finished talking with Pei Xiu, the Wind Master stuffed the whisk into the back collar of her robe, stood up, and smiled at Xie Lian.

"Your Royal Highness the Crown Prince. I've heard much about you."

To Xie Lian, "heard much about you" really wasn't a compliment. But nonetheless, it was just meaningless pleasantries, so he smiled back. "I'm sure it's nothing. I've heard much about you as well, Lord Wind Master."

"Sorry about before, by the way," the Wind Master said.

Xie Lian paused. "Before? What happened before?"

"Didn't you all run into a windstorm in the desert?"

Thinking back, Xie Lian could almost taste the mouthfuls of sand. He replied, "Yes?"

"I started that," the Wind Master said.

"..."

The Wind Master explained, "That windstorm was meant to stop you all from going near the Kingdom of Banyue, but not only did you not get blown away, you went around and ended up in Banyue anyway."

The longer Xie Lian listened, the more he felt that something wasn't right. First she used a windstorm to stop them from getting to Banyue Pass, and now this whole thing was suddenly out in the open. What did it mean?

Xie Lian didn't respond, biding his time to see what the other would say. The Wind Master then continued, "But in regard to this whole ordeal, it would be best if Your Highness got no further involved."

Xie Lian stole a look at Banyue curled up on the ground and felt his dread rise.

He was already worried that if this scandal were to reach the Upper Court, the officials could easily muck up the truth, add strokes where they shouldn't, and have Banyue take all the blame while Little Pei ran off scot-free. With Wind Master's sudden appearance, telling him not to get further involved, didn't this cement that they would protect Little Pei?

Without any change in expression, Xie Lian stepped forward to stand in front of Banyue, hiding her behind him, and said warmly,

"But I'm already further involved, so telling me to leave it now is fairly pointless, no?"

The Wind Master flashed a smile. "Don't worry. You can take the State Preceptor of Banyue away with you."

Now that was unexpected. Xie Lian was slightly taken aback, and the Wind Master continued. "While you were all in the pit, we heard everything from up here. Although the state preceptor has turned into a wrath, when I roamed the city, I saw that she had drawn the array to trap the Banyue soldiers and released all the captured mortals. She didn't hurt anyone and even saved people. The only ones I'm taking are General Pei Junior and Kemo; you don't have to worry about me placing undue blame on anyone."

Xie Lian relaxed. "Much ashamed! I was suspicious."

"It's normal to worry," the Wind Master said. "There's certainly an unpleasant culture in the Upper Court, after all."

The lady in black looked as if she couldn't stay for a moment longer and spoke up. "Are you done? If you're done, let's go."

The Wind Master rebutted, "*Tsk!* What's the rush? The more you rush, the more I wanna talk!" Still, she turned her head and smiled, taking out a folding fan from her waist. "Your Royal Highness, if there's nothing else, we'll see you in the Upper Court?"

Xie Lian nodded, and the Wind Master opened her fan. On the fan was the word for wind, "Feng," on a slant, and three inclined lines like wind on the back. That had to be the Wind Master's spiritual device. She fanned forward three times, and backward three times. Suddenly, a gust of wind blew from out of nowhere.

The wind drew dust and sand, and Xie Lian raised his sleeve to block the debris. When the wind died down, the two ladies, Pei Xiu, and Kemo had all disappeared, leaving behind only Xie Lian, San Lang, Nan Feng, and the curled-up Banyue on the ground.

Xie Lian dropped his sleeve, still a little dazed. "What just happened?"

San Lang casually strolled over. "A pretty good thing."

Xie Lian looked at him. "Is it?"

"Yeah. The Wind Master was trying to help you by telling you not to get involved."

Nan Feng walked over too. "That's right. You've dug too deep into this business already. The only thing left to do is to file a complaint to the Heavenly Emperor. Don't get yourself any more involved."

Xie Lian got it. "Is it because of General Pei?"

"Correct," Nan Feng said. "This time you have thoroughly offended him."

Xie Lian laughed. "I knew I was going to offend someone one of these days, I guess it doesn't matter who."

Nan Feng furrowed his brows. "Don't think I'm joking. After the Palace of Divine Might, the next most powerful martial palace is Ming Guang. General Pei thinks very highly of Little Pei and has long been trying to oust Quan Yizhen. He's gonna come knocking, looking for trouble."

"Quan Yizhen is the martial god that rules the west, right?" Xie Lian asked.

"That's the one," Nan Feng replied. "Quan Yizhen is also a new official. He ascended around the same time as Pei Xiu. He's young, and a little, um…but very powerful. General Pei intended for Pei Xiu to take over all the devotees of the west, and he's done well for himself, especially these past few years. Now with you dragging this scandal out into the open, it's not looking good for Pei Xiu; maybe he'll even be banished. If he gets banished, your luck is gonna turn for the worse too."

Xie Lian rubbed his forehead, mentally taking note that from now on he would have to be more mindful when eating, drinking, and walking.

San Lang, however, didn't think it was a big deal. "Don't worry. Pei Ming is too proud. He won't do anything underhanded."

Nan Feng gave him a look.

"What about the Wind Master?" Xie Lian asked. "She told me not to get involved, meaning she's the one who will file the complaint. In that case, wouldn't she become the one offending General Pei? I can't have that. Let's call her back. Nan Feng, do you know the password to her personal communication array?"

"You needn't worry about the Wind Master," Nan Feng said. "General Pei can hurt you, but he won't touch her. She may be younger than you, but she's much more successful in the heavens."

"..." Xie Lian wasn't shocked into silence but was instead thinking, *Who in the heavens is more of a failure than me? I don't think there's anyone.*

San Lang laughed. "With that backing, of course she's successful."

"Are you talking about the lady in black? She looks to be a strong character too," Xie Lian remarked.

"No," San Lang replied. "But she must also be one of the five elemental masters that make up 'Wind, Water, Rain, Earth, and Thunder.' I recommend not offending her."

The Wind Master could start a twister from nowhere, which was obviously powerful. But the lady in black was stronger. Xie Lian kept thinking that the lady had noticed something in San Lang and felt rather concerned.

"I agree."

Still, there were words that Xie Lian thought didn't need to be said, so he swallowed them. He thought, *Even someone with a strong backing may not be successful. Back in the day, the crown prince of Xianle had the support of the Heavenly Emperor who ruled all three realms for a thousand years. He was still a failure.*

Xie Lian picked up his fallen bamboo hat, dusted it off, and sighed in relief upon seeing that it wasn't flattened. He tied it back around his neck and looked at Nan Feng. "You weren't pursued and beaten up by those two ladies the whole time, were you?"

"Yes. We fought the whole time," Nan Feng replied, face dark.

Xie Lian patted his shoulders. "Thanks for your hard work." Suddenly, he remembered another hard worker and turned around. "Where's Fu Yao?"

"Wasn't he watching the bitten man?" Nan Feng responded.

Xie Lian didn't recall seeing Fu Yao after getting blown out of the Sinner's Pit. Actually, ever since A-Zhao revealed himself, there had been no sight of him. If he didn't leave then, he must've left when the wind blew.

Xie Lian wasn't actually that worried. He figured Fu Yao didn't want to get mixed up in this mess, so he ran off. But, having heard Nan Feng say "bitten," he snapped out of it, and they both cried at the same time: "The shanyue fern!"

"The sky is only just lightening, no rush," San Lang said.

However, there was no such thing as "no rush" when it came to saving lives. Even if they were far from the twenty-four-hour deadline, who knew if anything had happened in all this time? Xie Lian had no time to think about Fu Yao. He hurriedly lifted Banyue onto his back and ran toward the palace grounds.

Once at the palace, Xie Lian laid Banyue down and immediately picked a few large bundles of the shanyue fern. That mud face was still on the ground, its face a bloody mess among its white bones.

In the past, Xie Lian would've buried it, but first of all, he was in a hurry to save people, and second, that man had been buried in the ground for fifty or sixty years, he must not want to go back. But the corpse of the dead merchant was missing, and Xie Lian stopped, puzzled.

Just then, San Lang emerged from the palace with a small clay pot. When Xie Lian saw, he immediately called out, "Good, San Lang, thank you."

Banyue was weak and they couldn't rouse her, so Xie Lian shrank her and tucked her into the pot. With the ferns collected, the group rushed back. It had been about eight hours since they left.

Returning to where Fu Yao had drawn the circle, Xie Lian saw that many were still sitting properly within it, too scared to venture out. The old man who had taken Nan Feng's pill was doing all right, and after applying the herb to his wound and having him eat the plant, he was able to stand and walk after resting for a while. Xie Lian didn't think there was any need to tell them what the herb used to grow on.

After some time, the merchants settled down, and they began to worry.

"Where's Tian Sheng? Why haven't the others returned yet?"

Xie Lian had been too busy picking herbs to find him earlier, plus there was not a single Banyue soldier left in the ruins, so he hadn't bothered with Tian Sheng and the others. He was just thinking about going back to search for them when he heard the voice of a boy yelling as he ran closer and closer. Xie Lian turned his head, and sure enough, it was Tian Sheng. The boy had a large bundle of the shanyue fern in his arms, and behind him were two other merchants, all huffing and puffing.

Xie Lian asked them what had happened and learned that while on top of the walls of the Sinner's Pit, Banyue swept the soldiers down and captured Tian Sheng and the merchants. They were terrified, but Banyue only led them down from the pit and directed them where to go before sending them on their way. They escaped, picked the herbs, buried the dead merchant's body, and rushed back as fast as they could, yet they were still slower than Xie Lian.

In any case, Xie Lian escorted the caravan out of the Gobi Desert and ended this journey at last.

Before they bid farewell, Tian Sheng snuck out to find him and whispered mysteriously, "Gege, I have a question for you."

"Ask away," Xie Lian said.

"You're actually a god, aren't you?"

"..."

Xie Lian was astonished. But also, a little touched.

In the past, there was a time when he'd holler and announce to the world, "I'm a god! I am the Crown Prince, His Royal Highness!" and no one would believe him. This time, he hadn't even said anything, and the other party asked if he was a god. It made him both astonished and moved.

Tian Sheng added immediately, "I saw you use spells! Don't worry, I won't tell."

How would you even tell? No one would believe you... Xie Lian thought.

Tian Sheng continued, "If not for you, I would've gotten thrown into that pit by that bunch of ugly ghost soldiers. When I get home, I'll build you a temple and worship you."

Xie Lian watched him pat his chest and make "very big, very big" hand gestures, and couldn't help but let out a laugh. He smiled.

"Then thank you."

San Lang was standing to the side, and he chuckled lightly for some unknown reason. Xie Lian didn't think it was because he thought a child's naive words were ridiculous.

Although children had no idea just how much work went into constructing a temple, receiving such a promise, whether it would be fulfilled or not, was nevertheless a happy occasion.

After much hassling, he made up a random title, "The Scrap Immortal," to leave behind, then he waved and walked off in the opposite direction. Nan Feng drew another teleportation array and sent them all back to Puqi Shrine.

Opening the door, Xie Lian took the straw mat out, laid it open on the ground, and collapsed on it like a dead body. This was done all in one breath. San Lang sat down next to him and watched him, a hand propping up his chin.

Xie Lian sighed. "How long were we gone?"

"About three, four days," San Lang replied.

Xie Lian sighed again. "Only three, four days. Why am I so tired?"

Ever since he ascended, he was worked to the bone like a dog, no lie. After he was done sighing, Xie Lian looked up.

"*Hnn?* Nan Feng? Why haven't you gone to report back yet?"

"Report back where?" Nan Feng asked.

"Aren't you an official of Nan Yang Palace? Won't your general miss you after three, four days?"

"My general isn't in the palace right now, so he won't miss me," Nan Feng replied.

Xie Lian rolled over and got up. "All right. It'll be good too, if you stay."

"What are you doing?" Nan Feng asked.

Xie Lian looked at him cheerfully. "I'm going to cook you a meal. As a reward for your hard work."

Nan Feng's face dropped drastically. He raised his hand, pressed two fingers together, and touched his temple as if receiving someone's private communication. He got up and turned.

"There's an emergency at the palace, I'll see you later."

Xie Lian raised his hand. "What? Nan Feng, don't go! How can there suddenly be an emergency? I really want to thank you for everything..."

"There's an emergency!!" Nan Feng roared and ran out the door.

Xie Lian sat back down on the mat and looked at San Lang. "I guess he's not hungry."

There was a loud bang before San Lang could reply, and it was Nan Feng who'd run back, blocking the doorway. "You two..."

Xie Lian and San Lang were sitting together on the mat, and they both looked up at him. "What about us two?"

Nan Feng pointed his finger at San Lang, then at Xie Lian, words stuck in his throat, unable to speak. Then finally, "I'll be back!"

"You're welcome any time," Xie Lian said.

Nan Feng gave San Lang one last stink eye before closing the door and leaving.

Xie Lian crossed his arms and tilted his head like San Lang and said, "Looks like there really is an emergency."

He turned to look at the youth next to him and smiled cheerfully. "He's not hungry, how about you?"

San Lang smiled cheerfully back. "I'm starving."

Xie Lian grinned and stood up again, before turning around and casually tidying the altar table.

"All right, then. What do you want to eat, Hua Cheng?"

Behind him, there was silence. Then chuckling.

"I still prefer the name 'San Lang.'"

"CRIMSON RAIN SOUGHT FLOWER?" Xie Lian asked.

"Your Royal Highness the Crown Prince," San Lang replied.

Xie Lian finally turned around with a grin. "That's the first time I've heard you address me like that."

The red-clad youth sat on the mat and propped up a leg, also grinning. "How does it feel?"

Xie Lian gave it a thought and replied truthfully, "It feels...a little different than when others call me by that title."

"Hm? How so?" Hua Cheng asked.

Xie Lian tilted his head, his eyes squinting a little. "It's hard to say, it's just..."

When others called him "Your Highness," some were emotionless and all business, like Ling Wen. But most of the time, when people called him "Your Highness," it was laced with a sense of disdain, like how one would intentionally address an ugly woman as a beauty, somewhat sarcastic.

Yet when Hua Cheng called him "Your Highness," the two words were uttered with grave sincerity. So, while it was hard to describe, Xie Lian felt that when Hua Cheng called him "Your Highness," it was different from when others used that title.

He continued, "That night at Mount Yujun, the groom who whisked me away was you, right?"

Hua Cheng's smile deepened meaningfully, and that made Xie Lian realize his words may have been too ambiguous. He quickly corrected himself.

"I meant, the groom in disguise who led me away was you, right?"

"I wasn't disguising myself as a groom," Hua Cheng replied.

Technically speaking, Hua Cheng wasn't wrong. The young man at the time never said he was the groom or anything; in fact, he didn't say anything at all. He only stopped in front of the marriage sedan and extended his hand. It was Xie Lian who went with him willingly!

"Fine. Then, why did you appear like that?" Xie Lian asked.

"This question only has two possible answers," Hua Cheng said. "First, that I came specifically for Your Royal Highness; second, that I was passing by and was free. Which do you think is more believable?"

Xie Lian counted the number of days Hua Cheng had spent with him and replied earnestly. "Which is more believable I can't say, but you do seem to have a lot of free time."

His entire person and his gaze both circled around Hua Cheng, going back and forth, and after a long while, he said, "You're quite different from what the rumors say."

Hua Cheng changed his sitting position, but with a hand still propping up his cheek, he watched Xie Lian and asked, "Oh? And how did Your Royal Highness figure out that I am Crimson Rain Sought Flower?"

The images of that umbrella dripping with blood, that gently clinking silver chain, and those cold silver vambraces filled Xie Lian's mind. He thought, *It's not like you were trying very hard to hide yourself.*

"Even after all the probing, you gave nothing away, so you must be a supreme. You're dressed all in red like the maples, like blood, and seem to know everything, seem to be capable of everything, and know no fear. And such magnanimity—other than Crimson Rain Sought Flower, who all the heaven officials fear, there didn't seem to be anyone else you could be."

Hua Cheng laughed. "May I take those words as a compliment?"

Can't you tell they're compliments? Xie Lian thought.

"Sparing so many words, how come Your Royal Highness doesn't question my motives in coming close to you?" Hua Cheng asked, his smile curbed somewhat.

"If you didn't want to say anything, and I asked, would you tell? Or you might not tell me the truth," Xie Lian said.

"That's not necessarily true," Hua Cheng said. "Besides, you can always kick me out."

Xie Lian replied, "You're so powerful. Even if I kicked you out now, if you really wanted to do something bad, wouldn't you just change your skin and come back?"

The two met eyes and grinned. Suddenly, a small knocking noise broke the temporary silence in the shrine. They looked to where the sound came from and there wasn't anyone, only that small, black clay pot rolling on the ground.

It was the same pot Banyue was tucked in. Xie Lian had casually placed it next to the mat, but somehow it had tipped itself over and rolled to the door. Blocked by the wooden door built by Hua Cheng, it started hitting the door by rolling into it repeatedly. Xie Lian was worried it might break itself, so he opened the door, and the little clay pot rolled into the grass field outside.

Xie Lian followed behind it and saw that once the little clay pot made it to the grass field, it stood itself up. Even if it was only a pot, it gave the impression that it was gazing at the night sky.

Hua Cheng also emerged from the shrine, and Xie Lian called out to the pot. "Banyue, are you awake?"

Thankfully, when they returned from the Gobi it was already deep into the night; otherwise, if anyone had seen Xie Lian ask a pot how it was doing, they would probably make a huge fuss again.

A moment later, the sulky voice of a girl came from the pot. "General Hua."

Xie Lian sat down next to it. "Banyue, have you rolled out here to stargaze? Why don't you come out?"

Hua Cheng was leaning against a tree next to them and said, "She only just left the Banyue ruins. Probably best if she stays in there for a while longer."

After all, Banyue had stayed in Banyue for two hundred years, and the sudden change of environment might be hard to adjust to. Xie Lian said, "Then you'd best stay in there for a while longer and heal. This is where I train, so you don't have to worry about anything else."

The pot shook twice as if trying to say something. After chewing on his words, Xie Lian said, "Banyue, the incident this time actually didn't concern you. Your scorpion-snakes were..."

"General Hua, I couldn't move at the time, but I heard everything," Banyue said.

Xie Lian was taken aback. Only then did he learn that Pei Xiu only sealed Banyue's movement, not her senses. "Just as well."

If she heard everything, it was just as well.

The clay pot asked, "General Hua, what will happen to General Pei Junior?"

Xie Lian crossed his arms in his sleeves. "I don't know. But wrongdoings will always be punished."

Another moment of silence, the pot shook twice, and Xie Lian finally understood that the shaking was a nod in agreement.

"General Pei Junior is actually not a bad person," Banyue said.

"Is that right?"

"Mm," Banyue replied. "He's helped me before."

Somehow, many more memories suddenly came back to Xie Lian.

Banyue often received beatings, and in the words of the other Yong'an children, she bore a face that "asked for it."

It took a long time after Xie Lian met her before he learned of this, since no matter how many beatings Banyue received, she wouldn't tell anyone. It wasn't until one day, when Xie Lian saw a group of children pressing her face into the mud, that he learned where all those bruises on her face came from.

But when he asked her about it some time afterward, she only remembered that she had to wash the handkerchief from the boy who pulled her out of the mud pit before she returned it, and nothing else.

She remembered none of the ones who beat her. But the ones who saved her once, she remembered for a lifetime.

Banyue continued, "Although Kemo always said scornfully that I had my mind possessed, that I had been completely used, whether General Pei Junior used me or not, I know it was my own will to open the city gates."

Xie Lian didn't know what to say anymore, but he could feel some part of his heart soften. A moment later, he patted that clay pot. "All right, it's all in the past. Oh, by the way. Banyue, the name Hua Xie is fake, and I haven't been a general for a long time. You don't have to keep calling me General Hua."

"Then how should I address you?" Banyue asked.

That was actually a good question. If Banyue called him "Your Highness," seriously, it'd feel weird. Xie Lian didn't really care about his address either, he just wanted to change the subject.

"That's up to you. I suppose it's okay if you keep calling me General Hua."

Only, there was another here with the surname Hua, so that might cause some confusion. But then he thought, "Hua Xie" was a fake name he took from the first word of the title "Flower-Crowned Martial God," so "Hua Cheng" may very well be a fake name too. That they both coincidentally picked the same word, "flower," for a surname was rather interesting.

"I'm sorry, General Hua," Banyue said again.

Xie Lian turned back to look at her and said woefully, "Banyue, why are you always apologizing to me?" Did he really look that sorry to people?

From within the pot, Banyue declared, "I want to save the common people."

"..." Xie Lian was speechless.

"General Hua, you said that once," Banyue said.

"???" Xie Lian was speechless *and* confused.

He quickly pressed down on the clay pot. "Wait, hold on a sec!"

"Wait for what?" Banyue asked.

Xie Lian snuck a glimpse at Hua Cheng, who was still leaning against the tree with his arms crossed, and said in a low voice, "Did I really say that?"

That was his favorite saying when he was only ten-something years old. In the many centuries thereafter, he shouldn't have uttered those words at all, so hearing them so suddenly made it difficult to accept.

However, Banyue was firm. "General, those were your words."

Xie Lian still wanted to argue. "I don't think so..."

Banyue told him sternly and coldly, "Oh, no, you did say them. There was a time when you asked us all what we wanted to do when we were older. Everyone answered, and afterward you said, 'My dream since I was little was to save the world, the common people.'"

"..."

So that was it. "Um. Banyue. Why would you remember something so clearly said completely randomly?!"

Banyue was confused. "Randomly? But General Hua, I thought those words were said very earnestly."

Xie Lian gazed up at the night sky, feeling helpless. "Ha ha... really? Maybe. I don't remember whatever else I might have said."

"You also said, 'Do what you think is right!'" Banyue told him. "'Nothing can block your way!' 'Even if you fall in the mud a hundred times, you must get up with determination!' And a lot more similar sayings."

"*Pfft.*"

He didn't need to look back to know that it was definitely Hua Cheng under the tree who laughed at that.

Even smothering the pot now wouldn't help. Xie Lian thought, *What...nonsense! Why did I keep saying those kinds of things...? I'm nothing like that...am I?!*

"But I don't know what's right anymore," Banyue said.

Xie Lian froze at those words.

"I wanted to do as General Hua said and save the people," Banyue continued. "But in the end, I destroyed the Kingdom of Banyue."

Her voice was lost. "And it seemed that no matter what I did... the results were all horrible. General Hua, I know I didn't do things right, but can you tell me, where did I go wrong? How can I do as you said and...save the common people?"

"..." Xie Lian replied, "I'm sorry, Banyue. How to save the world, the common people...I didn't know the answer to that question back then, and even now I still don't."

Banyue was silent for a moment, then said dejectedly, "General Hua, to be honest, it feels like for the past two hundred years, I've had no idea what I'm doing. I'm such a failure."

Hearing her, Xie Lian became more depressed, thinking, *Doesn't that make me even more of a failure? And I've lived for eight hundred years too...*

Xie Lian left the little ghost Banyue in the pot to stargaze alone and calm down. He went back inside Puqi Shrine with Hua Cheng.

After closing the door, Xie Lian suddenly spoke up. "Banyue remained at Banyue Pass willingly. It wasn't because she became a wrath that she was trapped there."

She always remembered that it was she who opened the city gates and had never given any excuse, like saying she was doing it for the people. It was to help the Banyue soldiers vent their resentment, so they could leave this world sooner, that she allowed Kemo to lead them to murder her over and over.

Xie Lian shook his head. "If General Pei Junior really didn't want to leave those Banyue soldiers behind and also didn't want the heavens to find out, he could have easily sent a clone to secretly descend and take care of them. Why did he do it this way instead?"

"Clones don't have the same amount of power," Hua Cheng said. "You saw how Pei Xiu's clone A-Zhao was? He couldn't take care of so many Banyue soldiers, so feeding them the living was the fastest and easiest way to disperse their resentment."

"Why did it have to be so fast?" Xie Lian wondered.

"Maybe it's so little Banyue wouldn't have to hang so painfully as many times," Hua Cheng replied.

Xie Lian was silent for a moment. "But what about the mortals?"

Hua Cheng replied quietly, "They're heavenly officials. Mortals are nothing but ants in their eyes. Pei Xiu is a classic highly ranked god. As long as no one found out, killing a few hundred people is no different than stomping a few hundred insects to death."

Xie Lian glanced at him and recalled that when San Lang jumped into the Sinner's Pit, he wiped out all the Banyue soldiers in a flash. He turned to him and said, "Clones don't have the same amount of power? I see your clone is pretty powerful."

Hua Cheng arched his brow. "It would be, but I'm the real thing."

Xie Lian turned to look at him, somewhat surprised. "Eh? This is your true form?"

"One hundred percent authentic," Hua Cheng declared.

If anything must be blamed, it would have to be the look on Hua Cheng's face, like he was welcoming Xie Lian to test it out himself. Without thinking, Xie Lian raised a finger and poked Hua Cheng's face.

After poking, Xie Lian snapped back to himself in shock, yelping *Oh no!* in his head.

He was only curious to see what a Supreme Ghost King's fake skin would feel like, but apparently, his body moved faster than his mind and poked him! How extremely outrageous of him!

To have someone suddenly poke him, Hua Cheng looked somewhat shocked too, but he was always calm and collected, so his expression cleared instantly. He didn't say anything, but his arched brow raised even higher, as if waiting for Xie Lian to explain. The laughter in his eyes was apparent. Of course Xie Lian couldn't explain himself. He looked at his own finger and then hid it away, betraying nothing of his thoughts.

"...Not bad."

Hua Cheng finally burst out laughing, and he crossed his arms with his head tilted. "What's not bad? Do you mean this skin?"

"Yeah, it's quite good," Xie Lian said sincerely. "But..."

"But what?" Hua Cheng asked.

Xie Lian stared at his face and studied it for a moment. Then finally said, "But can I see your real face?"

Since he said "this skin," that meant that while this body was his true form, the skin wasn't his real one, and this appearance was not his true face.

This time, Hua Cheng didn't respond immediately and dropped his arms. Maybe it was all in Xie Lian's head, but Hua Cheng's eyes dimmed a little, and Xie Lian's heart tightened despite himself.

When the air froze, Xie Lian knew his question may have crossed the line.

Although for the past few days the two of them had gotten along well, that didn't mean they were so close that he could make this type of request. Without waiting for his response, Xie Lian quickly smiled.

"I was just asking; don't take it to heart."

Hua Cheng closed his eyes, and a moment after, he smiled softly. "I'll let you see it someday, if there's a chance."

If anyone else said that, it'd naturally be perfunctory. "Someday" usually meant "please forget it." But it was Hua Cheng who said it, so Xie Lian felt that "someday" meant "someday," and it would surely happen. That made him even more curious, and he grinned.

"Then I'll wait till the day you feel it's okay to show me. Let's rest for now."

After bustling about for half the night, Xie Lian had long since tossed the idea of cooking to the back of his mind and returned to lying on the straw mat. Hua Cheng also lay down next to him. No one bothered questioning why, after coming clean about their identities, a god and a ghost could still lie together on a crappy mat, laughing and chatting.

The straw mat didn't have pillows, so Hua Cheng used his arms, and Xie Lian imitated him in pillowing his head on his arms too. He mentioned casually, "The Ghost Realm seems so idle. Don't you guys ever need to report back to anyone?"

Hua Cheng not only used his arms as a pillow, but he propped his leg up too. He replied, "Report to whom? I'm the biggest one there is. Besides, we all mind our own business, no one bothers anyone."

So the Ghost Realm was made up of many disorganized bands of lost souls and feral ghosts. Xie Lian replied, "Is that so? I thought it'd be like the Upper Court, with a central government. If it's like that, have you met any other ghost kings before?"

"I have," Hua Cheng said.

"Even Green Ghost Qi Rong?"

"You mean that lowly, vulgar trash?"

Well, what do I say to that? Xie Lian thought. *Yes? No?*

Thankfully, he didn't need to say anything, as Hua Cheng continued, "I greeted him, and he ran away."

Xie Lian had a hunch that this "greeting" couldn't have been your regular sort of greeting. Sure enough, Hua Cheng said casually, "And then I received the moniker 'Crimson Rain Sought Flower.'"

"..."

So before, when he mentioned wiping out the lair of another ghost, he was talking about Green Ghost Qi Rong, and this "greeting" was carnage. *What an extraordinary greeting,* Xie Lian thought, rubbing his chin.

"Do you have something against the Green Ghost Qi Rong?"

"Yeah," Hua Cheng replied.

"What's that?"

"Can't stand his face."

Xie Lian didn't know whether to laugh or cry, thinking, *Did you challenge those thirty-three heavenly officials because you also didn't like their faces?*

"The officials of the Upper Court all call him vulgar, and even the Ghost Realm scorns him. Is that true?"

"It's true. Even Black Water is disgusted with him," Hua Cheng replied.

"Who's Black Water?" Xie Lian asked, then recalled, "Oh, is that the one called 'Ship-Sinking Black Water'?"

"That's right. He's also known as the Black Water Demon Xuan."

Xie Lian remembered that this Black Water Demon Xuan was also a supreme, but Green Ghost Qi Rong was only almost a supreme and just there for the headcount. He asked, interested, "Are you close with this Demon Xuan?"

"No," Hua Cheng replied lazily. "There aren't many in the Ghost Realm I'm close with."

Now Xie Lian was amazed. "Is that so? I thought you'd have many subordinates. Maybe our definition of 'close' is different?"

Hua Cheng quirked his brow. "Yeah. In the Ghost Realm, those lower than supreme have no right to speak to me."

It was an exceedingly arrogant statement, but Hua Cheng made it sound so indisputable and self-evident. Xie Lian smiled softly.

"You have it pretty good in the Ghost Realm. It's only so big, not like the heavens. I can barely remember the heavenly officials in the Upper Court, and there are many more waiting to ascend in the Middle Court; it's like an ocean of names."

"What good is it to remember them? Don't bother. It's a waste of your brain," Hua Cheng said.

"Ha ha, it's kind of offensive if you can't remember their names." The heavenly officials loved their reputations.

Hua Cheng clicked his tongue. "If they can be offended by such a small thing, then they're nothing but narrow-minded trash."

After chatting that much, Xie Lian didn't want to dig too deeply into the subject lest they touch on something sensitive, so he changed the topic away from the differences between the two realms.

He glanced at the closed wooden door and wondered, "Banyue, that child, I wonder when she'll come back in."

The bold words "I want to save the common people" returned and reverberated in his head, pouring a mess of images in his mind, and Xie Lian had to forcibly push them down.

Just then, Hua Cheng spoke up. "Those were good words."

"Which ones?" Xie Lian asked.

"'I want to save the world, the common people,'" Hua Cheng replied leisurely.

"..."

Xie Lian was thunderstruck.

He flipped over and curled into a shrimp, wishing for another pair of arms so he could cover both his face and his ears. He groaned, "...San Lang..."

Hua Cheng seemed to have nudged closer and deadpanned right behind him, "Hm? What's wrong with those words?"

Hua Cheng wouldn't back down and Xie Lian couldn't win against him, so he flipped back over and said helplessly, "It's silly."

"What's there to be afraid of?" Hua Cheng said. "To dare speak of the people of the world, whether to save or to destroy them, is admirable. The former is harder than the latter, so it's even more respectable."

Xie Lian shook his head, not knowing whether to laugh or cry. "If you dare to speak, you have to be able to follow through and actually achieve it."

He laid an arm over his eyes. "Oh, all right. I suppose that's nothing. What Banyue said was already pretty good. I've said sillier things when I was even younger."

Hua Cheng laughed. "Oh? Like what? Let's hear it."

Xie Lian was pensive for a moment, and he smiled softly as he chased his memories. "Many, many years ago, there was someone who told me they couldn't live on anymore. They asked me for the reason they were alive and what was the meaning of their life."

He glanced at Hua Cheng. "Do you know how I answered?"

It might have just been Xie Lian's imagination, but there seemed to be light in Hua Cheng's eyes. He asked softly, "How did you answer?"

Xie Lian said, "I told them, 'If you don't know how to live on anymore, then live for me! If you don't know the meaning of your life, then make me that meaning, and use me as your reason to live.'

"Ha ha ha..."

As Xie Lian spoke, he couldn't help but let out a small laugh and shook his head. "Even now I don't understand what I was thinking back then. How did I ever have the courage to tell someone to make me the meaning of their life?"

Hua Cheng was silent, and Xie Lian continued. "It really was something that could only have been said back then. Long ago, I really thought I was invincible and fearless. If you asked me to say the same words now, there is no way they would ever leave my lips again."

Xie Lian continued slowly, "I don't know what happened to that person afterward. But to become someone's reason to live is already a heavy responsibility. How dare I speak of the world?"

Silence blanketed Puqi Shrine.

After a while, San Lang said quietly, "Something like saving the common people, it really doesn't matter how you do it. But, although brave, it's foolish."

"Yeah," Xie Lian agreed.

Hua Cheng continued, "Although foolish, it's brave."

"..."

Xie Lian grinned. "Thanks."

"You're welcome," Hua Cheng said.

The two stared at the holey ceiling of Puqi Shrine in amiable silence, and Hua Cheng spoke up again after a while.

"You know, Your Highness, we've only known each other for a few days. Is it all right for you to say so much to me?"

"Well," Xie Lian huffed, "what's the problem? Whatever. Those who have known each other for decades can become strangers in a day. We met by chance, and we may part by chance. If we like each other, then we shall continue to meet; if we don't, then we shall part. At the end of the day, there's no banquet in the world that doesn't come to an end, so let's take it easy, and I'll say what I want to say."

Hua Cheng seemed to have chuckled, then suddenly he said, "If."

Xie Lian turned his head to face him. "If?"

Hua Cheng didn't turn around but continued to stare at the dilapidated ceiling of the shrine, and Xie Lian could only see this handsome young man's left profile.

Hua Cheng said softly, "If I was ugly."

"Huh?" Xie Lian gaped.

Hua Cheng finally turned his head slightly. "If my true appearance is ugly, would you still want to see it?"

Xie Lian was taken aback. "Is it? Although there's no real reason, I never thought your true appearance would be too horrible-looking."

"Who knows?" Hua Cheng said, half-jokingly. "What if I'm discolored, disfigured, ugly, monstrous, and horrible. What will you do?"

At first, Xie Lian thought this line of inquiry was rather fascinating. So the overlord of the Ghost Realm, the one called the devil incarnate and feared by all in the heavens, would care about his looks? But when he thought about it deeply, he didn't think it was very funny anymore.

He vaguely recalled, in the many rumored backstories of Hua Cheng, one said that he was a disfigured child from birth, or something along those lines. If that was true, then he must've grown up discriminated against by others. Maybe that was why he was particularly sensitive about his appearance.

Thus, Xie Lian chewed on his words. "Well..."

He used his warmest, most sincere voice. "To be honest, the reason I want to see your true appearance is only because, you see, we're already like this..."

"Hm?" Hua Cheng piped up. "Like what?"

"...Well, we're sort of friends now, right? So if we're friends, then we should be honest with each other. My wanting to see your true appearance has nothing to do with how you look. You asked what I would do, but of course I won't do anything. Don't worry, as long as it's your real face, I'm sure I'll... Why are you laughing? I'm being serious."

When Xie Lian reached the last part, he could feel the youth next to him shaking. He froze for a moment at first, and thought, *Are my words so moving that he's touched like this?* and was too embarrassed to turn around to see. But after a while, the soft laughter from next to him very obviously leaked out. Xie Lian felt rather deflated and placed a hand on his shoulder to give it a little push.

"San Lang...why are you laughing so much? Did I say something wrong?"

Hua Cheng immediately stopped shaking and turned around. "No, you're very right."

Xie Lian felt even more deflated at those words. "You're so insincere..."

"I promise, you won't find another person more sincere than me in this world," Hua Cheng replied.

Xie Lian didn't want to talk anymore and flipped over, his back facing Hua Cheng. "Forget it, time to sleep. Don't talk."

Hua Cheng chuckled again, then said, "Next time."

Even though he was determined to sleep, hearing Hua Cheng speak, Xie Lian couldn't resist replying, "What's next time?"

Hua Cheng whispered, "The next time we meet, I will use my true appearance to greet you."

There was much to ponder about those words, and Xie Lian should've kept questioning him. But after a long night, an unstoppable drowsiness overtook him, and he couldn't hang on, falling into a deep slumber.

The next morning, when Xie Lian woke, the spot next to him was already empty.

He scrambled to get up and walked around the shrine in a daze. When he opened the door, there were no figures to be seen outside. It seemed like it was true. The youth had indeed left.

However, the fallen leaves had been swept into a pile, and next to that pile stood a small clay pot. Xie Lian took the pot inside and placed it on the altar. Right then, he suddenly noticed that there seemed to be something extra on his usually bare chest.

He raised his hand to touch it, and found just below the cursed collar there was an exceedingly thin chain, hanging loose and light.

Xie Lian immediately removed it from his neck. Turned out it was a silver chain, so thin and light that he hadn't felt anything on him before. And dangling from the chain, there was a crystal-clear ring.

THE STORY CONTINUES IN
Heaven Official's Blessing
VOLUME 2

Heaven Official's Blessing

TIAN GUAN CI FU

Character
&
Name Guide

Characters

The identity of certain characters may be a spoiler; use this guide with caution on your first read of the novel.

Note on the given name translations: Chinese characters may have many different readings. Each reading here is just one out of several possible readings presented for your reference and should not be considered a definitive translation.

MAIN CHARACTERS

Xie Lian
谢怜   "THANK/WILT," "SYMPATHY/LOVE"

HEAVENLY TITLE: Xianle, "Heaven's Delight" (仙乐)
FOUR FAMOUS TALES TITLE: The Prince Who Pleased God

Once the crown prince of the Kingdom of Xianle and the darling of the heavens, now a very unlucky twice-fallen god who ekes out a meager living collecting scraps. As his bad luck tends to affect those around him for the worse, Xie Lian has spent his last eight hundred years wandering in solitude. Still, he's accepted his lonely lot in life, or at least seems to have a sense of humor about it. Even for the perpetually unlucky, there's always potential for a chance encounter that can turn eight hundred years of unhappiness around.

Xie Lian has seen and done many things over his very long life and originally ascended as a martial god. While it was his scrap-collecting that saw him ascend for the third time, Xie Lian's feats of physicality are hardly anything to scoff at...though he'd sooner use them as part of a busking performance than to win a fight.

Hua Cheng
花城   "FLOWER," "CITY"

FOUR CALAMITIES TITLE: Crimson Rain Sought Flower

A fearsome king of ghosts and terror of the heavens. Dressed in his signature red, he controls vicious swarms of silver butterflies and wields a cursed scimitar known as Eming. He first gained infamy by defeating and humiliating thirty-three gods in combat and burning down every last one of their temples in a single night, dooming them to obscurity and oblivion.

His power and wealth are unmatched in the Three Realms, and for this he has as many worshippers as he does enemies (with considerable crossover between categories). Although he is an enigmatic figure who can shapeshift to any form to avoid detection, his butterflies have recently been sighted in the Mortal Realm...

San Lang
三郎   "THIRD," "YOUTH"

A young man who ran away from home and, through a chance encounter, made Xie Lian's acquaintance while hitching a ride on a passing ox cart. Dressed in fine clothing the color of blood-red maples and knowledgeable on topics obscure and esoteric, it seems that he grew up in the lap of luxury. However, he does not hesitate to sleep on a single straw mat in Xie Lian's humble home, nor to get his hands dirty doing household chores. Truly a remarkable person in every respect. So why does he seem so suspicious?

HEAVENLY OFFICIALS & HEAVENLY ASSOCIATES

Feng Xin
风信   "WIND," "TRUST/FAITH"

HEAVENLY TITLE: Nan Yang, "Southern Sun" (南陽)
The Martial God of the Southeast. He has a short fuse and foul mouth (especially when it comes to his longstanding nemesis, Mu Qing) but is known to be a dutiful, hardworking god. He has a complicated history with Xie Lian: long ago, in their days in the kingdom of Xianle, he used to serve as Xie Lian's bodyguard and was a close friend until circumstances drove them apart.

Fu Yao
扶摇   "TO TAKE FLIGHT (ONE WHO IS AMBITIOUS)"

A junior official of the Middle Court, hailing from the Palace of Xuan Zhen (Mu Qing's palace). He is cold, quick to judge, and even quicker to roll his eyes. Followers of General Mu Qing tend not to get on very well with followers of General Feng Xin, and Fu Yao is a proud follower of this trend; he is constantly fighting with Nan Feng.

Jun Wu
君吾   "LORD," "I"

HEAVENLY TITLE: Shenwu, "Divine Might" (神武)
The Emperor of Heaven and strongest of the gods. He is composed and serene, and it is through his power and wisdom that the heavens remain aloft—quite literally. Although the heavens are full of schemers and gossipmongers, Jun Wu stands apart from such petty squabbles and is willing to listen to even the lowliest creatures to hear their pleas for justice.

Ling Wen
灵文   "INGENIOUS LITERATUS"

HEAVENLY TITLE: Ling Wen

The top civil god and also the most overworked. Unlike the majority of gods, she is addressed by her colleagues and most others by her heavenly title. She is one of the rare female civil gods and worked tirelessly (and thanklessly) for many years to earn her position. Ling Wen is exceedingly competent at all things bureaucratic, and her work keeps Heaven's business running (mostly) smoothly. She is the creator and head admin of Heaven's communication array.

Mu Qing
慕情   "YEARNING," "AFFECTION"

HEAVENLY TITLE: Xuan Zhen, "Enigmatic Truth" (玄真)

The Martial God of the Southwest. He has a short fuse and sharp tongue (especially when it comes to his longstanding nemesis, Feng Xin) and is known for being cold, spiteful, and petty. He has a complicated history with Xie Lian: long ago, in their days in the kingdom of Xianle, he used to serve as Xie Lian's personal servant and was a close friend until circumstances drove them apart.

Nan Feng
南风   "SOUTHERN," "WIND"

A junior official of the Middle Court, hailing from the Palace of Nan Yang (Feng Xin's palace). He is uptight, serious, and prone to outbursts of swearing when angered. Followers of General Feng Xin do not tend to get on very well with followers of General Mu Qing, and Nan Feng hardly bucks the stereotype; he is constantly fighting with Fu Yao.

Pei Ming
裴茗   SURNAME PEI, "TENDER TEA LEAVES"

HEAVENLY TITLE: Ming Guang, "Bright Illumination" (明光)
FOUR FAMOUS TALES TITLE: The General Who Snapped His Sword
The Martial God of the North. General Pei is a powerful and popular god, and over the years he has gained a reputation as a womanizer. This reputation is deserved: Pei Ming's ex-lovers are innumerable and hail from all the Three Realms. Pei Xiu is Pei Ming's indirect descendant, and Pei Ming has taken him under his wing to help advance his career in the heavens. And when General Pei sets his sights on a goal, he doesn't take kindly to those who get in his way.

Pei Xiu
裴宿   SURNAME PEI, "CONSTELLATION"

A martial god and a distant (and indirect) descendant of Pei Ming. He's usually called "Little Pei" or "General Pei Junior" for this reason, and his own worship is tied to the worship of Pei Ming himself. He is often called in to clean up his ancestor's messes, but regardless of the circumstances, he always maintains his composure with a polite yet detached air. Always cold and composed, Pei Xiu is a tactician through and through. There are rumors that his ascension to godhood occurred because he led the charge to slaughter a city.

Wind Master
风师

HEAVENLY TITLE: Wind Master
The elemental master of wind, the Wind Master is as flighty and pushy as the element she commands, and as wealthy as she is generous with money. She possesses a strong sense of justice and will not be dissuaded by notions of propriety. She appears to be close

friends with the lady in black accompanying her, despite the latter's insistence to the contrary.

GHOST REALM & GHOST REALM ASSOCIATES

Banyue
半月　　"HALF-MOON"

Former state preceptor of the Kingdom of Banyue, now a wrath ghost. She is a small, frail young woman who nonetheless possesses the power to call upon and control deadly scorpion-snakes. Despite her gloomy disposition, she earnestly wishes to save others from suffering, even if it means that she must suffer in their stead.

Kemo
刻磨　　"MILLSTONE"

A former general of the Kingdom of Banyue, now a wrath ghost. He bears great resentment against the State Preceptor of Banyue and great hatred for the long-dead kingdom that destroyed his own, even long after his death.

Qi Rong
戚容　　"FACE OF SORROW"

FOUR CALAMITIES TITLE: Night-Touring Green Lantern

One of the Four Calamities, also called the "Green Ghost." Unlike the other three Calamities, he's actually only a wrath ghost, not a supreme. Gods and ghosts alike agree that he was only included in the group to bump up the number to an even four. (Also, he's just that big a pest.)

Ship-Sinking Black Water
黑水沉舟

FOUR CALAMITIES TITLE: Ship-Sinking Black Water

One of the Four Calamities. Ship-Sinking Black Water is a mysterious and reclusive water ghost that rules the South Sea. Like Hua Cheng, he won the bloody gauntlet at Mount Tonglu and wields the power of a supreme ghost.

White No-Face
白无相 "WHITE NO-FACE"

FOUR CALAMITIES TITLE: White-Clothed Calamity

One of the Four Calamities. Mysterious, cruel, and powerful enough to battle with the Heavenly Emperor himself—truly, a supreme among supremes. He destroyed the Kingdom of Xianle.

Xuan Ji
宣姬 "DECLARE," "CONCUBINE"

A former general of a fallen kingdom, now a wrath ghost known as the ghost bride. She is obsessed with Pei Ming, who rejected her affections after she tried to take their physical-only relationship to the next level. Her fury at being scorned led to the gruesome deaths of many happy brides-to-be.

MORTAL REALM & MORTAL REALM ASSOCIATES

A-Zhao
阿昭   "CLEAR" OR "OBVIOUS"

A local guide in the Banyue region who makes a living guiding merchant caravans through the treacherous landscape. Despite his taciturn nature, his guidance and knowledge of the area is immensely valuable to Xie Lian's group.

Tian Sheng
天生   "INNATE," OR "HEAVEN/SKY," "BORN"

Youngest member of the merchant caravan traveling through the desert near Banyue. Impulsive but kindhearted.

Old Man Zheng
郑老伯   SURNAME ZHENG, "OLD UNCLE"

Elder of the merchant caravan. When he is stung by a scorpion-snake, a rescue trip is mounted to get the antivenom.

Xiao-Pengtou
小彭头   "LITTLE," SURNAME PENG, "HEAD"

A hotheaded young man who is determined to hunt down the ghost groom and get the reward money. Refuses to listen to reason.

Xiao-Ying
小萤   "LITTLE," "FIREFLY"

A young human girl who assists Xie Lian in tracking down the ghost groom. She is softspoken and timid, but possesses a courageous, caring spirit (and makeover skills that will get you from zero to wedding-ready in no time).

SENTIENT WEAPONS AND SPIRITUAL OBJECTS

Ruoye
若邪   "LIKE/AS IF," "EVIL" OR "SWORD"

Xie Lian's sentient strip of white silk. It is an earnest and energetic sort, if a bit nervous sometimes, and will go to great lengths to protect Xie Lian—quite literally, as it can stretch out to almost limitless dimensions.

Locations

Banyue
半月   "HALF-MOON"

A long-dead, long-forgotten kingdom built upon a long-dead oasis in the Gobi Desert. It was well known in its heyday for its proud, mighty warriors. The ruined, decaying cityscape still has one monument that looms undaunted against the grind of centuries: the Sinner's Pit, which served both as a jail and method of execution for Banyue's worst criminals.

It was also infamous for its fearsome wildlife and unforgiving landscape. Sandstorms continue to be a frequent occurrence, and local guides warn that the deadly scorpion-snakes still lurk in the shadows to strike hapless travelers seeking refuge from the relentless desert sun.

Ghost Realm

The Ghost Realm is the home of almost all dead humans, and far less organized and bureaucratic than the Heavenly Realm. Ghosts may leave or be trapped away from the Ghost Realm under some circumstances, which causes major problems for ordinary humans and gods alike.

Heavenly Realm

The Heavenly Capital is a divine city built upon the clouds. Amidst flowing streams and auspicious clouds, luxurious palaces dot the landscape, serving as the personal residences and offices of the gods. The Grand Avenue of Divine Might serves as the realm's main thoroughfare, and this road leads directly to the Palace of Divine Might—the Heavenly Emperor's residence where court is held.

The Heavenly Court consists of two sub-courts: the Upper

Court and the Middle Court. The Upper Court consists entirely of ascended gods, while the Middle Court consists of officials who—while remarkable and skilled in their own right—have not yet ascended to godhood.

Mortal Realm

The realm of living humans. Often receives visitors from the other two realms.

Mount Tonglu
铜炉山 "COPPER KILN MOUNTAIN"

Mount Tonglu is a volcano, and the location of the City of Gu. Every few hundred years, tens of thousands of ghosts descend upon the city for a massive battle royale. Only two ghosts have ever survived the slaughter and made it out—one of those two was Hua Cheng.

Puqi Village
菩荠村 "WATER CHESTNUT"

A tiny village in the countryside, named for the water chestnuts (puqi) that grow in abundance nearby. While small and unsophisticated, its villagers are friendly and welcoming to weary travelers who wish to stay a while. The humble Puqi Shrine (under reconstruction, welcoming donations) can be found here, as well as its resident god, Xie Lian.

Yong'an
永安 "ETERNAL PEACE"

A fallen but once-prosperous kingdom that bordered Banyue. The two nations frequently squabbled over borders and territory, and Yong'an eventually annihilated Banyue in an all-out war.

Name Guide

NAMES, HONORIFICS, & TITLES

Diminutives, Nicknames, and Name Tags

XIAO-: A diminutive meaning "little." Always a prefix.

-ER: A word for "son" or "child." Added to a name, it expresses affection. Similar to calling someone "Little" or "Sonny."

A-: Friendly diminutive. Always a prefix. Usually for monosyllabic names, or one syllable out of a two-syllable name.

Doubling a syllable of a person's name can be a nickname, and has childish or cutesy connotations.

FAMILY

DI: Younger brother or younger male friend. Can be used alone or as an honorific.

DIDI: Younger brother or a younger male friend. Casual.

GE: Familiar way to refer to an older brother or older male friend, used by someone substantially younger or of lower status. Can be used alone or with the person's name.

GEGE: Familiar way to refer to an older brother or an older male friend, used by someone substantially younger or of lower status. Has a cutesier feel than "ge."

JIE: Older sister or older female friend. Also a familiar address by someone of lower status to refer to another in a higher position of power. Can be used alone or as an honorific.

JIEJIE: Familiar way to refer to an older sister or an older female friend, used by someone substantially younger or of lower status. Has a cutesier feel than "jie," and rarely used by older males.

JIUJIU: Uncle (maternal, biological).

MEI: Younger sister or younger female friend. Can be used alone or as an honorific.

MEIMEI: Younger sister or an unrelated younger female friend. Casual.

SHUFU: Uncle (paternal, biological). Formal address for one's father's younger brother.

SHUSHU: An affectionate version of "Shufu."

XIAOSHU: Little uncle.

XIONG: Older brother. Generally used as an honorific. Formal, but also used informally between male friends of equal status.

XIONGZHANG: Very formal/respectable address for elder brother. For direct blood-related only, and for any older brother, not just the eldest.

XIANSHENG: "Husband" or "Mister" in modern usage; historical usage was broadly "teacher."

If multiple relatives in the same category are present (multiple older brothers, for example) everyone is assigned a number in order of birthdate, starting with the eldest as number one, the second oldest as number two, etc. These numbers are then used to differentiate one person from another. This goes for all of the categories above, whether it's siblings, cousins, aunts, uncles, and so on.

EXAMPLES:

If you have three older brothers, the oldest would be referred to as "da-ge," the second oldest "er-ge," and the third oldest "san-ge."

If you have two younger brothers you (as the oldest) would be number one. Your second-youngest brother would be "er-di," and the youngest of your two younger brothers would be "san-di."

Cultivation and Martial Arts

GENERAL

GONGZI: Young master of an affluent household.

-JUN: A suffix meaning "lord" or "gentleman." May be combined with other titles.

SECTS

SHIDI: Younger martial brother. For junior male members of one's own sect.

SHIFU: Teacher/master. For one's master in one's own sect. Gender neutral. Mostly interchangeable with Shizun.

SHIJIE: Older martial sister. For senior female members of one's own sect.

SHIMEI: Younger martial sister. For junior female members of one's own sect.

SHISHU: The younger martial sibling of one's master. Male or female.

SHIXIONG: Older martial brother. For senior male members of one's own sect.

SHIZUN: Honorific address (as opposed to shifu) of teacher/master.

Cultivators and Immortals

DAOREN: Daoist cultivator.

DAOZHANG: A polite address for Daoist cultivators, equivalent to "Mr. Cultivator." Can be used alone as a title or attached to someone's family name—for example, one could refer to Xie Lian as "Daozhang" or "Xie Daozhang."

YUANJUN: Title for high class female Daoist deity. Can be used alone as a title or as a suffix.

ZHENJUN: Title for average male Daoist deity. Can be used alone as a title or as a suffix.

Pronunciation Guide

Mandarin Chinese is the official state language of China. It is a tonal language, so correct pronunciation is vital to being understood! As many readers may not be familiar with the use and sound of tonal marks, below is a very simplified guide on the pronunciation of select character names and terms from MXTX's series to help get you started.

More resources are available at **sevenseasdanmei.com**

Series Names

SCUM VILLAIN'S SELF-SAVING SYSTEM (RÉN ZHĀ FǍN PÀI ZÌ JIÙ XÌ TǑNG):
  ren jaa faan pie zzh zioh she tone

GRANDMASTER OF DEMONIC CULTIVATION (MÓ DÀO ZǓ SHĪ):
  mwuh dow zoo shrr

HEAVEN OFFICIAL'S BLESSING (TIĀN GUĀN CÌ FÚ):
  tee-yan gwen tsz fuu

Character Names

SHĚN QĪNGQIŪ: Shhen Ching-cheeoh
LUÒ BĪNGHÉ: Loo-uh Bing-huhh
WÈI WÚXIÀN: Way Woo-shee-ahn
LÁN WÀNGJĪ: Lahn Wong-gee
XIÈ LIÁN: Shee-yay Lee-yan
HUĀ CHÉNG: Hoo-wah Cch-yung

XIǍO-: shee-ow
-ER: ahrr
A-: ah
GŌNGZǏ: gong-zzh
DÀOZHǍNG: dow-jon
-JŪN: june
DÌDÌ: dee-dee
GĒGĒ: guh-guh
JIĚJIĚ: gee-ay-gee-ay
MÈIMEI: may-may
-XIÓNG: shong

Terms

DĀNMĚI: dann-may
WǓXIÁ: woo-sheeah
XIĀNXIÁ: sheeyan-sheeah
QÌ: chee

General Consonants & Vowels

X: similar to English sh (**sh**eep)
Q: similar to English ch (**ch**arm)
C: similar to English ts (pan**ts**)
IU: yoh
UO: wuh
ZHI: jrr
CHI: chrr
RI: rrr

ZI: zzz
CI: tsz
SI: ssz
U: When u follows a y, j, q, or x, the sound is actually ü, pronounced like eee with your lips rounded like ooo. This applies for yu, yuan, jun, etc.

Heaven Official's Blessing

TIAN GUAN CI FU

Glossary

Glossary

While not required reading, this glossary is intended to offer further context to the many concepts and terms utilized throughout this novel and provide a starting point for learning more about the rich Chinese culture from which these stories were written.

China is home to dozens of cultures, and its history spans thousands of years. The provided definitions are not strictly universal across all these cultural groups, and this simplified overview is meant for new readers unfamiliar with the concepts. This glossary should not be considered a definitive source, especially for more complex ideas.

GENRES

Danmei

Danmei (耽美 / "indulgence in beauty") is a Chinese fiction genre focused on romanticized tales of love and attraction between men. It is analogous to the BL (boys' love) genre in Japanese media. The majority of well-known danmei writers are women writing for women, although all genders produce and enjoy the genre.

Wuxia

Wuxia (武侠 / "martial heroes") is one of the oldest Chinese literary genres and consists of tales of noble heroes fighting evil and injustice. It often follows martial artists, monks, or rogues, who live apart from the ruling government, which is often seen as useless or corrupt. These societal outcasts—both voluntary and not—settle disputes among themselves, adhering to their own moral codes over the governing law.

Characters in wuxia focus primarily on human concerns, such as political strife between factions and advancing their own personal sense of justice. True wuxia is low on magical or supernatural elements. To Western moviegoers, a well-known example is *Crouching Tiger, Hidden Dragon*.

Xianxia

Xianxia (仙侠 / "immortal heroes") is a genre related to wuxia that places more emphasis on the supernatural. Its characters often strive to become stronger, with the end goal of extending their life span or achieving immortality.

Xianxia heavily features Daoist themes, while cultivation and the pursuit of immortality are both genre requirements. If these are not the story's central focus, it is not xianxia. *The Scum Villain's Self-Saving System*, *Grandmaster of Demonic Cultivation*, and *Heaven Official's Blessing* are all considered part of both the danmei and xianxia genres.

Webnovels

Webnovels are novels serialized by chapter online, and the websites that host them are considered spaces for indie and amateur writers. Many novels, dramas, comics, and animated shows produced in China are based on popular webnovels.

Heaven Official's Blessing was first serialized on the website *JJWXC*.

TERMINOLOGY

ARRAY: Area-of-effect magic circles. Anyone within the array falls under the effect of the array's associated spell(s).

ASCENSION: In typical xianxia tales, gods are conceived naturally and born divine. Immortals cannot attain godhood but can achieve great longevity. In *Heaven Official's Blessing*, however, both gods and immortals were born mortal and either cultivated deeply or committed great deeds and attained godhood after transcending the Heavenly Tribulation. Their bodies shed the troubles of a mortal form and are removed from the corporeal world.

AUSPICIOUS CLOUDS: A sign of good fortune and the divine, auspicious clouds are also often seen as methods of transport for gods and immortals in myth. The idea springs from the obvious association with clouds and the sky/heavens, and also because yun (云 / "cloud") and yun (运 / "luck") sound similar.

BOWING: As is seen in other Asian cultures, standing bows are a traditional greeting and are also used when giving an apology. A deeper bow shows greater respect.

CHINESE CALENDAR: The Chinese calendar uses the *Tian Gan Di Zhi* (Heavenly Stems, Earthly Branches) system, rather than numbers, to mark the years. There are ten heavenly stems (original meanings lost) and twelve earthly branches (associated with the zodiac), each represented by a written character. Each stem and branch is associated with either yin or yang, and one of the elemental properties: wood, earth, fire, metal, and water. The stems and branches are combined in cyclical patterns to create a calendar where every unit of time is associated with certain attributes.

This is what a character is asking for when inquiring for the date/time of birth (生辰八字 / "eight characters of birth date/ time"). Analyzing the stem/branch characters and their elemental associations was considered essential information in divination, fortune-telling, matchmaking, and even business deals.

Colors:

WHITE: Death, mourning, purity. Used in funerals for both the deceased and mourners.

BLACK: Represents the heavens and the dao.

RED: Happiness, good luck. Used for weddings.

YELLOW/GOLD: Wealth and prosperity, and often reserved for the emperor.

BLUE/GREEN (CYAN): Health, prosperity, and harmony.

PURPLE: Divinity and immortality, often associated with nobility.

CONCUBINES: In ancient China, it was common practice for a wealthy man to possess women as concubines in addition to his wife. They were expected to live with him and bear him children. Generally speaking, a greater number of concubines correlated to higher social status, hence a wealthy merchant might have two or three concubines, while an emperor might have tens or even a hundred.

CONFUCIANISM: Confucianism is a philosophy based on the teachings of Confucius. Its influence on all aspects of Chinese culture is incalculable. Confucius placed heavy importance on respect for one's elders and family, a concept broadly known as *xiao* (孝 / "filial piety"). The family structure is used in other contexts to urge similar behaviors, such as respect of a student toward a teacher, or people of a country toward their ruler.

COUGHING/SPITTING BLOOD: A way to show a character is ill, injured, or upset. Despite the very physical nature of the response, it does not necessarily mean that a character has been wounded; their body could simply be reacting to a very strong emotion. (See also Seven Apertures/Qiqiao.)

CULTIVATORS/CULTIVATION: Cultivators are practitioners of spirituality and martial arts who seek to gain understanding of the will of the universe while attaining personal strength and extending their life span.

Cultivation is a long process marked by "stages." There are traditionally nine stages, but this is often simplified in fiction. Some common stages are noted below, though exact definitions of each stage may depend on the setting.

◇ Qi Condensation/Qi Refining (凝气/练气)
◇ Foundation Establishment (筑基)
◇ Core Formation/Golden Core (结丹/金丹)
◇ Nascent Soul (元婴)
◇ Deity Transformation (化神)
◇ Great Ascension (大乘)
◇ Heavenly Tribulation (渡劫)

CULTIVATION MANUAL: Cultivation manuals and sutras are common plot devices in xianxia/wuxia novels. They provide detailed instructions on a secret or advanced training technique and are sought out by those who wish to advance their cultivation levels.

CUT-SLEEVE: A term for a gay man. Comes from a tale about an emperor's love for, and relationship with, a male politician. The emperor was called to the morning assembly, but his lover was asleep on his robe. Rather than wake him, the emperor cut off his own sleeve.

DAOISM: Daoism is the philosophy of the *dao* (道), known as "the way." Following the dao involves coming into harmony with the natural order of the universe, which makes someone a "true human," safe from external harm and who can affect the world without intentional action. Cultivation is a concept based on Daoist superstitions.

DEMONS: A race of immensely powerful and innately supernatural beings. They are almost always aligned with evil.

DRAGON: Great chimeric beasts who wield power over the weather. Chinese dragons differ from their Western counterparts as they are often benevolent, bestowing blessings and granting luck. They are associated with the heavens, the Emperor, and yang energy.

EIGHT TRIGRAMS MAP: Also known as the bagua or pakua, an eight trigrams map is a Daoist diagram containing eight symbols that represent the fundamentals of reality, including the five elements. They often feature a symbol for yin and yang in the center as a representation of perfect balance between opposing forces. (See also The Five Elements and Yin Energy and Yang Energy)

FACE: *Mianzi* (面子), generally translated as "face," is an important concept in Chinese society. It is a metaphor for a person's reputation and can be extended to further descriptive metaphors. For example, "having face" refers to having a good reputation, and "losing face" refers to having one's reputation hurt. Meanwhile, "giving face" means deferring to someone else to help improve their reputation, while "not wanting face" implies that a person is acting so poorly/ shamelessly that they clearly don't care about their reputation at all. "Thin face" refers to someone easily embarrassed or prone to offense at perceived slights. Conversely, "thick face" refers to someone not easily embarrassed and immune to insults.

THE FIVE ELEMENTS: Also known as the *wuxing* (五行 / "Five Phases"). Rather than Western concepts of elemental magic, Chinese phases are more commonly used to describe the interactions and relationships between things. The phases can both beget and overcome each other.

  ◇ Wood (木 / mu)
  ◇ Fire (火 / huo)
  ◇ Earth (土 / tu)
  ◇ Metal (金 / jin)
  ◇ Water (水 / shui)

FORTUNE SHAKER: A wooden jar full of thin bamboo sticks with varying degrees of good and bad luck inscribed on the bottom ends. The user shakes the jar with a wish in mind, and the first stick that drops out will dictate the outcome of the wish.

GHOST: Ghosts (鬼) are the restless spirits of deceased sentient creatures. Ghosts produce yin energy and crave yang energy. They come in a variety of types: they can be malevolent or helpful, can retain their former personalities or be fully mindless, and can actively try to interact with the living world to achieve a goal or be little more than a remnant shadow of their former lives.

GU SORCERY: The concept of gu (蛊 / "poison") is common in wuxia and xianxia stories. In more realistic settings, it may refer to crafting poisons that are extracted from venomous insects and creatures. Things like snakes, toads, and bugs are generally associated with the idea of gu, but it can also apply to monsters, demons, and ghosts. The effects of gu poison are bewitchment and manipulation. "Swayed by gu" has become a common phrase meaning "lost your mind/been led astray" in modern Chinese vocabulary.

HAND GESTURES: The baoquan (抱拳 / "hold fist") is a martial arts salute where one places their closed right fist against their open left palm. The gongshou (拱手 / "arch hand") is a more generic salute not specific to martial artists, where one drapes their open left palm over their closed right fist. The orientation of both of these salutes is reversed for women. During funerals, the closed hand in both salutes switches, where men will use their left fist and women their right.

HAND SEALS: Refers to various hand and finger gestures used by cultivators to cast spells, or used while meditating. A cultivator may be able to control their sword remotely with a hand seal.

HEAVENLY REALM: An imperial court of enlightened beings. Some hold administrative roles, while others watch over and protect a specific aspect of the celestial and mortal realm, such as love, marriage, a piece of land, etc. There are also carefree immortals who simply wander the world and help mortals as they go, or become hermits deep in the mountains.

HEAVENLY TRIBULATION: Before a Daoist cultivator can ascend to the heavens, they must go through a trial known as a Heavenly Tribulation. In stories where the heavens are depicted with a more traditional nine-level structure, even gods themselves must endure and overcome tribulations if they want to level up. The nature of these trials vary, but the most common version involves navigating a powerful lightning storm. To fail means losing one's attained divine stage and cultivation.

HUALIAN: Shortened name for the relationship between Hua Cheng and Xie Lian.

IMMORTALS AND IMMORTALITY: Immortals have transcended mortality through cultivation. They possess long lives, are immune to illness and aging, and have various magical powers. An immortal can progress to godhood if they pass a Heavenly Tribulation. The exact life span of immortals differs from story to story, and in some they only live for three or four hundred years.

IMMORTAL-BINDING ROPES: Ropes, nets, and other restraints enchanted to withstand the power of an immortal or god. They can only be cut by high-powered spiritual items or weapons and usually limit the abilities of those trapped by them.

INCENSE TIME: A common way to tell time in ancient China, referring to how long it takes for a single incense stick to burn. Standardized incense sticks were manufactured and calibrated for specific time measurements: a half hour, an hour, a day, etc. These were available to people of all social classes.

In *Heaven Official's Blessing*, the incense sticks being referenced are the small sticks one offers when praying at a shrine, so "one incense time" is roughly thirty minutes.

INEDIA: A common ability that allows an immortal to survive without mortal food or sleep by sustaining themselves on purer forms of energy based on Daoist fasting. Depending on the setting, immortals who have achieved inedia may be unable to tolerate mortal food, or they may be able to choose to eat when desired.

JADE: Jade is a culturally and spiritually important mineral in China. Its durability, beauty, and the ease with which it can be utilized for crafting both decorative and functional pieces alike has made it widely beloved since ancient times. The word might cause Westerners to think of green jade (the mineral jadeite), but Chinese texts are often referring to white jade (the mineral nephrite). This is the color referenced when a person's skin is described as "the color of jade."

JADE EMPEROR: In Daoist cosmology, the Jade Emperor (玉皇大帝) is the Emperor of Heaven, the chief of the Heavenly Court, and one of the highest ranked gods in the Heavenly Realm, lower only to the three primordial emanations. When one says "Oh god/lord" or "My heavens", it is usually referring to the Jade Emperor. In *Heaven Official's Blessing*, Jun Wu's role replaces that of the Jade Emperor.

JOSS PAPER: Also referred to as ghost paper, joss paper is a form of paper crafting used to make offerings to the deceased. The paper can be folded into various shapes and is burned as an offering, allowing the deceased person to utilize the gift the paper represents in the realm of the dead. Common gifts include paper money, houses, clothing, toiletries, and dolls to act as the deceased's servants.

KOWTOW: The *kowtow* (叩头 / "knock head") is an act of prostration where one kneels and bows low enough that their forehead touches the ground. A show of deep respect and reverence that can also be used to beg, plead, or show sincerity.

MERIDIANS: The means by which qi travels through the body, like a magical bloodstream. Medical and combat techniques that focus on redirecting, manipulating, or halting qi circulation focus on targeting the meridians at specific points on the body, known as acupoints. Techniques that can manipulate or block qi prevent a cultivator from using magical techniques until the qi block is lifted.

Numbers

TWO: Two (二 / "er") is considered a good number and is referenced in the common idiom "good things come in pairs." It is common practice to repeat characters in pairs for added effect.

THREE: Three (三 / "san") sounds like *sheng* (生 / "living") and also like *san* (散 / "separation").

FOUR: Four (四 / "si") sounds like *si* (死 / "death"). A very unlucky number.

SEVEN: Seven (七 / "qi") sounds like *qi* (齐 / "together"), making it a good number for love-related things. However, it also sounds like *qi* (欺 / "deception").

EIGHT: Eight (八 / "ba") sounds like *fa* (發 / "prosperity"), causing it to be considered a very lucky number.

NINE: Nine (九 / "jiu") is associated with matters surrounding the Emperor and Heaven, and is as such considered an auspicious number.

MXTX's work has subtle numerical theming around its love interests. In *Grandmaster of Demonic Cultivation*, her second book, Lan Wangji is frequently called Lan-er-gege ("second brother Lan") as a nickname by Wei Wuxian. In her third book, *Heaven Official's Blessing*, Hua Cheng is the third son of his family and gives the name San Lang ("third youth") when Xie Lian asks what to call him.

PHOENIX: *Fenghuang* (凤凰 / "phoenix"), a legendary chimeric bird said to only appear in times of peace and to flee when a ruler is corrupt. They are heavily associated with femininity, the Empress, and happy marriages.

PILLS AND ELIXIRS: Magic medicines that can heal wounds, improve cultivation, extend life, etc. In Chinese culture, these things are usually delivered in pill form. These pills are created in special kilns.

PIPA: A four-stringed lute, played by plucking with the fingers.

QI: *Qi* (气) is the energy in all living things. There is both righteous qi and evil or poisonous qi.

Cultivators strive to cultivate qi by absorbing it from the natural world and refining it within themselves to improve their cultivation base. A cultivation base refers to the amount of qi a cultivator possesses or is able to possess. In xianxia, natural locations such as caves, mountains, or other secluded places with lush wildlife are often rich in qi, and practicing there can allow a cultivator to make rapid progress in their cultivation.

Cultivators and other qi manipulators can utilize their life force in a variety of ways, including imbuing objects with it to transform them into lethal weapons or sending out blasts of energy to do powerful damage. Cultivators also refine their senses beyond normal human levels. For instance, they may cast out their spiritual sense to gain total awareness of everything in a region around them or to feel for potential danger.

RED STRING OF FATE: Refers to the myth in many East Asian cultures that an invisible red string connects two individuals who are fated to be lovers. The string is tied at each lover's finger (usually the middle finger or pinky finger).

SECT: A cultivation sect is an organization of individuals united by their dedication to the practice of a particular method of cultivation or martial arts. A sect may have a signature style. Sects are led by a single leader, who is supported by senior sect members. They are not necessarily related by blood.

SEVEN APERTURES/QIQIAO: (七窍) The seven facial apertures: the two eyes, nose, mouth, tongue, and two ears. The essential qi of vital organs are said to connect to the seven apertures, and illness in the vital organs may cause symptoms there. People who are ill or seriously injured may be "bleeding from the seven apertures."

SHANGYUAN: Shangyuan Jie (上元節), or the Lantern Festival, marks the fifteenth and last day of the Lunar New Year (usually around February on the Solar Calendar). It is a day for worshipping and celebrating the celestial heavens by hanging lanterns, solving riddles, and performing Dragon Dances. Glutinous rice ball treats known as yuanxiao and tangyuan are highlights of this festival, so much so that the festival's alternate name is Yuanxiao Jie (元宵節).

SHANYUE: The name of this fictional plant translates to "the benevolent moon."

SHRINES: Shrines are sites at which an individual can pray or make offerings to a god, spirit, or ancestor. They contain an object of worship to focus on such as a statue, a painting or mural, a relic, or a memorial tablet in the case of an ancestral shrine. The term also refers to small roadside shrines or personal shrines to deceased family members or loved ones kept on a mantle. Offerings like incense, food, and money can be left at a shrine as a show of respect.

STATE PRECEPTOR: State preceptors, or guoshi, are high-ranking government officials who also have significant religious duties. They serve as religious heads of state under the emperor and act as the tutors, chaplains, and confidants of the emperor and his direct heirs.

SWORDS: A cultivator's sword is an important part of their cultivation practice. In many instances, swords are spiritually bound to their owner and may have been bestowed to them by their master, a family member, or obtained through a ritual. Cultivators in fiction are able to use their swords as transportation by standing atop the flat of the blade and riding it as it flies through the air.

Skilled cultivators can summon their swords to fly into their hand, command the sword to fight on its own, or release energy attacks from the edge of the blade.

SWORN BROTHERS/SISTERS/FAMILIES: In China, sworn brotherhood describes a binding social pact made by two or more unrelated individuals of the same gender. It can be entered into for social, political, and/or personal reasons, and is not only limited to two participants; it can extend to an entire group. It was most common among men, but it was not unheard of among women or between people of different genders.

The participants treat members of each other's families as their own and assist them in the ways an extended family would: providing mutual support and aid, support in political alliances, etc.

Sworn siblinghood, where individuals will refer to themselves as brother or sister, is not to be confused with familial relations like blood siblings or adoption. It is sometimes used in Chinese media, particularly danmei, to imply romantic relationships that could otherwise be prone to censorship.

TALISMANS: Strips of paper with spells written on them, often with cinnabar ink or blood. They can serve as seals or be used as one-time spells.

THE THREE REALMS: Traditionally, the universe is divided into Three Realms: the **Heavenly Realm**, the **Mortal Realm**, and the **Ghost Realm**. The Heavenly Realm refers to the Heavens and Celestial Court, where gods reside and rule, the Mortal Realm refers to the human world, and the Ghost Realm refers to the realm of the dead.

VINEGAR: To say someone is drinking vinegar or tasting vinegar means they're having jealous or bitter feelings. Generally used for a love interest growing jealous while watching the main character receive the attention of a rival suitor.

WEDDING TRADITIONS: Red is an important part of traditional Chinese weddings, as the color of prosperity, happiness, and good luck. It remains the standard color for bridal and bridegroom robes and wedding decorations even today.

In traditional Chinese wedding ceremonies, the bride was always veiled when she was sent off by her family in her wedding dress. Veils were generally opaque, so the bride would need to be led around by her handmaidens (or the groom). The veil was not removed until the bride was in the wedding suite with the groom after the ceremony, and it was only removed by the groom himself.

WHISK: A whisk held by a cultivator is not a baking tool but a Daoist symbol and martial arts weapon. Usually made of horsehair bound to a wooden stick, the whisk is based off a tool used to brush away flies without killing them and is symbolically meant for wandering Daoist monks to brush away thoughts that would lure them back to secular life. Wudang Daoist Monks created a fighting style based on wielding it as a weapon.

YIN ENERGY AND YANG ENERGY: Yin and yang is a concept in Chinese philosophy that describes the complementary interdependence of opposite/contrary forces. It can be applied to all forms of change and differences. Yang represents the sun, masculinity, and the living, while yin represents the shadows, femininity, and the dead, including spirits and ghosts. In fiction, imbalances between yin and yang energy can do serious harm to the body or act as the driving force for malevolent spirits seeking to replenish themselves of whichever they lack.

ZHONGYUAN: Zhongyuan Jie (中元節), or the Ghost Festival / Hungry Ghost Festival, falls on the fifteenth day of the seventh month of the Lunar Calendar (this usually falls around August/ September on the Solar Calendar). The festival celebrates the underworld, and offerings are made to the dead to appease their spirits and help them move on.